Peas, Beans & Corn

Peas, Beans & Corn

a novel by
Jennifer Wixson

Book 2 in
The Sovereign Series

Published by

White Wave™

For more information contact:
White Wave, P.O. Box 4, Troy, ME 04987
or visit *www.thesovereignseries.com*

10 9 8 7 6 5 4 3 2 1

ISBN 978-0-9636689-5-0

eBook ISBN 978-0-9636689-6-7

Peas, Beans & Corn is a work of fiction. Names, characters,
(most) places, and incidents are the products of the author's
imagination or are used fictitiously. Any resemblance to actual events,
locales and persons, living or dead, is entirely coincidental.

THE SOVEREIGN SERIES
TRADE MARK
I went to Heaven—'Twas a small Town—Emily Dickinson

*This book is dedicated to the men
and women of the US Armed Forces*

AND

*to the Maine corn shop workers
of yesteryear, who fed them.*

Acknowledgements

My gratitude must first go to the loyal group of fans whose heart-felt enjoyment of *Hens & Chickens* spurred me to stretch my one little tale into four novels, creating *The Sovereign Series*. In addition, this book would not have been possible without the support of dozens of other folks, including: Professor Paul B. Frederic (University of Maine at Farmington), whose seminal work **Canning Gold** *Northern New England's Sweet Corn Industry: A Historical Geography* provided many of the stories and much of the inspiration for this novel about an old canning factory; Maine author John Gould, from whose humorous 1979 book, *The Shag Bag*, I've borrowed an anecdote or two; the inspirational American poet Emily Dickinson, upon whose words the plot twists and turns; and my old friend Master Sergeant Leonard Bruce Atkins Retired USMC, who lent to this story his military expertise and a whole lot more.

I'd also like to thank Betty Littlefield of the Brooks Historical Society, who shared several lively tales about the old canning factory in her town; Lucille Hodsdon of Norway, whose loan of lovely black and white photographs from the multiple corn shops in the town of Minot, Maine, helped me step into the lives of the people and the industry; Kate McBrien, Curator of Historic Collections at the Maine State Museum, and Museum Archivist Deanna Bonner-Ganter; Diane Nute, the town of Troy's Postmistress, whose encouragement and support propped me up on those down days; Russell Mitchell of Troy, whose irresistible story about Evelyn's swimming hole somehow wormed its way into these pages; once again, my awesome editorial team, who provided not just clarity but also continuity with *Hens & Chickens* – Marilyn Wixson, Rebecca Siegel, Stanley Luce, Laurel McFarland, "Aunt" Wini Mott, and Professor Frederic, who checked for historical accuracy; my proofreaders and darling nieces Joanna and Laurel McFarland; my creative conspirators from the Maine *Writers In Progress* Facebook group, Gail VanWart, Robin Follette, Kimberly Leute, Scott Fuller and Nancy Freedman-Smith; my talented artistic and design team Peter Harris Creative, including Peter Harris and Greg Elizondo; my advance readers, Dorothy Fitzpatrick, Tami Erwin, Viletta Knight, Adeline Wixson, Sally Beaty, Joanna Felts and Robin Follette; my super-supportive parents, Eldwin Wixson of Plymouth, N.H. and Rowena Palmer of Norway, Maine; and my mother-in-law Bessie Luce.

Last, but not least, I'd like to recognize my loving husband – the Cranberry Man – who ties on an apron in winter and takes over the household chores so that I might toss another stick of rock maple into the woodstove and write to my heart's content.

Jennifer Wixson

Troy, Maine
May 1, 2013

Front cover insert photograph and back cover ghost image are from the Don Mills Collection, Poland, Maine, courtesy of the Minot Maine Historical Society. Both pictures are of the same corn shop, Burnham & Morrill Co. Corn Shop #5, which was located at Minot Corner between the Methodist Church and the Little Androscoggin River.

Sweet corn being unloaded at a Maine corn shop, circa 1924.
Credit: Collections of the Maine State Museum, www.mainestatemuseum.org
See p. 283-285 for more corn shop photos.

Table of Contents

Chapter 1

"1 Went to Heaven – 'Twas a Small Town"

It is uncommon hard – downright difficult – to retrieve childish things once we have set those childish things aside. However, this only increases our longing for them.

Those who've matured gradually over time have probably never desired to return to the awkward, pinchbeck days of youth, where one changes personalities like cell phones. But those whose adulthood has been forced like paperwhite narcissus (with the possible exception of the Apostle Paul) often yearn for the lost liberties of their youth. Leonard "Bruce" Gilpin was such a one.

In 1996, while still a senior at Common Hill High School in Sovereign, Maine, Bruce Gilpin was informed that he was going to become a father. Stoically, he set aside his post-graduation plans to motor across the country in his restored 1969 AMC Rambler and shouldered instead the triple burdens of wife, work and family. Two years later, when his even younger wife decided that she herself was not ready to set aside those childish things, Bruce was left alone with a mortgage payment, an unfulfilling job, and an eighteen-month-old son. Thus the robin's egg blue Rambler was set aside for good, but not forgotten.

Five years passed. The child, a boy, Grayden "Gray" Gilpin, grew and started elementary school, and the frazzled father thought he began to see a light at the end of the tunnel. But just when the twinkle was returning to Bruce's friendly brown eyes and he found himself raising his head from his labors long enough to look around for a fun, loving companion (his wife having long since become his ex), the awful event that changed the world – 9/11 – occurred and Bruce Gilpin answered the call to further duty. He joined the Maine Army Guard, whose rallying cry of

"Bayonets forward!" recollects the turning point in the Civil War when Col. Joshua Chamberlain called upon his soldiers of the 20th Maine to "Fix bayonets!" holding fast at Little Round Top and saving the Union.

When our tale begins, in the fall of 2012, four tours of duty in Afghanistan and three tours in Iraq had left thirty-five-year-old Staff Sergeant Bruce Gilpin with very little of the juice of youth. I will not say that the jejuneness was entirely squeezed out of him, but I will admit he was settled into an acceptance that, for him, all play was probably over. If there was satisfaction to be gained, it would be won by further labor at the altar of duty, to which god Bruce had sacrificed (not entirely in vain) his youth.

Many times over the years the boyish-hearted Bruce had wanted to kick over the traces and gallop free like the wild mustangs on the plains. But today, at thirty-five, these desires caused him so much heartache and seemed so unrealistic that he was constantly schooling himself as to what must be his duty now that the accelerated draw-down in Afghanistan had released him from the National Guard. He was free to go where he pleased (sort of) and do what he pleased (ditto), with the only hindrance being his now sixteen-year-old son, and the duty he owed his parents for helping raise Gray during his decade-plus of soldiering.

Some people reap wonderful harvests from self-denial. And most Americans could use a healthy dose of self-abnegation in their diets. But Bruce Gilpin was not one of them. Still, he persisted. He was mentally cajoling himself now, as he waited for the bus to take him on the last leg of his journey home from Afghanistan.

Heck, she'll be thrilled if I propose to Trudy! She's been trying to get us together for thirteen years!

He stood in a crush of travelers at South Station in Boston, waiting to board the bus to Bangor. The "she" in question was his mother, Maude Hodges Gilpin, who had hinted in one of their last conversations on Skype, while he was still in Kandahar, that his childhood chum Trudy was as willing to tie the knot as she had been in fifth grade when she kissed him beneath the bleachers. Bruce didn't quite believe in Trudy's fealty, but he was awake to the benefits of such a match.

Gray won't be too far from Mom and Dad then, and it'll be good for him to have someone else to consider.

It was early October, and the fall rain and faded skies of the overcast afternoon helped sharpen into focus throughout the city of Boston the

reds and oranges and yellows of the New England foliage. Every grada-
tion of leaf color was revealed to the wondering eye, from the blood-
splattered red of the Japanese maples to the girlishly blushing oak leaves.
Even the black fungal spots on the fading green of the pin oaks contributed to the display, turning the fall leaves into flying tree frogs. But
Bruce Gilpin, intent upon his course of self-instruction, was blind to the
magnificent exhibition, which originated from a god of a different stripe.

Lost in thought, Bruce neither saw nor smelled the damp ground beneath his feet. He was dressed in new jeans, sneakers, and a Maine Army
Guard jacket. The crowd for "destination Bangor" undulated closer to
the idling bus and he automatically moved with it. At six-foot-one, he
was a solid-looking man, inheriting the beefy frame and Maine farm boy
good looks of the men in his mother's family. The Hodges men sported
acorn-colored hair and fun-loving brown eyes, but most prominent was
their impish, almost pointed ears, which telegraphed their true natures
more truly than any common facial expression. Bruce's mother often
bragged that her handsome son looked nothing like his father, the skinny, wizened, Sovereign shopkeeper Ralph Gilpin, and she was right.

The low-key jostling of boarding the bus soon began and Bruce
perked up. The drill of boarding and disembarking was a quantum com-
ponent of any soldier's career, and he instinctively fell in with the forward motion of the line. Once his body returned to automatic pilot, his
brain resumed its mental plotting and cajoling.

*We could live with her father – Trudy would never leave Leland. He must be
close to eighty now! And it's a great opportunity for Gray to work on a farm, instead
of being in the store with Dad all the time.*

As Bruce stepped up into the bus, following the vague form in front
of him, he had nearly convinced himself that it would be in the best
interest of everyone involved (except himself, of course) to return home
and marry a woman whom he didn't love. Thus, preparing himself a future life of dutiful misery, he returned to the work at hand. He glanced
up to scan for a vacant seat, and faltered momentarily at the sight – not
of soldiers in their familiar DCUs (Desert Camouflage Uniforms), but
of civilians of all ages, shapes, sizes and costumes. He hesitated, suddenly disoriented, head filled with the buzz of words. He grasped onto
the back of the nearest bus seat experiencing a sense of déjà vu. The
college student boarding behind him bumped into his back.

"Sorry, man," said the youth, stopping.

"No problem," Bruce replied. He lurched forward toward what appeared to be the nearest open window seat, about half-way up the aisle. When he reached the seat, he halted again. This time his progress was arrested by the sight of a petite young woman curled up comfortably next to the window. She was reading something on her eReader, her hand cupping a soft cheek and her feminine wrist nearly swallowed up by an oversized wool sweater. Neat folds of shiny black hair were held in place on top of her comely head by some sort of plastic gewgaw, similar to one he'd once see his sister Penney wear, though certainly not as effectively.

Bruce hesitated in the aisle. He preferred a window seat so that he could keep his eyes on the road, a side effect from his convoy driving days in Iraq and Afghanistan, when he vigilantly scanned the passing landscape for potential ambushes and IEDs. However, his heart was pulling him in an altogether different direction. When was the last time he'd had the opportunity to sit next to a beautiful woman?!

As he hesitated, she glanced up at him from her eReader. A pair of searching purplish-blue eyes sized him up at a glance – but she didn't dismiss him. Although he possessed the courage to drive from Kandahar to all the forward operating bases in Afghanistan, over roads potentially laced with hundreds of IEDs, Bruce Gilpin suddenly discovered he couldn't muster the courage to ask a pretty girl with eyes the color of late season asters if the seat next to her was available.

That she was pretty, no one could doubt, especially not a soldier freshly back from the front. Her hair, the color of burnt wood, was thick, lustrous and inviting. Dark, shapely eyebrows and thick lashes accentuated the warm rosy glow of her cheeks. Her eyes sparkled like the waves on Unity Pond on a fall afternoon. All thoughts of Trudy Gorse and his harebrained schemes for the future scattered like birdshot.

That longing for his youth – for the innocent, ardent love of youth – could no longer be repressed, and desire exploded exquisitely in the back of his brain. He felt rather than saw white shooting stars and rapidly twinkling lights as spellbinding as the tail-end of Fourth of July fireworks. A shot of adrenaline rushed through him, jump-starting his tired heart, and leaving the hair on the back of his neck and arms standing at attention. Bruce felt more alive than he had in years, and he gawked at the girl, stupidly wanting to gush boyishly: "Where have you been all my life?!"

She smiled. "Go for it," she said, indicating the aisle seat with a nod of her head. She balanced her eReader on her right knee, and, with an easy motion, slung her purse from the vacant seat to the floor.

Bruce promptly folded his muscular frame into the seat. Bottleneck removed, the line of humanity once again started forward, pressing past the two of them, now snug in an intimate cocoon. When the aisle was clear, he stood up again, shrugged out of his jacket and stuck it into the overhead compartment. Then he reclaimed his seat, sank back and exhaled deeply.

He had expected her to resume her reading, but she did not. Instead, she toyed absently with her necklace, a hand-carved wooden ornament dangling from a strip of rawhide. His right hand beat a tattoo against the armrest, as he contemplated what to do next. He pushed up his shirt sleeves, and attempted to appear nonchalant. "Whatcha reading?" he asked.

Her eyes dropped momentarily to the eReader in her lap. "Emily Dickinson," she replied. Her tone was light-hearted, and her eyes, which now returned to his, signaled an interest in pursuing the conversation.

There was an awkward pause, while Bruce cast about for something to say. He had never heard of Emily Dickinson, and yet the young woman seemed to expect that he would know who she was. The background light on her tablet switched off, giving him an idea. He was grateful for the portable internet at the base that had enabled him to stay connected with the outside world. "Isn't she the one that wrote *50 Shades of Grey*?"

The young woman burst out laughing. "Not likely!"

Bruce felt the heat of humility rise up his neck. He shifted uncomfortably in his seat.

"Oops, I'm sorry! I didn't mean to embarrass you—it's just too funny!" Her blue eyes confirmed her sincerity. "Honestly, you've never heard of Emily Dickinson?"

He berated himself for trying to appear with it. "Nope. I've been, uh … otherwise engaged for the last eighteen months. I thought I was keeping up with stuff, but I guess not."

She offered a quick, self-deprecating grin. "Oops, again," she said. "Emily Dickinson has been dead for about a hundred years."

This time, Bruce broke into laughter. "Ha, ha! What a nerd!"

"I think there's only one nerd here, and it's not you." She paused. "Army?"

He nodded. "National Guard."

"Have you been in Afghanistan?"

"Yep."

"Are you home for good, now?"

"Back to being a full-time civilian!"

"I bet your family is thrilled to have you back!"

But Bruce didn't want to talk about himself; he wanted to learn more about her. Searching for someplace to begin, he reverted to the original topic. "What kind of stuff does your dead lady write?"

"Poetry," she said, in a musical lilt, which stretched the one word into an enchanting *po-et-try*.

"No wonder I never heard of her!"

"Don't sell yourself short – you might like her!"

"Yeah, right. Poetry. Every soldier's dream."

"Listen …" She picked up the eReader, and, as the words flashed back onto the screen, began to read slowly: *"I went to Heaven – 'Twas a small Town – Lit with a Ruby – Lathed – with Down…"*

Bruce closed his eyes, and listened to her hypnotic, dulcet tones. He relaxed back into the comfortable seat, and drew in a deep breath. As she recited the poem, he pictured his hometown of Sovereign, Maine – the fields, the early morning dew, the fragile butterflies and the strange hummingbird moths of summer.

When she stopped reading, Bruce, who had been lulled into a state of repose, exhaled deeply. He felt lazy, relaxed, fulfilled. "You're right, I do like her," he said, opening his eyes. "Sounds like she's describing my hometown."

"You see!" she cried triumphantly, "I said not to sell yourself short."

"Don't tell anyone, though."

She laughed again. "Seriously, what did you think?"

"She's right on about most of it – the fields being quiet when dew falls, and stuff like that. But what's meckling mean? That's a new one."

"*Mechlin*," the girl corrected, lightly. "It's a Belgium lace from the 19th century. Back then ladies' fans were covered with the stuff – it's a very fine lace – so an ingénue could screen herself from her beau, yet still get a good look at him." She mimicked a coquette using a fan.

"I only half understood what you just said," he admitted with a grin.

She rewarded him with another giggle. To Bruce, starved for youthful, feminine companionship, the moment of intimacy pierced his habitual emotional armor. Time jumped the tracks. He heard a ringing in his ears and felt his juices flowing again. He thought that he would like to be one of those guys from the 19th century, crazed with passion, trying to peer beyond the fan to get a good look at her face. He wanted to know everything about her, from the tip of her tiny feet to the top of her graceful head. But he didn't know where to begin, it had been so long.

"Where do you live?" she asked, easily. She set the eReader down into her lap, and, with a practiced move, pulled the clip from her hair, and stuck it in her mouth. She bent her head slightly and a waterfall of dark locks spilled down, screening her face like the ingénue with the fan.

His heart filliped at the sight of those loose flowing tresses. The floral scent of her shampoo suffused their cozy cocoon. He wanted to wrap her hair around his hand like a silken scarf, and draw her close. But he restrained himself. *Jesus!*

She lifted her head and looked up at him with innocent, dewy eyes, plastic clip still in her mouth. "Mou thaid the moem meminded mou of mour mometown?"

"Uh, my hometown?"

"Mmhmm."

"Sovereign, Maine. It's a small town just south of Bangor. We're only about a thousand people; you've probably never heard of us."

The clip dropped to her lap. "What?!" A torrent of hair followed, knocking the eReader onto the bus floor. The electronic device hit the rubber mat with a muffled thud.

"I'll get that," he said, eagerly reaching down to nab the electronic device. He retrieved the eReader and dusted it off. He handed it back to her. "Seems OK, but I think it shut itself off again."

She shoved the tablet into her purse, and regarded him with an air of astonishment. "But … you're a week early! They're not ready for you!"

"What?"

She quickly twisted up her hair and clipped it in place. "They're not ready for you!" she repeated, mysteriously.

"Whoa! – who's not ready for me?"

"The whole town! The Ladies Auxiliary is meeting at our house today—Mom hasn't even started on the banner! And *your* mother isn't even expecting you until next week, because Gray told me – he was over mowing our lawn last Thursday – that your mother wanted him to paint your bedroom this weekend—Oh, my God, I am so babbling! You don't have the faintest idea what I'm talking about, do you? Because you don't have the faintest idea who I am!" The young woman broke off, and stuck out her slender hand. "Amber – Amber Johnson. My Mom married Wendell Russell, and we live in the old Russell place. It's so cool to finally meet you!"

Yikes! Amber Johnson?! His inner pith turned to parchment.

He not only knew who she was, but he became painfully aware that the young woman over whom he had been mooning for the past half hour was "off limits." Heck, she was still in college! He winced as he recollected how his mother had described this newest resident of Sovereign in a recent email: "She's a pretty young thing – just a few years older than Grayden – and the poor boy has a terrible crush on her!"

He mentally kicked himself. *She's just a kid! Fool! What were you thinking, Old Man?!*

The sensation of timelessness burst like a giant soap bubble, awakening him to a cold, wet reality. He felt a faint disgust with himself, as though he had eaten too much.

It was all a fantasy, a cruel, tantalizing mirage, like water in the Iraq desert, trying to trick him from his path. He needed to get himself back on track, pronto! Fooling around with her like he was a fifteen-year-old! Hadn't he already decided that he was going to go back to Sovereign and marry his old school chum Trudy Gorse?!

She was waiting for him to consummate the introduction, hand earnestly outstretched, an expectant look on her heart-shaped face. Her lips were slightly parted, revealing a tantalizing glimpse of her teeth and tongue.

Jesus! It was all he could do to stop himself from leaning over and kissing her.

Interestingly enough, no sooner do we tell ourselves that we are not going to desire a certain object, than we desire that object even more. If we say to ourselves, "Don't eat that second piece of chocolate cake," we are almost guaranteed to devour not only the second piece, but also a third piece as well. This was the challenge now facing Bruce Gilpin on the bus ride to Bangor. After declaring to himself that Amber Johnson was "off limits," voices in his head, to which he knew he should certainly not listen, began clamoring for him to clasp that sweet outstretched hand and—devour the chocolate cake!

Chapter 2
· · · · · · ·
"1 Could Almost Taste Those Sweet, Buttery Kernels"

Amber Johnson, twenty-one, had glanced up from her Emily Dickinson and perceived the good-looking, thirty-something man faltering in the bus aisle. She registered it all in a flash. The beefy physique. The Maine Army Guard jacket. The classic butch haircut. Even the way he carried himself screamed, "Veteran!"

Generally, Amber paid scant attention to her unknown male travelling companions during the routine bus ride from Boston to Bangor. She had discovered during these bus rides – necessitated by the weekend intensives required for her online degree at UMass – that it was too easy during the four-hour trip to get trapped into unwanted intimacies with men from which it was difficult to backtrack after arriving in Bangor. She typically employed her eReader as a privacy device. But like most Americans, Amber had a deep respect for the US Armed Forces, and therefore she wanted to do her part to make his reentry into civilian life as easy as possible.

She smiled at him. "Go for it," she encouraged, indicating the vacant seat next to her. She set her eReader onto her right thigh and moved her purse.

As the bus lumbered out of the city and onto I-93, the Maine guardsman gradually opened up to her. He was attractive, in a diamond-in-the-rough sort of way, with a staccato laugh and a self-deprecating sense of humor, which matched the impishness of his elfish-looking ears. But Amber found herself drawn mostly to his hands: strong, capable, useful. She wondered what it was he had done in the service.

Some people believe that eyes are the windows of the soul. However, fortune tellers from every culture know that our hands reveal far more about our characters than our (often) lying eyes. And the young guardsman's hands, although momentarily resting peacefully on their appointed armrests, were yet not asleep, but wide awake, curious, hopeful, alert as an intelligent dog. As the bus hurtled down the highway, his hands began searching for something to do, something to fix or build or repair or even to lovingly caress. When he talked, his hands painted a clearer picture of his heart than his words, eagerly revealing an honest, hopeful nature to an adept diviner. Amber was an adept diviner.

Amber felt as though the two of them had entered a time warp, until he had stated that his home town was—Sovereign, Maine. At that point, the spell was broken, and the gentle cocoon in which they had been wrapped split open.

Was it possible? Could it be? Was she sitting next to Sovereign's hero of the hour? – Bruce Gilpin! – returning home from the war in Afghanistan?!

No! And yet … how many other returning war veterans were there for whom the Sovereign Ladies Auxiliary – which was meeting this very day at Amber's own house! – was preparing a parade and full-blown, town-wide celebration?

"It's so cool to finally meet you!" she exclaimed. She stuck out her hand, expecting an eager greeting from those alert first responders on the armrests. Instead, she was surprised and disappointed to discover that something within him had changed.

He woodenly acknowledged the introduction, shaking hands and quickly pulling away. In a blink of an eye, he had retreated back into a soldier, his face becoming painfully stern. His hands, once friendly and eager, lay stiff and cold, like weapons at the ready.

She pretended not to notice the metamorphosis. "I've heard so much about you, mostly from Gray," she continued, gaily. "Of course, he thinks you're perfect."

He forced a short laugh. "I hope he remembers that the next time I ground him."

"He's such a good kid! You must be proud of him."

"Thanks. But I haven't had much to do with it. My folks deserve all the credit."

More mundane chit chat followed. The landscape whizzed past. He stared out the window, as though he was enthralled by the fall foliage. But Amber suspected that he wasn't seeing any of it – he was using the scenery as a distraction, as a screen behind which to hide, much like the ingénue with the mechlin fan.

Hurt and frustrated, she sank back next to the cold window. She considered reclaiming her eReader from her purse and returning to Emily Dickinson. But she hesitated.

His left hand had begun to awaken, tapping lightly on the armrest, as though dispatching a message to her in Morse code. *"Help me!"* Amber translated the message perfectly. She would not give up on him.

"Gray and I are good buddies. We hang out, sometimes."

"So I've heard."

"He's really looking forward to having you around. I know how he feels, too. My Mom and I were alone for fourteen years until she married Wendell. My Dad died when I was eight."

This latest information appeared to disconcert him. His head turned back in her direction. "I thought your parents were divorced? Not that it's any of my business," he added, hastily. "That's just what my mother said once, in an email, I think."

Amber felt a dawning of comprehension. Ah, so she had been talked about! Of course! Sovereign was a small town. Everybody always talked about everything! She would have been expected to have heard of his relationship with Trudy Gorse. Amber realized that it was perfectly acceptable for an engaged man to flirt with a stranger on a boring bus ride, someone he knew he was never going to see again. But it was not so acceptable when that stranger turned out to be someone who knew that you were expected to come home and marry your childhood sweetheart!

Well, she wasn't going to change her behavior. What happened, happened. Certainly, she wasn't going to say anything. And if his heart was fixed on Trudy, the older woman had nothing to worry about. But, if his heart was not fixed …

Suddenly, Amber found herself hoping that his engagement to Trudy Gorse, of which she had recently heard, was more rumor than fact.

"My Dad drank himself to death," she blurted out. She wasn't sure why she said that; she just didn't want to lose the emotional connection that they had established.

He blinked, but said nothing.

"After my older brother was killed in a car accident."

"Yikes!" Compassion replaced the indifference in his ardent brown eyes.

"Dad blamed himself. He'd let Scott go to a party with some older kids and they were drinking and driving, of course, and the car crashed into a telephone pole. Scott was killed instantly."

"Jesus … how old were you?"

"Six. Fortunately, Mom hauled me off to a grief counselor. She begged Dad to come with us, but he said he didn't believe in head doctors. So he tried to drink the pain away, instead. It didn't work."

"Yeah, some of my buddies made the same mistake," Bruce commiserated. He fell silent, lost in thought.

Amber surreptitiously watched her seat mate. She recognized that a struggle was occurring within his breast, and felt both sorry for him and vindicated by her renewed efforts at intimacy. "Look at me, feeling sorry for myself," she declared, "to you – who's just come back from a war zone!"

He relaxed his grip, and looked up. "Seems to me you've got a lot to feel sorry for," he said.

"And you don't?"

He smiled. "Well, I wouldn't go that far. I've got a few regrets."

"About the war?"

"Nope."

"What then?"

His right hand inched closer, sending out an advance signal that he was "friend" not "foe," much like a sailing ship running up its flag. Amber's heart skipped a beat. He was back!

"Maybe I feel sorry that I never met a pretty woman like you earlier. Maybe then I wouldn't have been in such a hurry to rush off to war."

The heat of his suggestiveness hit her full force. Unprepared, she blushed. "If my math is correct, I would have been about ten when you joined the Guard," she replied. She attempted to cool her hot cheek with the palm of her hand.

"I bet you were still cute, though."

She smiled at him. "Flatterer."

"How'd you get your name? Was your Mom a hippie, or what?" he said, with a grin.

Amber giggled. "Not likely! I had a lot of hair when I was born, and I bet you can guess what color it was!"

"Ha, ha! The name still suits you, though."

But Amber didn't want to talk about herself; she wanted to learn more about him. "What are you going to do now?" she asked, curiously. "With your life, I mean," she amended hastily, as a devilish glint had appeared in his eyes.

"That's the million dollar question."

"You must have thought a lot about it?"

"Yeah."

"And … ?" The fingers of his hand brushed against hers, sending a little spark of electricity up her arm.

"Every soldier thinks about what he's gonna do when he gets home. He dreams about it for years, even," he replied, seriously. "The thing is, you always know it's only a dream, that it's not gonna happen. It's just a pleasant thing to think about so you don't think about getting yourself blown up by an IED or getting trapped in your truck and burning to death 'cause you can't get the damn door open." He glanced out the window, his gaze instinctively probing the passing landscape.

"I'm so glad you're out of there!"

"Me too. I was a nervous wreck whenever I drove out on a convoy," he admitted.

"I can imagine!"

"If you follow too far behind the guy ahead of you, you worry you might get lost over there and no one's ever gonna hear from you again," he continued. "But if you follow too close, and he hits the IED—wham! He flips his truck and you run into him. Now, both of you are on fire and in serious trouble! But you can't worry about that stuff all the time, if you did you'd go crazy. So you create this pretty dream for yourself about what you're going to do when you get back to the real world. But the whole time you're dreaming, you know that it's just a dream. It ain't ever gonna happen."

"Why not? Why can't your dream happen?!" Amber asked, earnestly.

He paused to collect his thoughts. "Because what I want to do isn't what I should do."

Amber understood immediately. "The classic moral dilemma: 'Should I follow my heart?' or 'Should I do the right thing?'"

"Something like that."

"Don't you think you've earned the right to do what you want?!"

"Nope. Not if it hurts others, like my parents and Gray."

"I can't imagine how it would hurt them!"

"That's because you don't know them."

Amber reflected a moment. She understood his concern for his family, and yet she knew – or thought she knew – that the young guardsman's family truly wanted him to be happy. She suddenly felt herself the font of therapeutic wisdom. "Disappointing others isn't the same as intentionally hurting them," she counseled. "If they're disappointed because your dream for you isn't the same as their dream for you, that's unfortunate, for them, anyway. But it shouldn't affect your decision to follow your bliss. I might not know your parents as well as you do – obviously I don't – but I know them well enough to know that unless you're happy, they're not going to be happy."

"Pretty wise words from a … " he broke off.

"Kid?" she finished for him, smiling.

"Yeah. How'd you get to be so smart?"

She shrugged. "The head doctor thing, remember? So … what's your dream?"

"Promise you won't laugh?"

"Nope. If you can't take it from me, you won't last long against your mother."

"Mom only wants the best for me," he replied, quickly.

"I know, I know! But there's only one person who knows what's best for you, and—it's not your mother, sorry."

"Don't apologize. I like it that you're honest with me."

He was silent for a moment, appearing to consider her advice. A boyish look suddenly came over his face. "Have you ever been down to the old canning factory, that big, run-down building in back of the train station?"

Amber was taken aback. "The canning factory? No, but I think I know what you're talking about. Wendell's mentioned it once or twice, only he called it the corn shop."

His eyes lit up. "That's the place! I bet you didn't know that Maine used to be the queen of the sweet corn canning industry?"

"You're kidding! I thought canned corn comes from places like Illinois and Idaho?"

"Maybe it does now, but it didn't always. For a hundred years Maine grew, canned, and shipped sweet corn all around the world. What would you say if I told you corn grown in Sovereign, Maine, fed the troops in the Civil War and the GI in the trenches of World War I and World War II?"

Amber was surprised. "I'd say that's pretty cool!"

"Clyde Crosby told me once that one Maine sea captain liked Sovereign's special blend of creamed corn so well he ordered eighty crates of it every year for his annual run to Australia!"

"Wow!"

"Old Clyde used to describe how the canning factory smelled when the sweet corn came in and I could almost taste those sweet, buttery kernels when he talked! It made my mouth water just listening to him." Bruce paused for a moment of pleasant reflection. "My Mom makes the best corn chowder, too! Not a stitch of meat in it, just a can of creamy sweet corn, Jersey milk, onions, salt and pepper, and lots and lots of butter."

"Stop, stop! You're making me hungry! But what happened to the canning factory? Was there a fire or something? Wendell told me the corn shop has been closed for, like, forty years!"

"In the early days of the canning industry – about 1860 – Maine had natural advantages over places like Illinois, Minnesota and Montana. We had cooler growing and harvest season temperatures, and lots of good rain, so we had better yields – more corn per acre, you know. We had better tasting sweet corn, too. We were the ones that came up with *White Crosby* and *Golden Bantam*. But improvements in technology – in the field and the factory, and even in transportation – took away our advantages. The guys out West caught up with us and after about a hundred years, the canning factories moved out of state. One day they were canning corn, and," he snapped his fingers, "the next day they shut down. Just like that, the sweet corn industry disappeared and most of the factories in Maine closed. Some of 'em, like the one in Sovereign, hung on into the sixties and seventies, canning some minor crops, like beans, peas and squash."

"Eeewww, squash!"

"Ha, ha, you don't like squash?"

"No!"

"You just never had good Maine squash before. That's one of the few crops still canned in the state. Over in South Paris."

Amber was completely fascinated. "How do you know so much?"

"I used to hang out at my Dad's store when I was a kid. My grandfather ran the general store then. All Grandpa's cronies – Clyde Crosby, Henry Gorse, Maynard Nutter – used to sit around the woodstove and shoot the shit. Sorry," he apologized, automatically, "shoot the breeze. They all worked at the canning factory at one time or other, and I loved sitting on the benches with them, listening to their stories. It all seemed so romantic to me. Everyone in town had some sort of connection to the factory, and a story or two to tell. Those were good days, when the corn shop was running! When the smoke was rising from the stacks it meant that the cash was coming into town. Even Grandpa had a hand in it. Grandma and Ma Jean would fry up donuts early in the morning and Grandpa would take 'em over with coffee at break time. When Dad was a kid – before he went over the road selling stuff for the store – he went to the corn shop with Grandpa and took lunch orders while the old man sold hot coffee and donuts."

"It sounds heavenly! I can almost smell the donuts frying. I wish we could turn back the clock!"

"Me too. I dreamed many a night while I lay in my bunk listening to the other guys snore about buying the old corn shop and starting it back up again. But …" he broke off. A dispirited sigh escaped him.

"But what?!" Amber encouraged, fervently.

"Aw, there's no going back. That place hasn't seen a penny of maintenance for forty years, plus the technology is hopelessly outdated. It's a dream. Just a stupid dream, something to think about so I didn't think about driving over an IED and becoming Afghan graffiti."

"But how do you know it won't work, if you don't try?!"

"I wouldn't even know where to begin."

"Oh, I'll help you, Bruce!" she cried. "I can't believe no one's thought of it before now! I've been involved with the 'buy local' movement for years, and I think canned local produce would be so cool! I can imagine selling sweet corn from Sovereign at the farmer's markets, especially in winter. People don't have time to grow and can their own sweet corn, but I bet they'd love to have it – if it was available."

"You're just saying that."

Amber shook her head energetically. "No, I'm not! And I know that everyone in Sovereign would want to help you, too, once they found out you wanted to get the canning factory running again!"

Pleased by her assurances, Bruce felt his spirits rising. They were both silent a moment, lost in their own reflections. "Well, then, now I am glad I came back early," he said, finally.

"You mean, you didn't plan it this way all along? To surprise your family?"

"Nope. I caught an earlier transport home, that's all. It happened so fast I didn't have time to notify the folks. Or even the Ladies Auxiliary."

Amber pictured him telephoning the mostly elderly members of the Ladies Auxiliary and giggled. "I'm sure they would have been your first call!"

"You don't believe me?" He pulled out his cell phone. "I've got Ma Jean on speed dial."

"Let me see that!"

Bruce teasingly lifted the phone just out of her reach. She made a little lunge for it, but he held it even higher. Her plastic hairclip popped off in the ensuing tussle over the phone, releasing cascading dark trusses. Temporarily blinded, she put her hands out to catch herself.

"Steady," he said, clasping her shoulders.

She felt his strong fingers taking command of her flesh, safely guiding her back down. Instinctively, she relaxed toward him.

He couldn't resist – he folded her into his arms. "God help me," he uttered, "I've wanted to do this from the first moment I saw you!"

Chapter 3

. . . .

The Ladies Auxiliary of Sovereign, Maine

When we last left our friends in Sovereign, Maine, the wispy yellow goldenrod of August was just coming into bloom and the rural farming community had very satisfyingly celebrated two weddings, including that of Lila Woodsum and Mike Hobart (whose adventures have been chronicled in a former tale), who relocated to Aroostook County shortly after their marriage. The second and more mature couple to tie the knot during the summer of 2012 – Rebecca Johnson, forty-eight, and Wendell Russell, sixty-five – stayed in Sovereign, making their home in the old Russell homestead, where Rebecca had been busy feathering her nest since being downsized from corporate America. With the support of Rebecca's daughter, Amber, the couple took over Lila's organic egg business, *The Egg Ladies*, and the little family of three was comfortably situated on the old home place, where, as a child, Wendell had helped his grandmother, Addie Russell, raise four hundred laying hens. When our story resumes a couple of months later, Rebecca and Wendell were therefore still enjoying the bliss one would expect from newlyweds.

"You're not leaving me!" Rebecca cried, seizing up the dish towel from the countertop next to the black soapstone sink and wiping the dusty flour from her hands. She tossed the towel back onto the counter, and transferred her hands to her curvaceous hips. She pouted at him, wisps of brown hair framing her pretty face. The tantalizing scent of molasses cookies filled the traditional eat-in country kitchen.

Wendell looked guilty, and hesitated at the escape route to the shed. He glanced longingly at the hot molasses cookies cooling on the wire rack on the kitchen table – tawny-colored cookies with thin, crisp edges, just the way he liked them. He could almost taste the burnt ginger, and his mouth watered. But he swallowed hard, and held firm to his purpose. "Wal, you know, there ain't no need for me to be heah. I ain't no lady."

Rebecca fastened her winsome blue eyes on him, and pushed a lock of soft brown hair back from her face. She pleaded her case. "But Wendell, dear, it's the first time I've hosted the Ladies Auxiliary. With Amber away, I … I might need you!"

Wendell faltered. He had never yet been able to say "no" to his bride. But there was a first time for everything.

"Wal, you know, 'tain't like you don't know everyone," he drawled. His years of travel with the US Navy had not been able to scrub the peculiar Maine accent from his voice. He hitched up his jeans, and returned his hand to the shed doorknob. Prior to their nuptials, Wendell, a bashful old bachelor, had never even called Rebecca by name. Since their wedding, he hadn't seen the need to change this policy, except, of course, when speaking of her to others. During those times he'd puff up like Bakewell Cream biscuits and proudly denote her as "Mrs. Russell" or "my wife." He was gratified by his pretty young wife, but perhaps not gratified enough to spend the afternoon with a flock of gaggling women. He fondled the cold iron doorknob.

"How do you think the great room looks?" The great room was the combined living-dining room of the old Russell homestead, at present attractively arranged for a gathering of twenty.

He peered obediently into the great room. Wooden chairs grouped about in threes or fours, and the antique oak dining room table was daintily spread with a lace tablecloth, cups and saucers, silverware, linen napkins and other accoutrements for an afternoon tea. "Looks awful shaap," he declared.

"You really think so?"

"Ayuh. You ain't got nuthin' to worry 'bout. 'Tain't like none of 'em nevah been heah before. There's jest gonna be Maude, Miss Hastings and Ma Jean."

"And Maggie Walker, the minister!"

"Don't worry 'bout Maggie. She won't stray too far from the food table." (This was not exactly a flattering portrait of yours truly.)

"And David O'Donnell! He'll be here, too."

"Wal, course, old David'll do the dishes for you, then." The one male member of the Ladies Auxiliary of Sovereign, Maine was openly gay, and well-known for his domestic abilities.

Rebecca sighed. "Oh, never mind," she said, smoothing down her apron. "You're right—I'll be fine." She smiled fondly at him, and indicated the molasses cookies with a quick shake of her head. "Help yourself, dear. Those burned ones are specially for you."

Wendell grinned broadly, flashing a gold upper incisor. "Don't mind if I do!" He reached out and secured four perfectly-burnt cookies from the wire rack.

"Just don't forget to pick up Amber. Remember, her bus gets into Bangor at four o'clock!"

"Ayuh." He carefully folded the cookies into a cloth napkin from the table. "'Til then, I'll be down to Ralph's store, if you need me."

"Oh, so that's where you go? Is that where they *all* go?"

Wendell nodded. "Thet's where the men go when the gals git together." He opened the shed door to exit, but she caught him before he made his final escape.

Standing on tip-toe, Rebecca pushed back his shaggy graying locks and gave him an affectionate kiss on the cheek. She dropped back down to her five-feet, two-inches and patted him on the arm. "That's just so you don't forget where you live," she said, suggestively.

He grinned broadly. "'Tain't likely," he replied. He winked.

Maude Gilpin, seventy-one, was the first member of the Ladies Auxiliary to arrive, about five minutes after Wendell had absconded with his rewards. She pulled slowly into the dirt driveway, which led to the rambling farmhouse and connecting barns and sheds. The fat, good-natured wife and grandmother was known in three counties for her culinary feats (her fiddlehead quiches were legendary), and she arrived a half hour early in order to unpack various goodies for the one o'clock tea meeting.

"There's more in the car," she said, handing off a stack of rubber tubs to Rebecca, who met Maude at the shed door. "I'll be right back."

"Oh, my goodness!" Rebecca exclaimed. "There's more?"

The Ladies Auxiliary of Sovereign, Maine, a local non-profit service organization, originated in 1850 when the need for a volunteer fire department in town had inspired the need to raise money to fund that fire department. (Four hay barns burned in that year while the townspeople stood by and helplessly watched.) If the men were to fight the fires, the women of Sovereign would raise money to equip them. Thus the first fundraiser ensued – the publication and sale in 1851 of a cookbook of favorite recipes – and the first fire truck, a horse-drawn affair, was soon secured. The Ladies Fire Auxiliary, as it was originally named, has raised tens of thousands of dollars (hundreds of thousands, if the truth were known) over the last one hundred and sixty years, utilizing every legal technique known to pick someone's pocket, including pie and cake sales, cookbooks, box lunches, breakfasts, suppers, and an occasional arts and crafts auction.

In 1987, however, the Sovereign Volunteer Fire Department was folded into the embraces of the tax paying citizens of Sovereign, and the Ladies services were no longer required. Although forced to drop the designation "Fire" from the name of their association, the Ladies determined to carry on with their charitable endeavors, and soon found many willing outlets for their cash (most notably our church and the Sovereign Historical Society). And so the pie and cake sales, cookbooks, box lunches, breakfasts, suppers, and occasional arts and crafts auctions continued.

Fifteen or so "ladies" (with apologies to David O'Donnell, who was present, as was I) shortly gathered in the great room of the old Russell homestead. After selecting platefuls of goodies from the dining room table, we settled into our seats. Rebecca, with a flushed, happy face, moved gracefully to and from the kitchen, keeping serving plates replenished and a blue stoneware pitcher of thick Jersey cream refreshed. A vintage 1980s coffee urn held down the far corner of the oak table, occasionally burping and gurgling, wafting the aroma of spicy black tea throughout the large, sunny oversized room.

"Tell me, dahrrrling – what's the secret of these WONDERFUL sugar cookies!" cried Miss Hastings, a diminutive eighty-seven-year-old retired music teacher who lived in an antique cottage located just a half mile further up Russell Hill. She teetered, china tea cup chattering, on the edge of her chair, looking not unlike her excitable pet chicken Matilda. Miss Hastings was dressed in her trademark black wool suit, dark nylons and frilly white blouse, and her wiry gray-black hair tumbled loose from the bun on the top of her head. "They are simply DELICIOUS!"

Maude, to whom the question was addressed, sat back into the over-stuffed couch, and looked coy.

"Caraway!" guessed Shirley Palmer, the former postmistress, recently retired after fifty years of faithfully sorting the mail and keeping (most) postal secrets. Shirley was married to the Road Commissioner,

Asa Palmer. "I kin see them queer-shaped seeds. You know the ones I'm talkin' 'bout, Miss Hastings? Ain't thet right, Maude?"

Maude acquiesced. "And … what else?"

"Oooo, a mystery!" exhorted Miss Hastings, eyes sparkling. Her tea cup rattled again. "I ADORE a mystery!"

"Careful," said Trudy Gorse (she who Bruce had been schooling himself to marry). Trudy was sitting next to the elderly Miss Hastings and leaned over and steadied the knobby, arthritic hand.

Shirley nibbled at the edge of the delicate shortbread cookie. She rolled the subtle-tasting morsel around in her mouth. "Mmmm … I kin almost taste it—it's on the tip of my tongue! Some kind of herb?"

"Butter," I suggested, winking at Trudy, whose fine Jersey butter, handmade in small batches, is sold in up-scale food markets in Maine and served in some of the best restaurants.

"That's a given, Maggie," said Maude, smiling fondly at Trudy. It was no secret in which pond Maude was angling for a new daughter-in-law. Trudy remained impassive, failing to rise to the bait.

"And it's the best butter, too!" I continued, quoting the March Hare from *Alice's Adventures in Wonderland*.

"What else?" said Maude.

I'm not much of a cook (domestic engineering not being a prerequisite for the ministry), but even I was intrigued. The butter cookies had a decidedly Victorian stamp to them and were incredibly addictive. My mouth watered, and I found myself hankering for the recipe.

"You'll never guess, so I'll tell you—rose petal jam!" Maude cried, sounding her trumpets.

There was a general chorus of disbelief. "Rose petal jam?!" "Oh, my goodness!" "I never would have guessed!"

Maude happily accepted the accolades. "It was a very good year for my old-fashioned roses – I brought them with me from Oaknole when Ralph and I were first married, you know – and so I made a batch of rose petal jelly. That only happens about once in a decade. Usually the petals brown up too early or the flowers hold tight to their buds and they're no good at all for jelly."

"I know jest whatcha mean about them holding tight to the buds," Shirley commiserated. "Once Asa bought me one of them new tea roses – 'twas a yeller one – and I could never get the darn thing to bloom. That thing jest sat next to the porch for two summers holding tight to its bud

23

like 'twas too precious for a country place. Wal, I got so mad at the darn thing I dug it up the next summer and planted it over next to the barn, right where we used to throw the manure out the hoss stall window. I'll be jiggered if that yeller rose hasn't bloomed every year since, sometimes twice!"

"Ladies, ladies – can we begin?" interjected Ma Jean, lightly rapping the wooden gavel on the coffee table. The unflappable eighty-two-year-old proprietor of Ma Jean's Restaurant was the President of the Ladies Auxiliary. "May we have the Secretary's Report, please?"

Trudy obediently flipped back a page in her notebook and read aloud to the group her succinct, hand-written report of the September meeting. At thirty-four, she was much more collected and serene than she had been at age ten, when she trapped and kissed Bruce Gilpin behind the bleachers at the Sovereign Elementary School. She was about five-feet, nine-inches, thin, with large hands and angular features. Trudy had never been beautiful but to my mind, she was the epitome of the "tomboy next door." A short mop of ash-brown hair and intelligent hazel eyes animated her high cheek bones. She had the double misfortune at birth to lose her mother and to be christened "Gertrude Rowena Gorse" by her somewhat elderly and romantic father, Leland Gorse, with whom she resided, and she had wisely chosen to abbreviate her given name almost as soon as she could talk.

"Thank you, Trudy," said Ma Jean, as the younger woman concluded her report. The President called for a vote accepting the minutes, and then briskly turned to Sheena Howe, who was situated on the opposite side of the room. "And now the Treasurer's Report."

Sheena, the only non-Anglo member of our group, likewise offered up her report in short order. She and her husband Paul, an IT expert at Unity College, had moved to Sovereign about a decade ago, discovering that the open and accepting farming community was an ideal place to raise their bi-racial family, which now consisted of five children of various shades of brown. Before the birth of her third child, Sheena had worked in financial services, and therefore handled the club's money and investments. "Unfortunately, the interest rate is still low," she continued, "so what we're earning on principal is extremely modest. But I still think it's safer staying in the CDs and bond funds rather than going back into stocks at this time, especially given the size of our balance."

There was a murmuring of agreement from the group.

"Any amendments or additions?" said Ma Jean. "Hearing none – all in favor of accepting the Treasurer's Report as written?" The vote was unanimous and Ma Jean raised her gavel, and brought it down with a sharp rap. "Minutes accepted as read."

The old business was moved through with the same rapidity, as everyone was anxious for the new business at hand – which was the grand celebration being planned for the return of our local hero and favorite son, Bruce Gilpin. A week from Saturday had been bespoken as Parade Day to celebrate Bruce's expected return, and would include, in addition to the parade, a chicken barbecue at the Fire Station. The Ladies Auxiliary was hosting both the parade and the barbecue. On that Sunday the Auxiliary would also host a church breakfast, a fund raiser specifically for our church, the Sovereign Union Church, of which I am the minister.

"Who wants to purchase the chicken?" asked the President.

Maude raised her hand. "Ralph can get us a discount through the store."

"Put the Vice President down for the chicken. And the paper products?"

"Ooo, I'll do that!" cried Miss Hastings. "It's the least I can do!"

"Very good – Jan."

Ma Jean was one of the few who called the town's beloved retired music teacher by her given name. Although only five years apart in age – Miss Hastings was the elder – the two ladies were polar opposites in character. Miss Hastings was extremely feminine and emotionally over-the-top, and Mabel Jean Edwards Brown was blunt, brusque and masculine. However, Miss Hastings and "Ma Jean" had been friends since childhood.

"And now about the banner … perhaps I should tell the group that last week I took the liberty of asking Rebecca to sew a 'Welcome Home' banner. How's that coming, Rebecca?"

"Oh, dear. I haven't started the banner, yet," Rebecca admitted. "But I promise I'll have it done by next Tuesday!"

"Very good." Ma Jean continued down her list with alacrity, grilling each member of the group as to her or his duties. After forty-five minutes, she reached the end of her list, and there was a momentary lull. The gingerbread clock on the mantle *clanged* three o'clock. Unfazed, Ma Jean glanced at her gold heirloom wrist watch, as if seeking confirmation of the time. "Is there any other business that needs to come before the group?" She raised her gavel warningly. "Hearing none – the October meeting of the Ladies Auxiliary is adjourned!"

The members broke up into little cliques, laughing and chatting as people do on a warm fall afternoon in Maine when they're in no hurry to be some-place else. Maude, always nimble on her feet despite her size, made her way easily through the crush to the dining room table, where Trudy was helping Rebecca clear away the dirty dishes. She clasped the younger woman's hand and squeezed it affectionately. "He'll be home soon, Sweetie!" she cried, her simple heart overflowing with pent-up, motherly feelings. She lifted a linen napkin from the table and daubed at her tears. "I almost can't believe it!"

"I'm so happy for you, Mrs. Gilpin," Trudy said, sincerely.

Maude's large breast heaved with emotion. "After all these years, Trudy, can't you call me M—Maude?" She caught herself just in time; she had almost said, "Mother."

Trudy smiled. "I've been calling you Mrs. Gilpin for so long now it seems like your first name. To change now would be like Father starting to call Abel—Cain, and Cain—Abel." These were the interesting Biblical names of her father's draft horses.

"But, Sweetie ... " Maude started to protest.

"You shouldn't get your hopes up, Mrs. Gilpin," Trudy said, gently. "You know I love Bruce – like everyone else in town – but he's going to need a lot of time to get reacquainted with us all. Sovereign has changed quite a bit in the eleven years since he's been in the Guard."

"He's been home several times!"

"What are a few months over the course of eleven years? Think of how we've all changed," Trudy urged. "Think how many new people have come to town." Maude's eyes instinctively sought out the figures of Sheena Howe and David O'Donnell. "Think how many farms have disappeared, and how many new houses have been built where there used to be pasture." A dairy farmer, Trudy was especially conscious of the loss of hay ground.

"But you're still here, Sweetie," said Maude, patting her hand. "And you're just the same as you've always been!"

Trudy recognized that Maude would not be talked down from her enthusiasm, and so she deliberately switched course to a direction that she knew the doting grandmother would follow. "And how is Gray do-ing? He's a junior now, isn't he? I hope all the excitement over his father's return hasn't affected his schoolwork?"

"Oh, no!" Maude hesitated. "Well, not much." While the old mother hen didn't want to admit that this particular chick was less than perfect, she also couldn't honestly give the impression that Grayden was anything like a stellar student. "He'll settle down once his father is back in the house, I'm sure."

"Bruce intends to live with you, then?" Trudy asked artlessly. She blushed when she realized the intimate nature of her question.

Maude patted her hand again. "Don't be embarrassed, *you've* got a perfect right to know that, Sweetie." She lowered her voice, signaling that Trudy's rights indeed trumped those of the rest of the group lingering around the table. "I wouldn't say this to anyone else, but I think Bruce doesn't want to be alone for the first few months."

"But he'd have Gray with him – he wouldn't be alone, would he?"

"Oh, no, he wouldn't take Grayden away from his home! We're so much like his real family now, and we're so handy to the store. You know Gray works with his grandfather every chance he gets."

"I see Gray in the store a lot. He's just like his grandfather. The customers love him."

"I wasn't sure for a while after that terrible incident with Tinkerbell, whether we were going to get Gray back in the store or not. He was so embarrassed to face everyone."

"Nobody blames him for shooting the white deer, Mrs. Gilpin. We all know that was an accident. He's a teenager. Accidents happen."

Maude shuddered. "We're so grateful that Mike Hobart was still around then, to rescue Grayden, or he might have been lost in the woods forever!"

At the mention of Mike Hobart, Trudy changed course again. "And when is Lila's baby due?"

"At the end of March. Or is it the first of April?" She turned toward where yours truly was standing next to the plate of Maude's rose petal sugar cookies. "Maggie – when are Lila and Mike expecting?"

"April Fool's Day," I replied, reaching for my third (or possibly fourth) cookie. "That is, if my sources are correct."

Ma Jean, who was passing like a queen from the room, overheard our conversation and paused in the doorway. "I'm sure they are. You've got more sources for information than I've got for sugar, Maggie Walker."

I laughed. "People do tell me things," I agreed. "But then, I know when to keep my mouth shut."

"Except in the pulpit?" someone suggested.

I laughed heartily, and some good-natured ribbing followed. It was well-known not only that I could be long-winded, but also that when my sermons ran long, Shirley's husband, Asa, kindly brought this to my attention by opening a hymnal and loudly *thunking* the book shut several times, not wanting to delay his dinner a minute past the noon hour. Fortunately for me, the question was rhetorical, and shortly after that the members of the Ladies Auxiliary of Sovereign, Maine dispersed like the mist that often rises up from Black Brook.

Chapter 4
The Men's Club

Prior to 1980, the Ladies Auxiliary always met at seven o'clock in the evening, and always on the second Wednesday of the month. But in 1980, the official meeting time was changed to one o'clock in the afternoon, and the date was changed to the second Monday of the month, Ma Jean's Restaurant being closed on Mondays.

To this day, most folks in town believe the time change that necessitated the day change occurred because the Ladies, many of whom were not as young as they used to be, decided that they didn't want to be out at night, especially in winter. Some of the Ladies even believed this explanation themselves. However, nothing could be further from the truth. The time change occurred because the husbands, fathers and sons of the ladies of the Auxiliary decided they didn't want to be away from their comfortable firesides after dark, and thus convinced their wives, daughters and mothers that it would be more convenient for the ladies if the Ladies met during the daytime.

What I admire about the Men's Club (a.k.a. the "Old Farts"), the loosely-knit bunch that gathers regularly to kibitz at Gilpin's General Store and always when the Ladies Auxiliary meets, is that they have no purpose beyond securing their general comfort of an afternoon. The Old Farts are not out to save the world nor do they want to find a cure for cancer. The most pressing concern is generally whether or not Ralph Gilpin, the seventy-six-year-old proprietor of the store, in keeping with the tradition started by his great-grandfather, Charlie Gilpin, has enough hard cider left to go around. Self-sacrifice is a worthy notion, but I've noticed that if a person keeps on giving and giving, quite often that person ends up with nothing. A soft seat next to the woodstove, a hot cup of coffee and a piece of apple pie go a long way toward the necessary rejuvenation of the human body and spirit.

When I first moved to Sovereign about fourteen years ago now, I'd occasionally catch the Old Farts in concert at the general store. "Pull up a chair, Minister!" Leland Gorse would bellow at me, as affectionately as though he attended church on a regular basis. "Nice to see ya!" And I did pull up a chair and joined them.

At that time, the little group of six or seven men occupied the front south corner of the store, next to the hot woodstove. However, when Ralph replaced the woodstove a couple of years ago with the new outdoor wood boiler, he took the opportunity to relocate the Men's Club to the back of the store, most likely so that he could place more tempting eye candy up front. This was met by such a chorus of moans and complaints from some of his best customers that the shopkeeper shortly acquiesced, and to this day the group remains happily ensconced in the corner by the big front window, holding fast to their traditional facing benches. The woodstove was replaced by a newfangled propane fireplace, making everything quite comfortable.

In the first few years of my duties as minister of the Sovereign Union Church, I made more progress finding my sea legs in town with the Old Farts than I did with the Ladies. The men welcomed me with no prerequisites, no categorizing, and no effort at handicapping my entrance into society. They were open, honest, friendly – and took me at face value. If I said I could do something, the men believed me, which naturally encouraged me to believe in myself.

Once I had received the blessing of the men, it was a somewhat shorter step to securing the women's blessing. The bar for the women, however, was set significantly higher than that of the men. For example, at the Ladies' church supper fundraisers I was politely invited to contribute a large, garden salad, which request seemed initially gratifying, until I learned the strict food hierarchy of the Church Supper. Believe it or not, baked beans, hot dogs (always red hot dogs), salads, breads and rolls, beverages, desserts – each has its place in an unwavering order of prominence, which order thus confers relative glory upon its maker or baker. Therefore, no lady willingly gives up her spot on the ladder to glory, and no lady moves up a rung in the female hierarchy until someone—drops dead. While salad is not at the bottom of the ladder, it is certainly not at the top.

"Don't feel bad," consoled David O'Donnell, at the fourth church supper to which I'd brought a salad. "When I first moved here they asked me to bring ketchup." Condiments are at bottom of the ladder.

When Wendell Russell met up with the Men's Club on this particular afternoon, there was much good-natured joking and ribbing. "Good of you to join us, Wendell!" "Warn't sure if you was gonna git away!" "Where's yer apron?"

In response, Wendell grinned at the group. There was a slight shuffling on one of the long benches and the newlywed hitched up his jeans and appropriated his usual spot. "Wal, you know, I warn't sure if I was gonna make it down myself," he admitted. His honest answer was met with more laughter, and some collegial back-slapping.

Ralph, who *was* wearing an apron, sidled up to the group, rubber sole shoes squeaking on the heavily-varnished wood floor. He balanced a large platter on his left arm, upon which multiple pieces of a cut pastry were gracefully arranged. He placed the platter and a handful of paper napkins down upon the low center table, and surveyed the buttery pastries with no little pride and satisfaction.

"Gawd almighty," exclaimed Leland Gorse. He picked up and examined a luscious-looking piece of the flaky pastry. A chunk of brown-sugared apple oozed out and plopped seductively onto the plate. "What's Maude cooked up for us today?"

"'Tain't baklava, is it?" worried ninety-three-year-old Clyde Crosby, loudly. "I never liked baklava. Too sweet."

Ralph glared at Clyde. "'Tain't likely."

"Looks darned good," interjected John Woods, spying the shopkeeper's spark of contumacy and quickly stomping it out. The seventy-year-old Sovereign selectman was a politician of the old-school variety, and completely understood Ralph's doting pride in his wife of fifty-three years. John's wife, Ruth Woods, held the penultimate position on the female food ladder, baker of yeast rolls, while Maude Gilpin held fast to that sacred top spot, desserts.

"It's Maude's apple strudel!" Ralph declared, putting his hands to his skinny hips.

Leland bit into the gooey dessert, and rolled his eyes toward heaven. "Gawd almighty!"

"I keep tellin' ya, my Maude is the best cook *evah*! This here is an old family recipe from her folks ovah to Winslow, and ..."

"What?! What's that you're sayin', Gilpin?" shouted Clyde, cupping his right ear. "I cain't hear ya!"

The shopkeeper raised his voice. "I said – Maude only bakes it *once a year*, during *Christmastime*! But she wanted to do somethin' special for the Men's Club *today*."

"You tell Maude we're mighty appreciative," Woods said smoothly. He helped himself to a large slice of strudel. "If we started every selectman's meeting with some of Maude's cooking, we'd get through our agenda with a lot less complaining, and probably a lot quicker, too."

Ralph appeared vindicated, and disappeared to refresh beverages.

The rest of the little group eagerly helped themselves to the cinnamon-laced apple strudel, and conversation flagged – unless the gentle cooing and billing that accompanies satisfied eating and drinking counts as conversation – until the strudel was completely consumed. At that point, Ralph pulled up a chair and joined them. This was the slow time of day in the store, when the wizened shopkeeper could afford to sit and rest his weary bones.

"Maude must be downright giddy, expecting Bruce next week," Woods continued. "We're real happy for you both. Tell Bruce when he gets home we've been keeping his seat warm on the bench here." And the selectman patted an open space on the comfortable cushioned seat next to him.

"Is he a-going back to work at General Agglomeration, or where evah 'twas he worked in Bangor afore he joined the Guard?" asked Leland. "They're supposed to keep his job open, ain't they?"

Now, this was a point upon which Ralph and his wife differed. Maude was anxious that Bruce should pick up the traces of his former life and get back to work. She was even willing to toss in a new wife, to help her son steady the load and share his burdens. But Ralph harbored the notion that, after more than a decade of fighting in two different wars, Bruce had earned some time off. Maybe now was the time for his son to liberate Charlemagne from the garage and drive cross country. ("Charlemagne" was Bruce's blue 1969 AMC Rambler, which he had appropriately named after the legendary war horse belonging to the 20th Maine's Col. Chamberlain.)

"We ain't sure yet jest what he's gonna do," Ralph admitted, absently twisting the dish cloth in his hand. "They got his job held for him, alright, but I ain't sure he's gonna take it. He's saved up a lot of money over the past few years, what with Gray living with us and all, so Bruce don't need to rush right back to work."

"I hope he don't, then," allowed Asa Palmer, the town's unflappable Road Commissioner, notorious for driving his yellow Cat-12 grader down to the general store when his truck wouldn't start. In an unusual burst of energy, Asa slapped his palm on the arm of the wooden bench. "I hope he don't. There's no hurry at-*tall*."

"Here, here," agreed Wendell, who himself had retired from the US Navy a few years earlier.

Ralph grasped at these straws of hope. "Thet's right – ya didn't rush right back to work, now didja, Wendell!" he said, eagerly.

"Wal, you know, I ain't quite as young as I used to be."

"What's Bruce say himself?" Woods inquired, shifting his lanky frame to a more comfortable position on the bench.

"He ain't saying much. He's keeping his cards pretty close to his chest, likely so his mother don't see 'em. But now that you mention it, John, he did want me to ask you a question."

"Shoot."

"He was wantin' to know if the town still owned the old corn shop."

"Gawd almighty! I ain't thought of thet place in ages," said Leland. "Father and I used to grow corn for thet old corn shop. Thet was afore Cain 'n Abel, course."

"We know all about it, Leland," said Asa.

"Oh, we still own the canning factory alright," answered Woods. "And we'd be happy to unload it, too."

"And Clyde here used to work in the retort room, putting them cans under pressure. Ain't thet right, Clyde?"

"Eh?"

"RETORT! Remember thet?!"

"Yessuh, by gawd, I do!" Clyde thundered. "I ain't never blew a retort, but I heared as some thet did! Stahted goin' to the corn shop with Mother when I was 'bout knee-high." And he lowered his arthritic paw to a corresponding height off the varnished oak floor.

"Was she a husker?"

"Eh?"

"Did she HUSK the CORN?"

"No, Mother worked the desilker."

"Now, why do you suppose Bruce is interested in thet old corn shop? He ain't queer, is he?" worried Asa. (By the term "queer" Asa kindly meant "touched in the head" from his military experience, and not that Bruce might be gay.)

"I'm sure Bruce has got his reasons for inquiring," Woods interjected. "And while we'd like to dump the property, Ralph, we certainly wouldn't like to dump it onto your boy."

Ralph equivocated. "Oh, I ain't sayin' he wants to buy it – he jest wants me to ask you 'bout it."

"Send him over to see me when he gets home. I'll tell him everything he wants to know, and then some."

Another agreeable memory occurred to Leland, and he elbowed Clyde on the bench next to him. "Member them gals from Boston?" he chaffed.

"What?!"

"Them GALS from BOSTON."

"Guess probbly I do!"

"Them the gals that took their summer vacations in Maine one year so as they could pick string beans?" Asa inquired.

"Ayuh. They worked for me and Bob Cooley. I paid 'em 6¢ a pound— ain't thet right, Clyde? SIX CENTS a pound!"

Clyde guffawed.

"'Twas twice what I paid t'others!"

"Thet's cause the young fellers paid you 4¢ a pound so as they could pick with 'em," said Asa, "*Didn't* them gals like to pick beans with their shirts off!"

The double-glass door to the general store *whooshed* open, and a mother with a young child clinging to her leg entered. She smiled at the group, and the members of the Men's Club nodded pleasantly in response.

"Hush," said Ralph, in a lowered voice. "'Tain't proper talk for a public place."

The young mother, Jessica Gould, approached the shopkeeper. "Do you have any pumpkin pie filling, Ralph?"

"Yep. Got some *One-Pie Pumpkin* down back. Maude likes the *One-Pie Squash* best, though."

Unfortunately, Clyde, whose face was turned toward the propane fireplace, hadn't heard the shopkeeper's caution or seen the woman's approach. "Sometimes them gals from Boston took off their BRASSIERES, too," he bawled.

Jessica Gould put her hands over her son's ears, and quickly trundled him off toward the back of the store.

Ralph hopped up. "Now you've done it!" he said, angrily. "No more corn shop stories!" He twisted adroitly, and disappeared in hot pursuit of his customer.

"Nice work, Clyde," said Asa.

"Eh?"

"We was jest getting stahted, too," lamented Leland, who had already wound himself up with another tale.

"I bet you were," said John Woods, reaching for his cup of cold coffee. "I bet you were."

Not long after this exchange, the store's pendulum wall clock chimed 3 p.m., releasing the Old Farts from their agreeable afternoon labors. They stretched, and exited the general store to retrieve their women from the Ladies Auxiliary.

Chapter 5
. . . .
The Natural Order of Things

"No parade, Mother," Bruce said. This edict was laid down gently but firmly the morning after his return to Sovereign. Having drunk from the Fountain of Youth during the four-hour bus ride with Amber Johnson, there was no going back for him. His adolescent hopes and dreams, so long repressed, had burst to the surface.

The prior evening the Gilpin household had been filled with laughter, hugs and tears, including an emotional reunion between father and son. But not much in the way of meaningful conversation had occurred as Maude's long-absent chick was snuggled back into the family nest. Now, however, morning had broken, and Bruce had sharpened his spurs. He dawdled at the breakfast bar in the family's 1918 Sears® manufactured house (the quaint Greenview Model), toying with his coffee mug. Ralph had just left for the general store and Gray, despite the teen's protests, had been dispatched on the school bus. A doting Maude was hovering over her chick, taking every opportunity she could to press his flesh, as though she couldn't believe he was really back in the nest.

Bruce took another sip of coffee, and began the hard work of undoing all of his mother's hopes, schemes and dreams. "No parade," he reiterated.

"No parade!" a shocked Maude echoed. She set the glass coffee pot down onto the granite countertop across from him with a *splot*. About ten years ago a doting Ralph, who had inherited the home from his grandfather, had added onto the kitchen in order to support his wife's culinary activities. He'd doubled the size of the room and, in addition to the large breakfast bar, the kitchen now boasted two convection ovens, a six-burner gas range, double refrigerator and a commercial dishwasher, all in matching stainless steel.

"And no barbeque, either," Bruce continued. "I want to go back to having a normal life as quickly and quietly as possible."

His mother offered up a little gurgling noise. "You can't be serious!"

"I am serious." He stood up from the bar, bringing his height and all of the weight of a returning war veteran up to bear upon the situation. The granite gulf between them widened.

"But, Sweetie, it's all planned out," cried Maude, clasping her fat hands together in despair. "All of us Ladies have our little jobs – I'm getting the chicken, and Rebecca's even sewing a 'Welcome Home' banner!"

Bruce rested the palms of his capable hands on the polished granite countertop and leaned toward her. "I'll reimburse anyone for any money that's been spent so far."

"That's not the point! Nobody wants your money – we want *you*!" Her eyes welled up. "The whole town wants to officially welcome you home!"

He smiled, the winsome, Hodges' smile he knew she never could resist. "The best welcome people can give me is to let me have my own way."

A desperate Maude played her ace in the hole. "But Miss Hastings will be so disappointed!" Now, Miss Hastings had been Bruce's favorite teacher in elementary school, and their fondness for each other was legendary. "She's been looking forward to riding in Charlemagne with you – you're to be the lead car in the parade!"

But Bruce was not to be turned from his adjudication. "I'll go see Miss Hastings and explain everything to her myself. She'll understand."

Disappointed, the air of éclat fizzled from Maude's fat frame. She sagged against the breakfast bar, head and shoulders drooping.

"Sit down, Mother," he said. He moved around the end, and gently steered her into one of the tall stools.

She shook her head in stunned disbelief. "We thought you'd be proud of your service to your country! Your father and I certainly are!"

"I am proud. But I just did my duty, like a lot of other guys – only I'm one of the lucky ones who brought all my parts and pieces back home."

She gazed up at him, her adoring eyes searching his handsome face. Was there ever a chick more wonderful than this?! Surely, she could be happy without parading him through town! Every step he took, every word he uttered made her simple heart sing.

"I want to take it one day at a time," he continued. He pulled up the stool next to her and sat down. "Become a regular citizen, just like everyone else in Sovereign."

Maude perked up at these interesting words, "just like everyone else in Sovereign." Her thoughts turned to the other scheme that lay near and dear to her heart. "Trudy is so looking forward to seeing you," she said, coyly.

"And I'm looking forward to seeing Trudy again," he said. "But ..."

Maude's heart fluttered with frightened expectation. "But ... ?"

"I'm not gonna marry her."

This was too much for Maude Gilpin. She burst into tears.

Bruce let his mother cry. He reached for a box of tissues from atop the microwave, and set them on the counter. "Here," he said, after a minute or two. He tugged two or three fluffy sheets from the box. "Blow your nose, and we can talk."

Obediently, his mother did as she was ordered. She let out a sigh of disappointment, and tucked the soiled tissue into her apron pocket. This day – so long hoped for! – was not turning out at all how she'd envisioned!

"You know I love you, Mom," he said, taking her by the plump hand. (This was rewarding. He only called her "Mom" in moments of extreme affection.) "I can never repay you and Dad for everything you've done for Gray and me."

"Oh, that was nothing!"

"It was everything. But now he and I need to get to know each other again. The last thing Gray needs is for me to stick Trudy in the middle of the mix."

"But Gray and Trudy are old friends!" Maude protested. "She's a good woman and she'd be a great mother! And you know yourself she'd make some man a wonderful wife!"

"Yeah, but that man ain't gonna be me."

Maude searched deep into his brown eyes for some sign of hope. "Are you sure?" she pleaded. "Don't be too quick to decide! After all, you haven't even seen her in eighteen months; she's quite lovely now."

"I'm sure she is. She always was pretty. You know we've been good friends since we were kids. But I'll never be able to ... to care about her, at least not in the way you want me to care about her."

This last pronouncement was too much for the heart-sore Maude. She rose up from her seat emotionally. "Oh, you young people don't know what real love is! It's not all wine and roses, and waves crashing on the beach. It's downright uncomfortable sometimes. Look at your father and me – we've been married for fifty-three years now – and it wasn't all smooth sailing, I'll tell you! But there's not another couple in Maine as happily married as we are."

Bruce chuckled, and slung an arm around his mother's rounded shoulders, squeezing her affectionately. "That's the problem – you and Dad have set too good an example. Did you marry Dad because you thought he was going to be a good husband?"

"Well, I certainly didn't think he was going to be a bad husband!"

"Or … did you marry Dad 'cause you thought he was about the hottest thing going when he pulled into Grandpa's farm in that flashy 1957 Rambler Cross Country Station Wagon?"

Maude made a little sound of protest. He stopped her. "Too late, I've heard the story too many times. The two of you were crazy about each other. You married Dad because you didn't think you could live without him. If that isn't the waves crashing on the beach, I don't know what is!"

Maude was completely conquered. "Oh, just don't go telling your father I can't live without him," she said, tartly. "He's got a big enough head as it is."

Bruce released his grip. "I'm pretty sure he knows it by now."

Mollified, Maude reclaimed her seat. "But, Sweetie, I hate to think of you without any woman in your life at all, except me and your sister!"

"I'm not ruling out women entirely. I'm just ruling out Trudy."

Something in the tone of his voice made Maude's motherly heart quake. What did he mean? Was there someone else? Was he going to drop another bombshell on her!

Her voice faltered. "Is there … someone else?"

Bruce's memory tempted him with the last image he had of Amber Johnson, gaily waving goodbye to him as she and Wendell drove out of the yard. He reverently recalled her bright blue eyes, her gentle encouragement, and her exuberant spirit. "Not at the moment," he lied.

Maude fell silent, a thousand thoughts piling up in her head. She knew that Wendell had dropped Bruce off at the house last evening, and that her son had returned on the same bus as Amber Johnson. Had the two met on the bus? Had they chatted? Was there something that Maude, as a careful, doting mother, needed to be chary about?

The possibility of a Bruce-Amber connection had worried her ever since Rebecca Johnson (now Russell) and her lovely daughter Amber had moved to Sovereign. It was not only the fact that Maude herself had already selected Trudy as her next daughter-in-law but also that she believed the age gap between her son and Rebecca's daughter as insurmountable. She experienced a twinge of conscience now as she recollected that she had even attempted to forestall such a romantic possibility by making it generally known at the Russell homestead that Bruce and Trudy were all but engaged.

She hesitated. "What do you think of Amber Johnson? Isn't she pretty?"

"Is she? I hadn't noticed."

"How could you not …" Maude broke off. He was teasing her. Her son was a man. He'd noticed.

Bruce burst out laughing. "Ha, ha – give it up, Mom! I know where you're going, and you can stop it right there."

"I don't know what you're talking about!"

"Oh, yes, you do."

Maude was relieved to note that his tone was carefree, somewhat cavalier. If there was an attraction between Bruce and Amber, it was most likely of a sexual nature, which certainly wouldn't last. "I just don't want you to get your heart broken."

"Why not me, as well as any other guy? Besides, who says Amber Johnson would break my heart?"

"I don't think she would intentionally. She's just a child, after all. She's not much older than Gray."

"Yeah, and I'm really old."

"You're not old!" his mother protested. "You're still a young man."

"Then what's the problem?"

"There's too much of an age gap between you. It wouldn't be natural!"

"There's five years between you and Dad," Bruce pointed out, sagely.

"Five years is certainly not the same as fifteen years!"

"What is that, some kind of new math? Amber Johnson is almost twenty-two and I'm thirty-five. That's only thirteen years difference."

"That means she was three when Gray was born," his mother quickly shot back.

This new angle on the age difference did give Bruce a moment's unease. Was he too old? Was she too young?

Maude saw his discomfort, and pressed her attack. "I really, really don't think it would work! There's a Natural Order of Things, like in a vegetable garden." A true farmer's daughter, she easily appropriated a suitable metaphor for her course of instruction. "You don't plant corn before you plant peas; you plant seeds in their proper order: peas, beans and corn. Why? Because if you plant the corn too early in the spring, the seeds will rot. And if you plant the beans before the peas, the late spring frost will kill the buds and the beans won't blossom. If the beans don't blossom you can't harvest any string beans, can you? Everything has a season, and in that season everything has an order. You had the season of the peas, but Amber's is the season of corn."

His mother's philosophy had so much of the ring of truth about it that her words gave Bruce pause. Was there a Natural Order of Things? And did this Natural Order preclude him from a romantic relationship with Amber Johnson?

He dutifully tried to quench the hope that had thrilled him to the bones since the bus ride yesterday. But it was to no avail. His heart would not be talked back down.

Maude sensed that she had gained some ground, and wisely decided not to push her luck. She remembered how stubborn her son could be; he had inherited that trait from his father. Once Bruce's mind was made up to something, it was very difficult to turn him. She didn't want to accidentally push him into Amber's arms. Instead, she returned to the original and most pressing topic, how to officially welcome him back into the community.

"Will you at least come to the church breakfast?" she pleaded. "Give us that much, please, Sweetie!"

He stood up. "I'll think about it," he said. He reached for his jacket.

"Where are you going?"

"I'm taking Charlemagne out for a drive, just to see what's new. Then I'm going over to the farm to see Peter."

"You're going to Oaknole?!"

"Don't look so terrified – it's only twenty-two miles to the farm. You forget where I've been for the past eighteen months. I think I can safely go to Winslow and back in time for supper!"

But Maude had forgotten nothing. This was another page from her lesson book, The Natural Order of Things, a page with which her son would become familiar someday soon. When a fledgling chick has left the nest, the mother hen still worries about her progeny, but that disquiet is little more than a nagging concern. But whenever a fledgling returns to the nest, even for a brief visit, all the mother hen's original anxieties return and the chick is once again subject to the clucking and fussing once bestowed upon the newly-hatched banty.

"I don't know what happens when you're not here, but when you're under my roof, I worry about you! Now, don't be late for supper."

"Five o'clock still?"

Maude stood up. She automatically gathered up his dirty coffee cup and teaspoon. "You know your father!"

He grinned. "Good to know some things never change."

And the hero of the moment turned and walked out the door, just like any other human being. But his mother, despite her disappointment, still considered him the finest cockerel in the flock.

Chapter 6
. . . .
Across Town

Across town, at the old Russell homestead, a similar conversation was about to occur. Shortly after nine o'clock that same morning, Amber returned to the house from the attached hen pen having tended the family's flock of three hundred organic layers. She doffed her Muck™ boots in the shed, and entered the comfortable country kitchen in her stockinged feet. She placed a dozen eggs for the household on top of the counter next to the black soapstone sink and washed her hands. The eggs that were for sale remained in the cold storage room that Wendell's ancestors had built into the cool earth below the shed.

Amber poked the fire, and helped herself to a cup of hot coffee from the eight-cup percolator pot that was warming on the back edge of the woodstove. She spooned some of Wendell's honey into her coffee, stirred the steaming beverage, and then settled into her customary chair at the antique oak table. She flattened a section of the Bangor Daily News that had been left temptingly near her calico placemat, and began reading.

Hearing her daughter return from her morning chores, Rebecca, who was in the great room sewing, stopped stitching a tear in one of Wendell's flannel shirts. She lightly entered the kitchen, and dropped a kiss on her daughter's head.

"How many did we get today, dear?" she inquired, opening the cover of the gray, corrugated egg box. She admired the large, farm-fresh brown eggs.

"Two hundred and ten," Amber replied, without looking up from the newspaper. "Those new pullets of Lila's are really starting to come on line now."

"Are the old ones still laying?"

"Mmm. They seem to be. Wendell said to turn the light on earlier and keep it on later, and that's helped. The chickens haven't seemed to notice that we're losing daylight."

45

"I'm glad for that!"

Me too, Amber thought, pausing in her perusal of the newspaper. But she said nothing aloud. Since taking over *The Egg Ladies* from Lila Woodsum, after Lila's marriage in June, Amber had noticed that the organic business had a serious cash-flow problem. The money was mostly going one way: out! Amber knew that her mother harbored deep anxieties about money (or lack thereof) and so she had made the decision to say nothing to either her mother or Wendell until she had not only assessed the situation, but also come up with a potential solution.

"Are you making the egg delivery to Belfast today, or is Wendell?" Rebecca continued, now happily frying up two farm-fresh eggs with their deep yellow yolks. The smell of toast and hot coffee wafted through the warm country kitchen.

"Wendell said he'd do it," Amber replied, glancing up. "I've got some studying to do today." She adjusted her thick ponytail, and gazed out the south-facing kitchen window. The sun was just beginning to work its way around the east side of the hen pen, and a few rays spilled over into Amber's lap. She noticed that Wendell's truck was missing from its customary spot in the dooryard. "Where'd he go? I hope he hasn't forgotten."

"He's gone down to Ralph's store to get something, some material for his latest project. He won't be long." Rebecca laid a clean calico napkin onto the matching placemat in front of her daughter, and added a set of silverware neatly on top.

"Thanks, Mom." Amber instinctively arranged the silverware, and slid the cloth napkin down into her lap. "What's he working on now?"

"Some kind of thingamajig to catch those flying squirrels in the shed."

"The Mouse Motel won't work on the flying squirrels?" The "Mouse Motel" was a wire cage with extended compartments that Wendell had built months earlier, and with which contraption he caught, kept and (when the motel was full) transported live mice far away from the old Russell homestead.

"I guess not." Rebecca had returned to her cooking, and now grasped the handle of the cast iron frying pan with a pot holder and used a wood-handled metal spatula to expertly flip the eggs. "He says the Mouse Motel is too small – that the squirrels won't go in there, no matter what he uses for bait."

"I'm surprised he didn't get the stuff when we were in Bangor yesterday," Amber mused.

"You know how he likes to give Ralph as much business as he can." Rebecca felt a twinge of guilt as she strayed from complete veracity. The truth was that she had asked Wendell to vacate the premises so she could have a heart-to-heart talk with her daughter. After listening to Amber chat eagerly about Bruce Gilpin last night upon her return from Boston, Rebecca had thought she had better set her daughter on her guard.

"Too bad it won't work," said Amber, taking a rewarding gulp of coffee.

"What?" Rebecca gave a little start.

"The Mouse Motel – too bad it won't work. But I can't wait to see his new thingamajig. Wendell is so good with his hands." This statement suddenly reminded her of Bruce Gilpin's capable hands, and her heart skipped a beat. She relived their intimate moments on the bus yesterday in all of their deliciousness. She also felt a twinge of guilt. She had spoken a few words about Bruce to her mother, but she certainly hadn't shared everything that had occurred on the four-hour bus ride. She could still feel the sensitive touch of his strong fingertips on her arms, and shivered with satisfaction.

"Cold, dear? I can throw another piece of wood in the stove?"

"Uh, I'm OK. It just was damp in the hen pen this morning."

Rebecca finished her culinary preparations, and set the breakfast plate – piled high with bacon, toast and eggs – in front of Amber. She stepped back with a satisfied smile, wiping her hands on her apron. "Want some jelly, dear? Wendell opened a jar of raspberry this morning."

"I'm good," Amber said, attacking the hot plate hungrily. "This is great, Mom, thanks."

Rebecca refreshed her own coffee, and sank down into the chair at the head of the table, her customary seat. Before she was married, they all had their appointed seats at the table: Lila, Rebecca and Wendell. When Lila left, Rebecca had appropriated the head chair. After her wedding to Wendell, nothing had changed, except that Amber had taken her mother's chair after switching from a residency to an online program at UMass, thereby joining the household fulltime. The biggest change at the old Russell homestead was that Amber had taken over Lila's day to day operation of the organic egg business.

Rebecca smiled at her daughter. "I'm glad you got to meet Bruce Gilpin yesterday. Isn't he handsome?" she asked, in a back-handed attempt at opening her romantic intervention. "Maude showed me a picture of Bruce in his uniform a few months ago."

"You think any man in uniform is handsome, Mom!" Amber teased.

"As well I should. But tell me, what did you think, dear?"

"He didn't have his uniform on, but he's still pretty hot."

Rebecca winced. This was discouraging. A big worry since she'd moved to Sovereign was that the dashing guardsman would return from Afghanistan and run off with her daughter's heart. Amber was innocent, affectionate, impulsive, and only twenty-one-years-old. Bruce Gilpin was thirty-five, had fought in two wars, and was likely world-weary, battle-scarred and suffering from PTSD. Rebecca also was cognizant of the fact that Amber had a habit of searching for her next "cause." (This was not necessarily a bad thing; after all, they had ended up in Sovereign partly because of Amber's dedication to the organic food movement.) What cause could be more appealing to a young woman like Amber than a handsome, brooding veteran?

"Did you get a chance to talk to him on the bus?"

In a split second, Amber's mind was opened to her mother's intent. "We sat next to each other, Mom. Not on purpose. It just happened. We talked."

"My goodness!" Rebecca exclaimed, her prejudice slipping out before she could stop it. "The whole four hours?"

"Don't look so shocked, Mom. It was just a bus ride. He didn't propose, or ..." Amber broke off. She had almost added the words "or anything," until she realized that "or anything" to her mother would probably include the ardent words dropped from Bruce's lips as he held her in his arms. She smiled at the memory.

"Oh, Amber! Don't get involved with Bruce Gilpin, please!"

Amber set her fork down onto the plate, and girded herself up for battle. "Mom, what do you have against Bruce Gilpin? After all, he's spent the last eleven years fighting for us! Don't you think he deserves our respect?"

"He can have my respect – he does have my respect. But not my daughter!"

Amber sat up straight. "C'mon Mom, I'm twenty-one-years-old – almost twenty-two!"

"I know, I know, I don't have any authority over you anymore!"

"Plus – it's not like I'm going to stay single all my life! At least, I hope not."

"Oh, dear! I just don't want you to run off with a battle-scarred war veteran!" Rebecca's soft blue eyes filled with tears. "At least, not yet."

"Not yet?! When, then?"

"When you're forty-eight. Then you can run off with whoever you choose, like I did with Wendell. I promise, I won't say a word, then!"

Amber relaxed. "Very funny. I thought you wanted grandkids? I'm not going to bring you many grandkids at forty-eight!"

This was problematic. The whole situation was problematic! Rebecca knew that the more she argued against Bruce Gilpin, the more romantic she was making him appeal to her impressionistic daughter.

"Darling, I just want what's best for you!"

"I know, Mom. But I also know there's only one person who knows what's best for me, and …"

"It's not me," Rebecca finished, sadly. She sat her coffee mug down on the placemat. "Sometimes I'm sorry I ever took you to that psychiatrist."

"No, you're not." Seeing the look of despair on Rebecca's face, Amber jumped up and gave her mother an affectionate hug. "Don't worry, Mom. There's too much of the practical, pragmatic you in me for me to go too far wrong in picking a man."

"It's not my DNA that I worry about – it's your father's," replied Rebecca, honestly. She reached up and brushed back a few strands of wayward dark locks that had escaped from her daughter's ponytail. "You know what Dad was like. He was so impulsive and, and …"

"Hot-tempered?"

"Emotional and vulnerable."

"Oh, Mom! Even if something does happen between Bruce and me – and I'm not saying that anything is going to happen – who's to say I'll be hurt? Maybe we'll fall madly in love and live happily ever after?"

Rebecca slid her arm around her daughter's trim waist and hugged her close. "Promise me one thing – no matter what happens, you'll be happy, dear?"

Amber hugged her mother back. "Now, that I can promise!"

A little commotion was heard in the shed, and the door to the kitchen popped open, interrupting the mother-daughter tête-à-tête. Wendell stuck his head in. "Wal, was I down to Ralph's long enough?" He grinned, gold tooth flashing. "You gals all dun jawin'?"

The two women burst out laughing. "Perfect timing," said Amber, releasing herself from her mother's loving clasp. "I've got to go study."

Rebecca kept silent. She wished in her heart that her husband had stayed away another half hour. Another thirty minutes or so and she might have effectively planted the seeds of doubt in Amber's mind. In addition, she had a little plan of her own in regard to another potential suitor for her daughter, Ryan MacDonald. Ryan was a high-powered attorney for Perkins & Gleeful, the Boston insurance company for whom Rebecca and Lila had once worked. At thirty-three, Ryan was a handsome man-about-town, and still single. He had once romantically favored Lila Woodsum, but after Lila's wedding Rebecca thought she had perceived a growing attraction to Amber. Ryan had last visited the farm in August, during which time a little group of friends (including Amber) had taken a trip to the Maine coast. Yesterday she had received a text message from Ryan saying he was coming north yet again. Rebecca had wanted to lay the groundwork for his visit – to sow the seeds of another suitor in her daughter's mind. She had lost one opportunity, but there would be other chances to glorify Ryan before his arrival.

Amber retreated upstairs to the snug space on the second floor landing of the stairwell where she had parked her schoolwork, books and laptop. She had claimed this small bit of sunny space, about six-feet by eight-feet, next to the tall, west-facing window where Wendell's grandmother, Grammie Addie, used to work on her sewing. Fortunately for Amber, her mother preferred to keep all of her sewing accoutrements downstairs in closer proximity to the daily egg customers, so she was able to appropriate the cozy space for herself. Amber had relegated Grammie Addie's old treadle sewing machine to the open chamber but kept the drop-leaf maple table for a desk, and joined with it a comfy floral-pattered wingback for a chair. A headless, old-fashioned mannequin, partially-dressed in an unfinished burgundy silk dress, eavesdropped from the corner, and two 1920s Charles Sawyer landscape prints adorned the floral-papered walls.

Amber settled herself into the Queen Anne's chair, her right arm pressed against the side, her delicate chin and cheek resting against her palm. She gazed out the window at the serene view that opened up before her appreciative eyes. Golden fields dotted with colorful wildflowers sprawled down over the hill toward the western horizon, where Amber caught a tantalizing glimpse of the dusky purple tops of the White Mountains. The fields were lined with glorious fall foliage, sharply-colored reds, golds, oranges and yellows. Mare's tails in the sky added a splash of white to the azure blue, making the panorama appear surreal and impressionistic. In summer, the leafy green maple trees that protected the front of the house screened out most of the view from the second story, as well as the hot sunlight, however, now, in autumn, when the fiery leaves had begun to fall, the ancient weathered trees complemented the view rather than obscured it.

Amber sank back deeper into the soft chair. A restful sigh escaped her. From this state of luxuriating repose, her mind reverted to those precious moments of yesterday with Bruce Gilpin. Until those indelible moments, Amber hadn't believed in love at first sight. A practical young woman (if somewhat enthusiastic when considering her latest cause) Amber had always been suspicious of the intense romantic feeling experienced by many of her college friends. Perhaps a little too much professional counseling combined with a prolonged college course in Freud's theory of transference had led her to believe that those feelings her friends experienced were figments of their imaginations. Now, she wasn't so sure.

God help me—I've wanted to do this from the first moment I saw you!

What open-hearted young woman could resist such a plea?! Not many. Not her.

And Amber hadn't resisted. As she lay against his muscular chest, his capable hands gently stroking her hair, she felt as though a new chapter in her life had been opened up to her, a chapter from a sacred book. Once upon a time, her emotional sun had risen and set upon her older brother, Scott. She had soothed him when he was tired and made him laugh when he was sad. His death had not just killed him, but also had annihilated her daily sunshine. A new *raison d'être* had been revealed, however, while resting in the arms of Bruce Gilpin. She suddenly discovered that she needed to love and be loved by—him.

She had never experienced such a feeling of perfect contentment as she did in those few minutes on the bus listening to the steady *thump-thump-thumping* of his heart and feeling his strong fingers caress her face and scalp. None of us ever knows the multitude of heavy cares and earthly weights that we have piled upon our hearts (either consciously or unconsciously) until those weights and chains are made to fall to the ground, like supplicants, when true majesty approaches. It is a sacred experience when those earthly cares give way, bowing before this Greater Power that boldly pushes into the temple where we have been worshipping our false gods.

When the bliss arrives, and our priorities are appropriately reordered, we wonder: How could I have been so foolish? Running after false gods and setting my sights on that which is not worth the paper upon which it is printed!

And yet, how quickly we forget from which source the bliss has sprung! And how often we need to be reminded, that there is but one god that shalt remain upon our altars, and that god is unconditional love.

They lay together for the briefest of moments – and yet the longest of eternities – before he broke away, embarrassed and chagrined. He gently set her back in her own seat, apologizing profusely. "I'm sorry," he said. "I'm really sorry. I didn't mean that to happen!"

Dazed, Amber leaned her head against the cold glass of the bus window, and attempted to gather herself together. Her hair. Her heart. Her thoughts. What did it mean? What could it mean? She pulled her sweater a little further down over her wrists. She felt as though she needed to make some sort of response, but she suddenly found herself tongue-tied.

"Don't ... I don't ... I don't know what to say," she admitted. Relieved to reveal the truth, she laughed. "I usually have all the answers, but now, I ... just don't," A glorious light shone from her eyes.

"Ha, ha – me, either!"

They smiled at each other with perfect understanding.

Some of that light could be seen in her eyes now as she gazed out the second story window of the old Russell homestead. She was awakened to the present by the rumble of an approaching vehicle. Traffic on the Russell Hill Road was notoriously slow, except during the early morning and afternoon rush hours, when four or five cars might go by in a row. Her ears perked up. Perhaps it was an egg customer? That would be a good thing! Even after the delivery to Belfast today, *The Egg Ladies* would still have twenty dozen or more eggs to sell this week. Some of the eggs would keep for next week, when she had promised to provide enough for the church breakfast. But she had agreed to sell those eggs to the Ladies Auxiliary at half price, which was below the cost to produce them!

She leaned closer to the window and peered down at the road. A slow-moving, sky-blue vintage automobile motored past the house. They weren't stopping, then. Too bad!

From her awkward point of view, Amber couldn't see the driver, but she could imagine the teenage boy that must be behind the wheel. Unwittingly, she pictured Gray Gilpin, who had only recently received his driver's license.

Cute! she thought, before turning mindfully to the open textbook on her desk. *Totally cute!*

She read a paragraph or two; a thought wormed its way up into her consciousness. *Wait, why isn't Gray in school?*

Her eyes flew back to the window, but the car had already motored out up the hill of sight. Was it *him*, then?

Chapter 7
Oaknole Farm

After the negotiations with his mother, Bruce liberated his 1969 AMC Rambler from its sacred resting spot in the family's detached two-car garage and prepared to hit the road. During the prior evening, he had plugged the automobile's stored battery into a charger and thus once Charlemagne's heart was restored the car rumbled to life, frame shaking, crouching body eager to be set free.

Bruce idled his old friend in the driveway for fifteen minutes, throwing open the hood and checking various nuts, bolts and other attachments. All the while he listened to the deep-throated flutter of the motor with the practiced intensity of a doctor. Satisfied, he climbed in, and motored off slowly down the North Troy Road. He waved "goodbye" at the front of the house, knowing rather than seeing that his mother was still watching him from the living room window.

It felt at once strange and yet perfectly natural to be maneuvering Charlemagne around the eight-inch rocks, rusty beer cans and other debris that Asa Palmer's grader had dragged back into the center of the North Troy Road. A colonnade of flaming orange rock maples lined the damp dirt road, and Bruce felt as though he was driving into the past, into 1995, the fall during his senior year in high school, before his sixteen-year-old girlfriend, blonde-haired, blue-eyed Sheila Quimby, had come and told him that she was pregnant. He rolled down his window, and inhaled a deep breath of fresh fall air, filling his lungs with the scent of decaying leaves, dank moss and autumn sunlight.

The image of a woman's face entered his mind, but instead of his ex-wife's limpid eyes, he beheld a pair of fervent orbs the color of late-season asters. *Amber Johnson!* He smiled, and shook his head. *What are you thinking, Old Man!* Nevertheless, the song in his heart matched the cheerful chirping and warbling of the flock of finches flying madly to and fro in the adjacent fields, preoccupied with their own mysterious autumn missions.

He hesitated at the intersection of Route 9/202, overcome with a deep-seated desire to turn left and cruise up the Russell Hill Road to see if he could catch a glimpse of Amber. But duty demanded that his first visit be paid to his father at Gilpin's General Store, and so he urged Charlemagne to the right and shortly pulled into the paved parking lot.

The store hadn't changed much since his last leave from the Guard (even the outdoor wood boiler was not new to Bruce), and the usual clutch of American-made pickup trucks littered the lot. He was soon inside shaking hands with five or six of the Old Farts, still lounging over their morning coffee and donuts at the store.

"Gawd almighty!" roared Leland Gorse. He rose up and clasped the soldier into a quick, fatherly embrace. "Good to see ya, son! Sit down here with me." And he elbowed ninety-three-year-old Clyde Crosby to make room on the padded bench.

"Next time, Leland," Bruce said, making his excuses with a pleasant smile. "I've got quite a few other visits to make this morning. I just got home last night."

"He cain't sit around and jaw all day like we do," Asa Palmer interjected, thrusting out his arthritic paw for a handshake. "Welcome home, son."

"I don't know why not," said Wendell, grinning. He stood up to collect his handshake. "Nice to see you, Bruce."

From behind the hardwood check-out counter, Ralph Gilpin was puffed up like a rooster, eyeing the unofficial welcoming ceremony with gratification and pleasure. To the seventy-six-year-old shopkeeper, this moment of his son's return from Afghanistan – shared with his comrades on the facing benches – was one of the high watermarks of his life. Ralph leaned his way forward into the conversation. "Ya goin' ovah to see Ma Jean, son?"

"Course he is!" Asa declared. "He ain't gonna go another minute without a piece of Ma Jean's apple pie!"

"He don't look very hungry," said John Woods. "Likely his mother didn't let him out of the house this morning without eating a mountain of food first."

After a few more minutes of good-natured joking and laughing, Bruce again shook hands all around. When he turned to exit, he noticed his father daubing his eyes with a cloth dish towel. Bruce's own throat constricted. God, it was good to be home!

"Later, Dad," he said, his heart swelling with affection as he pushed through the double-glass doors. "See you around five o'clock."

"Ayuh. Show up then and there might be some dessert left!" his father called after him. And Bruce heard the chortles and chuckles of the old men as the door closed behind him.

His next stop was indeed Ma Jean's Restaurant, a quaint, thirty-seat restaurant, formerly a small house, on the Bangor Road. By 9:30 a.m. the breakfast crowd had mostly dispersed, and he was able to pull up a prime stool at the bar. Ma Jean spotted him through the server's window, pulled off her apron and bustled around to greet him with a fond squeeze, a rare display of emotion from the matriarch.

"I heard you were home," she announced. "Pulled a fast one on your mother, did you?"

"I wasn't trying, Ma Jean. It just worked out that way."

"Some things work out for the best. You saved her an extra week's worth of worry."

"I like your perspective!"

"And Bruce," she continued, laying her hand regally on his arm, "don't you worry about raining on our parade. We'll survive."

So, his mother had already shared that bit of information, too!

During the short half-hour that Bruce was at the restaurant, several townspeople, spotting Charlemagne outside, stopped in to shake hands and wish him well. The returning guardsman began to feel that he had seen everybody in Sovereign that morning—everybody except the one person he most wanted to see!

After the obligatory slice of hot apple pie and two cups of coffee, Bruce was allowed to escape Ma Jean's with a box lunch under his arm. He headed Charlemagne north on Route 9/202, drove a short ways and turned right onto Russell Hill Road. It was about ten o'clock when he motored slowly past the old Russell homestead – noting with satisfaction that the Staircase Tree was still intact – yet there was no sign of Amber Johnson in the yard. Had he only looked up, however, he would have seen her daydreaming from the second story window.

The day was fine, what we would call an Indian Summer day in Maine, with the ambient temperature about 65F and rising. Bruce, who was driving into the sun, pulled over and shrugged out of his jacket. He tossed it onto the passenger seat, and shifted the Rambler back out onto the road.

He cruised around town, visiting all of the special places near and dear to his heart: Evelyn's fishing hole, the old schoolhouse, the dilapidated canning factory, and many other boyhood treasures. About noontime, he pulled into the turnout on top of Common Hill, where he ate Ma Jean's box lunch while appreciating the vista of sprawling hayfields dotted with grazing black and white Holsteins. The cows reminded him of his intended visit to his uncle Peter, and, when he had finished the chicken sandwich, pasta salad and piece of chocolate cake, he pointed Charlemagne east toward his uncle's farm.

Oaknole Farm is one of the oldest continuously operating dairy farms in Winslow, and the property has been in the Hodges' family for nine generations. It hadn't always been a dairy farm, of course. In the early days of the 18th century, when the white settlers first tentatively pushed out past the safety of Fort Halifax, the original homestead was little more than a hardscrabble farm. But Abel Hodges, of the second generation, was a shrewd man, and correctly reckoned that the future was in lumber. Abel built a sawmill on the property at the confluence of the Sebasticook River and the outlet stream from a nearby pond. The Hodges family was content to pad their pockets with proceeds from the mill for about one hundred years, until an unfortunate fire put them out of business. After that, Charles Hodges experimented with several different types of animal husbandry – chickens, cows, pigs, race horses, and finally Bruce's great-grandfather, Joel Hodges, settled down to raise a registered herd of Jersey cows. The dairy farm had passed next to Leonard Hodges, Bruce's beloved late grandfather, for whom Bruce had been named (we must not forget our hero's given name is "Leonard") and for whom he had worked every summer since the age of twelve. When Bruce's ninety-five-year-old grandfather had died in 2010, his mother's younger brother, Peter, who had worked the dairy farm with his father for the past forty-five years, became the sole owner and operator of Oaknole Farm.

At fifty-six, Peter Hodges was fifteen years younger than his sister, Maude. In addition, Peter was youthful at heart, and thus he and Bruce were more like best friends than uncle-nephew, the awkward designation "Uncle" having been dropped sometime after Bruce's sixteenth year. The two men resembled each other – both six-feet tall, brown-haired and well-muscled, although Peter's back was beginning to permanently bend, betraying the effects of his daily labors. Peter was an intelligent, sensitive man, an educated farmer of the old school, having attended the University of Maine where he had received a degree in agricultural engineering. A long-time bachelor, he was popular in the community, having once been active in 4-H and also having entertained hundreds of local kindergarteners over the years on the five-year-old's annual field trips to the farm.

Oaknole Farm is officially designated by the US Postal Service as being located on the Garland Road, however, in order to gain access to the house, barns and outbuildings one must turn off the paved road onto the farm access road known as Oaknole Lane. The dirt lane runs about a mile down through a copse of ancient oak trees, from which leafy verdure the property takes its name. The traditional white, two-story, two-hundred-year-old farmhouse sits like a prize at the end of the lane, occupying a height of land that offers a panoramic view of the Sebasticook River Valley to the west. To the east, open fields spread capaciously across rolling hills lending a sense of graciousness to the grounds. Gigantic pines, balsams and mixed hardwoods march forward like an army to meet the fields, but wisely stop short to reconnoiter from a distance. Without prejudice, I can say that Oaknole Farm is one of the prettiest spots in Kennebec County.

When Bruce arrived at the still-green, grassy promenade to the house and barns, a small herd of Jerseys, with their tawny brown skin and dusky black eyes, was congregating, jostling and *mooing* in the turn-out pasture situated next to the large red tie-up. Bruce parked the car in front of the milk room, and glanced at his watch. Two o'clock. Peter was right on schedule.

He entered the milkroom, the screen door squeaking as it had for the past thirty years or more. He stepped carefully onto the damp concrete as his eyes adjusted to the dark. The milkroom was attached to the tie-up like a barnacle and housed the sweating steel bulk tank (which cooled and preserved the milk), a large double sink, shelves of cleaners and farm supplies, and other implements of the dairy trade. Bruce smelled the familiar scent of sour milk and cleaning detergent, and his heart squeezed in painful, pleasant anticipation of the hearty welcome he knew he would receive from his uncle. Under the stainless steel double sink he spied a couple of spare pairs of black barn boots, and he stopped long enough to swap out his sneakers for the tall rubber boots.

He bent his head and pushed through the swinging wooden door into the tie-up portion of the connecting barns, where he was greeted by the endearing odor of cow manure intermingled with the sweet scent of hay. Two or three wild barn kittens scattered behind loose hay bales. Bonnie, his uncle's border collie, was waiting for him eagerly on the other side of the door and she whined for attention. He fondled her head; her tail wagged happily. Bruce stepped forward, ducking automatically to avoid hitting a low-hanging light bulb, but not before noting that Peter had switched from incandescent to compact fluorescent bulbs.

His uncle was attending the bevy of bovines, which creatures were gingerly following one another into the barn like beauty pageant contestants taking the runway for the first time. There was a soft clinking of chains as Peter, with long accustomed practice, secured each cow into her appropriate stanchion, catching the metal ring that dangled from their leather collars and snapping it fast. He moved deliberately, dropping soothing words of endearment intermingled with snatches of a popular song. He had a deep baritone voice and a fondness for singing, especially in the barn. Peter patted each animal gently on the rump to forestall the bovine's instinctive side kick from the blind spot.

Bruce, who still recognized many of the cows and knew them by name and nature, spotted the renegade Marigold standing innocently in Velvet's stanchion, as though she had been tied up there every day of her life. "C'mon old girl, that's not your spot," he said, grasping the iron bars and swinging his body gymnastically through the stanchion, turning the errant cow back into the center aisle that separated the two rows of stanchions. His uncle heard his voice and straightened up.

"Hey, Bruce!" Peter exclaimed, tipping back the brim of his Boston Red Sox cap as if to get a better look. "I thought you weren't due in until next week?!"

"I caught an earlier transport; I got home last night."

Somehow the two men maneuvered through the milling and *mooing* cows, and heartily embraced in the sawdust strewn center aisle. Neither uncle nor nephew made any attempt to hide their emotion, only laughing a little in masculine embarrassment. Peter broke away first, wiping his eyes on the back of his flannel shirtsleeve. "God, it's great to see you!"

He readjusted his baseball cap. "I hadn't even got my hopes up about how soon I would see you and … here you are!"

"Mom was pretty surprised too."

"I bet she was! I wish I could have seen the look on Maude's face."

"She was happy as a clam … until I told her 'no parade.'"

Peter chuckled. "Not going to be paraded around town like a prize bull, are you?"

"Nope. No blue ribbon for me."

"I don't blame you, son."

The two men chatted easily, soon reverting to the job at hand. A sensation of peace and harmony stole over Bruce as he helped his uncle secure the cows in the tie-up. When the last cow was snagged, Bruce stood up and surveyed the barn. He was startled to discover that nearly half of the one hundred stanchions were empty. He turned to this uncle, concerned. "Where's the rest, Peter?"

"Gone. I had to sell 'em."

"What! Why?!"

With a sorrowful shake of his head, Peter indicated the rolling grain bin. "I couldn't afford to feed 'em, plain and simple. The drought out West has sent the price of grain through the roof. My grain bill last month was $8,000."

"Yikes!"

"And remember, that's with only half my herd. We're working for the grain man more than ever, these days. I've even given some consideration to growing all my own feed – adding oats and chopped grass to the hay – and cutting out the grain man altogether. The Amish in your neck of the woods are already doing that. They don't like GMO corn, or paying the grain man, either, I suspect."

Bruce was at a loss for words. He had no idea things were so bad at Oaknole. He glanced around the barn again, looking for further signs of hard times. "Did you sell the replacement heifers, too?"

"Some – not all," Peter admitted. "They're still outside." He began to push the grain cart down the outer aisle, doling out the evening's rations of grain to the expectant cows. Bruce idled along with him. "I sold the girls to a Canadian dairy farmer," his uncle continued. "He wanted 'em to raise the butterfat content of his Holstein herd. Gave me good money for 'em, too. Of course, he took my top milkers. But I couldn't turn him down. I'm just glad your grandfather isn't alive to see this day."

"Boy, you're not kidding!"

"It's almost enough to make a farmah wanna move to Canada," Peter joked, flashing the impish trademark grin of the Hodges' men. "Almost, but not quite."

By 3 p.m. the compressor was running and Bruce found himself washing down cow udders in preparation for milking. Oaknole Farm still used the forty-year-old pipeline system installed new by Leonard Hodges, which vacuum system moved the fresh milk from the sealed access port above every stanchion out to the milkroom. Peter, who generally worked alone, milked three cows at a time, taking turns checking and changing out the portable teat-cup hose assemblies from cow to cow. As soon as he hooked the teat-cups up to Daisy, a stream of hot urine erupted from the cow and splattered on the cement floor. Bruce, standing next to Daisy's neighbor, received some of warm salt mist in his face. He wiped his face with his arm.

"Welcome home," said Peter, grinning. He scootched down and hooked the third hose assembly to Velvet. The steel and rubber contraption resembled a large black and gray spider, and made four distinct *slurping* noises as the teat cups were attached. "Seen Maggie yet?"

Bruce was momentarily befuddled. "Maggie?"

"Maggie Walker. The minister."

"Right! I always forget you and Maggie are friends. I don't think Mom knows that," Bruce added, thoughtfully. "She never mentions it."

"Your Mom was in high school when Maggie and I started kindergarten. She didn't pay much attention to us. Maggie was born on the dairy farm just down the road ... well, it used to be a dairy farm, anyway. The old Walker place. She and I both went to Halifax School. We rode the bus together."

"Yeah, you told me that once. She's actually on my list of people to see."

"Need to make a confession?"

"Ha, ha. I'm sure I should! No, Maggie gave me some advice after Sheila left me. It was her first year in Sovereign, I think. I just wanted to touch base with her."

"She likes to give advice. Maggie lives for that."

"It was pretty good advice, too," Bruce said. He regarded his uncle curiously. "What, was Maggie one of your old girlfriends, Peter?"

"Something like that."

Daisy, whose hairy, de-horned head Bruce had been rubbing,

interrupted the conversation with a little bleat of annoyance. She kicked at the hose assembly attached to her udder. Her front right mammary gland, smaller than the other three, was milked out, and the teat cup *blithered* repeatedly as the sucking mechanism kept trying to squeeze more milk from the dry organ. Without thinking, Bruce leaned over and flicked off the teat cup, silencing the annoying noise and satisfying the bovine. When he stood back up, he discovered his uncle watching him with an amused look in his brown eyes.

Peter leaned lightly against Velvet's fawn-colored back. "Looks like you can take the soldier out of the farm," he said, "but you can't take the farm out of the soldier!"

Bruce smiled. "Some things you don't forget," he replied. Nonetheless, he was pleased with the compliment.

The sun had already dipped behind the western skyline when Bruce prepared to leave Oaknole Farm. Before he departed, he secured a promise from his uncle to accompany him when he visited the corn shop in Sovereign. "Probably the old equipment should all be consigned to the scrap heap," he admitted, after explaining to Peter his interest in restarting the canning factory. "But I want to check it out anyway. And I'd like to get your opinion."

"I'm not sure my opinion would be good for much, but I'd be curious to see the place. I've heard a lot about the canning industry over the years. Your grandfather used to grow *Golden Bantam* for the corn shop in Clinton. That was before my time, but Maude would probably remember it. He said he used to drive a wagonload of sweet corn down to the factory and come back with cash money, which was pretty important in those days! He'd also bring back a free wagonload of husks and cobs to feed to the cows in winter. It was a pretty good deal."

"The grain man got the short end of that stick!"

"The grain man got his just deserts, I'd say. Let me know when you want me to take a run over. I've been meaning to visit Sovereign for a while now, anyway."

"What, to visit your old girlfriend?" Bruce joked, never believing for a moment that his bachelor uncle might actually be interested in paying a visit to the minister of the Sovereign Union Church.

Peter pushed back his baseball cap, and looked innocent. "May-be."

Chapter 8
· · · · · · ·
Miss Hastings

Bruce spent the next few days at the Armed Forces Reserve Center in Bangor, dealing with the paperwork and other tasks necessary for his ETS with the Maine Army Guard. While there, he toured the new, 108,000-square-foot Regional Training Institute, which was situated next door to the Reserve Center. Its official ribbon-cutting ceremony had just been held on the prior Friday. A state-of-the-art training facility, the Training Institute would be used to develop a wide variety of military skills, including combat arms training and medic education classes. The Training Institute had been built entirely during Bruce's last tour in Afghanistan, and he was blown away by the size and modernity of the building.

"Totally amazing," Bruce proclaimed to the affable sergeant first class, after a tour of the new facility. "I wish we'd had this when I joined up."

The youth saluted. "We're pretty proud of it, sir," he acknowledged.

Bruce felt uncomfortable. "I've hung up the uniform for good, now, sergeant, you don't need to salute."

"I believe you were with the 286th, sir?"

"Yeah, Combat Sustainment Support Battalion, Kandahar."

The sergeant saluted again. "Welcome home, sir."

In between visits to the Reserve Center and Training Institute, Bruce stopped by the Sovereign Town Office, hoping to meet with John Woods to discuss the old canning factory. Woods, who was chairman of the three-member Board of Selectmen, made himself available to citizens for complaints or compliments (and there were generally more complaints than compliments) on Tuesdays and Thursdays, except during the hours of morning coffee break and lunch. At those critical times of day Woods could be found at Gilpin's General Store and Ma Jean's Restaurant, respectively.

"Come on into the office here," invited the lanky selectman, flipping on the light switch in the formal office set aside for private meetings. He lowered himself into a tattered desk chair, and pulled up to a 1960s-style metal desk, which was covered with overflowing manila folders, letters, catalogs and town reports. "Betty, can you bring me everything we've got on the old corn shop?" he called out to the front office. "I don't do a thing around here except sign the stuff they put in front of me," he continued, clearing off a space on the desk with a little shove. He waved Bruce into the wooden chair opposite the desk. "Those girls do it all for us. You been to the VA yet?"

Bruce took the proffered seat. "Not yet," he said. "I've been up to the base a couple times, though."

"Better sign up for those veteran's benefits before they decide to take 'em away," suggested the seventy-year-old Woods, himself a veteran.

"It's on my list."

Betty Peabody, the stylish, sixtyish Town Clerk, entered the office carrying a two-foot-high stack of manila folders and papers. "Where do you want these?" she asked, peering over the top of the stack.

"Jesus," said Bruce, jumping up to help unburden Betty.

"Set 'em all here," Woods replied, patting the empty spot on the desk. "I tried to warn you, Bruce. She isn't pretty. Takes a lot of letter writing and lawyering to acquire a property as dilapidated as the old corn shop."

"Or try *not* to acquire it," quipped Betty Peabody. Hands free, she offered a cheek for the younger man to kiss. "Welcome home, dear. We heard you were back. Have you seen Miss Hastings yet?"

"Not yet," said Bruce, resuming his seat. "She's on my list."

"Coming to the church breakfast next Sunday?" the chatty Town Clerk continued. "Your Mom's running the kitchen. I know a lot of folks are hoping to see you there, Bruce."

"He'll put it on his list, Betty," Woods answered for the younger man. "Now, skedaddle, or we'll never get through this pile of junk before lunch."

The two men waded through the stack of documents, attempting to trace the history of the old canning factory from the Westcott family of Portland to the Town of Sovereign, Maine. The property had gone through multiple stages of liens over the prior fifty years, during which time the town had acquired both the real estate and the personal property inside the building.

"Does the town own all the machinery, too?" Bruce asked.

"Every nut, bolt, screw and conveyor belt," replied Woods. "Town took it for unpaid personal property taxes. That ole interest adds up pretty quick after the first decade!"

Bruce left the Town Office two hours later toting the pile of manila folders. Before he departed, he had arranged a tentative date to visit the old canning factory with the Board of Selectmen and his uncle Peter.

It was not until Friday afternoon that Bruce found himself with enough time on his hands to telephone his favorite former teacher and to invite himself over for afternoon tea. Instead of Charlemagne, Bruce drove his late model pickup across town to Miss Hastings' home. He had purchased the chocolate-colored, four-wheel drive on his last leave, and had left the vehicle at a local storage facility during his final tour in Afghanistan.

This time Bruce was in luck. When he approached the old Russell homestead, he spotted Amber Johnson outside at the Staircase Tree. She was attempting to plant an eight-foot, wobbly wooden stepladder on the uneven ground beneath the *Eggs For Sale* sign that dangled from the ancient maple. He pulled into the yard, and switched off the pickup.

"Just in time, soldier!" she greeted him, one hand on her hip, eyes sparkling. Her dark hair was confined to one thick, long braid that hung down to the small of her back.

He stepped out of the truck, and appraised the situation. "Trying to get yourself killed?"

"Thanks for the vote of confidence! I'm trying to hook this thing … " and she held up a carved wooden *Butter For Sale* sign "… onto the bottom of that thing." She pointed up to the matching egg sign hanging several feet above her head. "We're selling some of Trudy's homemade butter here, now."

"Hey, that's great," he said. But his heart sank a bit as he recalled another unpaid visit that was on his list.

"She's taking our eggs with her to the farmer's market tomorrow, too, and she's going to peddle some to her restaurants on her next butter run. Her chefs are all organic. The least we can do is sell Trudy's butter to some of our egg customers!"

"My grandfather always said, 'Fahmahs gotta stick togethah,'" Bruce drawled in an exaggerated Maine accent. "Now, move over and let me hang that thing."

Amber obediently stepped aside, but not before he caught a tantalizing whiff of her familiar shampoo. The delicate scent started his heart throbbing. He wanted to slip his arm around her slim waist and pull her to his chest; however, he schooled himself to focus on the task at hand.

She gazed up at him hopefully, expectantly. *Jesus.*

He propped open the ladder, climbed up a step or two and easily secured the butter sign onto the protruding metal loops in the egg sign. He hopped back down and brushed his hands together. "What's next? Need some help cleaning out chicken coop?"

"Oh, to be six feet tall!"

"What?! You don't like being short?" he joked.

"I'm not short – I'm five-four!"

"Yeah, and I'm the Dark Knight."

They both laughed.

Bruce was amazed by how easily he could talk with her. He had expected some initial awkwardness, especially given the intimate nature of that accidental incident on the bus. Yet here they were conversing naturally, almost as though they had known each other all their lives!

"I like what you've done to the tree," he continued, indicating the colorful chickens that decorated the Staircase Tree, one original, heavily-varnished chicken setting on each of the twelve steps. The Staircase Tree was an ancient maple whose trunk had been split dramatically in half by lightening. Half of the tree stood upright at the edge of the road guarding the entrance to the old Russell homestead like a sentinel, and the other half bowed to the ground as though greeting royalty. The grounded limb resembled an elephant's trunk, weathered and gray, and into this battle-scarred trunk someone had carved a dozen steps leading up into the leafy canopy.

"Pretty cool, isn't it?" Amber agreed. "Mike Hobart put the chickens on the steps as a surprise for Lila. Miss Hastings' kindergarteners made them out of *papier-mâché.* They're supposed to represent her pet chicken Matilda."

Bruce examined one of the shellacked paper chickens. "How'd Hobart attach these things?"

"Wooden pegs. We can move the chickens around, or bring them in in bad weather. Mike carved the egg sign, and Wendell just finished carving the butter sign this morning. Pretty cool, huh?"

"Wicked cool," he said, teasingly.

"Make fun of me if you will, but I wouldn't be here if it wasn't for the Staircase Tree! That's what made my Mom and Lila fall in love with this place at first sight."

Bruce was dutifully impressed. "No kidding!"

"No kidding. They took one look at the Staircase Tree and they were hooked. It makes the place seem so special. Of course, nobody knows who carved the steps in the tree – that's what makes it magical. The steps just appeared one day."

"Oh, did they?" Bruce queried. He leaned back against solid tree trunk, folded his muscular arms across his chest and looked smug. "I know who carved the steps."

"You do not!" she countered. "It's one of the big mysteries in Sovereign!"

"Maggie knows who carved 'em, too."

"Maggie? The minister!"

"Yep. I'll tell you the story, if you promise not to laugh!"

"This time, I *do* promise not to laugh." Amber eagerly sank down onto a step on the stepladder, and rested her chin in her cupped hands. "Tell me, tell me!"

"OK, I confess—I made the steps."

"You?!"

"Cut 'em out with a chainsaw, one at a time."

"But … the Staircase Tree has been here forever!"

He shook his head. "Nope. Only about thirteen years. I did it after Sheila – my ex-wife – left me."

"Oh? I'm so sorry," she replied.

"That she left me? Or that I made the steps?" He advanced a little over the leaf-strewn ground, to where she perched on the stepladder. The slippery leaves rustled beneath his feet. He grasped the wooded ladder with his left hand, and gazed down at her heart-shaped face. "Because I'm not sorry she left. Not now, anyway."

Amber didn't pretend to misunderstand his meaning. His eyes revealed open admiration. She blushed, and dropped her eyes. As if on cue, a red squirrel that had been eavesdropping from an adjoining maple, hopped over to the Staircase Tree and began scolding them loudly.

Startled, Bruce dropped his hand. "Ha, ha! You didn't tell me you had a body guard!" He picked up a small stick and tossed it at the jabbering heckler. "Get away, romance-killing rodent!" The creature easily sidestepped the throw, but temporarily suspended its harsh chatter.

"I wonder why Maggie never said anything," Amber mused. "How did she find out?"

He kicked at a pile of dry leaves, but said nothing. He enjoyed the sound and smell of the decaying foliage.

"There's more to the story, isn't there?" she guessed.

He leaned back against the tree. "There could be."

"Tell me," she entreated.

"Well, when Sheila left me, I was pretty angry. It's hard for me to believe now, but I almost made myself sick over it. I didn't know who to talk to – certainly not my parents! So, out of desperation, I went to see Maggie. She'd just moved to town and I knew the old men liked her. After listening to me vent for about two hours, she suggested that I turn my anger into something positive, like a piece of art. At first, I took her advice with a big grain of salt. But a couple of days later when I came over to mow the lawn – I was caretaker of the place when Harold Russell owned it – I saw this downed tree limb. It was the third limb broken off that summer, and I decided it was time for this old soldier to go." He patted the tree trunk affectionately. "I was getting my chainsaw out of the back of the truck, when it occurred to me that this could be my piece of art. So instead of cutting down the tree, I carved these steps. That was a lot of work—took me all afternoon!"

"I bet!"

"I called 'em 'Steps to Nowhere,' because my marriage to Sheila went absolutely nowhere. When I told Maggie about it later we both had a good laugh. Pretty silly, huh?" He surreptitiously checked her reaction. "Disappointed?"

Amber shook her head in astonishment. "Only with myself! I'm embarrassed that I ever tried to give you any advice."

"Aw, you probably didn't expect a tough guy like me to admit to seeing a shrink, much less a minister."

"Outrageous *and* courageous! I'm impressed!"

"Then I'm doubly rewarded for my efforts!" He glanced up at the thinning golden canopy. "Hey, have you ever climbed up to the top? There's a great view of the Western mountains up there! Before I went off to Iraq, I used to sit up there and daydream. Nobody can see you in summer, when the leaves are full." He paused, thinking of those days gone by. "All my hopes and dreams are in this tree," he added, somberly.

The pathos in his voice was irresistible. Amber abandoned her perch on the ladder and quickly moved to his side. She touched his arm comfortingly. "I'm so sorry that your marriage didn't work out."

"Thanks."

She followed his gaze up into the canopy of the tree. "What did you dream about, up there?"

He slipped his arm naturally around her slender waist and pulled her close. She didn't resist. Instead, she lay trustingly against his muscular chest. He cradled her in a gentle embrace, his chin resting lightly on the soft hair of her head. "Maybe I dreamed that a pretty woman would come along," he whispered, "and want to love me as much as I loved her."

Amber felt herself trembling. "Has she?"

"Buck, buck, buck, ddddtrrrrrrrrr!" The red squirrel scolded annoyingly.

They broke apart, laughing, their intimate moment extinguished. "Ha, ha! Not today, apparently!"

She started to move away, but he caught at her hand boyishly. "Hey, come up to Miss Hastings' house with me! She's expecting me but she won't mind another visitor, I know. We can leave my truck here, and walk up."

To his delight, Amber assented. The two of them strolled up the hot-topped road, hand in hand like teenagers, not caring if a car came by to see them together. The vigilant red squirrel followed them for a tree or two, but once satisfied that he had done his job, returned to guard the Staircase Tree. The October day was bright, and the afternoon sun felt warm and pleasant against their face and hands. Late season crickets tuned up their orchestra, and monarch butterflies added poignant blotches of color to the fading brown of the autumn fields, fluttering from one fragrant, fading flower to another. The couple dawdled along, wallowing in a sense of other-worldliness. Time overtook them like a passing stranger.

Miss Hastings lived in an antique home, an awkwardly-designed, two-story cottage situated about half a mile above the old Russell place. The retired music teacher, who had been watching out the window for her expected guest, met them at the shed door. "Dahrrrlings!" she cried, in her rich, operatic voice. "Come in, come in, you DAHRRRLINGS!"

The petite woman hugged them both, and ushered them through the mudroom past the squawking Matilda and into the comfortable country kitchen, where a small fire was burning in her wood cookstove. A tea kettle filled with steaming water misted the room. The kitchen table was set for two for tea, but Miss Hastings quickly added a third place setting and shooed them into the comfy cushioned chairs.

She turned at once to Bruce. "Tell me all about it, dahrrrling," she instructed him, pouring out the tea. She seemed to accept as perfectly natural that Bruce and Amber should be visiting her together. She passed around a plate of frosted, raisin-filled cookies. "I want to hear EVERYTHING."

Bruce gave Miss Hastings a quick rundown of what he had done during his first week at home. "I've even been over to Oaknole to see Peter," he concluded, helping himself to a third cookie.

"OOoo, you've been to Oaknole!" Miss Hastings cried. She quickly turned her attention to Amber. "Dahrrrling, don't let him take you over there," she teased, "or we'll never see you again!"

"What's Oaknole?"

"That's the name of our family farm in Winslow," Bruce explained. "It's a dairy operation; my uncle Peter runs it now."

"Dahrrrling, if he gets you over there, you'll never want to leave— the two of you will spend the rest of your days clishmaclavering among the cows!"

Amber smiled. "I don't know what clishmaclavering means, but it sounds heavenly!"

Bruce pictured Amber frolicking with him in the green pastures of Oaknole, and he decided it might be a good place to keep her. "Once you see the place, you might not want to leave," he agreed.

"Haahaa! I told you DAHRRRLING!" The diminutive lady suddenly recollected her hero. "What are you going to do with yourself now, dahrrrling?"

Bruce told her about his interest in the canning factory, and shared with his former teacher the particulars of his meeting with John Woods at the Town Office. When he was finished, he was surprised to discover that Miss Hastings herself – like so many residents of Sovereign – had an important personal connection to the old canning factory. "You moved to Sovereign because of the corn shop?!" he exclaimed.

"That's right, dahrrrling! We moved here in 1929."

"But I thought you'd always been here!"

"Haahaa! That's only because I've been around FOREVER! No, Father moved us here during the Depression. He was an engineer in the old country, but they left just before the October Revolution. He and my mother landed in New York, and kept moving further and further north, desperately looking for work. One day Father saw an ad in a Massachusetts newspaper for a superintendent of the Westcott Canning Factory in Sovereign. I was about four-years-old at the time. In addition to being an engineer, Father ran the retorts at a canning factory in the old country. So, we all boarded the train for Sovereign, and, thank the Good Lord, Father got the job!"

Amber was deeply moved. "What an amazing story!"

"I remember Father's pay was $50 a week," Miss Hastings continued, "because he told me it took him one week to earn what it had taken him and mother months together to earn before they could get married."

"I never knew your father was superintendent of the corn shop," Bruce mused.

Miss Hastings nodded. Tears filled her eyes. "That's because you never knew him; he died before you were born. He was such a DAHRRRLING man! Everyone ADORED him. Father was so grateful to get the job that he just wanted to make everyone else as happy as he was. We bought this lovely house and settled down. Mother gave piano lessons to the local children, and, well, here I am!"

As the elderly lady reminisced, Bruce groped under the table for Amber's hand. Finding it responsive to his touch, he squeezed affectionately. She squeezed back. Their eyes met across the tiny table, sending and receiving looks of mutual appreciation.

"I ADORED Father," the retired music teacher continued. "And I LOVED visiting him at the canning factory. Clyde Crosby's mother took him to work with her – there wasn't any child care in those days – and Clyde and I used to play together. I had a terrible crush on him. Clyde was a few years old than me—still is, I guess!" She cackled loudly again. "Haahaa!"

"What is Clyde – ninety, now?" Bruce guessed.

"He's ninety-three if he's a day! I'll be eighty-eight in December and Clyde is five years older than me! OOoo, he was a HANDSOME fellow, Clyde Crosby! Wait, I've got a picture of the old corn shop crew I can show you." And Miss Hastings disappeared for a minute and returned shortly with clutch of black and white photographs. She slipped one of the pictures from the group, and placed it on the table in front of them. It was a black and white of thirty-five or forty people – men, women, and children – lined up on the front steps of the canning factory. The men were dashing in their long-sleeved, high-collared striped shirts with contrasting dark ties, and the women were homey in their long dresses and full-length, white pinafores. A large sign above their heads proudly proclaimed: *WESTCOTT'S CANNING FACTORY, First Quality Corn, Grown and Packed in Sovereign, Maine.*

"There's Father!" Miss Hastings cried, pointing to a handsome, middle-aged man. "And there's Clyde!"

Bruce examined closely the image of a big-eared, mischievous-looking child. "Ha, ha! That's old Clyde Crosby?"

"Isn't he DAHRRRLING?! Look at this one – these are some of the corn huskers – aren't they ADORABLE?" And the elderly lady slid another black and white onto the table.

"I love their outfits," gushed Amber. "Imagine getting all dressed up like that to husk corn!"

Miss Hastings passed the pile of vintage photographs across the table to Bruce, who began flipping through them. Fascinated, he spread them out on the table for all of them to see, creating a collage of people, buildings, and outdated machinery. The displayed images covered the kitchen table, offering a seductive glimpse of days gone by. Seeing the black and white photographs all together, Bruce felt as though he was peering through a keyhole, onto a particular moment in the past. "Quite a piece of history you have here!"

"Aren't they DAHRRRLING? But what's a used-up old coot like me to do with all of them? I know these old photographs belong in a museum, but I hate to see them leave town!"

"Amen," agreed Amber, examining the pictures reverentially. She glanced up at Bruce. "This is amazing! You're definitely onto something here. I'm not sure what it is, but it's huge!"

Half an hour later, Miss Hastings watched as her two guests strolled down the driveway, hand in hand. She daubed a tear from her eye, and then gathered up the vintage photographs and returned them to the leather-bound trunk in her downstairs bedroom. Inside the fabric-lined trunk, she spied a colorful musical revue poster from the 1940s. "Come hear *The Songbird of Sovereign!* Sweetest singer in the world harkens from a tiny town in Maine!" the New York City poster announced. She lifted the poster, and exposed a framed, black and white snapshot of a thin young man seated casually on a set of wooden steps that led up into an institutional type building. He was smiling into the camera, and was dressed in a light-colored, single-breasted suit with notched lapels, a white shirt, and a patterned tie. A lock of his dark hair fell rakishly over his left eye and several others dangled nearly to his shirt collar in back. She carefully removed the vintage picture from the trunk and set it on her dresser. The pretty five-by-seven frame was a wood filigreed table-mount style, with a center hinge so that the image could be tilted backward or forward to suit the whim of the owner.

Miss Hastings tilted the frame so that the friendly-looking young man's eyes smiled into her own. "I'm still here, Henry, my dahrrrling!" she proclaimed, lovingly. "But it won't be long, now, and we'll be together again!"

Chapter 9
. . . .
Fathers and Mothers

I'd like to take the opportunity to say a few words about Sovereign, Maine, and the nature of the people who inhabit this small town (pop. 1,048). As you might have noted, Sovereign residents are good-humored, even-tempered and big-hearted. In my afore-mentioned tale, I described Sovereign as a frost pocket of goodness, a place where evil doesn't exist because the killing frost arrives just in time to quench all budding attempts at small-mindedness and mean-spiritedness. I was roundly criticized for that discourse by a few readers, apparently appalled to discover theological thought in a 21st century novel (thinking perhaps at the very least they should have been warned that the book contained no gratuitous sex). Duly chastised, no such sermon shall spring forth now. However, I would like to offer up a few words of context.

Just because the residents of Sovereign prefer good to evil, doesn't mean that they aren't occasionally foolish or proud or vain. Silliness, vanity and pride are not evil in themselves, merely the result of an imperfect casting of divinity, from which parent our human natures are supposedly copied. An imperfect casting renders a blemish here or there, perhaps an indelible stain. But these blemishes have value because, by their very nature, they point the way toward perfection.

In a perfect world, we humans would have no need of silliness, vanity and pride. However, our world – even the world of Sovereign, Maine – is not perfect, and these three qualities (and others of a similar nature) help point us in the right direction. Without silliness, we might never savor the fruits of joy. Without pride and vanity, we might be altogether ignorant as to how we are doing on our march toward our unattainable goal of perfection.

But what of humility, you might ask? Isn't humility a necessary attribute to acquire in our quest for perfection?

The short answer is—no. Humility is not a characteristic to be deliberately acquired, like a new suit of clothes or an app on our smartphones. Rather, humility is a by-product of our spiritual growth, much like rinse water is a by-product of laundry. We can't consciously aromatize ourselves with the sachet of rinse water, but we can turn the dials on the washing machine so that there is a possibility this fragrant by-product will be produced.

In short, one does not need to be perfect or even humble to live in Sovereign, Maine; one only needs the desire to use the washing machine. Many newcomers have moved into town over the fourteen years that I have lived here, and they come and they go, much like lady's fashion in the city or the latest electronic devices. They are interesting to note, but for some reason they don't fit into our little community. But a precious few, such as Rebecca Johnson (now Russell), do fit, and choose to stay, discerning perhaps that the town of Sovereign is not just a good place to live but also a catalyst for self-correction. They mingle with the natives – good humored, even-tempered and big hearted – but also foolish, vain, and proud. Without them, we would have no story.

Rebecca heard their chatter and laughter before Amber and Bruce reached the driveway at the old Russell homestead. She glanced at her image in the shaving mirror that still hung judiciously next to the black soapstone sink. Wendell, like his grandfather Pappy before him, preferred to shave in the warm kitchen every morning, utilizing the small oval mirror, rather than the medicine cabinet mirror in the cold bathroom. Dissatisfied with her reflection, Rebecca made a little grimace.

"'Tain't like he's going to notice you," drawled Wendell, who was dawdling at the table in the traditional eat-in country kitchen.

She turned around to face him. "Thanks a lot, darling husband."

"Wal, you know, Bruce has mostly got eyes for Amber."

"Oh, dear! That doesn't help, either."

"You look awful shaap, though," he submitted, with a cheeky grin.

She laughed, momentarily appeased.

Within minutes, the introductions were made, and Rebecca found herself offering Bruce Gilpin the contents of her larder, which she thought on the whole was better than offering him her daughter. "I've got some lemon sponge cake. And farm-fresh custard pie!"

"The custard is awesome," proclaimed Amber, taking her usual spot at the table.

"Thanks," replied Bruce, who remained standing next to the shed door. "But we just had cookies up at Miss Hastings' and I shouldn't eat anything else." He glanced at his watch. It was nearly five o'clock. "I've got to get home soon so my mother can stuff me full of food."

"You ain't missed many meals ovah there, I see," Wendell quipped, noting the ex-soldier's beefy frame.

"Ha, ha – there wasn't much else to do in Kandahar but eat and sleep."

"What did you do in the Guard, Bruce?" Rebecca asked, politely. She hoped against hope that his exploits in Afghanistan weren't of a particularly heroic nature.

"Maintenance and ordnance support with the 286th Combat Sustainment Support. We took care of four companies and four detachments of warriors."

"How nice," she replied, without the least understanding of what constituted an ordnance, let alone ordnance support.

Amber rested her chin on her hands. "What's that mean?"

"I fixed stuff. For the guys on the front lines."

"Bruce here kin fix jest about anything," Wendell proclaimed. "One time he even got the town's old Viking-Cives plow truck goin' when Asa Palmah himself couldn't git the thing stahted." Both men chuckled at the recollection. "'Twas 'bout six feet of snow thet day, too," he added.

Rebecca groaned inwardly. The look of open admiration on her daughter's face as Wendell praised Bruce Gilpin was causing her considerable anguish. How could she quickly dispatch the young veteran?

Bruce unexpectedly came to her aid. "My grandfather taught me how to keep stuff running at Oaknole," he explained. "And speaking of things running …" he glanced at his watch again, "… I've got to go. If I'm not home by five o'clock, Mom will send out the Guard. Ha, ha!"

That evening in the marital bed Rebecca lightly chastised her husband for his defection. "You made him look like such a hero, dear," she said, fitting herself into the waiting crook of Wendell's arm. They snuggled contentedly into the center of a six-inch thick featherbed, finding just the right position amongst the eiderdown for their evening's slumber. This was Wendell's favorite part of the day. An old bachelor, he had awakened late in life to the fruits of feminine companionship and was now savoring them. Light cast from an antique floral table lamp bathed the room in a warm glow, and the hand-hewn ceiling beams threw dark, interesting shadows against the figured wallpaper.

"Did you see the look of adoration on Amber's face?" she continued. She snuggled closer to her husband's solid warmth, absently smoothing a wrinkle from the colorful, hand-stitched quilt.

"Wal, you know, 'twas jest the truth – he did git thet old snow-plow goin' agin." Without disturbing her, Wendell reverently rear-ranged a stray lock of her copious brown curls. At times he couldn't believe she belonged to him—they belonged together. And at other times he couldn't remember what his life was like before she moved to Sovereign.

"Whose side are you on?"

"I ain't on nobody's side. I was jest tellin' a story."

"Some stories are best left untold."

"Ain't you bein' a bit harsh? He did go ovah to I-raq and Afghanistan …"

"Oh, I know, I know! And I'm grateful to him, truly. But not grateful enough to give him my daughter!"

Wendell thought that perhaps Amber was no longer his wife's prop-erty to give away. However, he wisely held his tongue.

"If I know Amber, she's going to find a veteran like Bruce much more appealing than … than … " Rebecca broke off, not wanting to reveal too many of her cards.

"Than a big city lawyer?" Wendell guessed. "Don't tell me yer plan-nin' to throw Ryan MacDonald in her face?!" He poked an elbow into the featherbed and hoisted himself up a few inches to get a good look at his wife. She looked guilty.

She defiantly pulled the quilt up to her chin. "So what if I am! What's wrong with Ryan?"

"Ain't nuthin' wrong with him, far as I kin see. But if I was a young girl – and I had my druthers – I know which man I'd prefer."

"Oh, dear!" said Rebecca.

Wendell sank back into the fluffy pillows, and resettled his wife lov-ingly in his arms. He relished his role as comforter-in-chief. "Kin you tell me what yer scairt of?" he inquired, hoping to help alleviate her fears.

"Oh, my goodness! Just think how much emotional baggage Bruce must be carrying! All those tours of duty in Iraq and Afghanistan! And that awful divorce from his wife!"

Wendell allowed Rebecca to vent for ten or fifteen minutes, dropping nothing more than a word or two of encouragement. She discoursed eloquently about the horrors of PTSD (she'd looked it up on the internet), her daughter's past emotional distresses (including the loss of her father and brother), and the age difference between the Amber and Bruce (although she seemed to overlook the fact that Bruce Gilpin and Ryan MacDonald were approximately the same age). She concluded with the heart-felt cry: "Amber deserves to be happy!"

Wendell finally saw his opening. "Wal, you know, you ain't givin' Amber much credit," he pointed out. "She's pretty shaap. I think she kin figure it out for herself."

Rebecca started to interrupt, but he stopped her. "You done a real good job mothering," he continued, soothingly. "You ain't got nuthin' to worry about. If she's half as spunky as her mother, she'll turn out jest fine."

This avowal from her husband was said in such a reassuring fashion – and was so flattering – that Rebecca suddenly discovered she was exhausted, and relaxed into his arms. Within five minutes she was asleep. Wendell, however, kept the table lamp lit for another fifteen minutes, in order that he might lovingly tend stray curls. He meditated upon her pretty face, and listened to her shallow breathing with something approaching awe. Mother, thy other name art Husband!

Across town, in another marital bed, a similar scene was occurring. Ralph and Maude Gilpin had settled themselves into their queen-sized mattress for the evening, much like they had every night for the past fifty-three years. They had never spent a night apart since their wedding day, not even when Maude's ninety-five-year-old father was dying and she went to live at Oaknole Farm to help her brother Peter take care of him. For four months, every evening after Ralph closed up the general store, he motored the twenty-two miles over to Winslow to eat his supper and sleep with his wife.

Maude reached for the ladies magazine that was lying on her bed stand. "They walked up to Miss Hastings' house together," she announced, flopping the magazine on her ample bosom without even glancing at the glossy cover. "Shirley Palmer saw them."

Ralph recognized the move, and knew he was in for a long night of it. He fumbled with his table light, in an effort to ward off the discourse that he knew was coming.

"They were holding hands! Can you imagine?!"

Ralph, who *could* imagine holding hands with a pretty girl like Amber Johnson, wisely held his tongue. He switched off the light.

"What if Trudy had driven by?!"

The good-hearted Ralph could not allow this protestation to pass unchallenged, for the rhetorical question savored of wrong-doing on his son's part. He would put up with a good deal of female silliness, especially at bedtime. But he wouldn't accept the suggestion that his son intentionally had done wrong. He switched his light back on. "They ain't engaged, Maude," he said, in what he knew was probably a wasted effort to correct his wife's understanding. "Bruce and Trudy ain't engaged. And from what I kin see, they ain't never likely to be."

"Did I say they were engaged, Ralph Gilpin? You misunderstood me!"

"'Taint likely."

One giant tear squeezed from her eye, and rolled down her fat cheek. "Bruce knows how much Trudy cares for him. If he had any consideration for her feelings at all, he certainly wouldn't be parading up and down the Russell Hill Road like a teenager!"

This response was difficult for Ralph to contradict and correct, for his wife's words did contain a grain of truth. "The boy's had a hard go of it ovah the last few years, Maude. I think you oughtta let him have some fun."

She sniffed. "A fine example he'd set for Grayden, then, toying with a young girl's affections!"

"I ain't suggestin' he take advantage of her!"

"I hope not!"

"I'm jest suggestin' thet you lighten up a bit, is all."

Maude pretended to be offended. She lifted up her magazine and began flipping loudly through the pages. Ralph switched off his light.

She dropped the magazine abruptly, her bosom heaving with pent-up emotion. "No parade! No chicken barbeque! No Trudy!" she sobbed. "It's almost more than a mother can bear!" She burst into tears.

Ralph scooted over next to her in bed. Their toes touched, and intertwined. "Tut, tut," he said, pulling his wife into his skinny arms. "'Tain't the end of the world, now is it? He's alive, ain't he? Thet's more 'n many a mother kin say tonight!"

Maude Gilpin's soft heart was touched, as she thought of the mothers of all the children who hadn't come home from the war. She was so moved by her good fortune, that she cried herself to sleep.

Chapter 10
. . . .
The Rusticator

Several days later, in the afternoon, a late-model, four-door sedan with Massachusetts plates motored tentatively down the North Troy Road, unfortunately without that efficacy of skill with which Bruce Gilpin approached the newly-graded gravel road. Instead of swerving to avoid obstacles, the driver of the dark, expensive-looking vehicle kept the car in its appropriate lane, surfing noisily over the eight-inch rocks, rusty beer cans and other debris that Asa Palmer's grader had dragged back into the center of the North Troy Road.

For those readers not familiar with the workings of a small town in Maine, some rural context might be helpful. The Road Commissioner in tiny hamlets such as Sovereign is generally elected by the voters annually (or bi-annually) and charged with the responsibility of maintaining the roads in winter, summer and mud season. The job is a thankless one, requiring frequent contact with unhappy citizens as well as inclement Maine weather. Pay is modest at best (perhaps $1,000 per annum) although there is a certain amount of glory in seeing the title "Road Commissioner" attached to one's name. And yet the position of Road Commissioner is one of the most hotly contested races in any small town election. Why? Because the Road Commissioner has the power to hire out the road work, offering state wages to his contractor, which in many cases is—himself. Such municipal simony, which would be considered a shocking conflict of interest in larger cities such as Lewiston or Portland, is overlooked out of sheer necessity in small towns such as Sovereign. For if the Road Commissioner isn't allowed to pad his pockets somehow, the road work simply wouldn't get done. Given the price of diesel fuel, no outside contractor would bother to bring his heavy equipment to town for the small amount of dollars going begging.

This only partially explains why Asa Palmer, the Road Commissioner, was responsible for the eight-inch rocks, rusty beer cans and other debris cluttering up the North Troy Road. The rest of the story is simply that Asa had once again forgotten to attach the rock rake to the back of his yellow Cat-12 grader when grading this stretch of road. Therefore, when Asa pushed his mould board down over the edges of the ditch to haul the gravel back up into the center of the road, building up a three-inch crown, he fished up a mess of other junk that was normally snagged and removed by the rock rake that trolled behind the grader. When Palmer reached the Troy town line and turned his grader around for the return trip, he beheld his mistake. "Dang it," he said. But he continued to carry on.

Needless to say, after the late-model, four-door Massachusetts sedan had travelled about a mile down the road, it picked up a rusty nail from an old board, and within five minutes, the driver, our old friend Ryan MacDonald – a tall, slender handsome man in his early thirties – was standing alongside his vehicle, examining a flat rear tire with something approaching disgust. He was dressed in neatly-pressed khaki pants, a new Pendleton® shirt and leather loafers. He sighed, and reached for his smartphone. A life-long city dweller, Ryan not only had never changed a flat tire in his life, but also it would not occur to him that, if a flat tire needed changing, he should be the one to do it.

Alas, alas! When Ryan tried to call for roadside assistance from Triple A, he discovered he had no cell service. He stared glumly at the phone, and then at the flat tire. This was not a good omen for his return visit to Sovereign.

Ryan, a corporate lawyer from Boston, was once a co-worker at the insurance company Perkins & Gleeful with Lila Woodsum and Rebecca Johnson. He had followed Lila to Sovereign in a vain attempt to kindle their flame of friendship into romance, but he had failed in that attempt. While sojourning in Sovereign with the Russells over the summer he had felt oddly at home in the quirky community. An only child whose parents were deceased, he had perhaps appreciated the warmth of Sovereign's residents even more than most visitors. Therefore, he had applied for and received a six-month leave of absence from his employer, packed up his clothes and laptop, and headed for a course of winter rustication in Sovereign. He was on his way to Mike Hobart's post-and-beam cabin on the North Troy Road, which he had rented for six months, and where he intended to pass his time in mature reflection and in re-reading Henry David Thoreau's *Walden* and books of a similar nature. He was less than a mile from his destination, when overtaken by this not-so-natural disaster.

Ryan glanced up the road to the north – where he noted more road debris, maple trees and stone walls – and swiveled to look down the road to the south. Here, he was somewhat more successful, for a pickup truck was approaching, deftly maneuvering the obstacle course.

Bruce Gilpin pulled up to the left of the distressed vehicle, and rolled down the passenger window. "Need help?"

Ryan indicated the rear wheel with a listless gesture. "I've got a flat."

Bruce hopped out of his vehicle. "Where's the spare?"

In short order, the former army mechanic had located the spare, jacked up the car and changed the tire. For Bruce, after working on M-ATVs (the military's $500,000 Mine-Resistant, Ambush-Protected, All-Terrain Vehicles), the tire change was little more than an exercise to stretch his muscles.

Job completed, he wiped his greasy hands on a cloth rag kept in his pickup for just such opportunities. "Nice car," he said. He offered up the clean appendage. "Hey, I'm Bruce Gilpin."

They shook hands. "Any relation to Ralph and Maude?"

Bruce admitted the filial connection. The two men leaned back against their respective vehicles, and began to chat easily. They were close in age, yet nothing could have been further apart than their upbringing and life experiences to date. However, the obligation of the service rendered instantly endeared them to each other, and they were soon prattling away like crows in a cornfield.

"And so the road is not usually like this?"

Bruce laughed heartily. "Ha, ha! Asa just forgot his rock rake, that's all. The rake is a big iron thing ... " Bruce stretched his arms wide "... he drags behind the grader. Catches all the junk the mould board pulls up from the ditch."

"Didn't he notice he didn't have it?"

"Probably."

Ryan looked askance. "Why did the man keep on going once he saw he didn't have the … thing attached?"

"That's Asa for you. He'd have had to walk to our house and call one of the selectmen to bring him the rake. Asa's in his seventies. He's not gonna get down outta the grader and walk."

"I noticed there's no cell service here."

"Wouldn't matter if there was service, Asa doesn't have a cell phone – wouldn't carry one to save his life. He'd be afraid his wife would find him. As it is, Shirley's got to get in her car and run him down when she wants him to do something."

"I don't think I've met him yet. Asa?"

"Asa Palmer. The Road Commissioner."

Ryan shook his head. "Nope, I'm sure I'd have remembered that name. It's pretty Biblical."

"Come to the church breakfast on Sunday," Bruce suggested in a friendly fashion, "and you'll get your chance. Then you can tell Asa what you think of the road."

"I don't think I'd do that," Ryan replied, unsure whether or not the other man was joking about telling the Road Commissioner his thoughts. "But I would like to attend the breakfast. What time?"

"Six to nine. Everybody in town will be there. Including me."

This last bit was added in such a dispirited tone, that Ryan couldn't fail to notice. "Don't you want to go? I know for a fact that there are some good cooks in Sovereign, including your mother!"

"Aw, I'm afraid they'll make a fuss of me." And before he knew it the newly-minted veteran shared his tale with the big city rusticator. "I was only doing my duty," he concluded. "It wasn't that big a deal."

Ryan thought the other man's eleven-year service to his country was a big deal. "If it was me, I'd wear my uniform everywhere," he said, "if nothing else, than to impress women!"

"Ha, ha. I'll lend you my fatigues; I'm not using 'em."

Ryan hesitated. "Do you know Amber Johnson?" he asked. "She's moved up here with her mother, Rebecca Russell. I knew her in Boston."

Bruce felt a shock to his heart, as though he'd accidentally touched a high tensile electric fence. He shortly brought the conversation to a close, and, as he motored off toward home, he didn't feel quite as friendly toward the other man.

The sun was beginning to set when Ryan MacDonald reached the neat-looking log cabin he had rented from Mike Hobart. He parked his car underneath a towering pine tree and proceeded to settle into his winter home.

A passive-solar home, the cabin's windows were oriented toward the south, and the temperature was nearly 70F when Ryan entered. The cabin boasted ceiling and support beams three-and-a-half feet thick, and knotted pine boards on the walls. An open floor plan featured a west-facing kitchen, and a combined living-eating area. The wood tones added a warm pleasantness to the dwelling. Two pair of antique snowshoes decorated the north wall by the stone fireplace, into which massive chimney a cast iron woodstove was inserted. Framed photographs of white tail deer, black bear and moose decorated the walls, and several nature guides and Maine books populated the built-in bookshelves. The cabin was both rustic and comfortable, and, after unpacking his own assortment of books and putting away his clothes, Ryan felt completely at home.

He had delayed provisioning the kitchen, knowing that he could purchase most of what he'd need for groceries from local farmers and growers. He'd buy his eggs from *The Egg Ladies*, of course, but first he would head to Gilpin's General Store to pick up a few other necessities.

This time Ryan easily maneuvered back down through the obstacle course on the North Troy Road to Route 9/202. When he pulled into the parking lot at Gilpin's, the clock had just struck five, and Ralph was already closing up. "I'm on my wintah hours," Ralph explained, after greeting the Boston lawyer outside the front door. "Whatcha got to have MacDonald?"

Ryan explained that he required milk, bread and butter to get him through the morning. "But I don't want to trouble you, Ralph," he said. "I can take a run into Unity."

"Tut, tut – 'tain't no need for thet!" The skinny shopkeeper disappeared back into the store.

The lawyer didn't know whether to follow him or not, so he remained standing outside, feeling stupid, with his hands in his pockets. Ralph returned in a couple of minutes with a paper bag filled with the requested groceries, plus some additional items (such as toilet paper) that the experienced shopkeeper thought right to include.

"How much do I owe you?" Ryan asked, pulling out his wallet.

Ralph waved the money away. "I'll keep a tab on ya," he said. "We'll settle up later."

Ryan was pleased. To him, extending credit was tantamount to an official acceptance into the close-knit community. "That's great, Ralph, thanks."

"They're sellin' Trudy's buttah ovah to Wendell's now," Ralph continued. "I didn't git ya none, 'cause I figgered you'd be goin' ovah there."

"That's my next stop!"

In truth, Ryan had saved his visit to the old Russell homestead for last, calculating that if he timed the stop with the dinner hour he might be invited to partake with the family. Rebecca had known he was coming, but he hadn't texted her that he had arrived.

Rebecca answered his knock on the door of the shed. "Ryan! I was just beginning to get worried about you." She gave him a quick hug, and ushered him into the cozy kitchen where Wendell was washing up a few cooking pots. "Look who's here," she announced. "Just in time for supper!"

"I don't want to trouble you …" the lawyer said.

"Don't be silly – it's no trouble!" (In point of fact, Rebecca had hopefully set an extra place at the dining room table.)

Ryan acceded, and allowed her to relieve him of his winter jacket.

"You won't need that in here! There's a fire in the woodstove." She disappeared for a moment to hang the coat in the shed.

Wendell grinned. "I like it hot," he said. He wiped his hands on the dish towel, and greeted the younger man cheerfully. "Nice to see ya, MacDonald. Pull up a chair." Wendell, who had been apprised of the attorney's intended visit, lowered himself into his customary spot at the kitchen table. "Still lawyerin' down to the big city?"

Ryan slid into the opposing seat, next to the shed door. "Not at the moment. I'm taking a six-month leave of absence from Perkins & Gleeful. I need some time for reflection," he added.

"Thet sounds like a good i-deah," said Wendell, accepting the news as a matter of course.

Rebecca reappeared in time to hear his last words. "My goodness, Ryan! I didn't realize you were taking that much time off!"

"I've rented Mike Hobart's cabin for the winter," he acknowledged. "Thanks for your offer to stay here, Rebecca, but I wanted some place by myself to read and think. Maybe even do some writing. Sovereign seems like a pretty good place to rusticate."

Hearing voices in the kitchen, Amber wandered in from the great room. "Who's rusticating? You, Ryan?" she said. "That's so cool!"

"He's taking six months off, dear. I'm so glad!"

Ryan rose up eagerly. "Amber! I was just beginning to think they were keeping you down with the chickens."

She smiled. "They let me out for meals."

He remained on his feet, hoping that if he did so she might cross the room to shake his hand. Instead, she leaned back against the wood door frame, hands behind her back. Her dark glossy hair was piled on top of her head in a pompadour style (her first attempt at copying the hair-dos of the women in the old corn shop photos). She was dressed in snug jeans and a loose-flowing purple blouse, and looked at once glamorous and casual. Ryan thought he had never seen a more desirable woman in his life. He silently congratulated himself on his decision to return to Maine to seek a life companion. Amber Johnson – beautiful, intelligent, educated and imbued with all the womanly spirit a man could want – was currently at the top of his list. But was she still available? A discerning man, Ryan had duly noted the change in Bruce Gilpin's attitude toward him when he had mentioned Amber's name.

Seeing that Amber wasn't going to approach him, Ryan reclaimed his seat. "I hope they give you some time off, too. I've been looking forward to more outings, like our picnic at the Millett Rock and the excursion we took to the coast in August."

"I thought you were rusticating?" Amber teased.

"Voluntary rustication allows for all sorts of interesting opportunities."

"Sounds so Thoreau."

"My hero, Henry David. Actually, I think it was Dr. Channing who coined the term 'voluntary rustication,' when he suggested that Sophia Peabody pay a visit to Cuba for her health."

"I'm surprised you know who Walter Channing is!"

Ryan smiled. "You Amherst girls never give us Harvard boys enough credit. You forget to what alma mater the Channings owe their allegiance."

Amber shot back. "Was that before or after Walter Channing was rusticated from Harvard?"

"Well, that's not exactly the type of voluntary rustication the good doctor advised for Sophia Peabody, I'm sure."

Wendell, who had been struggling to follow the verbal volleys between the two young people, saw his opening. "Is Sophia any relation to Betty Peabody?" he asked, referring to the Sovereign Town Clerk.

Both Amber and Ryan MacDonald laughed. "Not likely," said Amber. She explained that Sophia Peabody, artist and illustrator, was the wife of author Nathanial Hawthorne, who penned classics such as *The Scarlet Letter.* The couple, as well as Dr. Walter Channing and his brother, the famed preacher William Ellery Channing, had been part of the Transcendentalist Movement of the 19th century.

"Wal, you know, jest 'cause she's dead, don't mean they ain't related," the old chicken farmer sagely pointed out.

"Well, you know, Wendell," Amber said, "you could be right!"

Chapter 11
· · · · · · ·
The Church Breakfast

Early mornings always found Amber in the hen pen, the attached, two-story, wigwam-style shed that Wendell's grandfather had renovated for Grammie Addie's laying hens. On the morning of the church breakfast, Amber arose extra early in order to collect the balance of the eggs necessary to feed the two hundred guests that were projected to attend the Ladies Auxiliary's fund raiser. Two hundred meals required four hundred eggs—thirty-four dozen! Normally, Amber would have been thrilled with the size of the sale; however, in this instance she had agreed to provide the organic eggs at half-price. At $2.25 per dozen, *The Egg Ladies* was losing money. But the business had carried a balance of fifteen dozen eggs into this week's production of one hundred and twenty dozen, so she was happy to move them, even at a loss.

A grayish-pink ribbon of the pre-dawn was visible when Amber wound her way down the tight wood and metal spiral staircase to the chicken coop, which was situated on the ground floor. She switched on the electric fluorescent lights, flooding the cavernous white-washed area with brightness and awakening the sleeping fowl. Several of the roosting birds croaked and shuddered out of their slumber. Two or three, squatting in the nest boxes, hopped down to the ground, their business now completed, sending up a dry spray of dust from the ankle-deep sawdust as they scratched on the floor.

Egg collecting was Amber's favorite part of her daily routine, as it had been for her predecessor, Lila Woodsum. She lifted Grammie Addie's watermelon-shaped wicker basket from the square-headed iron nail sticking out from the old barn boards adjacent to the door of the hen pen. She slipped the latch on the chicken coop, and let herself into the screened-in area. Carefully, Amber felt through the warm sawdust in the three dozen nest boxes that Mike Hobart had built, searching box by box for the large brown eggs. Several of the New Hampshire reds were still setting, and they fluffed their feathers and nestled down to shroud their treasures. One of the chestnut-colored hens looked askance at Amber, offended that she could dare to raid such precious gems. Amber dropped a few words of encouragement, slipped her hand beneath the smooth feathers and secured two eggs.

"*BBuckbuckbarrwk!*" screeched the chicken, sending sweet-smelling sawdust flying as she flapped out of the nest box.

"Go get em, girl!" Amber said, laughing. She continued gathering the eggs.

Heavy layers of sawdust and cobwebs deadened the sound of the outside world, and Amber sometimes felt when working in the hen pen as though she were in the belly of Jonah's whale. Therefore, she didn't hear the arrival of the chocolate-brown pickup that parked at the east end of the building nor the tell-tale *creak* as the barn door opened. Rather, she felt a rush of cool, fresh air into the ammonia-laden odor of the chicken coop and instinctively turned around. She was startled to see Bruce Gilpin entering the hen pen from the rarely used ground entrance to the east. "Bruce!"

He came quickly forward to greet her, an eager look in his animated brown eyes. He was dressed in blue jeans and a gray Maine Army Guard sweatshirt. Her heart leapt at the sight of him.

Unfortunately, he had forgotten to close the door behind him, and several of the more alert chickens took advantage of this unexpected opportunity and darted outside into liberty. "The door!" she exclaimed, clutching the egg basket in one hand and gesturing toward the fleeing hens with the other.

"Yikes!" he cried, and leaped back outside to try and capture the escaping birds. But the faster Bruce chased after the fleet-footed fowl, the faster they scurried in different directions on the grass. One or two other curious chickens poked their red heads out the door and stood gravely on the stoop considering the situation.

Amber burst out laughing. It was too funny! She set the basket down, and retrieved a pail of scratch corn. When she made her appearance in the doorway, the errant chickens instantly recognized the hand that fed them and hustled toward her. She turned and tossed a handful of corn behind her into the coop, and the sinners were soon returned to the warm fold; that is, all the sinners but the very repentant perpetrator of the crime.

Bruce hung back, feeling foolish and guilty. "I can't believe I did that! You'd never know I was raised on a farm."

"Get in here, so I can shut the door!"

"I was just so happy to see you!"

He followed her into the hen pen, and she closed the door behind the two of them. When she turned around, she was practically in his arms. With an involuntary movement, he clasped her to his breast, and unclipped her hair. The dark tresses tumbled down over her shoulders, and before she knew it he was running his fingers through her hair, muttering little words of endearment into her ear.

Amber didn't resist. She couldn't resist. Her heart accepted his will with perfect contentment. Once again, her earthly cares dropped away: the lackluster egg sales, the high cost of organic grain, the unexpected arrival of Ryan MacDonald. She pressed against his muscular chest, her blood matching the rhythm of his pounding pulse. Heaven on earth knows no paradise such as lovers reuniting!

He leaned down and kissed her on the eyelids and lips, and just as abruptly pulled away. Desire darkened his eyes. Amber languidly reached up and lovingly fondled his face. "Don't stop," she pleaded, her womanly body aching with desire.

He captured her wrist, and pulled her hand away. "Oh, no! I made that mistake once in my life and I'm not gonna repeat it!"

"It wouldn't be a mistake!"

"Yes, yes it would." He firmly pushed her away from him, and released his grip. He ran his hand over his short brown hair. "God! How hard it is to do the right thing in this world!" He smashed his fist against the barn door, and it gave a little jump.

"Careful," she said, "don't break my door."

"Ha, ha! What about my poor hand?"

"That, too."

The spell was broken. "I'm sorry, I just couldn't wait a minute longer," he vowed. "I haven't seen you in nine days!" There had been phone contact since the walk to Miss Hastings' house; however, other responsibilities had intervened to keep them apart, including opening day of deer hunting season, which he necessarily spent with his son.

"Couldn't you wait a few more hours 'til the breakfast? It's only 4:30 a.m.!" she protested. Nevertheless, she was gratified by his simple declaration.

"Then I'd have to share you."

She eyed him suspiciously. "How do you know about the back door to the coop?" She wasn't sure if she suspected something nefarious or if he was just blessed with uncanny abilities to find her.

"I used to care-take this place, remember? I know every nook and cranny of the old place. Especially the haymow!"

"I bet you do!"

He grinned, and patted her shapely bottom affectionately. "I'm actually here to get the eggs for the church breakfast, Sweets. At least, that's my excuse. Mom told me last night that you were going to bring 'em with you down to the church, but I thought I'd come over and see if I could get lucky … er, help."

"Some help!" she retorted. Heart singing, she re-secured her hair, and returned to her egg gathering.

He leaned back against a white-washed support post to leisurely watch her. "Let me know if I can do anything."

"Mmmhmm."

The fluorescent lights were bright and cheerful, and she began humming a little tune. She was dressed in an oversized flannel shirt, faded jeans and a pair of tall barn boots. His heart constricted longingly as he beheld her, and he knew in that moment that he wanted to spend the rest of his life with this woman. A vague image popped into his head of the two of them, in a field of wildflowers, chasing after two or three dark-haired, pointy-eared kids like he had chased the chickens moments earlier. Oh, God! If only it could be true!

Until he met her, he had never believed in destiny. He would have said that life was a stern, sacred duty; that one carved his lot from a hard, inflexible world much like a worm in sandstone. Now, he felt the freedom of water – liquid joy – tumbling down from the mountainside, eagerly seeking its fate. There was no other choice except to flow merrily downward and embrace the arms of the willing, waiting sea.

Into this intoxicating daydream floated the face of Ryan MacDonald. With a twinge of fear, Bruce recalled the handsome man asking him: *Do you know Amber Johnson? She's moved up here with her mother, Rebecca Russell. I knew her in Boston.* And he again regretted that he had invited the other man to attend the church breakfast.

He pushed resolutely away from the support post. "Sit with me at breakfast," he commanded. He took the heavy egg basket from her arms, and pushed a stray strand of hair gently away from her smiling eyes.

"I can't!" she wailed. "I'm one of the waitresses."

"Oh, I thought it was a buffet," he said, disappointed. He had wanted to show everyone, especially Ryan MacDonald, that she was his – the two of them belonged together.

"We still have to pour coffee, clear plates, and stuff. We don't get much chance to sit down. Besides, you're the hero of the hour! I wouldn't be able to get close to you even if I wanted to—I'd have to shove aside all the old ladies!"

He sighed, and offered up a wry grin. "Being a hero isn't all it's cracked up to be."

She patted his arm. "I think you can stand a little more adoration."

By 5:30 a.m. they had cleaned the eggs, and placed them in gray, corrugated cardboard flats. Bruce loaded the necessary flats into the passenger side of his pickup, and carefully closed the door. "See you soon, Sweets," he said, hopping into the driver's seat.

Amber's heart thrilled at the recognition of this new term of endearment. *Sweets!* It wasn't just the nickname, it was the joyful way in which he said it that gave this sobriquet such poignant appeal. *Sweets!*

She couldn't let him go without at least acknowledging a return of such affection. "Hey, if you want to sit in my section, sit in the way back!" she called loudly after him. "Behind the cash table!" She saw an ardent flicker in his eyes through the glass windshield, and knew he had heard her direction.

After a quick shower, Amber donned a pretty white blouse and jeans. She drove to the church, Wendell and Rebecca having gone on ahead. By the time she reached the 1960s annex to the church where the breakfast was being cooked and served, a short line had formed at the door. Amber entered the antiquated kitchen by the side door, and was greeted by the scent of fresh cinnamon rolls, the moist heat from the gas range and the excited buzz of ladies' voices. Maude, in her roll of captain-on-deck, was wearing the Ladies' traditional pinafore over a full skirt, and was issuing orders in a calm, controlled manner. Amber received her instructions, and obediently slipped into her quaint matching pinafore. She began filling the water pitchers and insulated coffee pots.

Maude was in high good humor. Bruce had arrived, and, after unloading the eggs, her son was making his way good-naturedly through the little crowd of women in the kitchen. Hugs and kisses were exchanged all around, and Maude was basking in a proud, motherly glow. She knew where the eggs had come from, of course, and from whose hands he had taken them. But at this moment, she didn't care. She had seen him greet Trudy Gorse with an affectionate squeeze and a few words, and that was enough to satisfy her for now.

The large dining room held twelve banquet tables, each covered with a white linen tablecloth, and was set for the first seating of one hundred. At 6 a.m., Miss Hastings perched her petite frame like a bird at a small table in the front of the room, and the doors were thrown open. Despite her age, she had not forgotten any of her former pupils, and Miss Hastings greeted everyone either by name or endearment. "Callie, dahrrrling!" she cried, accepting the $7 breakfast donation from the hand of a chubby child. "So good to see you, dahrrrling!" She beamed at the youngster's parents. "So good to see you, too, you DAHRRRLINGS!"

Platters of homemade cinnamon buns, muffins, scrambled eggs, farm-raised bacon and sausage, blueberry pancakes, toast and jams and jellies of every variety tempted the hungry throng from the linen-draped serving tables set up in front of the banquet room. Amber maneuvered cheerfully from table to table in the back of the room, filling coffee cups, refilling cream pitchers, fetching glasses of orange juice and ice water. She kept an eye on Bruce as she worked, watching him laughing and joking with the crush of well-wishers. Old men slapped him on the back and shook his hand, and their wives put themselves forward for hugs and kisses.

In forty-five minutes, Amber noted that Bruce had worked his way to the back corner of her section. He appropriated one of the folding metal chairs at the end of an empty table, and sat down. But as she tried to make her way to him, the aisle quickly became impassable. He winked at her apologetically over the sea of heads, as if to say, "See? What did I tell you!" She smiled in response, and felt a tug of love in her heart. She turned on her heel to refill the coffee pot, and bumped into—Ryan MacDonald.

"Ryan! I didn't expect you so early!" she exclaimed. She attempted to pull back, but he was too quick for her.

He took her by the elbow, keeping the two of them close together. "I wanted to get here before they ran out of food. Looks like I'm just in time! Tell me, where should I sit?" He glanced around. At six-feet, two-inches, Ryan could easily see over the crowd, and he spied Bruce Gilpin holding court in the back corner of her section.

Amber was about to direct Ryan to an open table on the opposite side of the banquet room, when a loud "Hallo!" from Ralph Gilpin arrested her. "Hallo, MacDonald! Ovah heah, son!" The skinny shopkeeper had seen the younger man's dark head, and was waving him over to the table where several of the Old Farts now sat with Bruce.

Ryan returned the shopkeeper's wave, and dropped his head closer to her ear. "See you later?" he asked hopefully.

Amber hesitated. She could almost feel the jealous gaze of Bruce Gilpin's eyes boring into her back. "Uh, I've got lots of studying to do," she replied, trying to fob him off.

"Oh, – OK, he said, deflated. "I thought we could continue our conversation about the Transcendentalists." He released her arm. "Your mother invited me over for dinner, though," he added, apologetically.

"Ya comin' or ain'tcha, MacDonald?" shouted Ralph. "I cain't keep ya seat open fer long!"

Without another word, Ryan slipped past her and made his way to the back table. Amber felt a rush of shame. She should have been nicer to him, but she didn't want to lead him on. She had suspected signs of a growing affection from the Boston attorney this summer, and she had been careful not to encourage him, considering Ryan more of a friend of her mother's than a potential romantic partner.

Amber retreated to the kitchen, where she refilled the coffee pot. Quickly, she retraced her steps, making her way to the all-important back table, where the old men were salivating over their food, clamoring for more coffee.

"Thet decaf?" asked Asa Palmer, pushing his mug forward.

"Not this pot, sorry."

Asa quickly put his palm over the top of his cup.

"Gawd almighty, Palmah, yer awful picky," exclaimed Leland Gorse, thrumming his spoon against the rim of his stoneware mug, indicating he desired a refill.

"I cain't sleep at night if'n I drink caffeine."

"I'll bring you some decaf on my next trip," Amber promised.

"Steady, boys – Bruce first," interjected John Woods.

She poured the hot coffee into Bruce's cup, avoiding his eyes. She knew that Ryan MacDonald was closely watching the two of them. She felt Bruce's firm hand slip insinuatingly through the gap in the back of her pinafore, and—splashed coffee all over the white linen tablecloth.

"Now ya dun it!" Leland declared. "Maude'll probbly fire yer arse."

The whole table burst out laughing. Relieved at the interruption, Amber sopped up the mess with the dish towel she carried over her arm. She finished pouring out the regular coffee and returned to the kitchen for the pot of decaf. Then she unassumingly filled Asa's mug, melting into the background like a good waitress. The men were now deep in conversation, even Ryan and Bruce hardly noticed her. All eyes were on the hero of the hour, and she eagerly eavesdropped on their conversation.

"Ain'tcha goin' back, then?" asked Asa.

"Nope, I think I'm gonna open a little garage," Bruce replied, taking a swig of coffee. He set the mug back down onto the table, and toyed with the handle. "Turn a few wrenches, maybe."

"By Gawd, we could use a garage in town!" Leland exclaimed. "I got that old Lippart-Stewart dump truck I cain't git stahted. Been haulin' firewood 'round town with Cain 'n Abel."

"We know all about it, Leland."

"Sounds like a good plan," said John Woods, thoughtfully. "We could use a good mechanic in Sovereign."

Ralph, who was sitting next to Bruce, fondly threw his skinny arm across his son's broad shoulders. "My boy kin fix anything!" he stated, proudly. "He worked on them big M-ATVs in Afghanistan. You seen the size of them things?!"

"She ain't stahted in probbly two years," Leland complained, scratching his head. "I been under her, 'n worked on her some, but there's a fittin' there I jest cain't seem to get off."

"Wal, you ain't as young as you used to be," Wendell pointed out.

"Never mind that now, Leland," said Woods.

Bruce, however, wasn't as quick to dismiss Leland Gorse as the rest of the men. He turned to the old farmer. "You still using that big Stillson wrench?" he asked, with true interest.

"Ayuh."

"That's your problem, Leland. That fitting you're trying to remove is not a nut on a thread, it's a cap and it's held on by a collar. Put your cold chisel to the collar and break it. The collar will fall off, and for a few bucks you can buy another collar to replace it."

Impressed murmurs and mutterings broke forth from the men at the table. "Well, I'll be hornswoggled!" "I told ya! My boy kin fix anything!" "I'll betcha five dollars he's got thet one right!"

Leland looked at Bruce, eyes agog. "By Gawd, you jest save me hunnerds of dollars!"

"Let's see if I'm right, first. I'll be over some afternoon to look at the old dump truck, OK?"

"It's good to have ya back, son!" cried Ralph, his heart overflowing with fatherly pride and affection.

Bruce glanced up, and noticed Amber listening to the conversation. Their eyes met. He smiled, and she smiled back. For a moment, it seemed as though there was just the two of them in the buzz of people. But several other sets of eyes, including those of Ryan MacDonald, had noted the non-verbalized connection between Amber Johnson and Bruce Gilpin. Not much in Sovereign happens without the whole town knowing it—especially a budding love affair!

Chapter 12
. . . .
The Old Canning Factory

The Thursday following the church breakfast, just after coffee break, John Woods and the two other members of the Sovereign Board of Selectmen met at the Town Office to prepare for their tour of the old Westcott Canning Factory with Bruce Gilpin and Peter Hodges. After signing a few checks and documents for Betty Peabody, Woods folded his long legs into his colleague's pickup. He called out a last minute instruction to the Town Clerk, who had followed him out the door. "Tell 'em they can find us down to the corn shop," he said. "That is, if anyone needs us that bad."

"Will do, Chief!"

Woods tugged the passenger door closed. "I hate when Betty calls me that," he grumbled. "Makes me feel like a dang Indian."

"Native American," corrected Bob Jessup, the most junior selectman. Young, short and fat, Jessup had been relegated to the awkward middle of the truck's bench-style seat as a result of his subordinate status on the board. "That's the politically correct way to say Indian," he added.

"You worry all about that, Bob. And while you're worrying about that, I'll worry about getting over to the corn shop before the roof falls in. Let's go, Maynard."

Without comment, Maynard Nutter, eighty-five, the other long-time selectman, obliged. He put his 1989 Ford F1 into gear, and headed carefully across town to the old corn shop.

"Sure you're OK to drive?" Jessup worried, glancing at Maynard's frail frame and blue-veined hands.

"Shut up, Bob," said Woods, and the younger man temporarily obliged.

The remains of the Westcott Canning Factory are situated on a private dirt road running from the defunct train station on the southeast side of Sovereign, near the Thorndike town line. The trip to the corn shop took about fifteen minutes, during which time Jessup, a first-year selectman, loosened up again, and chatted like a nervous magpie. Needless to say, both Woods and Nutter were glad when they arrived.

The best view of the old canning factory was from the rear of the building. The front side of the building, once a field, was now grown up to a forest of lanky hardwoods, Japanese knotweed, and sumac. However, in back of the three-story wood-shingled building a PWA project bridge from the 1930s still carried local traffic across Black Brook. From this heavy concrete bridge, it was possible to get a decent idea of the scope and size of the old canning factory, since only a few old soldiers (mostly ash trees) survived the regular spring flushing of the brook to screen the view of the towering mass of boards and tin.

The main building that once housed the daily canning operation was longer than a football field, and ran length-wise along the edge of Black Brook, only about five feet away from high water in springtime. The ground beneath the building was uneven, sloping down to the dark moving water from the high ground in front of the factory, once a flat, grassy pasture. Picturesque gray boulders covered with moss, lichen and colorful autumn leaves added to the pleasing posterior prospect, and the view from the bridge was highly photographed in fall. The building sat on leviathan wooden posts, which world-weary Atlases still stood perfectly straight even after more than a hundred years of labor. The top two floors of the building (the two visible and accessible from the front), were last painted a beige-yellow and trimmed a rich chocolate-brown. The boards were still solid, and the paint, although faded and flaked, revealed a tantalizing glimpse of the grandeur of those earlier days. The insignificant bottom level, only glimpsed from the rear, was a weathered gray, having never been painted, and was now all but invisible, blending naturally into the gray rocks and tree trunks lining the brook. Miraculously, much of the single-pane glass remained in the sixteen, eight-over-eight windows visible from the rear, and the corrugated metal roof, although bleeding large patches of orange rust, was also still intact, thereby ensuring that the building might remain standing for quite a few years yet.

Maynard Nutter paused on the weight-limited bridge, so that the three selectmen could contemplate the old canning factory from a distance. "Don't thet bring back memories, though," he said, shaking his head somberly. Four generations of Nutters had grown peas, beans and corn for the Westcott Canning Factory.

"Makes you realize how fast time goes by, don't it?" replied Woods, rolling down his window to get a better look. "My father grew squash for 'em, at the end of it."

"Seems like jest yestiday I was down there on them rocks tryin' to steal a kiss from Ma Jean!" Maynard continued. "Course, she was Mabel Jean Edwards, then. Didn't she hate thet name – Mabel!"

Woods chuckled. "Likely she married Harold to try and get rid of it," he suggested. "Too bad they never had any kids."

"Poor Mabel," Maynard agreed, sighing deeply.

"Why's she called 'Ma,' then?" asked Bob Nutter, his curiosity piqued. "If she never had no kids?"

"Oh, somebody – Henry Gorse, maybe – knew how badly Mabel Jean wanted a family," Woods explained, "and just started calling her that, in an affectionate sort of way. The name just caught on, and she's been 'Ma Jean' ever since."

"Poor Mabel," Maynard repeated. "She's been alone a long time; it's been goin' on thirteen years since Harold died! Don't seem possible, do it?"

Woods shook his head. "Nope."

While the selectmen reminisced, Bruce Gilpin and his uncle suddenly appeared around the side of the building. Oblivious to the onlookers on the bridge, the two men poked their heads into the dark maw of open space beneath the old canning factory.

Woods' eyes narrowed. "They're checking out the footings," he said. "Smart place to start, boys."

"Wonder why he wants this old place?" Maynard muttered, more to himself than the other two.

"He's gonna get the factory up and running again. Doncha know?" Jessup answered confidently.

Woods shook his head. "Oh, I don't know about that. I don't know as Bruce knows himself what he wants." He slowly rolled his window back up. "But I do know those Hodges men ain't fools. Let's get on with it, Maynard."

Half the town had wanted to accompany Bruce on his maiden tour of the old canning factory and for the sake of simplicity he'd had to take the strict position that this foray was official town business in order to thin down the crowd. Therefore, only those with some sort of official standing were allowed to be present. Unfortunately, this meant that the one person whom Bruce most wanted to accompany him – Amber Johnson – was not of the advance scouting party. She herself had pointed out that it would be difficult to justify her attendance while at the same time keeping away the Old Farts, all of whom were clamoring to go.

"It's not fair to them," she said. "After all, Clyde and Leland and Asa were some of the ones who got you interested in saving the corn shop in the first place! It wouldn't be right for me to go and not them."

When this exchanged occurred, Bruce and Amber were cuddling in his vintage blue AMC Rambler, which was parked at the overlook at Common Hill. They had snuck away from their respective homes for a quiet afternoon drive in Charlemagne. "But I wouldn't be doing this at all, if it wasn't for you," he pleaded. "I want you with me when I first step inside!" He looked down at her upturned face and flashed his winsome Hodges' smile, the smile that always worked on his mother.

But Amber didn't budge. "Nice try, Love," she said. "But it won't work."

"That's pretty hard-hearted, except for the love part, of course."

She snuggled closer, as a consolation prize. "Maybe you'll take me on a private tour sometime, when it's just the two of us?" she suggested.

"Aw, you're just saying that to make me feel better." He dropped a kiss on the top of her head. "But keep it up—it's working."

"Just put yourself in Clyde Crosby's shoes and you'll know I'm right."

"Ha, ha! I don't think I could ever fill those shoes!"

Interestingly enough, Ryan MacDonald, had made the cut. After hearing about Bruce's fascination for the corn shop at the church breakfast, the Boston attorney had good-naturedly offered free legal advice. Instead of reading and rusticating, Ryan had spent the past three days going through the folders Bruce had retrieved from the town office. In addition, Ryan had motored down to the registry of deeds in Belfast and performed the arduous title search on the property, ensuring that the town owned the old corn shop and the equipment free and clear of any other liens. After all that, Bruce had felt obligated to invite the other man, who offered to attend as the project's legal counsel.

Bruce felt his hackles rise at Ryan's suggestion he might need legal advice. "I don't think I need a lawyer," he said. He was too much of a gentleman to say what he was thinking, however, which was: "You city people are way too quick to sue!"

"Well, let's make sure you don't," Ryan replied, smoothly. "It won't cost you anything if I'm right, but it could cost you a lot if you're wrong."

Thus, despite the fact that Bruce suspected Ryan's intent – correctly perceiving him as a rival for Amber's affections – he had invited the other man to come along.

When the selectmen pulled up to the front of the building, Ryan was loitering at the bottom of the wide, paint-flaked wooden steps. He greeted the others with a stiff nod. "They're down back," he said, with a little indication of his head in the direction of the brook. The four men waited awkwardly on the gravel-covered ledge. Birds cat-called from the tops of the tall ash trees and the sound of rushing water could be heard from the brook.

Bruce and Peter shortly joined them, and the necessary introductions were made. The six men regrouped, as men do, shuffling around until each secured a comfortable piece of ground. The little group thoughtfully regarded the dilapidated factory. The sign plastered across the front of the building was barely legible, with just a shadow of the black paint declaring *WESTCOTT'S CANNING FACTORY, First Quality Corn, Grown and Packed in Sovereign, Maine.* A paper *Keep Out!* sign had half-peeled from the left side of the front double door, and flapped mildly in the light breeze. While they stood there, a bird darted out of a broken window on the top floor, and zoomed off into the late-morning sky. Although it was the first of November, the air was unusually warm for a fall day in Maine, continuing a weather pattern that had been in place since summer.

"Well, let's give her a go, boys," said Woods. "Did somebody remember to bring a bolt cutter? Betty couldn't find the key."

Bruce produced the necessary item from the back of his truck. "Got it," he said, brandishing the bolt cutter. His heart picked up in anticipation of the consummation of his long-time dream. During his last tour in Afghanistan, he had spent many a long night envisioning this moment, when the door to the old canning factory would be thrown open for the first time in nearly half a century, exposing her treasures.

"Good man."

"Watch the steps," advised Ryan MacDonald. "They're in bad shape."

Bob Jessup put a foot on the bottom step and heaved his heavy carcass upward. A loud crunch was heard, as his thick leg pierced the spongy wood. "Dammit!"

"Too late," said Maynard Nutter, unable to keep a note of glee from his voice. Although Maynard was forty-five years older than Jessup, he was easily one hundred and fifty pounds lighter, and with the aid of a shaky railing, the old man nimbly ascended the steps to the upper landing.

An eight-foot-long wooden deck wrapped around the front of the building, connecting the front to the factory's side loading dock. Maynard peered down the long western edge of the building. "We used to pull up here 'n git weighed in," he reminisced. "All of us kids crammed in like sardines amongst them barrels o' string beans in the back o' the truck. Then we'd go 'round 'n unload the beans, 'n we'd run right back through to git weighed up agin. Mrs. Mitchell – she was one o' the office gals who worked the scales – she kept a pretty close eye on us six kids to make sure we was all back in thet truck afore we got weighed agin."

"Making sure your father didn't get paid a little extra, was she?" said Peter Hodges, chuckling.

"Ha, ha," said Bruce, looking at Maynard's slight frame. "That might have cost 'em – what? An extra dollar? I bet you didn't weigh sixty pounds when you were a kid, Maynard!"

"A dollar a day, seven days a week adds up mighty fast," Woods pointed out. "Especially when you multiply it by six kids."

"Oh, Father always made sure to keep a few o' us in the truck, to try 'n confuse Mrs. Mitchell, you know. But he couldn't git nuthin' past her; she was awful shaap!"

Bruce nervously approached the wooden door. The Westcott family had left the building locked, but the soft metal had corroded so much that the bolt cutters made short work of it; one bite, and the lock hit the deck. The rusty latch *creaked* as he folded it back. He stepped away from the sagging door. "Who wants to do the honors?" he asked, eagerly.

"Go ahead, son," Woods encouraged. "We're all here on your account."

The five men moved back so that Bruce could swing open the wide wooden door, which had once served as the main entrance to the old canning factory. A rush of cool, dank air reminiscent of a musty dirt cellar escaped, and it seemed to Bruce as though the old place groaned a little, as though unhappy to be woken from its long slumber.

Despite the many windows, the inside was dark, nearly as dark as an in-ground cemetery vault that Bruce had peeked into one summer. The spiders, barn swallows, pigeons, dust and dirt had had their way with the windows for decades and the grimy glass was now nearly opaque. He hesitated at the entryway for a moment, waiting for his eyes to adjust to the dim light.

"Anyone think to bring a flashlight?" Woods inquired, peering over his shoulder.

"Dammit, no," said Jessup.

Bruce moved forward a few feet. Once he was out of the bright sunlight, the mass of antiquated machinery began to creep towards him from the shadows, like old farm equipment does when you first step into a darkened barn. With the exception of a long conveyor belt, none of the machinery looked familiar. Everything was covered by a blanket of dust, grime and cobweb residue, which gray thickness rounded out all the sharp edges. "Jesus," he said. He glanced around, attempting to take everything in: the pulleys, the chains, the belts, the giant flywheels, the cast iron pipes and fittings, the humungous beams overhead, the caps, the sealing machine, the old electrical wiring, push carts covered with empty aluminum cans. A row of ladies straw hats and old-fashioned umbrellas dangled from Shaker-style pegs, decorating one of the walls. On the opposing wall, framed black and white photographs and newspaper clippings nearly obscured the painted wall. Bruce felt as though he had opened the door to a giant time capsule.

He approached the conveyor belt, scuffing across the dirt and dried bird droppings that littered the floor. "Look at this," he said reverentially, his brain immediately engaged in an attempt to decipher the flow of the canning operation from the unfamiliar nature of the residual machinery. He moved cautiously, mindful of the aged wooden floor, working his way down the line from the capping machine toward the head of the conveyor belt. He could almost hear the faint echo of laughter, and he remembered a practical joke Henry Gorse, Trudy's grandfather, had told him, about the time he had put a mud turtle on the conveyer belt along with a pile of shucked sweet corn. Henry had watched from behind a barrel as the women doing the corn inspection spied the mud turtle and scattered in terror. Bruce imagined Miss Hastings' father, the corn shop Superintendent, alerted by the women's screams, hurrying to the scene, and then the good-natured laughter that followed all around as the renegades (both the turtle and Henry) were captured.

"She's in pretty hard shape," allowed Woods, hard on Bruce's heels. The selectman's words brought him back to the present. "I'm afraid she's worth more at the junkyard than anything else, son."

"This place looks like a museum!" exclaimed Ryan MacDonald. His nose wrinkled in slight disgust at the faint odor of ammonia. "Except for the pigeon droppings, of course."

Bruce felt his heart sinking with every step he took. His experienced eyes could see at a glance that there was no hope of restoring the old canning factory to its former glory. Even if he could get everything running again – and that was a big IF – the machinery was hopelessly outdated. He knew – or thought that he knew – that the equipment in the corn shop would never pass today's worker safety codes. An image came to mind of the stainless steel commercial kitchens he had seen in the service, and he told himself that nothing here would ever meet the new, more stringent FDA standards for safe food preparation, either.

The disappointment was almost overwhelming. Worse was imaging how he could possibly break the depressing news to Amber. He hated to think of the sparkling glow of excitement and enthusiasm fading from her pretty blue eyes. Once again, he mentally kicked himself for not having had the courage to demand her presence. She should have been with him – by his side! Everything would have been so much easier!

Bruce felt a strong hand on his shoulder. "Don't let it throw you," said his uncle, reassuringly. "Things always look worse than they really are."

He turned around. "You're just saying that to make me feel better, Peter," he said, a bit defensively. Nevertheless, he did feel better.

"May-be. But just because I'm saying it, doesn't mean it isn't true."

The group of men spent more than an hour peering into every nook and cranny of the old canning factory, ferreting out some of its hidden treasure. On the second floor they discovered the can loft, where thousands of tin cans and hundreds of wooden shipping boxes were still stored. "Here's the desilker!" announced Maynard Nutter, from a small room next door. Bruce thoughtfully examined the abandoned piece of equipment. He recalled the black and white photograph of the young Clyde Crosby he had seen at Miss Hastings' house, and imagined young Clyde running free through the old corn shop, while his mother worked the desilker.

"And here's the double husker!" Maynard continued, triumphantly. "Who'da thunk they would have kept this old junk?"

"It does seem strange they hung onto it all," replied John Woods. "Especially as the Westcotts were from Portland, not Sovereign."

Ryan, who had been content to tag along quietly, now put himself forward. "I believe the Westcotts hoped for a long time that they might can sweet corn again in the future," he said. "At least, that's what I interpreted from some of the documents and correspondence I reviewed earlier in the week."

Jessup sniffed disdainfully. "Flatlanders," he pronounced.

"They continued to pay the personal property taxes on their equipment, long after the town had foreclosed on the real estate," the lawyer added.

"I'll be goddammed," said Woods, impressed. "Did they really?"

Ryan nodded, pleased to finally have brought something to the table. "They knew that the town couldn't or wouldn't sell the real estate until the personal property—" he waved his hands indicating the old equipment "—was removed. Looks to me like the Westcotts just kept hoping that one day their fortunes would change and they'd be able to get the factory back up and running again. They never did, obviously."

In spite of himself, Bruce was affected by the extraordinary effort Ryan had taken on his behalf. "Thanks for that, Ryan," he said. Their eyes met, and he read in the other man's face the gratification his words had given. "I'm glad you came with us," he said sincerely.

John Woods glanced at his watch. "I'll be jiggered – lunchtime, boys!" he announced. "If we don't get down to Ma Jean's soon, there won't be any pie left!"

Even before the promise of pie, Bruce had begun to feel his spirits recover. He turned to address little group. "Let's make it a party – I'm buying! Who's in?"

There was a little chorus of "yeas" and agreeable chuckles.

"Come along, then," Bruce declared. He turned to his uncle. "You coming, Peter?"

"Nope, thanks. I've got a few stops to make," Peter said, giving a little tug to his baseball cap. "I'll just have time to fit 'em in and get back to Oaknole in time for milking."

"Going over to see your old girlfriend?" Bruce joked, never believing for a moment that his uncle might indeed be planning a visit to yours truly.

He winked at his nephew. "May-be," he said.

Chapter 13

. . . .

Forever Friends

Most of us, I suspect, have that one special person from childhood, that one friend, ally, bosom buddy, confederate, partner and playmate from whom no confidence is withheld and with whom every hope and dream, no matter how silly or how small, is shared. Sometimes these confidantes are of the same sex. Sometimes, particularly when the bonds are formed very young, they are of the opposite sex. My comrade of childhood was of the opposite sex, and his name was Peter Hodges.

Although Peter and I were vaguely aware of each other's existence before age five (our families operated dairy farms about a mile apart on the Garland Road in Winslow), we didn't bond until we started Kindergarten. On the first day of school, the kindly bus driver Carl Horn, also a dairy farmer, carefully parked Peter and me together in the seat directly behind him so that he could keep an eye on us until we arrived at Halifax School. About every mile or so, Mr. Horn would glance up into the bus' rear view mirror and wink at us reassuringly. Sometimes, when it was very cold, the big-hearted bus driver would let us sit up above the bar on the metal heater located to the left of his long legs. On those days, Peter and I snuggled happily together (although probably not very safely), feeling incredibly important on our toasty perch, from which we enjoyed a dazzling and dizzying view of the world beyond the expansive bus windshield.

To ensure that we weren't separated once we got to Halifax School, Peter and I held hands when we disembarked and were shepherded away to our classroom. Once inside, we selected abutting desks, two small wooden stations up at the very front of the classroom where nobody else ever wants to sit. We stayed together at lunch, too, sitting elbow to elbow, trays touching, at the long cafeteria table in the school's basement. Even though children weren't supposed to talk during lunch (Maine's education system was strict in the 1960s), our thoughts and feelings were an open book to one another and pieces of food moved back and forth from one plastic brown tray to the other. Peter always took my peas and carrots, knowing I didn't like them, and, generous as he was, he almost always gave me his desserts in exchange for the vegetables. Now, that's a friend.

One day I was caught talking at lunch – I couldn't resist telling Peter about the new litter of barn kittens that had been born that morning – and I was reprimanded by the vigilant lunch monitor, who ordered me to pay a visit to the principal, a dead ringer for Almira Gulch, to repent of my sins. I did repent – repent that I had ever been born. Terrified, I slipped outside the two-story brick building, and hid behind the large black iron trash barrel that guarded the front door to Halifax School like a gargoyle. My loyal companion, although safe from censure himself, bravely joined me, not only so that I wouldn't be on the lam alone but also so that when we were caught (and we figured it would take a couple of days for them to find us) I wouldn't suffer the horrible punishment by myself.

We were discovered about fifteen minutes after lunch, when the classes started up again and our little wooden desks were obviously empty. Peter and I were marched like prisoners of war up to the second floor, to face "Miss Gulch" in her office. Now, Miss Gulch kept a mean-looking leather razor strap dangling from a wooden peg on the wall next to her desk. (Corporeal punishment was still allowed at school in those days.) Tales of student floggings with the razor strap, perhaps more hagiographic than real, were whispered from student to student. Peter and I hung our heads, and stood penitential in front of Miss Gulch's magnificent oak desk, our five-year-old knees quaking. Before I knew what he was doing, Peter stepped forward and confessed to the crime. I never knew what love felt like until that moment.

Miss Gulch lectured both of us on the evils of talking during lunch, gave us some hard candy from a drawer in her desk, and sent us back to the classroom with a stern warning never to be seen in her office again. And despite the enticement of more hard candy, we never showed our faces there again. From that day forward, Peter has been my hero.

I could go on and on, telling stories about the adventures we had together, like the time Peter dared me to dog-paddle out to the middle of the slimy, pollen-covered frog pond to pick the one lone yellow water lily that tempted us from afar. "If you get it, you can be Queen for a day," he pronounced. "I don't want to be Queen for a day," I sniffed. "I want to be King!" And I was King for that day, and possibly every day after that.

Just before our seventh birthdays (Peter and I were born in late August, only a few days apart), my father decided to improve our family situation. Dad had seen the writing on the wall for Maine's small dairy farms (in the 1950s there were 51,000 herds of dairy farms in Maine; today there are 306). He elected to pursue higher education as a vocation by which he could feed his growing family. So we split from the extended family of three generations of the Walkers on the Garland Road, sold our farm and moved away from the nest.

Peter was devastated. I promised to write him faithfully, at least once a week, no matter where I lived and no matter what was happening in my life. And I've kept that promise for fifty years either by letter, email, text, direct message or tweet, except for the weeks I've been with Peter in person. Growing up, my parents, burdened with five other children in addition to myself, easily agreed to let me spend most of my school holidays and summer vacations with my Winslow grandmother, and between our letter writing and our summer sojourns, the special bond that Peter and I shared has never been broken, not through the natural course of lovers (and lost lovers), nor the deaths of dearly beloved friends and family members. We've always been there to support, console and validate each other. When I gave birth to an illegitimate daughter (my lovely Nellie, who's now twenty), Peter was the first friend to visit me, bringing a large bouquet of yellow roses to my hospital room in Bangor. Certainly, none of my classmates from seminary showed up, embarrassed and ashamed as they were to know a minister-in-training who proudly gave birth out of wedlock. Peter Hodges and I are forever friends.

"So, Bruce is thinking of doing something with that old canning factory," I said, setting a piece of pumpkin pie on the kitchen table in front of Peter (a personal visit from Peter was like a rare wildflower, given his responsibilities on the farm). A new bouquet of fall flowers graced the table, which was covered with a figured oil cloth. My forever friend had appeared without warning on the doorstep of my two-story cottage on the Cross Road in Sovereign shortly before one o'clock. After our initial hug, he'd shared with me Bruce's interest in the old corn shop, and gave me a brief run-down of the official tour of the abandoned building that had occurred that morning. I knew Peter couldn't stay long because of the milking, that silken bond which confines a dairy farmer's movements three hundred sixty-five days a year. I fed him a grilled cheese and to-mato sandwich, and now we were lingering longer than we should have been over our beverages and dessert. "He doesn't know what he's getting himself into this time."

Peter spooned a large dollop of Wendell's honey into a mug of steaming tea. (Most Maine communities have at least one beekeeper, and Wendell is our resident expert.) The spoon made little clacking noises as Peter stirred his tea. "Oh, I think Bruce has a pretty good idea of what he's up against, after looking around this morning." He knocked the spoon against the rim of the mug and set it down onto the oilcloth.

"Do you think there's any chance he could get that rusty old machin-ery running again?"

"The kid can get anything running again. You know how he is, Maggie. There isn't a tractor on the farm he can't fix or M-ATV he can't overhaul."

"But where's he going to get the money?"

"That's the real question," Peter agreed. He leaned his weight onto his sturdy elbows. "God knows I don't have any money to give him."

Mutual friends have asked me over the years if I didn't think Peter Hodges was handsome. I never know how to answer them, because I never see Peter as he is, I always see him as the short, elf-eared kid who stepped onto the bus three minutes after I did with that same terrified look in his eyes. Over the years, he grew to become about six-feet tall, and, thanks to the Hodges' genes and the physical labor on the farm, he muscled up nicely. (He never did outgrow those pointy-ears, though.) Today, he is somewhat stooped and his acorn-colored hair is now peppered with gray, and almost always capped with a Red Sox baseball hat. I suspect that Peter is bald now, but I don't know or care since I haven't seen him without his baseball cap in more than thirty years.

"What's the latest on the Farm Bill?" I asked, knowing that the last Federal termagant had expired, which meant that the price guarantees for Maine's dairy farmers like Peter were going to expire at the end of the year, unless Congress got off their duffs and passed a new Farm Bill or extended the old one.

"Don't get me started on that, Maggie," he warned. "That damn thing is stuck in committee. I'm losing money every day, what with the high price of grain, but nobody in Washington gives a hoot." He picked up his mug with both hands, blew across the top and took a swig of tea. He returned the mug to the table, and toyed with the handle.

"Is that because of the drought?"

"They say it is. But I'm not sure there's not some price gouging and outright thievery going on as well." When he got wound up on any topic related to farming, Peter could be pretty energetic.

"Why don't you give it up, Peter?" I urged.

"Quit farming? You know I can't do that, Maggie."

"Why not? Now that your Dad is dead, you don't need to carry on, do you?"

"What am I going to do with myself? I'm only fifty-six."

"Thanks for reminding me how old I am."

"What if I told you to stop working? Would you do it? Could you do it?"

He had a good point. I wouldn't stop working even if I could afford to, since I love the ministry too well to give it up. "Mine's a calling," I replied. "There's a difference."

"Like Hell there is."

"Maybe you can cut down the size of your herd? So you won't have to work so hard?"

"I guess you haven't been out to the farm in a while."

"Not since your Dad's funeral."

"Two years ago, when Dad died, I was milking one hundred cows. Now I'm down to about fifty. My whole herd – replacement heifers, calves and all – is less than a hundred animals."

"Damn."

"Nice language for someone with a calling."

"I've used worse. Sometimes in a sermon."

"Yeah, and who taught you those swear words?" And Peter and I had a good laugh over some of our youthful follies. The heartfelt bond we shared surfaced long enough for us to catch a glimpse of it, like the giant pickerel we occasionally spotted as kids while fishing in the tall weeds on the Sebasticook River. He stretched his thick arms across the table and clasped both of my hands with his calloused paws. "Why didn't you ever marry me, Maggie?" he lamented.

The question was rhetorical. Peter didn't expect an answer and I didn't offer one. We loved each other, and we knew it. That was more than enough. I gently retrieved my hands, but not before I noted the growth of the hard knobs of arthritis forming on his wide knuckles.

Peter turned naturally to the other not-so-secret longing of his heart – the disposition of Oaknole Farm after he died. "You know how much I was hoping Bruce would come home from Afghanistan and take over the farm," he said. He sighed deeply, and I felt his pain. "That's part of what's kept me carrying on at the old place, especially when Dad was sick. That and I didn't know what else to do with myself."

"Did Bruce say outright he doesn't want to farm?"

"He didn't say it in so many words. He said he'd help me with the haying, and fixing equipment and stuff like he always did. And he'll give me a day off whenever I need it. I know he's not ready to get tied down three hundred sixty-five days a year, and I don't blame him a bit. But if I'm not carrying on the family farm for him, who am I carrying on for? There's nobody else."

"Penney?" I suggested, naming Peter's niece, Bruce's older sister, who ran an organic greenhouse in Thorndike.

He shook his head. "Penney's not interested, and her boys aren't either. They don't stray too far from their electronic gadgets these days."

"What about Gray?"

"You and I both know that old Ralph has been grooming Gray to take over the store since he was a baby. Ralph saw early on that he wasn't going to get Bruce to take over; he always wanted to be at Oaknole, with his grandfather and me. He couldn't stay away. That's why I'm so disappointed, now, I guess. I hadn't realized until his visit the other day how much I'd been hoping Bruce would come back to the farm when he got done in Afghanistan."

"Damn kids never do what the old folks want, do they?" I said, perhaps thinking more of my daughter, Nellie, than of Peter's nephew Bruce. "That's what your grandfather used to say, anyway." We chuckled, thinking that we were the old people now.

"What's up with Nellie?" he asked, kindly, easily following the course of my thoughts.

"You know she was in Australia over the summer? And then she was home with me for about five minutes before she went back to her friends in New York. It's enough to break a mother's heart."

"But she's still in school?" he said, concerned.

I nodded. "Still at Columbia. She's one of those kids who'll be in school the rest of their lives, I think. She's talking about a PhD, now, and she hasn't even finished her bachelor's degree yet!"

"But how can you afford that, Maggie?" he worried, glancing around the cozy country kitchen, looking for tell-tale signs of any unusually-stringent household economy. "You aren't skimping on yourself, are you?"

"No more than I have been for the past twenty years."

"Remember, you promised you'd come to me if you ever need anything?"

"I do, and I will. But I'm not broke, yet. Besides, you just told me you don't have any money to help Bruce!"

"Giving money to Bruce to bring the corn shop back is not the same as helping an old friend. I've still got plenty of money for you and Nellie, Maggie. I've got the red pine plantation I can harvest." (Farmers in Maine always have an extra woodlot or two they keep in their back pocket, just in case there isn't enough money left over after paying the grain man to cover the real estate taxes.)

"Don't harvest your woodlot on my account. The Sovereign Union Church took me on full-time. I even get health insurance now, and a few pennies a month set aside for my retirement."

"You didn't tell me about that! What, did the church rob a bank?"

"Very funny. Last year Miss Hastings donated an oil painting to the Ladies Auxiliary and they sold it at James Julia's winter art auction for $50,000. It was something her father brought over with him when the family escaped the Bolshevik Revolution."

"I'll be damned! You definitely forgot to tell me that."

"Miss Hastings has another painting by the same artist she's donating this year."

"And the Ladies gave the whole $50,000 to the church?"

"Half of it. They never give away more than half of what they raise – that's Auxiliary policy. They invest the rest."

"Lucky for you they decided to give the $25,000 to the church!"

"It wasn't luck; it was blackmail. I had a job offer, a full-time position, from a Universalist-Unitarian church in southern Maine. I guess I forgot to tell you that, too. When I told my parishioners I might be leaving them, they decided they were too old to break in a new minister. So, they offered me a real job."

"Your book hasn't upset the apple cart too much, then?" he said, referring to that afore-mentioned chronicle, *Hens and Chickens*, which was published last summer.

"On the contrary, I think they liked it, especially the part about me running naked through the goldenrod every August."

"By the way, you forgot to tell me about that, too."

Chapter 14

. . . .

"It's a Perfect Chance for Them to Tell Their Stories!"

After the tour of the dilapidated canning factory, Bruce had wanted to rush back to the old Russell homestead to share his experiences, disappointing as they were, with Amber. But life had intervened to keep them apart. While lunching at Ma Jean's Restaurant with Ryan and the selectmen, Gray had texted and asked his father to accompany him deer hunting that afternoon. School had let out early, and the boy naturally wanted to spend time with the father who had been so long absent. In addition, there had been that worrisome incident earlier in the year when Gray had accidently shot and killed Sovereign's famed white deer. Bruce, who was as proficient with guns as he was with machinery, thought it would be a good opportunity to give his son some hands-on firearms training. He calculated that the hunting foray into the town forest would delay his visit to Amber by only a few hours, since the November sun would set by 4:30 p.m. What he hadn't calculated upon was that his son would shoot a deer, which necessitated tagging and tending the carcass. Therefore, by the time the evening's work was accomplished and Bruce had showered and changed, he discovered to his chagrin that it was too late for country visiting. Instead, he placed a quick call to Amber, with whom he had spoken briefly earlier, and promised to be with her by one o'clock the following afternoon.

When he arrived at the old Russell homestead the next day, he was further chagrined (and more than a little angry) to discover Ryan MacDonald's vehicle parked in the driveway before him. Jealousy is a fiendish worm, able to locate our soft spots and eager to take advantage of them. When Bruce Gilpin spied the dark, late-model sedan with Massachusetts plates, he felt the worm of jealously gnawing at his gut.

Under that bitter influence, he hardly knew how he made his way out of his pickup and into the kitchen. But shortly, there he was, being welcomed to the table by the woman he loved, and the man whom he suspected of loving her. The two of them had obviously been dining and chatting together for quite some time, the remains of their luncheon were not yet cleared away.

"So cool! Ryan's been telling me all about it!" Amber exclaimed, greeting Bruce affectionately. "I couldn't wait for you to get here to tell me what you think!"

I couldn't wait for you ... was all that he heard. His face darkened, as he pulled up a chair.

"Well? What do you think?!" she continued, excitedly, resuming her seat at the head of the table. "Ryan says the place looks like a museum!"

"I'm sorry, Gilpin," the other man said, apologetically. He was sitting directly across from Bruce. "I just assumed you came over yesterday. I didn't mean to steal your thunder."

Bruce felt the worm thrusting in through the very fibers of his heart. He put his elbows on the table, and hid his face in his hands. *Oh, God! Must he lose everything?! The dream of getting the canning factory operational again? His youthful hopes and dreams? Her innocent, perfect love?!*

It would have been better to have had no hope at all, than to feel the hope dashed!

A little groan escaped him. Alarmed, Amber leaped up and rushed to his side. She pressed her hands against his arm and shoulder. "What's wrong? Is it Gray! Did something happen to Gray?!"

"He's fine," Bruce said, almost roughly. But he couldn't bring himself to look at her.

"What is it, then?!"

Ryan, who had an inkling of the young veteran's emotions, spoke up. "It's my fault, I'm afraid," he said. "I stuck my foot in it. I'd better leave." He stood up to go.

Bruce forced himself to face his rival. He glared at him. "Don't bother," he said. "I'm OK, just, my heart – Jesus! – I hurt!" He cupped his face in his hands again, and burst into tears.

Amber was truly concerned. She didn't know what was going on nor did she care. What mattered was that the man she loved was in pain, and he needed comforting.

She dropped to her knees, reaching up to caress him. "Shhh! It's going to be OK, Love," she reassured him. "Whatever it is, we can get through it together!"

He continued to sob, chest heaving with emotion. She lifted a cloth napkin from the table and began daubing the precious fluid that seeped through his fingers. She murmured little words of encouragement, and rubbed his back and shoulders. "Shhh, shhh!"

In a few minutes, the waterworks stopped. Bruce dropped his hands to the table, drew in a shaky breath, and straightened himself back up. "My God, I needed that!" he pronounced. He laughed tenuously. "Ha, ha! I didn't realize how much emotional stuff I had bottled up inside me!"

Amber instantly thought of PTSD. "Thank God you got it out!"

"I'm sorry, Gilpin," Ryan said. He was still standing, awkwardly, across the table.

Bruce pulled the pretty calico napkin away from Amber and used it to blow his nose. He regarded the cloth apologetically. "Oops, I thought it was a tissue." He set the soiled napkin onto the table.

"I didn't mean to rain on your parade," the other man continued.

"Heck, I should thank you, MacDonald!" Bruce declared. "I never would have got all that stuff out if I hadn't been stark raving mad with jealousy."

Amber pushed herself up off her knees, comprehension beginning to dawn. "Jealousy? Is *that* what's going on?" She turned from one man to the other, seeking confirmation. Both men looked guilty. "I don't believe it," she continued. "Fighting over me like … like eighth graders?!"

Bruce hardly knew what to say. How could he explain to her how sick he had felt when he pulled into the driveway and saw Ryan MacDonald's car?

Ryan, however, wasn't a high-powered attorney for nothing. He had been in many an awkward situation in and out of court, and thus he had learned the hard way that sometimes it was best to tell the truth and take your lumps. "There seems to have been a misunderstanding," he admitted. "I guess I read more into your mother's words and emails than was actually meant to be there. I got the impression – erroneous, I know now – that you would be happy to see me again, Amber."

"But I was happy to see you again!" she protested.

"No, not that kind of happy. I mean, you know, 'happy to see you'!" he said, clumsily attempting to throw some amour into his voice.

Amber blushed. "Oops!"

"Exactly. Like I said, I misunderstood or misinterpreted some cues from your mother, probably because I wanted to hear what I wanted to hear. I wanted her encouragement to be encouragement coming by proxy from you. But since I've been here, I've discovered my mistake. It's obvious your affections are already engaged—understandably so, if I might add. And then," he continued, turning to his rival, "to make matters worse, I accidentally stepped on your toes today, Gilpin. Once again, I apologize. Now, all I need to do is to find some way to get myself gracefully out of this kitchen, which is what I'm sure you've both been wanting for the past half hour." He retrieved his coat from the back of the chair, and slipped an arm into the sleeve.

"Wait, MacDonald!" Bruce interjected. "Don't go." A boyish look came over his face. "I need your help!"

Ryan hesitated, jacket dangling awkwardly. "You do?" A hopeful light flickered in his dark brown eyes. "Don't tell me you're seriously considering renovating that old place?!"

"Well, let's just say I'm not giving up," he replied, smiling.

"I knew it!" Amber exclaimed, affectionately clasping Bruce's arm.

"But it's gonna take all of us – maybe the whole town – to pull this thing off!"

Ryan slipped out of his coat, and returned it to the back of the chair. "You surprise me, Gilpin!"

Amber quickly cleared the dirty dishes from the table. "I'll go get some paper so we can begin planning," she said. She disappeared into the great room.

Ryan reclaimed his seat. He leaned eagerly forward on his elbows. "You think it's salvageable, then? The place looks in hard shape to me."

"Yeah, you're right about that," Bruce admitted. He picked up a pen that had been lying on the table, and tapped it assuredly against the wood. "But I heard what you said when you stepped inside—it didn't register with me at the time. But now I think you're right."

Ryan looked perplexed. "What I said? What did I say?"

"You said, 'The place looks like a museum.'"

Amber returned to the kitchen in time to overhear this remark. She flopped two fresh yellow legal pads on the table. "A museum? Did I miss something?" she asked, setting the tea kettle onto the woodstove to heat up.

Ryan leaned back in his chair. "A museum? You might be onto something!" he allowed.

Bruce threw an arm over the back of his chair. "I'm sorry, Sweets," he said, turning in her direction. "I know you were hoping we could get the old corn shop going again so we could can local food! But that's just not gonna happen. Those days are gone forever, at least at the corn shop, anyway. But ..." he continued, leaning forward to address them both, "the place looks like a museum because it should be a museum! We have a great chance here, what with all that old machinery still intact and some of the folks who used to operate the machinery still alive, like Clyde Crosby, to turn that place into a first-rate museum! Almost everybody over seventy in this town has some sort of connection with the old canning factory, and we can ask each of 'em questions and video tape their answers. It's a perfect chance for them to tell their stories! If we do this thing right, fifty years from now – a hundred years from now! – people will be able to visit our museum and step back into the past, just like we did yesterday, only much, much better. We can save an important piece of Maine history. Now, what do you say to that?!"

Ryan thumped his fist on the table, an expression of sheer joy on his face. "I say, you're a genius, Gilpin!" he declared. "Now, why didn't I think of that?!"

"Ha, ha! You *did* think of that!" Bruce said. And the two men laughed. Bruce was reminded of how much he had initially liked Ryan MacDonald when they had first met on the side of the North Troy Road.

Bruce glanced anxiously at Amber, trying to read her expression. "What about you, Sweets? I hope you're not too disappointed! I know how much you were hoping to can local produce."

He was rewarded with a brilliant smile. "I'm not disappointed in the least! I think a museum is an awesome idea," she said. "In fact, I've been doing a little research of my own, and guess what?!"

Bruce started to speak, but she continued, enthusiastically. "You'll never guess, so I'll tell you—Maine already has two new food processing plants! One of them is up in Aroostook County but the other is right down the road in Belfast! Do you believe it?!"

"Yikes! Talk about timing!"

"I told you processing local food was a timely idea! They are both state of the art operations, of course."

"Ha, ha! That's something the old corn shop would never be!"

"That's excellent news, Amber," interjected Ryan. "I've really been enjoying all the fresh local food around here. I'm glad you turned me onto the 'Eat Local' movement last year."

"But preserving the past is just as important as preserving vegetables," she continued, seriously. "That's why I love your idea of turning the old canning factory into a museum!" She poked the fire, and moved the tea kettle onto the hottest spot on top the woodstove. "But where would we begin? I wouldn't even know how to go about it!"

"Me either," Bruce admitted, toying with his pen. "I just know we've got a great chance to save a piece of history, and we shouldn't waste it."

But the attorney's mind had already leaped three steps ahead. "I know what we need to do," he said, easily. He reached for Bruce's pen, and scratched out a few words onto one of the legal pads. He held up the pad and showed them both. *501(c)3 – non-profit organization.* "We need to set up a non-profit," he said, "so that we can get tax-deductible donations for the project. It's going to take a lot of money to turn that place into a workable museum."

"You got that right!" Bruce said. "The underpinnings of the building are still solid, but she needs a new roof, new paint and new windows – and that's just for starters! Even with volunteer labor, I figure it'll take us at least $50,000 to get off the ground. But aren't the legal fees for setting up the non-profit gonna cost us a lot of money?"

Ryan shook his head. "Not any more than the filing fee, which is $400-$850, depending upon the estimated gross annual receipts for the first four years. I can do all the paperwork for the 501(c)3, gratis, of course; it's not too difficult, really. But we do need to elect a volunteer board of directors first, which," he continued, surveying first Bruce and then Amber, "I'm assuming won't be much of a problem!"

Bruce felt the hair on his arms and neck standing up. "I told you we needed you, MacDonald! I can feel it! It's like I felt walking in there yesterday, seeing everything as it was when the workers shut down the conveyor belt after their last job. It was just like walking into a time capsule!"

Ryan continued this thread. "Only they didn't know it was their last job, when they closed the doors that day," he said earnestly. "They thought they would be back the next day, or the next season. Or the season after that! When the workers left that last day, they had no idea the doors would be closed forever. They even left their hats." He paused, as a thought occurred to him. "Funny, we never do know sometimes when we say our final goodbye to something, do we?" he added, poignantly, thinking more about his lost romantic possibilities with Amber than about the corn shop workers losing their livelihoods.

Amber read his mind. "Oh, Ryan, I'm so sorry!" She went to him and threw her arms affectionately around his thin frame.

He unfurled her arms, and squeezed her hands. "It's not your fault, Amber. I had no justification for thinking that you cared about me."

She started to speak, but Ryan stopped her. "Don't say it, please."

Bruce felt his heart quicken at the raw emotion in the other man's voice. The lawyer's honesty not only increased his respect for Ryan MacDonald, but also fanned the flames of his own ardent longing for Amber Johnson. He wanted her in his arms, and he wanted her there *now*.

Nothing makes a woman more desirable to a man than the desire of another man for that same woman. As he watched Amber attempt to comfort Ryan, he longed to clasp her to his chest, and rain kisses upon her willing face. His jealousy had been quashed, but he did begin to feel the urge to claim his prize.

Immediately, he felt ashamed. Amber loved him. He knew she loved him! He was the winner, and the other man the loser. And the more Bruce watched the two of them, appreciating her gifts, the more he recognized what his opponent had lost. He began to feel truly sorry for Ryan MacDonald, and felt as though he wanted to do something to alleviate the other man's suffering. But he certainly wasn't going to share Amber's affections!

Was there no love to be found for Ryan MacDonald in Sovereign, Maine, then?

Inadvertently, Bruce thought of his old school chum Trudy Gorse, for whom his mother was always playing matchmaker. Perhaps two could play at that game, as well?!

"What about Trudy?" Bruce suggested. "Maybe we should ask her to be on the board of directors? Trudy knows everybody in town, and she'd be great at collecting stuff like old pictures. What do you think?" He winked surreptitiously at Amber.

Amber's eyes widened slightly, as she perceived Bruce's intent. "I think Trudy would be an awesome addition to the board!" she seconded.

"Trudy?" queried the lawyer, shaking his head, doubtfully. "I don't think I know her, do I?" He turned to Amber for confirmation.

Now, Amber knew perfectly well that Ryan MacDonald had met Trudy several times over the past year. Trudy had accompanied them all to the seashore this summer, and Amber had even seen her speak a few words to Ryan at the church breakfast. Unfortunately, Trudy Gorse, despite her height, never stood out in a crowd. The older woman rarely put herself forward, and when she did, her reserve made her difficult to get to know. Amber herself had only recently discovered Trudy's true caring nature, after she had offered to help *The Egg Ladies* move all those dozens and dozens of unsold eggs.

Feeling generous toward both Trudy and Ryan, and worshipping at the altar of love herself, Amber was eager to ensnare another pair of hearts, especially two hearts so obviously wanting to love and be loved as Ryan MacDonald and Trudy Gorse! "Well, I'm not sure you have met Trudy," she prevaricated. "But she's perfect for the museum board! You'll enjoy working with her, Ryan. She's the research librarian at the high school, and, and ... you know, she makes the butter we're selling, now," she added, as an afterthought.

Ryan's face brightened. "I had some of that butter! That was the best butter I've ever eaten!"

Encouraged, Amber continued. "You should see Trudy's farm, too. She's got the sweetest little cows!"

"Her father, Leland, used to grow beans and corn for the canning factory," Bruce added.

"She certainly sounds like a good fit for the board," the attorney agreed. "I'd like to meet her."

"Come over for dinner next Sunday, and we'll have Trudy, too! We'll make a party of it! Mom's been looking for an excuse to have a party for quite a while."

Ryan gratefully accepted the offer. "Count me in," he said.

"Am I invited?" Bruce said. "Hint, hint."

Amber put her hands on her hips and smiled at him. "Could I keep you away?"

"Not likely, Sweets!"

The tea kettle sucked in a deep breath, and wobbled a whistle. Three hearts felt their spirits rise at the cheerful sound. We never know when these moments of perfect contentment will occur in our lives. Fortunately, such ignorance only serves to heighten our bliss.

Chapter 15
. . . .
Chicken Coops and Churches

Despite his burning desire to clasp Amber to his breast, claiming his sweet reward, Bruce had departed the old Russell homestead that afternoon with only the briefest of embraces. His ardent longing had not cooled during the initial museum planning session. No, if anything, his hunger to hold her had only increased as he watched her slip around the table, serving the tea and cookies. She accidentally brushed against his shoulder and he groaned inwardly. It took heroic effort for him to restrain himself from grasping her by the slim hips and pulling her onto his lap.

He himself had been responsible for the lost opportunity, however. The tea had been drunk. The cookies devoured. The plan of attack had been scribbled down on the fresh legal pads, with each of them having their own list of action items. Ryan had risen to leave, generously offering to vacate the premises first so that Bruce and Amber could spend some time alone before Wendell and Rebecca returned from their Bangor excursion.

When the attorney had stood up to exit, Bruce rose as well. "I'd better run, too," he said. "I told Gray I'd help him with his homework. Like that's gonna do any good!"

"Don't go on my account, Gilpin," Ryan said, somewhat wistfully. "I'm sure you and Amber have a lot to … talk about."

But Bruce had correctly read the longing for love in the other man's breast. To stay with Amber now would be rubbing the attorney's face in his loneliness and defeat. Bruce was too soft-hearted to take advantage of his rival's discomfiture. "Nah, I gotta head out. I'll call you later," he said to Amber.

Both men retrieved their jackets, and Amber followed them into the shed. Ryan thanked his hostess for lunch, as well as for the tea and cookies. "No problem," she said, sincerely. "And I'll text you as soon as Mom gives me the go-ahead on the dinner."

"Great, thanks," Ryan replied, smiling. He stood on the top step, his handsome face catching the rose-colored rays of the late-afternoon sun. "I'm pretty much available these days. In the meantime …" he indicated the yellow legal pad under his arm, "… I'll get cracking."

When Ryan turned and advanced down the steps toward his car, Bruce seized his opportunity. He snaked his arm around Amber's waist and roughly pulled her to him. He rained a few kisses down upon her willing lips. "And I'm pretty much available, too, Sweets," he whispered, insinuatingly. He thrust her away. "I'll see you later," he added, mysteriously.

"Don't go!" she entreated, heart throbbing for more. She reached for his hand to hold him back, but he had already leaped down the wooden steps, taking them two at a time.

Ryan turned to wave. "Thanks again!" he called to her.

Amber tried not to look guilty as she lifted her hand in response. Ryan climbed into his black sedan and shut the door. She put her hand to her eyes to shield the setting sun, and her heart sank as she watched Bruce hop in his truck, and follow the attorney out the driveway. She wondered what he had meant when he had said, "I'll see you later." She thoughtfully closed the shed door and returned to the kitchen.

Since his return home to his parent's house, Bruce had been wishing for a place of his own. He was grateful to his parents for having provided a home for his son and a temporary home for himself whenever he was on leave from the Guard. Now, however, all that was changed. He'd completed his final term of service; there would be no more tours of duty for him in Iraq or Afghanistan (or wherever else the President decided to send American troops). Finally, it was time for him to get on with his life, and that meant that this soldier needed to find a home base.

When he had first thought about where he would live after his ETS (while still in Afghanistan), he had expected to stay with his folks for six months, perhaps longer. That was back when he was considering coming home and marrying Trudy Gorse. He'd realized then that it wouldn't make sense for him to buy a home of his own if he'd shortly be living with Trudy and Leland at Scotch Broom Acres on the Ridge Road. Now he knew that he was not going to marry Trudy. Instead, he was hoping to marry someone else, someone with eyes the color of late season asters. And for that ambition to be realized, he would need a private place in which he could actively woo his young sweetheart. He didn't expect she would fall into his arms immediately, but after today he was much more hopeful that his mission to secure Amber Johnson as a permanent help-mate would ultimately be successful.

While it might be perfectly acceptable for a teenage boy, like his son Gray, to operate a strategic romantic campaign from the home of his parents or grandparents (after all, such home was the boy's home, too), he didn't think it was either appropriate or satisfactory for a man of thirty-five to be found making out with a young woman on his mother's living room couch. And he wanted that home soon! Sneaking around finding opportunities to be alone with Amber was not Bruce's style. By his nature, he was direct, honest, above-board. He was beginning to feel desperate, and he didn't like the feeling.

Some of what Bruce was experiencing, Amber unconsciously felt herself. Over the summer, when her mother and Wendell were first married, she had moved out to Bud's place, a small rustic cabin, which had once housed Grammie Addie's hired hand. The cabin was situated in the woods about a hundred feet from the house, and her removal there had offered her parents some privacy during the early weeks of their married life. But Bud's place wasn't insulated, and when the cold weather arrived, Amber had moved back into her upstairs bedroom in the old Russell homestead. As she cleaned up the tea dishes following Bruce's departure, she wished she hadn't been so quick to abandon the three-room cabin. She fanaticized about his strong hands having their way with her on the small cot in Bud's place and smiled in secret delight. She had been saving herself for the man she loved, the man she planned to marry. And she couldn't wait to see him again!

The next day was Saturday. By the time Amber completed her chores and returned to the kitchen, she still hadn't heard from Bruce. She had been half-hoping, half-expecting that he'd magically appear in the hen pen in the early morning hours, much like he did on the morning of the church breakfast. So she'd kept an ear out for the sound of his truck. But the egg collecting, cleaning and other chores had been accomplished in solitude (if one can consider working among three hundred squawking chickens as solitude), without the excitement of any unexpected visitors.

"Any calls?" Amber asked her mother, upon returning to the kitchen. She helped herself to a cup of hot coffee, and awaited her answer. Given the eagerness of Bruce's parting embrace – and his last mysterious words

– she'd certainly expected to hear from him by now. But when she had checked her phone a few minutes earlier, there had been no messages.

Rebecca paused from kneading a loaf of whole wheat bread. She pushed back a stray strand of soft brown hair with the back of her hand. "Just Miss Hastings. She phoned to say she's coming to our dinner party!"

"Cool," Amber said, trying not to show her disappointment.

As Amber had expected, Rebecca had enthusiastically signed onto the Sunday dinner party. In addition to Miss Hastings, their confirmed guests now included Trudy and Leland Gorse, Bruce and Gray Gilpin, and Ryan MacDonald. Amber hadn't told her mother that match-making had spurred the idea for the dinner party, calculating that it was best for Trudy and Ryan if they were brought together before unsuspecting eyes. Amber herself would take the necessary steps to ensure that the couple was seated next to each other, and then she would leave the rest to fate, to fate, and to their individual longings to love and be loved.

"Expecting an egg call, dear?" Rebecca continued, as she shaped the bread into a comely loaf. The scent of fresh dough permeated the toasty kitchen.

"What? Oh, maybe. Did you reach Clyde Crosby?"

"Wendell's gone over to his house. Clyde has such trouble under-standing things over the phone, you know."

"Great," she replied, now only half listening.

There had been some prolonged discussion about who (and who not) to invite to the Sunday dinner. Rebecca had felt obligated to include Maude and Ralph Gilpin; however, Amber had strongly opposed that idea. She knew that Maude was angling after Trudy as a daughter-in-law, and thought that such open machinations by Bruce's mother would be off-putting to Ryan. Whether or not to include Leland had been another dicey issue. Soft-hearted Rebecca thought that the older man shouldn't be left alone while his daughter enjoyed a dinner out, but Amber had worried that the farmer's uncouth remarks might scare off the big city at-torney. Wendell had naturally wanted to invite his buddy, and so Leland's name was added to the list. Last to be considered for an invitation had been the very elderly Clyde Crosby.

Clyde's name had come up in reference to the museum project, and once again Rebecca's soft heart was moved to issue the lonely widower a dinner invitation. "It'll be perfect!" she had pronounced. "We'll have all of them together at the table – Miss Hastings, Leland and Clyde – and they'll tell us all sorts of wonderful stories about the old canning factory!"

Amber had almost regretted she hadn't revealed to her mother that next Sunday's dinner was meant to be a match-making opportunity for Ryan and Trudy, not a preliminary information gathering session for the museum project. But she held fast to her original intent to keep mum.

She took a hot bath, hoping to disperse her disappointment and a growing sense of malaise. Unfortunately, soaking in the old-fashioned clawfoot tub, in silken, rose-scented water, only afforded her the luxurious opportunity of daydreaming about Bruce. After drying and dressing, Amber realized she was just as dejected as before her bath.

It was almost 11 a.m. and she had yet to hear from him! Where was he?!

Amber was about to disappear upstairs to the comforts of her soft chair and study nook, when her mother stopped her. "Maggie called while you were in the tub," Rebecca said. "She'd like you to run two dozen eggs down to the church for her."

Ordinarily, Amber would have been thrilled with an egg sale, even one as modest as the minister's. At the moment, however, she just wanted to curl up in her comfy chair with her eReader and escape to the world of Emily Dickinson. "Now?" she asked, with some exasperation.

"She says she needs the eggs right away," Rebecca replied. Suddenly, a new thought occurred to her. "Do you think we should invite Maggie to our dinner party?"

Amber threw up her hands. "Why not?" She felt as though she was rapidly losing control of the party. "I'll invite her when I drop off the eggs."

The November morning was cool and raw, so preliminary to her drive to the church Amber donned an over-sized, hand-knitted sweater, scarf, and matching sky-blue hat rolled up at the bottom. She had picked out the outfit earlier that morning, knowing that the pretty colors highlighted her eyes. She'd naturally hoped that Bruce would enjoy the result of her efforts. Instead, she collected the two dozen eggs from the cold storage room in the hen pen, and headed down to the little white church preparing to share her youthful beauty with—me, a middle-aged, female minister.

The Sovereign Union Church, a traditional small New England church, is located on the Bangor Road, about fifty yards from the turn-off to the Russell Hill Road. The church has been non-denominational for the last thirty years, although the sanctuary has served Methodists, Universalists and Baptists over the course of its nearly two hundred year history. Currently, I serve as pastor, having been called fourteen years ago, partly because I was a Universalist-leaning Quaker and partly because I was, well, less expensive than most of my male counterparts.

Amber pulled into the parking lot at the little white church not twenty minutes after my phone call. She was somewhat disconcerted to see that the parking lot was empty.

She wondered if perhaps her mother had misunderstood me. Perhaps I'd wanted the eggs taken to my home on the Cross Road? Just to make sure, she parked the car, and pushed open the solid oak door to the church, egg boxes firmly in hand.

The interior of the Sovereign Union Church is much larger than it looks from the outside, since it encompasses mostly one large room with an expansive cathedral ceiling and elongated leaded windows that stretch nearly from ceiling to floor. No matter the weather outside, the effect inside is one of uplifting brightness, for the room is filled with light from windows on both the south and north sides, and the walls, ceiling and pews are all painted with that highly-polished white paint that seems to be traditional in such New England churches. Recently, we replaced the old floor covering with a plush burgundy carpet, which added an aesthetic richness to the simplicity of the interior.

The overhead lights were off, but a pillar candle burned brightly on the altar, its flickering flame repeating itself in reflections from a pair of brass candlesticks. An enormous bouquet of colorful fall leaves also decorated the linen-draped table and the scent of autumn woods diffused the room. Amber hesitated a moment, admiring the cheerful view in the church's nave.

"Anyone home?" she called out. "Maggie?"

Amber listened, but heard only the soughing of the wind in the towering pines outside the single-pane, leaded windows. She moved slowly toward the vestry, a tiny room cobbled together in the front south side of the church that I used as my office. She hesitated at the double-crossed wooden door, which was shut, wondering if she should knock. She rapped lightly.

A high-pitched woman's voice emanated from within. "Come in, dear!"

She turned the brass knob, and swung the heavy door open, revealing a book-lined study, and—Bruce Gilpin grinning at her from behind the minister's desk!

"Bruce!" she exclaimed, dumbfounded.

"Come in, dear!" he coyly repeated, affecting – not very convincingly – an older woman's voice.

She was so surprised to see him sitting in the gothic-looking chair that she nearly lost the eggs. With a strong thrust, Bruce leaped over the paper-strewn mahogany desk just in time to prevent the corrugated boxes from hitting the red carpet. "Surprised you, didn't I?"

Before Amber had time to process what was going on, he had set the eggs into a matching empty chair, and relieved her of her hat and scarf. He gathered her into his arms, and began covering her cheeks and lips with fervent kisses. Overcome with desire, she swooned against his muscular chest. "Don't stop!" she cried, weakly.

Bruce, who had no intention of stopping now that his prize was finally in his arms, continued his advance. He wheeled the two of them around, and pressed her eager form up against the solid mahogany desk. With a deliberate move, he popped open her plastic ponytail clip, releasing a bounty of dark, curling waves. "Ahh, I've been dreaming of this!" he declared victoriously. He wrapped her hair around his wrists. "You can't escape me, now!"

Amber nearly swooned, feeling their flesh meld together. Desire raged within her breast. She felt as though she couldn't get close enough to him, and she pushed back against his muscular hardness. In response, he lifted her easily up onto the desk, and, dropping his strong hands down to her hips, pushed her across the top. In the process, he accidentally sent a pile of papers flying to the floor. "Now I've done it," he said. He straightened himself up and ruefully regarded the mess, brown eyes laughing. "I hope that wasn't Maggie's sermon for tomorrow!"

At the mention of my name, Amber awoke to her senses. A strangled cry escaped her swollen lips. "Oh, my God! Maggie!" She sat up, and surveyed the tiny office, as though expecting me to pop up and reprimand the lovers at any moment.

"Relax! She's not here."

Dazed, Amber glanced first at the boxes of eggs resting in the padded gothic chair, and then back at Bruce. "What's going on? Where's Maggie?" she asked, suspiciously.

"Aw, Maggie was in on it the whole time," he admitted, with an impish grin. He ran his hand through his short hair. "I just wanted to get you to myself! I couldn't figure out any place to go, so … so Maggie suggested her office."

Amber was slightly shocked. "The minister suggested her office for … for a romantic rendezvous?!"

"She's not like a normal minister," he explained. "Well, at least I don't think she's like a normal minister. I actually don't know any other ministers! Ha, ha! Besides, I wasn't going to ravage you, Sweets! I just wanted to steal a few kisses."

Amber slipped off the desk. She resecured her hair, and knelt down to collect the loose white papers, taking the opportunity to regain her composure. She shook her head at him. "You never cease to amaze me, Bruce Gilpin!"

"That's my job, Sweets—to amaze and delight you, for the rest of your life!"

She paused, hands trembling. Her mind latched onto the last words of his statement. *To amaze and delight you – for the rest of your life!*

Her heart constricted with painful emotion. She so loved him! If only they could be together for the rest of their lives!

"I've got an appointment with a realtor on Monday," he continued, blissfully unaware of her thoughts. "We're gonna look at some houses for sale in the area. What do you think of that, Sweets? I'm gonna get my own digs!"

Amber sank back onto her trim haunches, and smiled up at him. "I think that's an awesome idea!"

He reached down and pulled her to her feet. He took the white sheets from her hands and clumsily restored the paper to the desk. "Come here," he said, tucking her back into his arms. "I can't keep chasing after you in chicken coops and churches forever, you know!"

He lowered his head to reclaim her lips. But his phone *jingled*, interrupting them. She giggled. "Are you sure Maggie's not watching, somewhere?" she said.

He relaxed his grip. "Sorry, I better get that. Asa's been having some problems with the town's plow truck." He released her, and retrieved his phone.

"Don't mind me," she said. She lifted the eggs from the seat of the gothic chair, and sank down into the soft plush seat. She watched lovingly as he talked with the Sovereign Road Commissioner. She could see that he enjoyed the idea of a mechanical challenge.

He paced the floor, his face lit up with eagerness and excitement. "Uh, huh. Hmm. Uh, huh. Yeah, right. OK, be right over." He ended the call and turned back to Amber. "Gotta go, Sweets! Asa can't get that old International started, and there might be some freezing rain tonight!"

Her heart overflowed with pride and love. "What about these?" she asked, archly, holding up the two gray boxes of eggs.

"Ha, ha! I'll drop 'em at Maggie's house on my way by."

Amber blanched slightly at the thought of seeing me again, knowing that I'd probably suspect what had occurred in her office. "I don't know if I'll be able to face Maggie again!"

"Don't worry, Maggie was young once – I think she'll understand."

So true! I was young once – I completely understand. And so would they both, when they reached my age (and certainly older). Ah, how little do any of us know when we're young, how much we'll be grateful for the flirtations and dalliances of our youth – our youth, so soon departed!

Chapter 16
. . . .
Evelyn's Fishing Hole

$\mathscr{A}$As anyone who has hosted a dinner party knows, a hundred seemingly insignificant details must be encountered and dispatched. The menu must be selected, of course, and the viands and victuals procured, but that's just the beginning. Therefore, after chores on Monday morning, Amber and her mother sat down together to create the menu, and to delegate the responsibilities for Sunday's dinner party.

"We should serve only local food," began Amber, who, in addition to being an organic farmer herself, had also been a long-time proponent of the Buy Local and Slow Food/Slow Money movements. "I can get a pork roast from the Sewalls, or a leg of lamb, if you'd prefer." The Sewalls were farmers in Thorndike who carried on a small animal meat operation. Amber frequently traded eggs with them for cuts of meat.

"A roast leg of lamb would be wonderful!" Rebecca said, savoring in her mind the delights of trussing up a leg of lamb for cooking. "I could use my own rosemary, and we could serve the roast with the rhubarb sauce I put up in the spring."

"OK, I'll get the lamb."

"But then, a little roast pork, you know, would be so lovely! We haven't had pork in ages – Wendell loves pork – and I could make fresh applesauce!"

"OK, I'll trade for some pork, then."

Rebecca sighed, regretting that they couldn't afford to serve both pork and lamb to their Sunday dinner guests.

"Mom, there will be other meals," Amber pointed out. "Pork or lamb? Or should I see what the Sewalls suggest?"

Rebecca's face brightened. "Do that, dear!"

Other preparations for their dinner party also included counting and polishing the silverware, selecting the china, ironing the large linen table cloth, and organizing serving dishes. The extra leaves to the antique oak dining room table needed to be rescued from the attic and cleaned, and two straight-back chairs must be rustled up from somewhere. Ten diners would be sitting down for Sunday dinner, and Rebecca wanted to ensure that each guest would feel comfortable enough to settle in for a delightful afternoon of dining and visiting.

In half an hour, Amber and Rebecca each had a long list of duties to accomplish before Sunday. In addition, Rebecca had a short list for Wendell. After her mother had hurried off about her chores, Amber scratched an addition to the bottom of her own list. *See Trudy.*

Thanks to her recent intimacy with Trudy Gorse, Amber knew the other woman's part-time work schedule at the high school. On Thursday afternoon, she pulled off the Ridge Road into the U-shaped dirt drive-way at Scotch Broom Acres, not long after Trudy had changed out of her professional work clothes and headed out to the barn for the afternoon milking.

As New England farms go, the old Gorse homestead, Scotch Broom Acres, was modest. An unpretentious white Cape-style house with red trim and a matching red tin roof was connected to a two-story barn by a short ell. The banked red barn, built for small-scale nineteenth century farming, boasted a sliding double door on the gable end, with a wide transom window overhead to capture every last ray of the winter sunlight. Inside, a ten-by-twelve horse stall to the left of the main area now served as a tack room hosting pitchforks, shovels, boots, medical supplies, buckets and other farming implements. To the right, the twelve cow tie-up held Trudy's four prize Jersey cows. Although modest, everything about the farmstead was neat and tidy, reflecting Trudy's personality probably more so than Leland's.

The double doors were open just wide enough to allow for a visitor, and Amber slipped inside. The barn smelled of sweet hay, and thanks to a ray of light from the transom window she noted that one of the upper lofts was chock 'o block full with new square bales. She peered around the corner into the tie-up and spied Trudy sitting on a three-legged iron stool, her cheek resting against the fawn-colored midribs of one of her pretty Jersey cows. The other three cows were patiently awaiting their turns to be milked, munching on the feed in their manger. Trudy was singing quietly, her back to Amber, as she expertly squirted milk into the stainless steel pail positioned beneath the cow's udder. She sang in a sweet alto voice:

The fox went out on a chilly night,
prayed to the Moon to give him light,
for he had many a mile to go that night
before he reached the town-o, town-o, town-o.
He had many a mile to go that night
before he reached the town-o.

Amber listened to the first verse, and then entered the tie-up, making some little noise on the battle-scarred wood floor to indicate her presence so that she wouldn't startle the older woman. "Hi Trudy," she said.

Trudy stopped singing. She craned her neck slightly to view her visitor, but her large capable hands continued their business, and the *squirts* against the side of the metal pail never missed a beat. She smiled at Amber. "Caught me singing in the shower," she said.

"You've got a beautiful voice! You ought to sing more often."

"Thanks. Miss Hastings gave me voice lessons when I was young. She was some kind of child prodigy herself. They used to call her *The Songbird of Sovereign*, you know."

"I didn't know. Sounds fascinating!"

"She had quite a career for a while. But I guess it wasn't what she wanted to do with her life, because she came back to Sovereign and taught music to all of us kids."

"She was probably homesick for Sovereign – I know I would be!"

"I used to sing in the church choir, too," Trudy mused. "Back when there were enough of us to have a choir, that is. I do miss it." Her hazel eyes glistered. "Eva Crosby used to accompany us on the piano. She passed away about ten years ago, now."

"Poor Clyde! I'm glad Mom thought to invite him to our dinner party."

"Me too. That was kind of her. Clyde's been alone for a long time." Trudy bobbed her head at a nearby hay bale. "Pull up a chair, and tell me about this interesting museum project I've been hearing about."

Amber perched comfortably on the square bale, and crossed her ankles. She wasn't surprised that news of the museum project had spread to the Gorse farmstead already. "The little birds have been busy already, I see," she joked.

"Father told me last night. Apparently, it's all the old men are talking about down to the store." The cow Trudy was milking exhaled a long, moist sigh. She patted the bovine's belly affectionately. "Almost done, Doris."

"I bet he didn't tell you that we want you to be on our board of directors!"

"No he didn't. We who?" Trudy asked, politely.

"Me, Bruce and Ryan MacDonald. We need five members for our 501(c)3, and we thought you'd be a great addition. We're going to ask Miss Hastings to be the fifth."

"Ryan MacDonald! On the museum board of directors? Now that surprises me."

"It was Bruce's idea; it just sort of happened." And Amber explained how the Boston attorney had performed the title search on the old canning factory, and how he had accompanied Bruce and the others on the maiden tour of the property. She outlined Ryan's important role in completing the legal paperwork for the museum project. "I don't see how we could make this thing work without him," she concluded.

"That's quite a commitment Ryan's making, for someone from Away."

Amber's heart sank at the faintly disparaging tone of the other woman's voice. "Doesn't sound like you have a very high opinion of him?"

"I don't really know him. But my impression of Ryan to date is that he's a bit of a social butterfly."

Amber paused, reflecting on Trudy's words. "He might appear flighty at first glance," she said carefully, "but I think Ryan's a lot deeper than he looks. It's taken me quite a while to get to know him, and I've known him a couple of years, now. He used to work with Mom and Lila in Boston, you know. He's an only child – that might explain a lot," she added, as an afterthought.

A solitary offspring herself, Trudy tipped her head in agreement. "It might," she allowed.

Amber recognized that her attempt to increase Ryan's appeal was barely working. She decided to pull out her big guns. "His mother died when he was a teenager, and his Dad passed away last year," she confided. "Poor Ryan's all alone in the world now!"

Trudy continued stripping Doris' rear teats. "I didn't know that," she said. "Well, I am sorry for him, then." She rose, pulling her iron stool up in one hand and the stainless steel pail, half-full of thick, creamy milk in the other.

Amber shifted her legs so the other woman could walk by her to the next cow. The sight of the rich, frothy milk in the pail reminded her of Ryan's remarks about Trudy's product. "By the way, he loves your butter!"

"Does he? Great! Another satisfied customer."

Amber sighed. This match-making business was problematic! Much more difficult than she'd expected! While she seemed to have made some progress in improving Trudy's opinion of Ryan, for any sparks to be kindled between Ryan and Trudy the other woman would need to be much more susceptible to potential romantic advances from the lawyer. Amber remembered that Trudy was once supposed to have been in love with Bruce, and she tried mentally not to compare the two men. She knew which one she preferred!

Despite the lack of encouragement, Amber determined to persevere. "I think Ryan's looking for a someplace to land permanently," she blurted out.

Trudy set the pail down with a *plunk*. She pushed her ash-brown bangs away from her eyes, a scornful expression on her face. Her soft mop of hair accentuated her high cheek bones, and Amber was reminded again how attractive Trudy was when she was animated. "And you think – what?" Trudy exclaimed. "That Scotch Broom Acres might be a good place for Ryan MacDonald to put down roots?!"

"Well, maybe I did," Amber admitted. "He's very nice!"

Trudy's gray eyes flashed. "Please, Amber! Take a look at Ryan MacDonald, and then look at me." She drew herself up to her full five-feet, nine-inches, and indicated her boyish-looking frame, oversized sweatshirt, worn jeans and rubber barn boots. "Can you see us together?"

"As a matter of fact, I can! I think you'd make an awesome couple. It isn't all about looks, you know. Don't write him off!"

"Can you picture Ryan MacDonald sitting down for supper every night with Father?!"

Amber's heart quailed. She herself had had some doubts about the big city attorney's acceptance of the uncultured but completely lovable Leland. "You're not ashamed of your father?" she retorted, bravely.

"Of course not! I'm just pointing out that Ryan MacDonald and I come from two different worlds. You can put me down for your board of directors, Amber. But don't put me down for Ryan MacDonald. You'll never see an 'old MacDonald' on this farm."

Even after that proud declaration from her friend, Amber still decided to place Trudy and Ryan side by side at the Sunday dinner table. She calculated that Trudy would be too much of a lady to make a fuss over the seating arrangement, and that Ryan would be gentleman enough to ensure his seatmate's comfort. She wasn't so sure it had been a good idea to give Trudy a heads up, in fact, she thought now it had probably been a mistake to suggest the possibility of a romantic relationship with Ryan MacDonald. She had obviously wounded her friend's pride, and had probably done more harm than good.

Rebecca had allowed Amber to make the seating assignments, though, and after much consideration, Amber had placed Leland at Trudy's left, around the corner from Bruce, who would sit at the bottom of the table. She thought this would be the safest place for Trudy's loquacious father. Wendell would appropriate his traditional chair at the head of the table, with her mother around the corner to his left, allowing her easy access to the kitchen. Maggie would face Rebecca across the table, with Miss Hastings opposite Ryan and Clyde across from Trudy. Amber had naturally settled herself at Bruce's left, next to Clyde and across from Leland. She prayed silently that Leland would say nothing during the dinner to embarrass his daughter.

Altogether, the first half-hour of the dinner proceeded remarkably well. Both a pork roast and a leg of lamb had been procured and passed around (Amber having been successful in trading eggs and butter for both selections). The meat was followed by a bevy of dishes, including sweet butternut squash, mashed potatoes and gravy, applesauce and rhubarb sauce, boiled onions swimming in creamy Jersey butter, and a selection of yeast rolls and breads. Conversation waned as the food made its rounds, and the guests eagerly partook of the sumptuous feast.

Clyde piled his plate high and eyed the food appreciatively. He slathered warm butter onto a honey yeast roll and popped half of it in his mouth. He gobbled the roll down, and smacked his lips. "Ain't thet awful good!" Since Clyde's wife died, he had received most of his food from Meals On Wheels, except when his friends invited him over to their homes to dine. He was a regular guest at Maude and Ralph's, as well as at Asa and Shirley Palmer's house.

"Plenty more where thet come from, Clyde," Wendell encouraged the older man. He proudly turned to his pretty young wife. "Ain't thet right, Mrs. Russell?"

She smiled, pleased with both the compliment and the rarely-used appellation from her husband. "There's a lot more in the kitchen! In fact, unless everyone helps themselves to seconds, dear, you'll be eating leftovers all next week!"

Leland shoveled a forkful of food into his mouth. "Where's your boy?" he asked Bruce, masticating conspicuously.

Amber glanced anxiously at Trudy, but her friend's face remained impassive.

"Down to the store," Bruce replied, liberally splashing hot brown gravy over his mashed potatoes. "Gray offered to work so my folks could have Sunday dinner with Peter."

"He's a shaap kid! A chip off the ole block!"

"My Dad's block, you mean," Bruce said, chuckling.

"Ayuh! He's jest like ole Ralph, ain't he?"

"Yeah, he's a lot more like his grandfather than me!"

"More pork, anyone?" Rebecca inquired. She lifted up the meat platter temptingly. "Maggie?"

I considered the opportunity, but finally waved her away. "No thanks. I'm saving myself for those cranberry-apple pies. I heard tell how good they are."

"Not too sweet and not too tart – jest the way I like 'em!" Wendell enthused. He had been methodically working through a mountain of food, but he slowed his pace, recollecting the pie and ice cream for dessert.

"You git them cranberries from thet fella down to Troy?" Leland interjected loudly. He leaned forward so that he could address Wendell down at the head of the table.

"Ayuh. Said he had a few berries this year thet the bugs didn't git."

"Thet's ole Phil Fernald's boy, you know," the farmer continued, more to the table at large than to Wendell. "Ole Phil used to go fishin' with us ovah to Evelyn's fishin' hole. 'Member thet, Clyde?" he added, raising his voice a decibel so that his hearing-impaired friend could catch his words.

"Guess probbly I do!"

Leland chuckled. "*Didn't* he have a hankering for dynamite! Phil 'most done us in one time down there, ain't thet right, Clyde?"

Clyde nodded. "Damn near kilt us!"

"Fishing with dynamite?!" Rebecca exclaimed. She dropped her fork, and the implement made a distinctive *clink* on the china plate.

"Ayuh. He was a hell of a fellow, thet Phil!"

"They're not interested in hearing about Phil, Father," Trudy said. Her tone was gentle, but deliberately discouraging.

Chastised, Leland glanced contritely at his daughter. He faltered. "Mebe not," he admitted. He pulled back a little and toyed with the remnant of a silver onion skin on his dinner plate.

"I'd like to hear the story," Ryan said, reassuringly. "I'm a fly fisherman myself, so I appreciate a good fish tale."

"Me too," I said, spooning some fragrant warm applesauce onto my plate next to a slab of roasted pork.

"OOoo, dahrrrling, do tell us the story!" Miss Hastings cried.

Leland needed no further encouragement. He pushed his plate aside and thumped his elbows on the table so he could lean forward and address the little group. He took a moment to wind himself up, satisfying himself in the process that he'd captured everyone's attention. He was a Maine storyteller of the old school, and knew perfectly well how to work a crowd.

Amber stole another glance at Trudy, but the other woman continued to eat, as though nothing of note was occurring. Amber looked next at Ryan. The attorney was peering over Trudy's bent head, regarding Leland with an interested, good-natured expression on his handsome face. "Well, let's hear it, Leland," he urged. "Don't keep us in suspense!"

Intent on her matchmaking scheme, Amber was startled when a strong hand caressed her thigh. She pivoted to face Bruce. He winked, his brown eyes twinkling with good-humor and love. She smiled at him, returning his affection joyfully. *Oh, if only this moment could last forever!*

"Wal, 'twas a hot summer day 'bout ten years ago," Leland began. "The hay was all in and there warn't much else to do, you know, 'cept go fishin'. A bunch of us fellas agreed to meet down to Evelyn's fishin' hole – thet's down in back of the ole corn shop," he added, for the edification of the newcomers. "We was there 'bout five hours without one goddammed bite. 'I know they're in there,' said Phil. 'I kin smell 'em.'

He was a determined kind of a fellow, always done what he said he was agoin' to do. And if Phil Fernald said he was agoin' to go fishin' he was agoin' to bring home fish."

Leland paused, partly to take a sip of water but mostly for dramatic effect. He plunked his glass down, and continued. "Wal, ole Phil went to the back of his pickup 'n pulled out a stick 'o dynamite. He was workin' on the roads back then 'n all them road workers carried dynamite in those days. He put a cap on it, scrounged 'round 'til he found a roll of Romex – house wire, you know – and he threaded 'bout thirty feet of Romex through a two-inch metal pipe. Phil stuck thet dynamite in thet pipe, 'n tossed the whole she-bang out into the middle of Evelyn's fishin' hole. When we was all reddy, he stahted up his truck and touched t'other end of the wire to his truck battery. Wal, we all waited but we didn't see nuthin' at furst. We heared a queer sound, though, and all of a sudden we seen there warn't a scrid o' water in thet brook! Not a scrid! We looked up in the sky, and Ho-ly Jesus!" Leland thumped on the table for effect. "Down it come! Water, fish, sticks, stones, mud turtles 'n everything! Ha, ha, ha!"

"Guess probbly we got a few fish thet day!" Clyde crowed.

The whole table burst out laughing.

"Jesus!" exclaimed Bruce. "I thought I lived on the edge in Iraq and Afghanistan, but that's nothing compared to the dangers you guys take around here!"

Leland shook his head. "Not no more," the farmer allowed, wiping away a few tears of laughter. "Times ain't nuthin' like they used to be! Not since ole Phil died, anyway. 'Tain't nobody else brave enough to set dynamite."

"Or foolish enough," Trudy said. "I think that's enough, Father," she added, quickly, as she spied certain signs that suggested Leland was winding himself up for another tale. "Let someone else talk."

Chastened again, Leland fell silent, toying with his dessert fork.

"Hey, don't stop!" Ryan urged. "Tell us another one." He flashed a charming smile at his female seatmate, but Trudy kept her eyes fixed determinedly upon her dinner plate. Failing to arouse her consent, Ryan leaned back in his chair, reached around her and clapped Leland affectionately on the shoulder. "I could listen to your yarns all day! Got another?"

"Who says they is yarns?!" Leland asked, innocently.

Ryan laughed. "Fish tales, then!"

"C'mon, Leland, give us another," Bruce prodded. "We all know you got plenty more."

Shored up again, Leland commenced to deliver one hilarious story after another with the perfect pitch of a Maine humorist. The pie and beverages were passed around without the old farmer missing a beat. The little party broke up three hours later, having been regaled with Leland's tales of cow tipping, bee lining and chicken hypnotizing.

"My goodness! I never knew Leland was so funny!" Rebecca exclaimed afterward. "I'll have to be sure to invite him to all my parties."

"Wal, you know, thet might not be a bad idea," agreed Wendell.

Amber wasn't so sure. She had kept a close eye on Trudy throughout the whole meal, during which time the other woman had remained cruelly impassive. Even after Ryan's obvious enjoyment of her father, the lawyer had netted only a few monosyllabic words from his seatmate, and the barest trace of a smile. Altogether, Amber rated her first matchmaking experience a complete failure.

Chapter 17
· · · · · · ·
Death of a Legend

The next few weeks passed quickly and quietly, with no major events occurring to interrupt the smooth flow of country life, not even a dinner party. Amber buckled down to her schoolwork and her organic egg sales, while Bruce fixed broken-down vehicles and sought a new home for himself and his mechanics garage. Ryan researched the 501(c)3 and Trudy continued her part-time work and butter making. The first two museum project meetings had been held at Miss Hastings' house, during which the nature and the scope of the project was outlined and the initial duties delegated. The next meeting was scheduled for the second week of December.

Just after Thanksgiving, however, the little world of Sovereign, Maine was upended by the death of a legend. Eighty-two-year-old Mabel Jean Brown (nee Edwards), better known as "Ma Jean," long-time proprietor of Ma Jean's Restaurant, passed away unexpectedly at her home on the Bangor Road. She died in her sleep, a gift for which many of us pray, especially the further we tread down the road, closer to our great reward.

I was called to Ma Jean's home that morning by Shirley Palmer, who discovered the peaceful corpse, still tucked away in her bed. When the restaurant had failed to open at 5:30 a.m. per usual, Asa had gone home to awaken his wife. Together they returned to Ma Jean's Federal-style brick home, situated about a quarter of a mile from the restaurant. Once Shirley recovered from the initial shock of losing her dear friend, she telephoned me. I arrived not long after Maude and Ralph Gilpin got there. Death generally draws a crowd.

"You're sure?" I asked, although the long faces of the little group cluttering up Ma Jean's neat kitchen assured me that death was present. In an attempt to overcome the pall, someone had started a fire in the Atlantic end heater and the smell of sulfur still lingered. I hoped that the odor was the remnant of a sulfur-tipped match and not Old Scratch.

"Deader 'n a doornail!" pronounced Ralph.

Maude began to weep. Ralph tossed an arm around his wife's fat shoulder, and gave her a reassuring squeeze. "Now, now, Maude! Ma Jean's had a good life!"

"It wasn't her time to go!" Maude wailed.

"I guess 'twas," he corrected her.

Shirley led me in to see the body, and the other three instinctively followed into the light-filled first floor bedroom. Ma Jean's lovely boudoir was decorated in vintage gold-striped wallpaper, an oriental rug, and striped drapes that were tied back to admit the early morning sun. A brass mantle clock ticked loudly over the white-painted fireplace, above which several old Edwards' family photos hung in oval wooden frames. Ma Jean lay stiffly on her back in the antique Jenny Lind bed, hands folded across her breast on a white Bates Mills bedspread. She had a satisfied expression on her face, as though she'd finished everything that she'd come to earth to accomplish. I was pretty sure after seeing Ma Jean's smile that if Old Scratch had been present, he'd gone away empty-handed.

Sometimes there is a sense of seraphic brightness like spiritual dust motes in a room when someone dies. Many times during my years in the ministry I've felt and sensed a soul vacate a body, seen them slip the corporeal bonds and escape with the last exhale. I've felt hallowed hands on my head as these astral beings make their way to a better world. This morning, however, it was obvious that Ma Jean had been dead for some time, and her spirit hadn't lingered.

We grouped around the bedside, and I offered a brief prayer. Then I began to recite the Twenty-third Psalm, which always seems to take the sting out of death, like the removal of a deep splinter. The others joined in with me, their voices tentative at first but gathering assuredness as we reached the last verse: *Surely goodness and mercy shall follow me all the days of my life, and I shall dwell in the house of the Lord forever.*

She was buried in the Russell Cemetery on top of Russell Hill, where so many Sovereign citizens have been laid to rest over the past one hundred and eighty-five years. The peaceful, sprawling cemetery offers one of the best views in town of the western mountains, a vista for which folks from the city pay hundreds of thousands of dollars. Perhaps this suggests that the old timers who first laid their loved ones to rest gave more consideration to their ancestors than they did to the Almighty Dollar. Or perhaps it suggests that nobody wanted to build their houses on a wind-swept hill in the old days. Nowadays visitors to the graves of their loved ones often sit and contemplate the view, taking the opportunity offered to ponder the great questions of life and death. In truth, the cemetery's serene setting is priceless.

Ma Jean left no family, but most of the town turned out to say their final "goodbyes" to the matron who had risen before daybreak for fifty years to feed them, their children and their grandchildren. The Ladies Auxiliary offered refreshments at the church annex after the service at the cemetery, but the mood there was glum and the guests departed before much of the cookies and cakes were eaten, the food perhaps a sad reminder that – without knowing it – they had all eaten their last pastry prepared for them by Ma Jean.

"I can't believe she's gone," Rebecca said, shaking her head. She and Amber had returned home after having cleaned up the annex. They were sitting at the kitchen table in the old Russell homestead, reviewing the day's events. The men had remained at the cemetery with the town's sexton, closing up the grave and replacing the neatly-cut sod. "I saw her Tuesday, and she seemed as strong as a horse!"

"Ma Jean always seemed so invincible to me. I was a bit afraid of her," Amber admitted. She lifted the hot lid of the teapot and peered inside. "I think the tea is ready – want me to pour?"

"Mmm, yes, thanks, dear," her mother replied, lost in thought. "I wonder what's going to happen to the restaurant?"

Amber poured the steaming tea into their matching floral teacups. The scent of the herbal tea suffused the warm kitchen. "I hope someone else takes it over and runs it! It'd be such a loss for the town if the restaurant was closed for good." Amber helped herself to some of Wendell's golden honey from a jar in the center of the table, and held the jar out to her mother. "Honey, Mom?"

Rebecca nodded, and took the glass jar from her daughter's hand. "And what about that beautiful brick house?!" she added, continuing the train of thought. "It's one of the oldest in town! She came from a very old Maine family. That was her family's homestead she and her husband lived in, you know. I remember the first time I ever went to Ma Jean's house, how proud she was to show me around! She knew the history of every piece of furniture in that place, every painting, every dish. Every stitch of linen, too! She had a lovely antique dresser under the hall stairway she kept her linens in, and she pulled open the drawers, took them out and showed them to me one at a time. Some of the hand-stitched linens were almost two-hundred years old!"

"How sad she had no family! I wonder what's going to happen to all those beautiful old linens, now?"

Rebecca helped herself to a sip of tea. She returned the delicate china cup to its matching floral-decorated saucer with a pleasing *clink*. "Shirley Palmer said she left everything to the Ladies Auxiliary. Some of the things will go to the Burnham auction, probably. I'm not sure what'll happen to the rest." The Burnham auction was local short-speak for the antiques auction held every Sunday at Houston-Brooks Auctioneers on the Horseback Road in Burnham. Well-attended by antiques dealers from around the state and even from other points in New England, the Burnham auction was the quickest place to liquidate an old homestead.

"That's good for the Auxiliary. But still sad."

Tears filled Rebecca's eyes. "It's probably sacrilegious to feel happy today, but I do feel happy! I'm so grateful for everything we have! Who would have thought a year ago that I'd be married to a wonderful man and living in Sovereign, Maine! I'm so lucky!"

Amber leaped up, and hugged her mother affectionately. "Oh, Mom! You *so* deserve to be happy!"

Rebecca lovingly smoothed back her daughter's dark hair. "I still can't help thinking about those linens, though," she admitted.

They both laughed.

Rebecca and Amber weren't the only ones considering the disposition of Ma Jean's worldly goods. Maude Gilpin, who knew almost to a word the contents of Ma Jean's will, had given the matter serious consideration, as well.

"I'm running down to the restaurant to check on things," she informed Ralph, when the couple had returned home from the funeral. Her scraggy husband was shrugging out of his rarely-used black suit. The funeral had made him consider his own short time on earth, and he was anxious to return to his daily routine, perhaps hoping by such speed to outrun the grim reaper. "After I change out of my dress, of course," Maude added.

"Whatcha hurry, Maude? We jest got Ma Jean in the ground!"

"Ma Jean wouldn't want all that food to spoil!"

He jerked off his tie. "Who died and left you in charge?" he asked, somewhat unkindly.

Maude sniffed. "If you must know, Ma Jean did!" she pronounced. "As the former Vice President of the Ladies Auxiliary, I'm now the President. Since Ma Jean left everything to the Auxiliary, I'm only protecting our assets. I'm giving Rebecca a call and asking her to come down and help me go through the freezers."

This announcement surprised her husband. Over the past few months it had seemed to him as though Maude and Rebecca had carried on an undeclared cookery competition, with one lady attempting to outdo the other in the kitchen. In addition, both women had made it patently clear that they were angling for alternative partners for their children. Maude was unhappy that Bruce continued to see Amber, and Rebecca's endeavors to tempt Ryan with her daughter hadn't gone entirely unnoted by the shrewd shopkeeper. Yet suddenly, Rebecca was the first person Maude was turning to for help? Ralph was pretty good at adding two and two, and today it was adding up to five.

Ralph eyed his wife suspiciously. "Ya ain't fixin' to git in there and start cookin', are ya?"

She put her hands on her ample hips. "Of course not! Well, at least, not right away. We don't have the proper licenses and certificates. But I think Ma Jean would want us to do something with the place!"

"You gals git thet restaurant goin' agin and I might never see ya!" he declared, beginning to get worried for his own personal comfort.

"Oh, go along with you now," she admonished, shooing him out of the bedroom. "Don't you fret, Ralph Gilpin – no matter what happens to Ma Jean's Restaurant, you'll still get your supper on time!"

He exited. "Five o'clock. Shaap!" he added from the hall, quite unnecessarily.

Maude wasn't the only Gilpin considering Ma Jean's assets. Bruce and the realtor had driven every mile of road in the town of Sovereign searching for a place for him to live and to set up a small mechanics garage. But to date their search had proved fruitless. Several suitable homes were for sale, but none of them offered the necessary outbuilding large enough to convert to a two-bay garage.

Ma Jean's home property on the Bangor Road included a grandiose, two-door, two-story carriage shed, where, before the advent of the automobile, the family's carriages, sleighs and sleds were stored when not in seasonal use. The doors were pretentiously tall, even for the time, and the first floor ceiling, to which the unused carriages had been hoisted up and hung from the rafters, was sixteen-feet high. Every time Bruce and the realtor had driven by Ma Jean's home he had pointed out to her that he was looking for a place exactly like Ma Jean's carriage shed.

After Ma Jean's unexpected death, Bruce began to think that there was no better place in Sovereign for him to set up shop than—her carriage shed, *if* he could get a lease for the building from the Ladies Auxiliary. The doors were tall enough to admit heavy equipment, even Asa's grader, and the high ceiling allowed for the installation of the two twelve-foot hydraulic lifts. The carriage shed was centrally located on the main highway, Route 9/202, and the circular drive offered easy access and plenty of off-road parking. Best of all, Ma Jean's husband, Harold, had installed electricity and plumbing in the building, having set up a small woodworking shop before he died in 1999. Bruce calculated he could use Harold's small shop as an office and renovate the second floor loft into a small apartment, where he could store his footlocker until he could convince Amber Johnson to marry him. After that, he and his footlocker would be at her disposal.

Although Bruce knew that the Ladies Auxiliary was Ma Jean's heir and that his mother was now the President of the organization, he elected to say nothing to his mother until he had spoken to Amber first. She was necessarily the first woman in his life.

He outlined his plan to Amber the evening following Ma Jean's funeral. "Whatcha think?" he asked eagerly, taking her by the hand. The couple was sitting side by side at the kitchen table in the old Russell homestead, which evening ritual had been established over the past few weeks. While Rebecca had yet to verbally give her blessing to the relationship between Amber and Bruce, she had given her tacit approval by abdicating her kitchen after supper so that they could have some privacy. Tonight, she had removed to the living room section of the great room, where Wendell was watching a loud, ubiquitous TV program.

"It's pretty quick to dispose of Ma Jean's assets, isn't it?" Amber worried.

"We're not disposing of anything, Sweets; we're putting the carriage shed back into use. If Ma Jean had lived, I would have asked her for a lease. The only difference now is that I'm getting the lease from the Ladies."

"Well, I have to admit, I've often wondered what's inside that place. It's a lovely building!"

"There's not much inside, now, probably. Harold cleaned the place out when he set up shop, and then Ma Jean sold off all his wood-working tools when he died a couple years later. When I was a little kid there used to be all sorts of carriages and sleighs in there, hanging from the rafters by old hemp ropes. I hated walking under 'em 'cause I was always afraid the ropes would break and the carriages would fall on my head. One day, when I was about eight, I dared myself to do it. I raced back and forth across the floor – twice! Pretty brave, huh? Nothing fell, obviously."

"Obviously! Oh, I wish I could have seen all those old carriages and sleighs," she added, wistfully. "I've always wanted to go for a sleigh ride. It's on my Bucket List."

"Yeah?" Bruce said, perking up. "I think I can help you cross that one off. The town holds a sleighing rally in January every year, and a couple of dozen teams show up from all over Maine. Leland even takes Cain and Abel, with Henry's old Portland cutter."

"Sounds wonderful!"

"There's a big bonfire, and lots of donuts and coffee. There'll be plenty of opportunities for sleigh rides at the rally, I promise. It'll be colder than you expect, though," he continued. "Maybe you won't like it?" He glanced over his shoulder into the great room, and, seeing Wendell and Rebecca occupied by the TV, slid her chair across the floor six inches closer to him.

"I'm not afraid of the cold – it'll give us an excuse to snuggle!"

He nuzzled her ear. "You think we need an excuse, Sweets?"

In response, she twined her arms around his bare neck, and pulled his head down. His eager lips claimed hers, and she blissfully gave herself up to his demands.

Chapter 18
· · · · · · ·
The Letter

The informal food feud between Maude and Rebecca ended almost the moment Rebecca entered Ma Jean's Restaurant the afternoon of the matron's funeral. Rebecca had received an enigmatic phone call from Maude while huddled over the teapot with Amber. The older woman had asked the younger to come down to the quaint restaurant, and bring a pair of thick gloves. Intrigued, Rebecca immediately drove down to Ma Jean's.

Maude met her at the door, and ushered her inside. "The pie's the limit," she said mysteriously, to her one-time culinary rival. She gestured expansively around the seating area of the small diner. "I want to keep the restaurant open, and I need your help! What do you think? Can we do it?!"

Rebecca's blue eyes lit up. "You had me at pie!"

The two women spent the rest of the afternoon happily inventorying the food items in the restaurant, in the pantry, refrigerators and ice-cold freezers. They took copious notes on Ma Jean's neat scratch paper, and then settled into one of the comfy red-cushioned booths to discuss everything. Over a cup of freshly-brewed coffee, they began to chart their course.

"I'll talk to Shirley about what we need to do legally," Maude said. "She's the administrator of Ma Jean's estate, you know."

Rebecca hadn't known. "Maybe Ryan can help with the legalities, too," she suggested. "He's been such a big help with the museum project. Should I ask him?"

"Please do. One of us also should contact the state and find out what we need to do to keep the doors open. Would you like to do that?"

Rebecca nodded, and added that detail to her list.

"I'll call the vendors and let them know what's going on."

"Speaking of which," Rebecca said, "should I call the phone and light companies?"

"Do, dear." Maude put down her pencil. "Same time tomorrow?" she inquired.

Rebecca's eager eyes telegraphed her agreement. "I can't wait for our first customer!"

The next day Bruce spotted their two cars at the restaurant, and pulled into the parking lot. "What's going on?" he asked, pushing through the front door.

The two ladies looked up guiltily from their corner booth, where they had been sharing the results of their assignments. "Bruce! You startled us!" his mother exclaimed.

"The door was open," he pointed out. "Anyone could have walked in – it just happened to be me." He strode over to the table. He was dressed in jeans, work boots and his gray Maine Army Guard sweatshirt. He looked handsome and happy.

Maude puffed up with motherly pride. "Coffee, Sweetie?" she offered, rising up eagerly.

"What! No pie?! No, no—I'm kidding! Sit down. I don't want anything, except permission to go into Ma Jean's carriage shed."

"Ma Jean's carriage shed?! Whatever for?"

He offered up that winsome Hodges' smile. "You have your secrets, ladies, and I've got mine! You'll just have to trust me, Mom."

Within an hour, Bruce was letting himself and Amber into the unlocked side door of the nearby carriage shed. The two-story, clapboarded building was positioned about fifty feet to the north of Ma Jean's Federal-style brick house, and about a quarter of a mile to the south of the restaurant. The outbuilding was white with black trim, which matched the black shutters and white trim of the brick house. The carriage shed sported a pretty slatted cupola atop its peaked roof, with an antique iron weathervane in the form of a running horse on top.

The side door led into the small woodshop that Harold Brown had built for himself, containing a carpenter's workbench, multiple wooden shelves, and a peg board for hanging hand tools. Two small windows admitted light into the shop, and Amber could see the tiny attached bathroom that contained a sink and toilet.

Bruce passed quickly across the wooden floor to the inner door leading to the double bays. He threw open the door, and reached for Amber's arm. "Careful," he advised, steering her into the relative darkness of the main compartment. "Let your eyes adjust to the light."

Amber heard the rumble of a big truck passing nearby on Route 9/202. The walls shook slightly. "Are you sure this is safe?" she asked, nervously. She was still on edge after Ma Jean's unexpected death, and almost expected the matron to walk into her carriage shed any moment and accost them.

"Don't worry, Sweets. The carriage house has been standing almost two hundred years; I think it'll last another day!"

The interior of the carriage shed had a hard-packed dirt floor and smelled like a combination of motor oil and wet newspapers. Wan November light entered from two tall matching windows situated north-east and south-west. As Amber's eyes adjusted to the gloom, she glanced around. The building was mostly empty. A few shovels and rakes rested alongside the wall next to the door, and some rusty paint cans littered a shelf along the back wall. Gigantic wooden beams splayed overhead, hoisting up the second story. The square posts and beams reminded her of the Lincoln Logs® her brother Scott had played with as a child. Before he died, she'd often sat and watched Scott assemble the logs, creating one fascinating wooden cabin after another.

Amber felt a deep-seated pain emanating from her solar plexus and recognized the all-too-familiar symptom of inextinguishable grief caused by the death of her older brother. There was a hole inside her that had never been filled—never would be filled. Nothing could replace her beloved brother. She could almost picture him there with the two of them, surveying the site, and idly wondered what Scott would think of Bruce as a brother-in-law.

"Hey, look at this!" Bruce called, interrupting her reflections. "The old rope's still here!" She moved to his side, and he directed her attention up to the hemp rope, now wrapped around the beams like tawny-colored snakes. "This place is perfect for my garage! The hydraulic lifts will go here – and here," and he indicated the appropriate spots on the dirt floor. "I'll have to pour a little concrete, but I was expecting that."

Amber, who knew very little about cars and even less about repairing and maintaining them, shook her head. "It's beyond me," she admitted. "I'll stick to eggs and Emily Dickinson."

"Ha, ha! We're quite a team; you handle the chickens and the poetry, and I'll handle the cars! Wanna see the loft?"

She nodded. "How do we get there?"

He moved toward a set of narrow wooden stairs hugging the back wall. "Follow me. But watch your step, Sweets, there's no guardrail."

She tentatively followed him up the weathered wooden steps, which opened into a large, peaked-ceiling loft. Cobweb covered windows lent an air of mystery to the dusty area, which contained old furniture in various stages of disrepair. The unorganized piles of furniture included five or six straight-back chairs with missing spokes, a drop-leaf table with a broken leaf, and a cane-seat rocker with a four-inch hole in the seat. Other interesting accoutrements included a red-painted wooden cradle, two potato baskets, several wooden sock stretchers dangling from square-headed nails, and even an old spinning wheel. Several leather-strapped trunks, wooden crates with colorful labels, an antique sled, and a woven fishing creel completed the unique historical collection.

Amber reviewed the cluttered loft with heightened enthusiasm. "OK, now I'm interested," she said. Despite her nagging qualms, she poked through the open area, picking up and examining one unique item after another. The wide, unfinished floor boards squeaked with her every step. "Quite a collection of outcasts," she said. "Everything's broken!"

He leaned up against the back wall, watching her progress. "Broken or not, I might need some of this stuff. I sold most of my furniture when I moved in with my folks ten years ago."

Amber spied a wooden contraption, strung evenly with knotted strands of hemp rope. "What's that?" she asked, intrigued. "Looks like some kind of torture device."

"Ha, ha! That's a rope bed," he replied, pushing away from the wall. He advanced with a devilish twinkle in his brown eyes. "Want me to show you how it works?"

"Not unless there's more to it than that!"

"Nope. The old rope bed went the way of the bundling board, I'm afraid. Too bad!"

The November sun dipped down behind the western horizon, splashing rose-purple rays against the bronze-colored wood. "We'd better get going," he said. "It'll be dark soon and I don't have a flashlight."

He took her by the hand and led her carefully downstairs and out into the fresh evening air. They climbed back to his truck, but instead of motoring back out onto the main road, Bruce pulled further up the driveway. The west-facing windows of Ma Jean's lovely old house captured the glow of the sunset. The red bricks were warm and rosy-looking, and the interior of the home appeared gloriously illuminated, as though every light within the house had been switched on.

"Looks like Ma Jean's having a party," Bruce commented.

"I hope she is – in heaven!"

Bruce drove slowly around the back corner of the house. He parked the truck next to an apple tree and switched off the engine. A white picket fence surrounded an ample back yard, which, in addition to several old fruit trees, included various herb and flower gardens, now withered down into their dark winter clothing. "Won't be long before the first snow," he said. "We'll have some fun, then!"

"Maybe in January," she replied, wistfully. "I'm so crazy busy with schoolwork right now I won't have much time to play!"

"Then I better take advantage of you now. Come here, you!" He reached for her with his strong, beguiling hands.

She obediently slid toward him, but suddenly, out of the corner of her eye, Amber spied another vehicle. "What's that?" she asked, pointing to a darkened pickup, partially-hidden by a hedge of crimson blackberry canes.

"That's Maynard Nutter's truck! I wonder what he's doing here?"

"I think I see someone moving around inside the house!"

Concerned, Bruce popped open his cab door. "I better make sure everything's OK."

"I'm coming with you," she said, determinedly. "Just in case."

"OK, but stay behind me."

The door to the rear entryway was unbolted, and Bruce pushed the door open and stepped into the laundry room. Amber followed him cautiously, her nerves on edge. She smelled the perfumed scent of soap powder, and noted Ma Jean's laundry soaps neatly stashed on a shelf above the white side-by-side washer and dryer. The house was so silent she could hear the *tick-tick-tick* of an old-fashioned clock from a nearby room.

"Anyone here?" Bruce called, keeping her safely behind him. "Maynard?"

In a few moments, Maynard Nutter sidled around the doorway that led from Ma Jean's kitchen. "I ain't breakin' 'n enterin'," he said, somewhat defensively. "Thet door was open." The eighty-five-year-old selectman was dressed in his usual outfit, a plaid flannel shirt tucked inside a pair of loose-fitting blue work pants. A well-worn gray farm cap was perched on his head, white hair poking out the sides like down feathers.

He looked frail and tired.

"Jesus, Maynard! What're you doing here?" Bruce demanded.

"Don't you worry, Bruce. I ain't doin' nuthin' wrong! I was jest re-trievin' some property."

"What kind of property?"

A contrary, puckered expression came over his weathered face. "Wal, if you must know, I was lookin' fer a letter."

"A letter?!"

"I wrote to Mabel 'bout a week afore she died, but I ain't heared nuthin' back from her. I was jest wantin' to know if she got my letter."

Amber felt her heart warm to the older man. He had written a letter to Ma Jean! It must have been some kind of a love letter!

Bruce was skeptical. "You wrote to Ma Jean? What for, Maynard? You saw her every morning for coffee, didn't you?"

Maynard clammed up. He looked down at the patterned linoleum, and shuffled his feet.

Amber touched Bruce on the shoulder. "I think it's a private matter," she whispered. "Don't embarrass him!"

The selectman overheard her caution. "'Tis a private matter!" he en-treated, plaintively. "But I ain't embarrassed. At least, not now, anyways."

Amber, who had been obediently standing behind Bruce, slipped around in front of him. "You didn't want anyone else to find and read your letter, did you, Mr. Nutter?" she guessed, in a kind voice. "Is that it?"

Encouraged, the selectman bobbed his head in agreement. "Thet's right, gal. I didn't want none o' the boys to make fun o' me 'n Mabel," he admitted, his thin, pointed shoulders perking up at her compassion-ate interest. "Warn't none o' their gol-danged business! I been wantin' to talk to Mabel privately for quite a while, but I didn't want to embarrass her. So I wrote her a letter and mailed it down to Unity. I've always had a hankerin' for Mabel Jean, since we was kids. I was even agoin' to ask her to marry me when she turned twenty-one, but I waited too long and one day this young fella, Harold Brown, come to town 'n opened a res-taurant next door to the Edwards. After thet, Mabel niver had no eyes for nobody but him!"

Amber was eager to know more, but she didn't want to offend him by further prodding. "I'm so sorry for your loss," she said, instead. "Her death must have been a terrible shock for you!"

Maynard's bright blue eyes filled with tears. He dashed them away with the back of his arm. "'Tain't what I was expectin'," he agreed. "I figgered I'd be the furst to go, surely."

Bruce, who had been listening to their exchange with growing interest, felt no such qualms about asking the older man intimate questions. "Didja ever get a chance to tell Ma Jean how you felt?"

Maynard shuffled his feet, and bobbed his head again. "Ayuh. In thet letter. Thet's why I was wantin' to know if Mabel had a chance to read it, afore she died."

"Didja find it?"

"Wal, I jest got here not long afore you come in, Bruce."

Bruce clasped the elderly selectman by the arm, and steered him back into the kitchen. "C'mon, Maynard, tell us what your letter looks like, and we'll help you!"

Maynard described to them the hand-written love missive, and the plain white envelope he'd used to mail the letter. The three then split up to search Ma Jean's home. The matron had obviously spent most of her time downstairs in the living room and kitchen, and the men began to hunt there. Amber, however, utilizing a woman's intuition, decided to search the bedroom. She calculated that Ma Jean – whom she'd once considered as stern and unapproachable – must have had a woman's heart, and regardless of her age, any woman would have kept a love letter in her bedroom.

Ten minutes later, Amber discovered the epistle. The letter had been stashed in Ma Jean's antique secretary, tucked by the matron into one of the fragrant wooden slots of the desk. Amber sank into the padded desk chair, and unfolded the off-white, blue-lined paper. She easily identified Maynard Nutter's scribbled signature at the bottom of the page, and quickly folded it back up without reading it. "I found it!" she cried.

Her curious fingers returned to the same slot, which contained several envelopes, searching for Maynard's mailer. But instead of the selectman's, she pulled out a different envelope – still sealed. The antique ivory envelope was addressed to *Mr. Maynard Nutter, Bangor Road, Sovereign, Maine*, and was stamped, ready to mail. It appeared obvious to Amber that Ma Jean had penned a reply to her elderly suitor, but instead of mailing it had set the reply aside for a few days, perhaps giving herself time to reconsider her words.

What a discovery!

Bruce strode into the elegant boudoir with Maynard hard upon his heels. "Didja find it?" "Did she git it?"

Wordlessly, Amber lifted up her prize to show them both. Her eyes gleamed. The selectman approached her, hungrily, hands outstretched.

He spied the antique ivory envelope, and hesitated. "Thet ain't it," he said. The disappointment hit him hard, and he grasped the back of her chair to steady himself.

He exhaled deeply, and she felt his warm breath against her neck. Amber suddenly felt shy. She touched him lightly on the arm. "I found your letter, and ... and something else besides, Mr. Nutter." She pushed the sealed envelope into his hands. "Here! Take a look at this, please."

Maynard straightened himself up and clasped the letter between blue-veined hands. He considered his own name, penned in black ink by a feminine hand, staring back at him from the thick, antique parchment envelope. He pushed back his cap and scratched his head, as if unsure what the return reply meant.

"She wrote back to you – she just didn't get around to mailing it before she died," Amber explained, gently.

Bruce whistled. "Yikes!"

The news was more than the elderly man could assay standing up. He moved back a few feet and sank down onto the edge of the Ma Jean's three-quarter sized bed, the bed in which the matron had died. "Should I open it?" he asked, trembling.

"Yes!" Amber replied, without wasting a moment for consideration.

Hands shaking, the selectman tore off the side edge, and clumsily pulled forth a pretty pink feminine notecard. Bruce stepped away, so that Maynard could have some privacy. The old man fumbled momentarily with the card, and then unfolded the note.

Amber waited with bated breath while Maynard slowly perused the contents. A minute later, his hands fell to his lap. He raised his watery eyes, but Amber could see that he was no longer present with them, he was someplace else. She spied in his blue orbs a vision of Heaven, a glorious, indescribable vista of gold-spun memories, eternal hopes and beloved dreams. For a moment, she thought she saw her brother, Scott, waving triumphantly from a puffy white cumulus cloud.

"She says, YES!" Maynard cried, sobbing. "Thank the good Lord Almighty – Mabel Jean says, yes!"

Chapter 19

· · · · · · ·

Emily Exposed

Ten days later, when Amber was hard at work on one of her three final papers for the end of her fall semester at UMass, Bruce sent her a cryptic text message telling her to meet him down at Ma Jean's carriage shed. Intrigued, and grateful for the excuse to shirk her studies for even a brief period of time, she saved her work on a memory stick and powered down her laptop.

He was already at the carriage shed when she arrived, greeting her at the side door. She allowed herself to be kissed, but when his hands started to wander she pulled away. "I haven't got much time," she chastised him. "I'm in the middle of a final paper!"

"Nice to know where I rate on your list of priorities," he chided. But she could see by the twinkle in his brown eyes that he was teasing her.

"You know what my priorities are," she replied. "School work and the chickens!" She reached up and lovingly ruffled his brown hair, which had grown more than an inch since they'd first met on the bus from Boston. "I love your hair, now!"

He grasped her wrist. "What a little liar you are – you said you liked it short!"

"I do like it short. I like it long, too!"

"Ha, ha! Follow me, Sweets – I need your help!"

He led her up into the loft, where she immediately noticed that someone had been at work inspecting and separating the clutter. The interesting historical artifacts that Amber had seen on her initial visit had now been sorted into two distinct piles. With the exception of the cane-seated rocking chair, most of the broken furniture was on one side of the room, and the rocker, spinning wheel, the cradle, the potato baskets and even the sock stretchers were on the opposite side.

"What's up?" she asked, her curiosity piqued.

Bruce surveyed the loft proudly. "What do you think?! I've taken a short-term lease on the carriage shed from the Ladies Auxiliary!"

She was surprised and somewhat shocked. "Already?! Ma Jean's only been dead two weeks!"

"She made her will thirty years ago, Sweets. Everybody in town knew what was going to happen when Ma Jean died; that's the way she wanted it."

"She couldn't have known you were taking over the carriage shed!"

"Nope, but she left everything to the Ladies Auxiliary with the instructions to raise the most money they could. Shirley was here the other day with an antique dealer, and he picked out the valuable stuff. They didn't want any of the rest of this," he indicated the pile of mostly broken furniture, "so I gave the Auxiliary $350 for everything. I need your help figuring out what to keep."

Amber felt a cold chill pass over her. She glanced around, warily. "I feel like we're vultures picking over Ma Jean's bones!"

"C'mon, it's not that bad," he pleaded. "You were so interested in this stuff before, I thought you'd jump at the chance to go through everything!"

She hesitated. She hated to refuse him! But she was beginning to feel uncomfortable with the speed at which everything had been moving since Ma Jean's death.

Seeing that he had so far failed to convince her, Bruce decided to shift gears. "Maybe it's not your job to worry about the administration of Ma Jean's estate," he suggested. "As somebody once told me, there's only one person – or group of people – who can decide what to do with Ma Jean's stuff and ..." he broke off, expectantly.

She smiled. "OK, OK, I get it. It's not me! Don't make me sorry that I ever shared that head doctor stuff with you!"

He grinned. "What goes around comes around! So, you'll help me?"

"OK, but I still think everything's moving a little fast."

He gave her a quick hug. "That's my girl!"

Amber couldn't resist first looking over the items that Shirley Palmer and the local antiques dealer had elected to send to the regular Sunday auction in Burnham. Most of the article choices appeared obviously valuable, but not all. She held up one of the wooden wool sock driers for Bruce's inspection. "They wanted this?"

"The antique guy said those sock stretchers can sell for as much as $25. Go figure!"

When she'd finished her quick review of the Auxiliary's auction items, Amber turned to Bruce's cache. She began poking through the piles of broken furniture, boxes and other historical paraphernalia that was stacked on the right hand side of the loft, under the slanted, unfinished eaves. With her peculiar interest in and attachment to the 19th century, Amber in truth would have been in Seventh Heaven, had it not been for her prick of conscience about Ma Jean's recent demise.

Bruce followed at her heels, tractable and obedient. He loved any excuse to be with her, and this salvage operation was revealing to him how well they would operate as a couple. He and his first wife, Sheila, had spent very little time together, and certainly had never been able to buckle into harness and accomplish anything as a team. Sheila hated to get her hands dirty, and never found the satisfaction in work that he experienced. In addition, Sheila got bored easily, and, although she didn't much like childcare either, she often used their baby as an excuse to slip away from work. He'd find her later in front of a blaring TV set, smoking a cigarette, with Gray playing quietly by himself in his crib.

"Ditch this," Amber said, arousing him from his momentary flashback by handing him an iron box, rusted beyond repair. "But this I think you can fix," she added, holding up the broken leaf of a maple table. She fitted the wood into the neatly severed edge of the nearby drop-leaf table. "See?"

He accepted both the rusted box and the broken leaf. "I can fix anything, Sweets," he bragged. "The question is – is it worth fixing?"

"Yes!" she said, returning eagerly to her selection process. "You need furniture, don't you?"

"You know it!"

"Let's look at the chairs next." She separated out of the pile four or five straight-back chairs, most of them with missing parts and pieces. She handed them to him one at a time. Wordlessly, he accepted the chairs and set them into a third pile with the table. She dropped to her hands and knees, and began searching for the broken spools and spokes. "I think this is the last piece," she proclaimed, fifteen minutes later. She stood up, brushed herself off and surveyed with satisfaction the little mismatched group of straight-back chairs. "Now you can have company over for dinner!"

"Pretty skimpy, aren't they?" he worried. He lowered his beefy frame down into one of the delicate chairs, and the frame made a *cri-i-icking* sound. But the chair held together.

"Just don't invite any fat people over and you'll be OK," Amber said. She regretted her thoughtless words as soon as they left her mouth. Too late, she recalled his plus-sized mother. "Oh, I'm so sorry – that was mean and rude!"

He stood up, and grinned. "Don't worry, Mom's used to it. I'll be sure to get myself a comfortable couch for her. Of course, my Dad will be able to sit anywhere!"

They continued this cheerful pattern for nearly two hours, the third pile expanding in proportion to the shrinking of the second pile. Amber was so engrossed with her work she barely noticed she was becoming thirsty and dirty. Her hair, which she had plaited into a thick braid early that morning, was beginning to come unraveled. She pushed a few stragglers away from her face, and flipped the braid back over her shoulder.

Bruce leaned over and wiped a few smudges of grime from her face. "Let's take a break, Sweets, and run next door for a cup of coffee," he suggested. "I know they're over there, just waiting for non-paying customers like us!"

"We're almost done! I've already looked at that stuff," she said, pointing to a little pile. "That can all go to the Unity Area Recycling Center. Just let me check out this old trunk and I'll be done." She dropped down onto her haunches, and patted the road-weary top of a small, leather-bound travel trunk with the initials *A.E.* painted in black on the side. "I'm surprised they didn't want this!"

He shook his head. "Too beat up."

"Did they look inside?"

"Yeah, it's mostly old letters and a few books. Nothing important, the antique dealer said. They might have pie today, you know," he tempted her.

"Mmmm, five minutes," she promised, unlatching the leather straps to the antique trunk and throwing open the lid.

But it was more than an hour later and the sun was beginning to set before he could pry her away, and even then, they took the trunk with them. She had discovered, by reading some of the letters and putting two and two together, that the antique piece of luggage had been the property of an Ann Edwards. The young woman had apparently died at an early age, and some of her beloved possessions had been packed away inside her travelling trunk. With the recent experience of Maynard Nutter and his letter still fresh in her mind, Amber couldn't resist reading some of the epistles. She had stumbled across one that was signed, *"Your dear friend, Emily Dickinson,"* and couldn't believe her eyes.

"Look at this!" she cried, waving the letter. "It's signed by someone called Emily Dickinson!"

"Ha, ha! That's the same name as your dead lady poet!"

She nodded, feeling the hair stand up on the back of her neck. "Strange coincidence, isn't it?"

Bruce scooted down next to her and took the letter from her hand. The signature was barely legible, but he did manage to make out *Emily Dickinson* at the bottom of the unusual half-sheet of paper. "Suppose it's any relation?"

"I don't have the slightest idea – but I'm going to see what else is in here!" Amber dove into the trunk with fresh enthusiasm. Some of the letters were loose, and some were carefully tied up with a pretty pink ribbon. She gathered up a pile of loose envelopes and one by one she reviewed the yellowed envelopes with their colorful cancelled stamps. "This one's from Amherst!" she blurted out. "And so is this! Oh, my God! *My* Emily Dickinson, as you call her, was from Amherst, Massachusetts!"

She was so befuddled she sat down onto the wide pine board with a little thud, still carefully clutching the fistful of yellowed envelopes. "These could have been written by the poet Emily Dickinson! We need to get them authenticated as soon as possible!"

Light was fading when they wrestled the trunk into the passenger side of the truck. Bruce had suggested setting the trunk in the bed for the short ride up to the old Russell homestead; however, Amber had quickly nixed that idea. She shuddered, picturing in her mind the top of the trunk flying open and the precious letters blowing out and littering the roadside like common trash.

The next morning, upon her instigation, Bruce placed a call to James D. Julia, Inc., an internationally acclaimed fine art and antiques auction house headquartered in nearby Fairfield. He explained the discovery in the old carriage shed, and made an appointment on the following day for a representative to come out and inspect the trunk and its potentially valuable contents.

In the meantime, Amber had temporarily abdicated her school work and was busy online searching genealogical information about Ann Edwards. She discovered that Ann was the child of Elizabeth and

Benjamin Edwards, who moved to Sovereign from Amherst in 1845. They were cousins of the Edwards already living in town, from which family Ma Jean – Mabel Jean Edwards – was descended. Ann had died of consumption – tuberculosis – at the age of twenty-two, and the letters, books and other ephemera had most likely been stored in her travelling trunk since her death. How the trunk ended up in the carriage house was a mystery, but the connection between the families was so close as to make its discovery perfectly tenable.

Amber also couldn't resist stealing back to the trunk again and again, like a honeybee returning to a tree of nectar-laden blossoms. She didn't dare to open and read the fragile letters, much as she wanted to. She was afraid she might accidentally harm one. However, she did poke carefully amongst the other papers and books in the trunk, unearthing in the process an unusual eight-page folio, with the interesting title, *Forest Leaves*.

Curious, she cautiously opened the cover of the small newspaper, and sought out the masthead. She gave a little start. It was the Amherst Academy school publication! Emily Dickinson had attended Amherst Academy for seven years as a girl! Further research on the internet revealed the magnitude of her new find. She placed the publication back in the trunk, and telephoned Bruce with the news.

"Emily Dickinson scholars will give their eye teeth for this!" she exclaimed. "A copy of *Forest Leaves* has never been found! This is huge! HUGE! You'll be able to have enough money for the museum project and a whole lot more!"

"If you say so, Sweets," he replied, not quite convinced. "I'm glad you're happy, anyway."

The next afternoon they received the visit from the auction representative. After examining the trunk, the appraiser decided the find was certainly of important historical significance.

"It never ceases to amaze me what wonderful things are found in attics and barns," the James Julia appraiser said to Amber and Bruce. The three were sitting at the kitchen table, and a fascinated Rebecca and Wendell hovered in the background, listening to the conversation. "If you're interested, I'll take the trunk and contents back to our office and we'll go through and catalog everything piece by piece. If the letters are indeed authenticated as having been written by the poet Emily Dickinson, they'll fetch quite a bit at auction." The appraiser turned to Amber. "And if you're right about that copy of *Forest Leaves* – that it's the only one known to exist – that will fan the flames of excitement even further."

"How much money are we talking about?" asked Bruce, resting his forearms on the table.

The appraiser reflected a moment. "It's hard to say, of course. So much depends upon the appetite of the collectors. Three years ago we sold a map of the battle of Georgetown done for George Washington for $1.15 million. That was the most expensive antique item ever sold at auction in Maine."

"Yikes! But this isn't a map of a famous battle," Bruce pointed out.

The James Julia representative shrugged. "In that same auction, a letter from Washington to his nephew sold for $120,000 – give or take a few dollars. Your letters aren't as old as the Washington material; however, Emily Dickinson is quite collectible. I'd say a conservative estimate at auction for everything you have would be $150,000 to $200,000."

Rebecca let out a little shriek, and quickly covered her mouth with her hand.

"Jesus!" exclaimed Bruce, slumping back in his chair.

Amber clapped her hands. "I told you you'd have plenty of money for the museum project!"

"And that's a conservative estimate, mind you," the James Julia appraiser continued. "Your items could bring quite a bit more."

"But … I can't keep all that money!" Bruce declared. "It wouldn't be right! The money should go to the Ladies Auxiliary."

Wendell, an old Maine horse trader always awake to an opportunity, put himself forward. "You bought all thet junk from the Ladies," he reminded Bruce.

"Yeah, but they didn't know what they had when they sold it to me!"

Wendell flashed his gold-toothed grin. "Them old gals snooze, they lose!"

"Do you have an attorney, Mr. Gilpin?" the James Julia appraiser asked. "We have a standard sales contract we use with our consigners, but given the nature of your discovery, perhaps you'd like to have an attorney represent you?"

Amber immediately thought of Ryan, but said nothing.

"As a matter of fact, I do have a lawyer," Bruce replied. "Ryan MacDonald. I'll have him give you a call tomorrow."

"Oh, Ryan will be so happy to help with this!" Amber declared, happily.

The appraiser jotted down the name. "Ryan MacDonald. Very good," he said, flipping shut his portfolio of hand-scribbled notes. "I think we should include the Emily Dickinson items in our fine art and antiques auction that's coming up in February. It's a three-day auction event, which always draws quite a crowd of bidders from all over the world. I think I can safely say at this point that the Emily Dickinson material will be some of the most anticipated items in our catalog." He rose and shook hands all around. Bruce helped him load the precious cargo into his vehicle, and then he was gone.

When Bruce returned to the kitchen, Amber was once again regaling her parents with the excitement of the discovery. Over the past forty-eight hours, she had been giving them all a crash course in the life, death and poetry of Emily Dickinson, the eccentric lady in white from Amherst, Massachusetts. Wary of publishing in her lifetime, Emily Dickinson left nearly 1,800 poems for her sister, Lavinia, to find in her desk after her death – and perhaps some additional words to be liberated from a trunk in Sovereign, Maine, one hundred and twenty-seven years later!

Chapter 20
. . . .
"What If 1 Burst the Fleshly Gate?"

In the months that she had known – and loved – Bruce Gilpin, Amber had never once thought about or even felt the thirteen-year difference in their ages. When her mother had worried aloud about the age gap, Amber had laughed away her mother's fears, chiding Rebecca for being pessimistic and old-fashioned. When Maude hinted about similar difficulties, Amber had shrugged off the remark as inconsequential, coming as it did from a woman whom she knew hoped for a different daughter-in-law.

To Amber, Bruce had always seemed so youthful at heart, and she herself felt so mature, that it had almost seemed as though they were of an age. But now as she sat silently watching and listening to Bruce, Ryan and Trudy chat about the museum project, she felt as though she were from an altogether different generation than the other three.

The third meeting of the Sovereign Canning Factory Museum Board of Directors was being hosted by Ryan at his cabin on the North Troy Road. It was mid-December, and Miss Hastings had not felt well enough either to host the group or to go out on a cold evening. Rather than postpone the meeting they had decided to meet without her. There was a roaring fire in the woodstove, and Bruce was sprawled in one of the two matching Windsor rockers on one side of the stove. Trudy was settled comfortably into the other rocker opposite him. Ryan was spread out on the couch, amongst a nest of books and papers. Amber sat on the rug, hugging her knees, somewhat apart from the rest. As she listened to the others laugh and joke, she felt confused and cross.

She couldn't believe the change to the group dynamics that the absence of Miss Hastings had unwittingly caused. When the elderly lady had been with them, their ages had seemed irrelevant. They had seemed a mixed group of people enthusiastically sharing a common interest. Now, however, without the spunky retired music teacher, it appeared patently obvious – at least to Amber, anyway – that the other three were analogous and she was an outlier. They were all about the same age – all so-called Millennials – mostly settled, secure and comfortable with themselves and their lives. In short, the other three were everything that Amber wasn't.

Bruce, with a new one-year lease from the Ladies Auxiliary, was cheerfully turning Ma Jean's carriage shed into a business and bachelor pad, and working at renovating the canning factory for the museum project on the side. Ryan was on leave from his high-powered career in Boston, adeptly juggling legal issues for the museum project, Ma Jean's Restaurant and the Emily Dickinson auction. Trudy was happy with her part-time job at the high school and her butter making business. Yes, Amber was the odd-person out. She was still a college student, still living at home with her parents, not even sure yet what she was going to do or where she was going to live when she graduated from UMass in May!

Adding to her present misery was the callous way in which – she felt – the town was treating Ma Jean's death. It seemed to Amber that everyone had accepted Ma Jean's death as a matter of course. After the funeral, with the exception of Maynard Nutter, there was no wholesale lamenting, no wailing or rending of clothing. Instead, Maude and Amber's own mother had been quick to appropriate the restaurant, and Bruce had taken over the carriage house. The Ladies Auxiliary had picked over the items in Ma Jean's home (as well as the carriage shed), and the Sovereign Historical Society had ventured to suggest that the antique brick house would make a good home base for them! Amber wondered that no one but herself could see how heartless they were acting!

She sighed, and tried to force her mind back to the business at hand.

"I've been cleaning up one of the old retorts. What a piece of work!" Bruce exhorted.

"What's a retort?" Ryan asked. "Sounds like canon fire."

"Ha, ha! You're not far off – an IED is more like it, though!"

"A retort is a high-pressure canner," Trudy explained to Ryan. She was using her librarian tone of voice with him, which made it obvious to Amber that, despite the attorney's efforts to strike up a friendship, Trudy had not yet warmed to him. "Canning factories used retorts to kill the harmful bacteria in the cans."

"You've got to come see these things, MacDonald; they look just like pressure chambers on an old submarine, only smaller," Bruce enthused. "They've got reinforced cast-iron sides, and old brass beam scales on top, with weights and counterweights, everything they needed to set the pressure just so. And each retort's got four large turnbuckles with two-inch screw stubs and big bolts to keep the door from blowing to smithereens!"

"They sound like quite the rig," Ryan agreed. "I can't wait to see them. I'm surprised we missed the retorts during our original tour of the factory."

"Aw, they stuck 'em in the back of the building, near the old boiler. That way if one of the retorts blew it would only take out part of the place. Clyde told me they came close to blowing a retort once, when he was a kid. Mickey Miller accidentally got the fire built up too hot in the boiler, and he was so scared he sent for the blacksmith. The guy put on a pair of leather gloves and reached in and yanked out some of the red hot coals. They saved the retort, but just barely!"

"Incredible!" exclaimed Ryan. "Thank goodness for the blacksmith!"

Even Trudy became animated. "I get goose bumps sometimes when the pressure in my stovetop pressure cooker starts to rise rapidly. I can't imagine what that must have felt like!"

"Those things must have been something awful to run," Bruce added, shaking his head in admiration over the workings of the factory-sized, steam-pressure canners. "I'll have to talk to Clyde about it. He ran the retort room, at the end of it."

"Oh, by the way, Bruce," Trudy added, "I spoke to Clyde yesterday, and he's thrilled about what we're doing."

"I'm glad you've seen him! I've been so busy I haven't had a chance to run old Clyde down."

Amber noticed that while talking to Bruce, Trudy's angular face lit up with genuine interest and excitement. The other woman was dressed in a comely wool sweater, and she thought she'd never seen her look prettier. Amber felt as though she herself had disappeared from their view, like the lowly dormouse at the Mad Hatter's tea party.

"We've got a date for next week," Trudy continued. "I'm going to borrow the school's video camera and tape Clyde. If you want, I'll start by asking him questions about the retorts. I'd like to get something done soon, just in case, you know."

"Yeah, it can't be soon enough; they're dropping like flies," Bruce acknowledged.

This callous remark from her beloved nearly sent Amber over the edge. But she stoically bit her tongue.

Bruce leaned forward in his rocker, giving Trudy and her notes his complete attention. "What else ya got for us?"

"I've started a preliminary list of some of the ephemera I've found," she replied. She lifted up her notebook so that she could read the list aloud. "Twelve boxes of assorted can labels with different brand names – apparently the factory canned corn under different labels for several large commercial accounts," she explained. "They waited until the orders came in to put the labels on the cans."

"Seems like a smart idea," said Ryan, who was perhaps anxious to get back into the conversation.

"I also found hundreds of bills of sale, some unpaid invoices, and dozens of black and white photographs. In addition, I also discovered a drawer full of receipt books containing copies of receipts to local farmers for their sweet corn, including some made out to my grandfather and great-grandfather."

Bruce whistled, settling back in the rocker. "Wow! That must have been quite a discovery for you."

Trudy's eyes glistened with tears. "For a moment I imagined my grandfather was still alive!"

"I'd give anything for a discovery like that!" Ryan declared, passionately. "How amazing for you to have such an interesting piece of family history!"

"You're doing a fantastic job, Trudy," Bruce said. "Keep it up!"

Both men eyed Trudy with obvious appreciation. She blushed, and looked down at her hand-written notes. Amber felt as though no one would notice if she arose, slipped out the door and started walking down the North Troy Road. She was glad she was wearing her lined L.L.Bean® boots.

"Well, I've got something exciting to report myself," Ryan added. He unconsciously straightened himself up on the couch. "The paperwork is filed for the 501(c)3, and it won't be long now before we can start taking tax deductible donations! We won't need them as much as we did before the Emily Dickinson discovery, of course, but the 501(c)3 will provide a mechanism for us to secure the additional funding necessary to maintain the museum in perpetuity."

Bruce had decided that he would equally split the proceeds from the sale of the Emily Dickinson items with the Ladies Auxiliary. The items were currently being cataloged for James Julia's February 2013 auction. He shook his head in wonderment. "You guys are amazing! I can't believe how much progress we're making with the museum project. Pretty soon we'll have 'em lining up at the door!"

Ryan laughed pleasantly. Trudy looked pleased.

"Speaking of progress, how's it going with your new garage, Gilpin?" Ryan asked, in a collegial tone. "I saw a cement truck there last week."

"Yeah. I got the floor poured and the two hydraulic lifts installed. Once I get my paperwork back from the state, I'll be open for business. Not sure if I'll have 'em lining up at my doors, though!"

"Oh, I'm sure you will, Bruce," Trudy assured him. "Everyone knows how good a mechanic you are!"

"Let's hope they remember. It's been a long time."

"We all remember," Trudy asserted. "This town has long memories."

Amber sniffed. She had just been considering how quickly the townspeople had seemed to forget Ma Jean. Fortunately, none of the others noticed her expression of disdain.

Ryan threw a long arm over the back of the couch. "Is your son going to live at the carriage house with you?"

"Nah, we talked it all over, and he's gonna stay with his grandparents for now. Funny thing, Gray used to say he couldn't wait for me to get home from Afghanistan. But now that I'm around 24/7, he isn't so keen to have me underfoot!" Bruce chuckled. "Typical teenager!"

The other two laughed. Amber bit her lip. She suddenly felt closer to Bruce's sixteen-year-old son Gray, than she did to Gray's father. And in point of fact, she was much closer to Gray in age!

"And how's that upstairs apartment coming?"

"George Palmer – that's Asa's grandson – is the contractor who's building me the little apartment over the garage. He's got his crew of four working full-time. Says he'll have it ready for me to move into next week."

"Excellent!"

"I can't wait to have my own digs. My folks have been great, but every guy likes to have his own place."

"Here, here," said Ryan, smiling. A considerate host, he finally realized that Amber hadn't spoken in nearly half an hour. "You're very quiet tonight, Amber," he added. "Is anything the matter?" He leaned forward, observing her closely.

Three sets of eyes turned toward where she was sitting now cross-legged on the rug, next to the coffee table. She was embarrassed by the unwanted attention. She felt the heat rising in her cheeks. "Not really," she said, somewhat crossly. "It's just crunch time for me, that's all."

"Crunch time?" repeated Trudy.

Amber shrugged. "Typical end of the semester stuff, you know. I've got three finals coming up and two papers to finish this week."

"I forgot you were still in college," the other woman replied, thoughtlessly.

Amber winced.

"Sorry, I didn't mean that like it sounded. Is there anything we can do to help?"

"Not unless you want to write a twenty-page paper about the early influences on the writings of Emily Dickinson."

"Ha, ha – that lets me out!" said Bruce.

"I might be able to help, though," Ryan offered. "I minored in 19th century literature, you know, Amber."

Amber hadn't known that interesting piece of Ryan's history. She perked up. "No wonder you knew so much about the Transcendentalists!"

Ryan waved a manicured hand toward his extensive collection of hardcover books, which had usurped Mike Hobart's lighter reading material on the built-in bookshelves. "Ralph Waldo Emerson puts me to sleep every night. Feel free to borrow anything you want – I know there was some sort of connection between Emerson and the Dickinson family. You might be able to use that angle. Emerson visited the Evergreens, Emily's brother's place, several times during his life, I believe. And if there's anything else I can do to help – anything legal and appropriate, of course – I'd be happy to oblige," he said, sincerely.

"Thanks, but unless you can make my days last forty-eight hours instead of twenty-four, there's not much anyone can do."

"You've just got to ask if you need help, Sweets!" Bruce interjected, beginning to feel uncomfortable. "Want me to take over the chickens for the next couple of weeks?"

"No, that's OK, Wendell's been helping with the morning chores."

"Why didn't you ask me?!"

"You've been so busy getting the garage going, and with the museum and everything, I … I didn't want to bother you," Amber replied lamely. She suddenly felt small again, and wanted to cry.

"I think it's time for some refreshments," Ryan suggested.

Out of the corner of her eye, Amber saw the attorney give Trudy a meaningfully look. She knew that Ryan was attempting to give her and Bruce an opportunity to be alone so they could talk. Suddenly, she realized she didn't want to talk about it at the moment. She stumbled to her feet. "I'll help you, Ryan," she offered. She immediately regretted her offer when she saw the mingled hurt and confusion on Bruce's face.

"Thanks, but you don't need …"

"I'll go," said Trudy, arising herself.

Amber sank back onto the floor. In a moment, Bruce was down by her side. He encircled her with his strong arms. "Jesus, Sweets! What's the matter?" With a gentle hand, he tilted her chin up, and pushed aside a few stray strands of dark hair. He dropped a light kiss upon her brow.

"It's nothing," she began—and burst into tears. He held her and soothed her as she cried.

She sobbed freely for a minute or so. She dried her eyes, and attempted to pull herself together. "I'm sorry – I don't know where that came from," she admitted. She had somehow ended up in his lap, and tried to free herself. But a few strands of her hair had twisted around the buttons of his blue work shirt, and pinched her when she pulled away. "Ouch!" she cried, putting a hand to her head to liberate herself.

"Hold still, let me fix this," he ordered, his nimble fingers easily untwisting the strands. He freed her hair, but as she moved to escape he caught her by the wrist. "Not so fast! I've got something to say first."

She obeyed, sniveling.

"I'm sorry, I'm such an ass," he said, earnestly. "I've been so busy, I haven't been paying attention to what's going on in your life. I forgot all about your papers and finals and stuff! What an idiot. Forgive me?"

She nodded, somewhat assuaged by his apology. "It's not all you," she admitted. "I've been feeling really weepy lately. I'm not sure why. For the last few weeks I've felt like there's something wrong with me. Like I don't fit in here; I don't belong." Tears surged back into her eyes, and a sob escaped her parted lips.

"Whoa! You do belong here, Sweets!" he proclaimed. "Where would I be without you?!"

"I'm sorry, I'm sorry! I've been feeling overwhelmed, that's all."

"Does this have anything to do with Ma Jean's death?" he guessed, shrewdly.

Amber hesitated. He'd hit the nail on the head. But how could she explain to him that her anger and depression didn't just relate to her own personal feelings about death, but also to how the community was treating Ma Jean's death. How could she tell him what she felt without sounding accusatory? *You people are acting really heartless!*

"I'm not good with death," she said, instead. She took the opportunity to slide out of his lap.

"Hey, I thought you were the woman with all the answers?!" Bruce joked, holding onto her hand.

She looked gloomy. "Maybe for everybody else, but not myself. I hate death. It sucks," she added, vehemently.

Ryan, who had returned to the living room area with a tray of hot beverages, overheard her plaintive remark. He placed the tray on the coffee table, and moved forward eagerly, interrupting their intimate conversation. "I know exactly what you're feeling, Amber," he disclosed, speaking in an unusually energetic tone of voice. "You can't let it get you down. I know from first-hand experience how devastating depression can be!"

She offered him a grateful half-grin, half-grimace. "So, what's *your* remedy for the dark side, Ryan?"

"My remedy? Ralph Waldo Emerson, Henry David Thoreau – and poetry."

"Poetry?!"

"You think only women read Emily Dickinson? I've been known to dip into Emily myself, usually when I've dipped a little too heavily into the sauce, though!"

Amber laughed, which was his intent. Encouraged, he reached down into his memory, and retrieved a well-loved poem. "'What if I say I shall not wait! What if I burst the fleshly Gate!'" he quoted, dramatically. "'And pass escaped – to thee!'" He broke off, somewhat abashed at his poetic outburst.

"Oh, don't stop, Ryan!" she said.

Emboldened, he continued, his face animated, dark eyes burning with theatrical excitement. "'What if I file this Mortal – off – *see* where it hurt me? That's enough. And wade in Liberty!'"

The attorney's ringing baritone voice reflected an emotional depth that Amber had never heard before. She realized it must be related to the unexpected loss of both of his parents. "Keep going!"

"'They cannot take me, any more!'" he cried, lifting his hand to his breast. "'Dungeons can call – and Guns implore! Unmeaning, now, to me – as laughter was an hour ago, or laces, or a travelling show. Or, … who … died … yesterday!'"

He ended with a melodramatic flourish. The room was momentarily hushed.

Amber clapped enthusiastically. "What a gift!" she avowed. "Thanks so much, Ryan!"

"Don't thank me," he replied, smoothly. He held out his hand, and gallantly helped her up off the wood floor. "Thank Emily!"

Chapter 21
. . . .
The Thunder Approaching

Overnight, eight inches of snow blanketed central Maine, putting the stone walls and abandoned hay bales to sleep for the winter. The giant balsam firs attempted to collect as much of the soft white stuff as they could, reaching upward with eager green arms, but the trees failed to gather it all in and the snow fell deep and thick through the night. Amber awoke to the rumbling of the snowplow and flashing orange light from the truck's strobe as the plow ascended Russell Hill. She struggled up in bed and glanced at her phone. Five-thirty. Time to get up – it was her morning to do the chickens.

She tossed aside the covers and peered out her upstairs window. It was still dark out and it was impossible for her to calculate how much snow they had received. The advent of the first snow reminded her of Bruce's words: *We'll have some fun, then!* And she wished now she'd let him give her a ride home from Ryan's cabin last night as he had wanted, instead of riding home with Trudy. Then they would have been able to talk everything over, and she would feel better this morning, instead of feeling as though she'd left something terribly important unsaid.

Last night, however, she hadn't wanted to talk. She hadn't wanted to feel pressured to explain what at the time had seemed inexplicable. Now, she realized that for the past week or more she'd been unconsciously angry. In addition to being angry over the callous way in which everyone was treating Ma Jean's death (and with death itself), she was angry with Bruce for having failed to define their relationship. True, they were a couple – there was no doubt of that. Everyone in town understood this, even his mother and her own. But what was to be their future? Why did he never speak about it? Was it because of his failed first marriage? Was he afraid to try again? Or was she being unreasonable, expecting him to declare his intentions when they'd only known each other for a few months?

She herself was so clear in her own mind that she had difficulty believing that he could be less clear. From the first moment she'd seen him – almost from the moment that he sat next to her on the bus – she'd known that she wanted to spend the rest of her life with Leonard Bruce Gilpin. He would always be the only man for her! If he died – God forbid! – or if he decided at some point that she was not the woman for him, she would pick herself up and march stoically forward, finishing out her days unmarried and childless.

While turning things over in her head, she was leaning against the cold glass of her single-pane bedroom window. She idly toyed with the liquid pockets of condensation in the upper corners of the glass panes, liberating teardrops of moisture with her index finger. She watched as they raced to the bottom of the wooden frames, and wondered that she was in such a similar hurry to race through her life.

Men were different than women, she chided herself. They were notoriously slow to make up their minds. She mustn't try to pressure him for a declaration. She should have more faith in him! And she should certainly have more faith in the being greater than herself, the One who surely brought them together, and who had created these instructive teardrops of condensation. Yes, she would try to have more faith!

She pulled away from the upstairs window, changed into her work clothes and descended cheerfully to the hen pen. When she returned to the kitchen several hours later, her mother greeted her affectionately, and in short order was placing a plate of toast and eggs in front of her.

"Maude wants to know if you can sell eggs to the restaurant for $2 a dozen," Rebecca mentioned, as she pulled up a chair and joined Amber at the homey table. "I told her I didn't think it would be a problem, but I wanted to check with you, first, dear."

Amber set down her fork. "We can't do that, Mom," she said, seriously. "I'd love to, of course – you remember I talked with Ma Jean about providing eggs to the restaurant six months ago. But we're losing money at $2 a dozen, and we can't keep on losing money."

"Oh, dear!"

"We could probably do $3.50. But even then, we're just breaking even."

"I don't think we could afford that, but I'll talk to Maude. She's handling the restaurant's finances."

They were silent for a minute or so while Amber resumed her breakfast. "When do you expect to reopen?" she asked, in between bites.

"January 2nd. I can't wait for our first customer!"

"I'm so happy for you, Mom!" Suddenly an ominous thought occurred to Amber. "When does your unemployment run out?"

"Not for another few months. I'm still on the extension." Rebecca had been downsized by the insurance company Perkins & Gleeful nearly a year earlier. She had started the business, *The Egg Ladies*, in partnership with Lila in lieu of looking for work each week.

"Do you think you'll make enough money at the restaurant to replace the unemployment, when it ends?"

Her mother laughed. "I'm not sure about that! But we'll have fun trying, anyway."

Amber frowned. "Fun might not be good enough," she replied, cryptically.

"Why not, dear? What's the matter?"

"Oh, Mom! I've been meaning to tell you – I just haven't found the right time! I had to use some of the money from my student loans to pay for our last grain shipment," she admitted.

A shocked expression came over her mother's face. "You took money from your student loans! For *The Egg Ladies*? Oh, my goodness! I didn't realize things have been *that* bad. Why didn't you say anything?!"

"I was hoping the business would turn around. But even with Trudy's help, we're not moving all our eggs. They're just too expensive for the locals, because they're organic. And it's too costly for us to take them to Portland, where people can afford to pay full price. In fact, we might have to take drastic measures soon, unless business improves."

"Now you're scaring me! Drastic measures? What does that mean?"

"Downsizing," Amber said, succinctly. She pushed her plate away. Suddenly, she wasn't hungry. "We might have to get rid of some or all of the chickens."

"Downsizing! My goodness, that's what brought me to Sovereign in the first place!"

"The recession has long arms, Mom," she conceded. "In fact, I was wondering – did you two look at Ma Jean's books before you decided to reopen?"

"No, that is – I don't think so. I didn't. I'm not sure about Maude. Why?"

"My bet is that Ma Jean wasn't making a profit. From what I've learned about her, she was probably keeping the restaurant open as a favor to her friends, bankrolling it from her own private resources. She was an only child, and apparently inherited a lot of money."

"Goodness, I hope that's not true!" Rebecca shuddered as she thought of the pitfalls that might lie ahead. "Thank goodness we've got Wendell's pension! And our mortgage is paid off!"

"We're in a shaky spot right now, but we'll manage somehow," Amber said reassuringly. She knew her mother was prone to worry about money, or lack thereof. "And if we have to sell *The Egg Ladies* and take our lumps, we'll do it – just like everyone else."

"Sell *The Egg Ladies!* But what will you do then, dear, without the business? You won't leave us?!" Rebecca implored.

"Frankly, Mom, I don't know what I'm going to do in May. I'll just have to find out when I get there!"

Both women fell silent again at the thought of how their worlds might change in six months when Amber graduated from UMass. Amber glanced out the window. With the arrival of the snow last night, the world outside appeared fresh and clean. She decided she'd postpone her studies for an hour or so. A brisk walk would clear her head, and help her refocus her energies from all of her many frustrations to her schoolwork.

She took a final swig of coffee, and pushed away from the table. "I'm going to walk up and see Miss Hastings," she said.

"Good idea," her mother replied. "I haven't seen her this week. In fact, I can't remember when I did see her last." She thought a moment. "My goodness! I've been so busy down at the restaurant I think I've only seen her once since Ma Jean's funeral!"

The first thing Amber noted as she waded through the eight-inch deep snow in Miss Hastings' driveway was that there was no smoke coming from the chimney. The dooryard wasn't plowed yet, but she didn't expect that it would be. She knew that Miss Hastings' plowman always came after the storm was over, so that he'd only have to plow once. He also would shovel the elderly lady's steps and walkway at the same time. But Amber knew Miss Hastings' routine well enough to realize that something was wrong. By this time of day certainly, Miss Hastings would have her woodstove going.

No one answered her knock at the shed, but she didn't really expect that, either. The door was unlocked and she stamped the fresh snow off her feet and pushed through the cold shed and mudroom, into the kitchen. The kitchen was also cold, and appeared lifeless. A few dirty dishes sat next to the sink, but there was no sign of the elderly lady.

"Miss Hastings? Are you here?!" she called, anxiously.

Amber detected a weak reply from the downstairs bedroom, and hurried through the dining room. She stepped around the corner into the back bedroom—and spied the elderly lady barely visible and unmoving beneath layers of thick blankets! In a moment, she was at the bedside, clasping Miss Hastings' thin, knobby hands, and crying out to her: "Are you sick?! What's the matter? Should I call an ambulance?!" Miss Hastings was alive, but her skin felt cold and waxy to Amber's warm touch.

"Dahrrrling, don't worry, I just didn't feel like getting up today," the elderly lady whispered. She tried to lift her head, but fell back against the lace pillowcase, her wiry black-gray hair askew. "Maybe you could be a dear and bring me a cup of tea and a bit of toast?" she asked, weakly.

Within half an hour, the house was full of people. Amber had telephoned her mother, who called Maude, who had called Shirley Palmer. The tea and toast had been procured, and the doctor sent for. Amber relinquished command of the situation, and returned to the kitchen to start a fire in the woodstove.

She was in the kitchen washing dishes when I arrived. News travels fast in Sovereign, especially news that relates to such a beloved member of our community.

"Oh, Maggie. Hi," Amber greeted me, when I let myself in through the shed. "She's not dead – she's just not feeling well today!"

"Relax. I'm not here with the holy water and prayer beads," I replied. "I'm just here as a friend."

"Oops, sorry," she said, drying her hands on a dish towel that hung next to the sink.

"No need to apologize. I'm glad you're keeping an eye on Miss Hastings; she's been a little down since Ma Jean died. I've dropped in on her several times since the funeral. But she's always been up and about during my visits. This is the first time she's stayed in bed."

"I hope this isn't going to become a habit," Amber worried.

"Death gets a lot harder to accept as you get older."

"I don't believe it! I don't think how you feel about death has anything to do with age. I've certainly been feeling Ma Jean's death, and I barely knew her!"

"Maybe I should amend my statement," I continued, easily. "Death is hard on the old *and* on the young. It's hard on the old, because when you've lost so many of your dear friends you begin to feel like a fish out of water."

"That's just how I've been feeling!"

"And when you're young, you feel that way, too, because death is not your friend—yet. Death is an uncomfortable foe that might strike at any time, and you never know who might disappear next, including yourself. As you get more comfortable with the cycle of life, you become less and less afraid of death itself, and more and more afraid of being the last one to go, the one left behind. Life is like a river rushing toward a big waterfall, and Miss Hastings is one of the ones who, instead of going over, snagged up on a rock and is now watching while all of her friends and loved ones get carried over the falls before her eyes. Must be an awful thing to watch."

"That's a fascinating metaphor for death – a waterfall," Amber mused. "I certainly don't feel very close to the edge."

"No, you're still young enough to think the falls are a long way off – you can't even hear the thunder approaching. And you're not old enough yet to find some comfort in death, like me. Don't rush it."

Amber shrugged into her winter jacket. "I see why people like to talk to you, Maggie," she said. "You've got an interesting perspective on life."

"Thanks. Stop by my office anytime," I offered, as she headed for the shed. "I'm usually in on Wednesday and Thursday afternoons. Of course, the rest of the time my office is available for romantic rendez-vous!" I called after her.

She poked her head back around the corner. "Oh, my God! I'm so embarrassed!" she exclaimed, putting her mittened hands to her face.

I winked. "Sorry. Couldn't resist! He's a good man – don't lose him!"

Doctor Bart arrived at Miss Hastings' house just as Amber was departing. He was driving his beat-up truck, per usual. He let himself into the shed familiarly. I met him in the mudroom, where he paused to doff his coat, scarf and cap. He stooped to say a few words to Miss Hastings' pet chicken, Matilda.

"Has anybody given her fresh food and water?" he asked, rising up. His white freckled face was grave, also per usual.

"'Hello, Aunt Maggie. Nice to see you,'" I twitted him.

Doctor Bart, twenty-nine, was the son of my dear childhood friend Jane Lawson from Albion. He worked out of the clinic in Unity, and had been Miss Hastings' family doctor since her last physician, old Dr. Wilson, had gone over the falls. When he was a baby, I used to change his diapers; therefore, I probably took more liberties with him than I should have. He was one of those redheads so homely he's adorable. I knew he was uncomfortable with his complexion, however, and would prefer the dark good looks of Bruce Gilpin or Ryan MacDonald.

His brick-colored curls had been smashed down by his tweed driving cap, and he ran his capable fingers through his hair now, attempting to liberate them. "Well?" he continued, ignoring my scold.

"I'm glad you're so concerned with the chicken," I replied, a bit tartly.

"C'mon Aunt Maggie, you know why I'm here. I just asked a question, that's all."

"OK, OK, I'll take care of the bird in a minute," I promised.

We moved into the kitchen. "How is she?" he asked, hoisting his black bag up onto the back of a chair. "I stopped in a couple of days ago, and she was fine. Maybe a bit down in the dumps, but her pulse was strong and her lungs were clear."

"Miss Hastings hasn't been herself since Ma Jean died, Metcalf."

He winced. His given name was Metcalf Bartholomew Lawson, an appellation of which he was not fond. Jane's maiden name was "Metcalf," an old English name to which she was attached. "Everybody calls me 'Bart', now," he pointed out.

"I see," I replied, in that tone of voice which implies that a person doesn't see at all.

Doctor Bart started for the bedroom, but hesitated in the doorway. "How's Nellie?" he inquired, momentarily abandoning his professional tone. "Is she coming home for winter break?"

"I hope so. But I never know with Nellie. She has a mind of her own. She might take off for the south of France, if someone suggests it, and they have the money to pay for it, of course." He was unmarried, and had a crush on my daughter, who was undeniably lovely. Unfortunately, Nellie rarely gave him the time of day. I knew he was probably too good for her. At this stage in Nellie's life she was selfish and self-centered; I hoped it was because she was young – she was still in college – not because she was like her father. But a mother couldn't ask for a better son-in-law than Doctor Bart. I made a mental note to be nicer to him.

"Maybe I'll stop in if she comes home," he suggested. "If you don't think she'll mind?"

"Drop in anytime, Metcalf—Bart," I amended hastily. "She'd love to see you." I crossed my fingers behind my back as I lied.

This time he didn't flinch. Instead, he hit me where it hurt. "By the way, Aunt Maggie, when was your last physical?"

I grimaced. I didn't like doctors, and he knew it.

He smiled, enjoying his *coup de maître*. "Make the appointment," he ordered, "or I'll make one for you."

I sighed. "Right."

He exited to his patient, satisfied that he'd done his good deed for the day; however, he'd ruined mine. Physicians – well-meaning or otherwise – always had a way of making me hear that approaching thunder of the falls.

Chapter 22

· · · · · · ·

"1 Didn't Think Girls Did That Anymore!"

Bruce was unhappy that morning, not with life, but with himself. He had been so busy getting the garage operational and the canning factory project up and running, that he hadn't paid enough attention to his sweetheart. Amber had been hurting, and he hadn't known anything about it! He who loved her better than anyone else in the world, had failed to notice over the past few weeks her sad eyes, drooping shoulders and lackluster smiles.

In addition, his pride was wounded because the person who had provided comfort for Amber was not himself but was the man he'd once suspected of desiring her affections. He wasn't afraid of Ryan MacDonald, now. He was too much assured of Amber's love for that. But he was afraid, after listening to the other man quote poetry last night, that he himself might lack something she needed.

They were so different – he and she! She was educated, professional, a part of the new world of the 21st century in a way he would never be. He was a small-town boy, a soldier, a family man who never had the opportunity to party or play or try all the different electronic toys and gadgets the world offered up these days. Maybe he was not enough for her? Maybe he would never be enough for her?

Some of these thoughts were passing through his head as he deftly maneuvered his pickup through the snow and slush on the Russell Hill Road, anxious to reach her house and clasp her to his chest once again. He had meant to come earlier in the morning; however, fate had intervened – as usual – in the form of a panicked phone call from Asa. The sander on one of the plow trucks wasn't working, and his mechanical skills were required immediately. Two hours later, the sander was back on the road, and Bruce was on his way to see Amber.

Thus was his state of his mind when he ran into her walking back from Miss Hastings' house, head down, apparently lost in somber reflections of her own. He pulled over, and rolled down his window. The precipitation had tapered off; nevertheless fat snowflakes covered her coat and hat with melting snow. "Hop in," he said, "and I'll give you a lift home." They were at the end of her driveway, and his words were meant as a joke.

But she, who had just left a frail and fragile Miss Hastings in her bed, failed to catch his humor. "We're already at the mailbox," she pointed out. "Did you hear about Miss Hastings?" she added, shivering. A finger of liquid ice had slid down her neck.

"No! What's up?"

In less than a minute, she was in his arms, within the warm comfort of the cab of the truck. Once she'd told him about Miss Hastings, he'd ordered her to stay put, pulled the pickup over to the side of the road and turned on his four-way flashers. Then he leaped out, scooped her up and climbed back inside. He brushed off the melting snow, then unfastened her winter coat and managed to get his arms around her slender waist. He hugged her. "Ahh! I wish I'd come sooner! Then you wouldn't have found Miss Hastings by yourself."

Amber rested her cold cheek against his shoulder. "Thank God she wasn't dead!" She shuddered at the thought. "I'm too young to discover dead bodies. I still think people should live forever!"

"I hope you live forever, Sweets! Or at least outlive me," he declared. "I don't know what I would do without you."

He took off her damp mittens, and briskly rubbed her cold hands. "And please! please tell me when anything is bothering you next time. I want to know! I'm awful numb sometimes, so if anything is wrong, you might have to just come right out and tell me. But my number one job is to help carry your burdens. You're the most important thing in my life, Sweets, and I want you to know it."

Her blue eyes glowed with gratitude and feminine adoration. "Thank you, thank you! I needed to hear that!"

His lips claimed hers; she met his demands eagerly. He kissed her slowly, sensuously, moving down from her neck to her collar bone. She sighed with ecstasy. The words "my cup runneth over" ran through her mind. She lazily fondled the tips of his ears. "I love your ears," she murmured.

He pulled back, taking the opportunity to nibble the tip of her nose. "My ears?"

"They're so cute – I can't resist them! It's the first thing I noticed when you sat next to me on the bus."

He feigned hurt. "Not my handsome good looks?"

"Your ears are part of your handsome good looks, Love," she pronounced, running her fingers through his short brown hair. "You'd be quite average-looking without them."

"Thanks a lot!"

She lifted his capable hand, and rested it against her throbbing breast. "I'd still love you," she said, softly, "no matter what you looked like."

His hand squeezed her breast possessively, painfully. A low moan escaped her. His lips became insistent, and she surrendered to their demands. His breathing was now harsh and ragged, and the sounds of his heightened desire added to the exquisiteness of her pleasure. He loved her! He wanted her!

The snowplow lumbered past the parked truck, sending shards of snow and slush pelleting against the side of the pickup. The driver honked loudly, several times. They broke apart, laughing.

"Ha, ha, that will be all over town by this afternoon!"

"I don't care in the least!"

"Good timing, too – I was getting pretty close to ravaging you."

She snuggled back against his chest. He stroked her hair. In her state of perfect contentment, she couldn't help but feel sorry for the elderly lady whose house she had just left. "How sad Miss Hastings never married! I wonder why?" she puzzled.

"My Mom said there was a man once, when she was very young."

"Did he dump her?"

"I don't think so; I think he died."

"She must have loved him very much … she's such an amazing woman, I'm sure she had plenty of other opportunities to get married."

"I meant to stop in and see her yesterday, but something came up," he berated himself. "Something always seems to come up!"

"You couldn't know – no one knew how she was feeling. We've all been so busy; we haven't had time to check on her like we should. Even my mother has only seen her once since the funeral."

"Should we go back there now?"

"No, no; somebody came in when I was leaving; I think it was the doctor."

"Doctor Bart? Did he have red hair?"

"I think so, yes."

He nodded, satisfied. "She's in good hands, then."

She turned around so that she was facing front, leaning back against his muscular chest. She contemplated the magnificent rural vista visible through the wet windshield. The fresh snow sparkled like blue diamonds. Chickadees flitted cheerfully from one side of the road to the other. The sky was the blue-green color of Maine tourmalines, which beautiful gems Amber had learned to love.

While they were thus reposing, I exited Miss Hastings' driveway, and motored past. I beeped and waved.

Amber felt her cheeks warming. "Oh, boy," she said. "That was embarrassing! Today was the first time I've been alone with Maggie since … well, since, you know."

"What? Did she scold you for our little office escapade?"

"No, no. She laughed it off. It was just awkward for me, that's all."

"You're pretty sensitive about that kind of stuff! Sometimes I'd swear you were a virgin," he joked.

Her heart began to pound, but she said nothing.

"Amber," he continued, in a questioning tone of voice, "you're not, I mean, …" he broke off awkwardly.

Still, she kept silent.

"Jesus!" he exclaimed. He tightened his grip on her elbows, and hoisted her around so he could see her face.

A glorious light shone forth from her eyes. She nodded, shyly. "I've been waiting," she whispered, lightly resting her fingertips against the curve of his chin, "for you."

The heat of desire surged through his loins. He groaned, and clutched her to his chest, shifting uncomfortably. He slammed his right palm against the hard steering wheel.

"Careful," she said, "don't break your truck!"

Her little attempt at defusing the situation worked, and in a few moments he felt his heartbeat return to normal, his blood flow subsiding. "I had no idea, Sweets! Why didn't you tell me?"

"What was I going to say – Oh, by the way, Leonard Bruce Gilpin, I've been waiting all my life for you to come along, and, well, you know. Not likely!"

"You could have given me a heads up!"

"I just did," she pointed out.

"Ha, ha – I guess you did!" His dropped a kiss on the top of her head. He felt almost overcome by a new sense of responsibility toward her, intermingled with increased respect. "I don't know what to say. I wasn't expecting it, obviously."

"Obviously!"

"I didn't think girls did that anymore!"

"It's coming back into style. I'm not so special."

With his free arm, he lifted her hand and kissed her tapered fingertips one by one. "Ahh, but you are special – you're very, very special – to me!" His throat constricted. "I love you, Amber Johnson," he said, gruffly.

Tears of joy filled her eyes. "I love you, Bruce Gilpin!" she cried. His lips claimed hers even before the exhale of her cry was complete. She felt him pulling her spirit into his lungs, into a sacred world where she was defended against the cruelties of corporeal existence. Eternity seemed within her grasp, like low-hanging fruit on an apple tree. She reached out to pluck the fruit—completely oblivious of the camouflaged serpent slithering down around the trunk of the tree!

Chapter 23
. . . .
Return of the Non-Native

The Emily Dickinson letters were soon authenticated by several experts, and the items were then listed for sale in the upcoming James Julia auction. Initial publicity initiated by the auction house created a sensation among museums, scholars, collectors, and devotees of the Amherst poet. Ryan, who was acting as the legal representative for both Bruce and the Ladies Auxiliary, shared the news with the little group of friends at the next meeting of the Sovereign museum project. The meeting was once again held at his cabin as Miss Hastings was still not well enough to attend.

"The experts say that the letters were absolutely written by Emily Dickinson," Ryan apprised them. "Not that any of us had much doubt."

"I knew it!" exclaimed Amber, clapping her hands. She was perched on the comfy couch, this time feeling a sense of belonging, almost the polar opposite of her emotions at their last meeting. Contributing to her metamorphosis was the fact that her semester had ended, and all of her papers and finals had been completed on time. "I can't believe I actually held in my hands something written by Emily Dickinson! What a gift!"

"The James Julia people are putting the Dickinson letters on the cover of their February catalog," Ryan continued. "Mark the date on your calendars—the auction is expected to be quite the event! They put the word out yesterday in the newspapers, and on Facebook and Twitter, and they've already had hundreds of calls and emails from around the world."

"That's fabulous," said Trudy. "Do we know anything more about their history?"

Ryan, who had met several times with the auction house representatives, was full of information. "Apparently, Ann Edwards was a student at Amherst Academy for several years with the young Emily Dickinson. When Ann's family moved to Sovereign, the girls exchanged letters until

Ann's early death a few years later," he explained. "In total, Emily wrote fourteen letters to Ann."

"She was a prolific letter writer," Amber interjected. "Oops, sorry, Ryan!" She was unable to repress her excitement, longing to share her personal knowledge of the poet whom she'd loved and studied for years.

"No problem," he demurred. "Go ahead."

"Emily wrote hundreds – maybe thousands – of letters in her life," Amber continued, eagerly. "She was almost a recluse at the end of her life – would you believe, she only talked to visitors from behind a closed door? But she corresponded with everybody who was anybody, just as though she went out and about everywhere! Oh, I wish I could have known her! How I would have loved to have her write a letter to me!"

"It seems like you do know her," Trudy pointed out. "She was writing to you, in her poetry, wasn't she?"

Amber nodded. "Sometimes I *do* get the feeling from Emily's poems that she's speaking directly to me. She has a way of capturing what I'm feeling – when I don't even know myself what I'm feeling! – and sharing that emotion back with me so that I can see it. Only instead of words, she paints a picture, which is much easier for me to comprehend."

"We women sometimes think more in images rather than words," Trudy agreed. "English doesn't seem to be our first language, does it?"

"Exactly!"

Ryan regarded Trudy with open admiration. She blushed. "Not that I'm any kind of an expert," she amended.

"Seems like you know a lot more than you give yourself credit for," Ryan said. "You've given voice to something about women that I've suspected for years."

Trudy appeared pleased by his praise. Amber wondered if her friend was finally warming to the handsome attorney? She was glad that the museum project had given the two an opportunity to get to know each other better.

"Strange bird," Bruce allowed, speaking of Emily Dickinson. He was only beginning to fathom the significance of the discovery in the loft. "I never would have known anything about her if it wasn't for you, Sweets! Those letters would have gone to the trash heap, for sure."

Amber shuddered. "Don't even say that!"

"It does make you wonder how many other important historical artifacts are lost every year," added Trudy, gently rocking in the Windsor rocker. She was thinking of her own recent discoveries at the dilapidated canning factory, including the hand-written receipts signed by her ancestors for the purchase of their sweet corn. "Every time I see the contents of an old family homestead in Sovereign being cleaned out, I wonder what's going to happen to all those old family photos and letters."

"Just go to the Burnham auction on Sunday and you'll see what happens to 'em," Bruce said. He shook his head. "Sometimes it's pretty sad!"

"I saw the transcriptions of Emily's letters, too," Ryan continued. "The James Julia people put them on their website so that anyone can go read them for themselves. The letters are very personal and sweet. She was still young when she wrote them, about sixteen, and they were written before Emily got into that esoteric, enigmatic literary style for which her later letters are known."

"You still think those fourteen little pieces of paper are gonna fetch enough to put a new roof on the old corn shop, MacDonald?" Bruce queried, somewhat jokingly.

"A new roof, new paint, new windows – as you would say, Gilpin, the whole she-bang! They're auctioning off the letters individually, of course, but the combined estimate – the low estimate just of the letters, mind you – is $125,000."

Bruce whistled. "I guess that'll get us a new roof!"

"But that's not all. Don't forget the rare copy of the Amherst Academy school publication *Forest Leaves*. Actually it's beyond rare; it's irreplaceable, as Amber so correctly surmised. It's the only copy of *Forest Leaves* known to exist. And there's something else I've been waiting to tell you all, especially you, Amber."

"Tell us!" she begged.

"There's also a short prose piece written by the young Emily in it!"

Amber was floored. "Oh, my God – I had no idea!" she cried. "That's fabulous!"

"As a result, the appraisers have had more difficulty valuing the *Forest Leaves*, but they've placed an estimate of $75,000-$100,000 on it. The James Julia people calculate that everything together will net somewhere between $200,000-$250,000, a little higher than their original estimate, thanks to the copy of *Forest Leaves*. Your share of that Gilpin will be $100,000 or more. The Ladies Auxiliary will get the other half, of course."

Bruce appeared stunned. "Go figure!" he said, shaking his head. "All that money for pieces of paper! If they're right, there's no end to what we can do with the canning factory!"

Amber couldn't contain her joy any longer. She hopped up off the couch, flew to Bruce and threw her arms around his bare neck. Through a blur of tears, she saw that his brown eyes had watered up, as well.

Oblivious of the others, he snaked his arm possessively around her slim waist, and pulled her onto his lap. "This is all because of you," he whispered, into her ear. His voice trembled with emotion. "If you hadn't invited me to sit next to you on the bus, Sweets, just think how different our lives would be!"

She squeezed his hand, unable to find words to express her felicity.

"Heads up, though, Gilpin," Ryan warned. "You'll be getting some calls from the press, not just the local press, either, the national and maybe even international press. The James Julia people envision generating as much publicity as they can from the Dickinson ephemera, and they think that you being a Maine National Guardsman returned from the war in Afghanistan lends additional cachet to the story."

Bruce grinned. "I only half understood what you just said, MacDonald."

"Heads up, the Huns are coming," Ryan elucidated. They all four laughed.

The forewarning came just in time. The next day Bruce received requests for interviews from three local Maine television stations, and two national morning news programs. Two radio stations in Massachusetts asked him to appear on call-in programs, and Amherst College, owner of the Emily Dickinson museum, dispatched representatives to view the collection, and to speak with Bruce in person about the discovery, hoping, no doubt, that more Dickinson items might be forthcoming from the carriage shed.

Bruce, whose mechanics shop had just received the necessary approvals from the state, arranged to meet all the interviewers at his newly-opened garage. Interviewed in the old carriage shed wearing his Maine Army Guard sweatshirt, he and the Dickinson letters made a compelling story. "I guess I got my fifteen minutes of fame and then some," he joked to Amber, at the end of a busy week of publicity.

Christmas Eve arrived in Sovereign with a blistering Nor'easter, burying the little town and its residents in a winter wonderland. On

Christmas Day, after completing her chores, Amber thoughtfully examined the fresh, white world outside the kitchen window, the aftereffect of the snowstorm. She concluded that the old homestead was a living embodiment of a Currier and Ives winter scene. The only thing lacking was a sleigh, with its jingling sleigh bells and team of horses—and that she was looking forward to at the Sovereign sleighing rally come mid-January!

She was sitting at the kitchen table with her mother, who was happily knitting. The knitting needles *clicked* comfortingly. On cold days, Rebecca preferred to work next to the warmth of the kitchen woodstove. Wendell was out plowing the driveway, and would shortly be reconnoitering the neighborhoods. A snowstorm in any small town in Maine always brings out the men in plow trucks, who appear to drive around aimlessly yet with a renewed sense of purpose.

"I'm so happy we came to Sovereign!" Amber blurted out, overcome with a rush of emotion.

Rebecca stopped her knitting, and looked over at her daughter fondly. "Me too," she agreed. "I can't imagine living anyplace else!"

Mother and daughter had decorated the interior of the old homestead with pine and balsam boughs, and the fresh astringent scent now mingled with that of the twenty-pound turkey already roasting in the oven. That afternoon the little family group was taking Christmas dinner – with dessert and all the fixings – up to Miss Hastings' house. Bruce and Gray, and Ryan would be joining them for dinner at 1 p.m. The general store was closed for the day, and Maude and Ralph were sharing their Christmas dinner with Peter over at Oaknole.

"Do you think we should have invited Maggie to dinner?" Rebecca worried aloud, on the short drive up to the retired music teacher's house. "I hope she's not by herself down there!"

Amber repositioned the hot boxful of fragrant yeast rolls and pies that was balanced in her lap. "Nellie came home from New York," she replied. "That's what Bruce said, anyway. She's only here with her Mom for a day or two, though."

"Nellie is such a lovely girl! But she doesn't look much like her mother, does she?"

"'Tain't very flatterin' to Maggie," said Wendell, who was driving. "Better not let her hear you say thet!"

"Oh, dear! I didn't mean it like it sounded!"

Modest gifts had been exchanged at the old Russell homestead on Christmas Eve. Amber had received a new hand-knitted cap and matching scarf from her mother, and an old multi-tooled jackknife from Wendell. The rest of the gifts were in the car, to be brought out and exchanged after the Christmas dinner was devoured. Bruce surprised Amber with a framed montage of copies of some of the Emily Dickinson letters, which he had put together with the help of a James Julia representative and a local frame shop.

"It's beautiful!" Amber cried, upon opening her gift. She carefully examined each letter, wallowing in a sense of timelessness and wonder. "This is the best present anyone's ever given me!" The moment the words left her mouth, she recalled everything her mother had done for her over the years, and regretted her hasty outburst. "Oops, sorry, Mom!"

Rebecca laughed. "Don't apologize! I know I can't compete with Emily Dickinson!"

Amber had given Bruce a solar-powered welding helmet, which utilitarian item he had put on his Christmas wish list. But after opening his gift to her, she felt as though she should have been much more creative and personal in her gift to him. "I'm sorry my gift is so boring!" she apologized.

"Hey, it's just what I wanted, Sweets," he said, cheerfully. "Now I can safely do my welding!"

She was sitting next to him, in a straight-back chair beside the window. He leaned over and kissed her full on the lips in front of the others, taking her by surprise. Amber felt herself blushing, but she eagerly returned his kiss. She was not embarrassed by their love!

"That's what I really wanted for Christmas!" he proclaimed, his brown eyes twinkling.

On January 2nd, Ma Jean's Restaurant reopened for business. Around 6:30 a.m., a horde of hungry Old Farts descended upon the little place, clamoring for bacon and eggs, toast, home fries and hot coffee. Rebecca and Maude were ready for their guests; and the sound of cheerful chomping and the scent of bacon frying soon filled the quaint eatery. The walls had received a fresh coat of yellow paint, and the cushioned red booths and matching bar stools had been cleaned and repaired. The old oak floor was sanded and varnished, ready to receive the next crop of scuff marks and dents. The restaurant looked fresh and neat, yet maintained the comfortable feel and the home-cooked menu that had made Ma Jean's legendary.

Bruce's garage was open for business as well, offering a much-needed service to the community. Instead of driving to Waterville or Bangor for repairs, the locals now brought their vehicles to him. In a shrewd marketing move, Bruce had decided to offer all his customers, regardless of the size of their bill, a coupon for a free piece of pie and cup of coffee at the restaurant next door. "It's a win-win for all of us," he explained to Amber. "They get pie and coffee, our mothers get a customer, and I get 'em out of my hair!"

Amber shook her head with bemused wonder. "You never cease to amaze me, Bruce Gilpin!" she declared.

He grasped her hand, and pulled her close for an embrace. "That's why ya love me, isn't it, Sweets?!" he bragged.

She tilted her head upward, awaiting his kiss, which was in truth the only answer he wanted in reply.

On Friday, just when Bruce was about to close up shop, a middle-aged woman entered his work area through the side door from the front office. She was chunky and nondescript, a washed-out blonde with a bloated face and watery blue eyes. Not recognizing her as a local, Bruce assumed she was someone from the city passing through, probably experiencing car trouble. He wiped his greasy hands on a rag, and politely approached her.

"Can I help you?" he asked, congenially.

She examined his handsome face briefly, and then offered up a bitter laugh. "How embarrassing! You don't even recognize me!"

Something in the timbre of her voice did sound familiar. He refocused on her eyes, which carried with them signs of a shared intimacy. Her face seemed vaguely haunting, but he still couldn't place her. She smelled like cheap perfume and cigarette smoke. Suddenly, everything clicked into place in his head. "Sheila!" he uttered, taking a step back.

She pulled her beige, waist-length parka closer around her turgid belly in a defensive fashion. "Finally! I was beginning to think I had the wrong husband." She critically surveyed his modest two-bay work area. "Quite a come down from your job at General Conglomeration in Bangor, isn't it?"

Bruce hadn't heard from his ex-wife in several years, and hadn't seen her in at least a decade. Since then, the world had obviously not been kind to Sheila. When she had first arrived in Sovereign, as a transplant from New Hampshire, she'd been a comely blonde-haired, blue-eyed teenager. All the youths at Common Hill High School had been infatuated with her. But it was with Bruce Gilpin that she'd quickly shared her favors. Now, she was an overweight, middle-aged frump, who appeared closer to fifty than the thirty-four years that he knew her to be. "What are you doing here, Sheila?" he asked, warily.

"Thanks for the welcome," she said. She glanced around the garage again, as if seeking reassurance that they were alone. "Where's Gray?"

"At home, with his grandparents."

She feigned displeasure. "The kid's not living with you?"

"If you wrote to him once in a while you'd know that," Bruce replied, quietly.

"Yeah, I know, I know! I'm a terrible mother. Maude never lets me forget that, even after all these years. Did you see what she wrote when she sent me his last report card?!"

A high-pitched wail from the shop office interrupted their conversation. "What's that!?" Bruce tossed the dirty rag onto the floor, and quickly crossed to the tiny office.

Sheila followed, hard on his heels. "Don't freak out, Bruce, it's just Olivia!"

Bruce threw open the door, and saw a second-hand baby carrier perched precariously in one of the restored antique chairs that he had placed into service in his office. He stepped to the chair, and examined the contents of the carrier. The roly-poly infant inside took one look at the unfamiliar face and shrieked even louder. Her fat arms flailed helplessly and her little pink fingers trembled with frustration and anger.

"Now you've done it," Sheila berated him. "You've scared her. Stop it, Olivia! You're perfectly fine." She collected the screaming child from the carrier and tossed the infant up onto her shoulder. She patted the baby's back, and joggled it up and down. The infant stopped its shrieking, and slurped in a lungful of air.

"Yikes! I didn't know you had another one!" Bruce grasped the top of the chair for support. Another baby! This would be Sheila's third child – and he knew for a fact that she had left her first two children with their respective fathers. "Where's her Dad? Still in the car?"

He quickly calculated that his ex-wife and her current partner must be passing through Sovereign, and had made an obligatory stop to see

Gray. He knew that Sheila had been married at least once since they were divorced thirteen years ago; however, he didn't know whether she was married to her current flame or not, or even in which state they were living. His mother was the one who kept the communication going between the little broken family. Much as Maude disliked Sheila, she believed that her grandson should have some kind of relationship with his mother. Maude knew that if she didn't instigate the communication with Sheila, Gray would never hear from her.

"Probably home in front of the TV set, drinking a beer," Sheila replied. A sullen expression came over her face. "He threw me out."

"What! With a new baby?!"

She nodded piteously. "Told me to take Olivia and go." Her blue eyes filled with alligator tears. "I didn't know where to go or what to do," she whined. "My parents are dead, and Taylor said after the last time he won't take me back." Taylor was her second husband.

A sick feeling began to form in the pit of Bruce's stomach. His ex-wife was alone, defenseless, with a new baby in tow. What was his responsibility to her now? Did he still owe her something, even after her abandonment of them all those years ago? Regardless of what she had done to them – to him and Gray – she was still the boy's mother!

"Have you got any money?" he asked. He was attempting to gauge the truth of the situation, but mostly he was stalling so he could have time to think. He kept some cash in a box in his desk drawer, and now he moved around in back of his desk to retrieve it.

"About enough to get a pack of smokes. He cut off my credit cards—the jerk! And I'm almost out of gas."

Bruce pulled open the drawer and retrieved the metal box. He opened the lid and took out two $50 bills. "Here, take this," he said, holding the cash out to her.

She shifted the infant higher up on her shoulder, and plucked the folded bills from his outstretched hand. She stuffed them into her jacket pocket. "Thanks, that'll get me the gas and the smokes, anyway. Do you mind if I crash with you for a while?"

Taken aback, he stared at her. "Jesus, Sheila! You divorced me!"

"I know, I know," she pleaded. "But I've got no place to go and a hundred bucks isn't going to take me very far! I won't stay long – I promise! Just until I get my act together. Besides, it'll give me a chance to see Gray again," she added, almost as an afterthought.

He groaned, momentarily covering his face with his hand. How could this be happening to him?!

A bellicose expression appeared on her face. "What, have you got some young thing with you, now?"

The door to his office swung open, and Amber stepped eagerly inside. She stamped the snow off her boots onto the welcome mat. She spotted Sheila and the baby, and gave Bruce a rueful smile. "Oops, sorry, Love!" she apologized, closing the door behind her. "Don't let me interrupt – I'll just wait upstairs!"

The infant sneezed, and Amber bent closer to make a few cooing noises near the fat face of the cross-grained child. "What a cutie!" she said. She straightened up and offered the other woman a bright smile. "Hi, I'm Amber Johnson," she said. She pulled off her mitten and held out her slender hand. "I don't think we've met?"

Sheila ignored the outstretched hand. "Obviously not," she replied, in a snarky tone of voice. "I'm Sheila Gilpin – Bruce's wife."

Chapter 24
. . . .
"Is It Supposed to Look Like That?!"

Before we correct Sheila's outright lie, we must leave our troubled trio momentarily and turn our attention to Scotch Broom Acres, where an even more pressing predicament was brewing. Ryan, Rebecca and Maude had driven past Trudy and Leland's neat red and white farmstead on their way to Shirley Palmer's place, where the ladies were to sign the official lease for Ma Jean's Restaurant, when Maude suddenly remembered she was out of butter. "Stop just a moment, please, Sweetie," Maude directed Ryan. "I need some butter."

Ryan good-naturedly stopped and backed up his black sedan. He pulled into the gravel drive and parked in front of the red banked barn. "So, this is where Trudy lives?" he asked, glancing around curiously. He had become increasingly intrigued by the reserved young woman over the past two months. Trudy's comments and remarks at the museum meetings were always thoughtful, intelligent and sincere. Occasionally, when speaking to the group, her face became quite animated and her sparkling gray eyes hinted at an emotional depth that Ryan decided he would definitely like to fathom. He perceived – or thought he had perceived – faint signs that might suggest she was warming to him.

"This is it – Scotch Broom Acres," Maude replied. She fumbled with her purse, removed some cash, and popped open the front passenger door. "I won't be but a minute."

"I'll come too," Ryan replied. He switched off the car's engine. "I'd like to look around." He pulled himself out of the vehicle, and stretched his long legs.

"Me too," said Rebecca, letting herself out of the back seat.

Despite the fact that it was January, the afternoon sun felt warm and pleasant against their faces. Ryan examined the unpretentious white antique Cape. The red front door was decorated with a balsam Christmas wreath, adorned with a Scotch-plaid bow. The tail end of the ribbon fluttered lazily in the refreshing southerly breeze. A tantalizing glimpse of frilly white curtains hinted at a very feminine hand at work inside the house. To Ryan's citified eyes, the Gorse homestead appeared charming and sweet.

The sliding barn doors had been left open about eight feet, allowing the afternoon sun to warm the inside of the barn. Maude stepped up inside. "Trudy usually has some butter in a fridge here," she said over her shoulder to the other two. They followed her lead into the barn.

Ryan blinked, as his eyes adjusted to the light. The scent of sweet hay filled his nostrils, and interesting pastoral images popped into his head. He surveyed the barn, noting the square hay bales neatly stacked in the upper lofts, and the clean hand tools hanging methodically in their places. *So much can be learned of a woman's true nature simply by taking an announced, impromptu stroll through her house, yard and gardens! And in this case, her barn! My grandmother in Winslow never left her house with dirty dishes in her sink. She was always afraid that she would receive an unannounced visitor while she was gone or that she would drop dead and be discovered to have left her housework undone.*

"Where's Trudy?" Ryan asked, turning around on an expensively booted heel.

Maude had found the fridge, and she and Rebecca were Ohh-ing and Ahh-ing over the variety of Trudy's hand-made butter and homemade Greek yogurt. "Still at school, Sweetie," she replied, absently. "I need six of the one-pounders, but that's all she's got. Do you think I should take them all?" she worriedly inquired of Rebecca.

"Oh, dear! Perhaps you shouldn't clean her out. We've only got a pound or two left at our place, and it's almost the weekend! I'm going to get some yogurt while I'm here."

Ryan peered over the ladies' heads into the old-fashioned fridge, where he saw various sizes of alabaster bundles of butter and quart-sized containers of yogurt. The packages were all decorated with pretty yellow stickers that proclaimed they were proudly made by hand in small batches at Scotch Broom Acres. Trudy's logo featured the quaint image of an old-fashioned plant broom – *gorse* being the common name of a dense evergreen shrub found in Scotland, closely related to its cousin *Scotch broom*. "How often does she make the butter?" he asked.

Maude, having grown up at Oaknole, was the resident expert. "Once or twice a week, depending upon the milk production. She uses the cream for her butter, of course, and the milk for the yogurt. Leland's sow gets the whey."

"I see," Ryan said, straightening up. But he didn't see at all. He didn't know anything about cows or even what whey was. But he was too embarrassed to ask Maude for further particulars, thus exposing his ignorance.

He abandoned the ladies to their butter quandary, and moved off in search of more clues that might help him understand the woman who was carefully keeping her heart at arm's length from him. He poked his head inside the tie-up, where his eyes were immediately met by three sets of dusky, long-lashed orbs staring back at him. As he stepped across the threshold, Trudy's prized Jerseys regarded his approach skeptically. The tail closest to him swished like a whip, and he jerked back, afraid of soiling his jacket.

Ryan had never been in close contact with a cow before, and he was somewhat taken aback by the intelligence revealed in their limpid black eyes. Trudy's Jerseys were much smaller than he'd expected them to be. He'd only ever seen their bigger-framed cousins, the black-and-white Holsteins, from a distant field. The animals were delicate-looking, with soft, fawn-colored skin and black faces. "Hello girls," he said.

One of the cows offered up a questioning *moo*, perhaps hoping he was bringing an offering of grain. Ryan held out his bare hand for her to sniff, and as he did so he heard an unnerving moan coming from the end of the tie-up. The pathetic sound chilled his heart and captured his attention. He peered down the window-lined barn, and spied a fourth cow, pacing restlessly inside a small stall in the north corner.

Ryan hesitated. His eyes and nose had noted the odorous brown islands of fresh cow manure splattered down the gangway. The afflicted animal moaned again, however, and unable to restrain his curiosity, he carefully maneuvered down the walkway, avoiding the islands, to the stall at the far end of the tie-up. The three other cows swung their heads around in unison to follow his progress.

Even to Ryan's ignorant eyes, this lone cow appeared to be experiencing some sort of distress. He rested his forearms on the top of the stall, and leaned forward, observing as she first lay down, then stood up, then lay down again, almost oblivious to her visitor. While Ryan kept watch, a glistening yellowish-whitish object protruded from her rear end, only to quickly disappear back inside. The cow released another teeth-clenching moan, and the protruding object appeared in view again, this time rising upward several inches as though straining to reach the low-hanging, whitewashed ceiling.

It was the strangest, most repugnant thing Ryan had ever seen, and he felt slightly nauseated. The pointed tip of the protrusion was the color of aged ivory and the rest of the thing was covered with a bloody blue film. He thought of a broken bone he had once seen on the football field in high school, and knew that something was wrong.

He heard a step behind him, and twisted around to see Maude and Rebecca approaching in search of him. "Is it supposed to look like that?!" he appealed to Maude.

Maude glimpsed the partially-exposed calf's leg, and uttered a little shriek. "Here, take this!" she said, roughly pushing the four pounds of butter into Rebecca's unwitting arms. "Let me see!"

Despite her butterball figure, Maude was always quick on her feet. In less than a minute, the seventy-one-year-old was inside the stall, examining the afflicted cow. She was wearing a down coat over her pretty print dress, nylons and winter boots, and now unfastened her jacket, in preparation for battle. "It's a breech!" she announced, looking Ryan squarely in the face. "You'll have to deliver it."

"Me?!" he choked. The horror of Maude's suggestion caught him by surprise, and he momentarily became overly conscious of his breathing. "I don't know anything about cows—I don't even know what you mean by a 'breech'!" he gasped.

"Backwards," Maude elucidated. "The calf is coming out backwards. And one of the legs is stuck. Now, take a deep breath – steady yourself," she ordered. Maude knew that agitated humans only served to agitate cows, and she didn't want to upset either the cow or the attorney further.

"Oh, dear!" cried Rebecca, clutching her quart of yogurt and the cold packages of butter to her chest. "The poor thing!"

Maude quickly assumed her captain-on-deck sensibility that was so successful at the church breakfasts. "I'll tell you both exactly what to do, and how I want you to do it," she stated. "If you follow my directions, everything will be fine. Understood?"

Rebecca and Ryan nodded as obediently as five-year-olds.

"Rebecca, put those things in the car, then go get a pail of hot water and some dish towels from the house. Get some soap, too, just in case I can't find the disinfectant." She trained her eyes onto the attorney's face. "Get yourself ready to deliver this calf, young man. Take off that coat, and roll up your shirt sleeves."

"But I ... I can't deliver a calf?!" he stammered, a near comical expression on his handsome face.

"You can, and you will." To Maude, in her take-charge demeanor, he was no longer 'Sweetie' but a chary farmhand who would most probably require strict supervision, explicit instructions and lots of encouragement. "I'll tell you what to do, step by step – I've had plenty of experience. I'd do it myself, only I'm just not strong enough. Now, you get yourself ready while I find the calving chains and the disinfectant."

Maude doffed her jacket and draped it over the far side of the stall. The silk dress she was wearing was one of her favorites; however, it must be sacrificed. Her winter jacket was more expensive than the dress, plus she was already feeling the heat of the upcoming battle. She eyed Ryan again, who had remained unmoved. "Do as I said – take off that useless coat and roll up those sleeves!" She marched off down the aisle to procure the necessary birthing supplies.

Almost before he knew what was happening, Ryan found himself alongside Maude in the stall with the restless cow. Rebecca had returned with a pail of hot water into which Maude had liberally splashed the disinfectant she'd found neatly shelved in Trudy's supply room. Ryan's hands had been swished in the orange antiseptic, and he was holding them up as ordered to drip dry.

The cow moaned again, and the one lone leg protruded even further, signaling, as Maude knew, that the other leg was trapped inside, hindering the calf's birth. She could tell by the way the toe pointed that it was a breech birth.

Maude tossed a dish towel into the pail and dipped her own fat hands into the orange water. She squeezed the excess water from the towel, and used the cloth to wash down the cow's dirty posterior. "You need to be as clean and as quick as possible," she instructed her wide-eyed pupil. "But you also need to be careful. You don't want to tear her. Do you understand?"

"Yes, I think so," Ryan said, heart in his throat. "What ... what do I do?"

"You're going to put your arm inside her birth canal, find the stuck leg and unstick it. Can you do that?"

He felt his legs quaking. "Yes," he replied hoarsely, in a voice that he literally didn't recognize as his own.

"Wait for the next contraction, then go with its flow. Push your hand and arm in, letting yourself get pulled back in." Maude gave a little air demonstration of how he should proceed.

"But how will I ..."

"Don't worry, you'll know!"

He followed her direction, and shortly was shocked to feel his arm sucked up, swallowed into the cow's birth canal almost to its elbow. The bovine paused in her contraction, bleating and gasping in pain from the additional intrusion. The pressure on his forearm was intense, much more than he'd expected. He gritted his teeth.

"Can you feel the other leg?" Maude asked, vigilantly regarding his progress.

Ryan slowly unfurled his long fingers and quickly struck against the calf's rear haunches. He groped the soft flesh, searching for the stuck limb. "I have it!" he cried.

"Good, good. Feel for the toe – be careful, don't let the toe tear the soft tissue."

"Ahh, gotcha!" he exulted, his brown eyes flashing victoriously.

The twisted leg was caught up in the birth canal like a branch in a stream catches upon a rock, impeding its natural flow downward. Ryan flexed the leg free from its trap, and rotated the limb back into position, in line with the other leg. The cow let out long, lowing, painful *moo*, and began pushing. Ryan's arm came out, along with the two matching toes, now side by side.

"We need to be quick now," Maude said, with more urgency in her voice. "Once that umbilical cord breaks, the calf will be trying to breathe on its own. It'll be sucking up nothing but the embryonic fluid and will drown if we're not quick. Hurry now, clean yourself up."

Ryan wiped the slime and manure that now covered his hands and arms onto his neatly-pressed jeans, and then dipped back into the pail for a sanitizing rinse. Maude expertly tied the calving chains to the calf's legs, putting a loop above each fetlock and a half hitch below.

"We don't usually do both legs at once, but time is of the essence," she explained. She handed the ends of the calving chains to Ryan. "Here, now, remember, we're working with the cow, not against her," she instructed. "This is not a battle, just a friendly tug of war – and you're going to win!"

Ryan poised for the next contraction, blood racing from the thrill of the challenge. He'd never felt more alive in his life. He tensed, inhaling deeply, sensing that another contraction was coming. He felt the pressure on the chains as the cow began to strain again and he began pulling, applying a small amount of pressure at first and then increasing it slowly, trying to time himself to the natural ebb and flow of the birthing cycle.

"Pull out," Maude directed. "Straight out. Oh, good heavens, you're too tall!"

Ryan scooched down a bit, and continued pulling.

"Harder!"

The rear haunches appeared. "Now, down," Maude cried, moving her fat torso and elbows in the direction she wanted him to pull. "Down!"

Ryan dropped to his butt on the hard barn floor, all of his physical and mental energies focused on pulling. He leaned his weight into the chains, and suddenly, with a loud *whoosh*, the tug of war ended abruptly. Ryan fell backwards, and the calf tumbled heavily into his lap, spewing blood and embryonic fluid everywhere.

Elated, he sat back up, wiping the bloody fluid from his eyes. "We did it! Haaahaa! We did it!" He affectionately patted the drowned-looking newborn calf.

But Maude knew it was too early to crow. "You're not done yet. Get yourself up and hold that calf upside down by its hind legs."

Ryan struggled to his feet, calf in his arms. Even with the fresh sawdust, the barn floor had become slippery. He juggled the calf and his feet until he secured them both. "Upside down?" he repeated, tossing his head back to move a moist lock of black hair away from his eyes.

"Yes, yes!"

The calf, which was fifty pounds of dead weight, nearly slid from his grasp when he took it by the ankles and dropped the head and shoulders. But he caught at the hocks, and lifted the calf as high as he could, arms straining with the unexpected weight. The burden of holding the unresponsive calf up was much harder than he'd expected, and he looked to Maude for signs of relief.

"Now, set it down. Carefully!"

He gently lowered the calf to the floor. Maude grasped a handful of hay from the nearby manger, and selected a stout piece. She bent down and tickled the calf's nose with the hay. The calf sneezed, opened its eyes and blinked. One of the legs jerked forward spastically.

"Oh, thank goodness, it's alive!" exclaimed Rebecca, who had been watching the birth with bated breath.

"Thank God!" Ryan exclaimed, a sob of relief escaping him. Exhausted, he staggered back, clasping the stall divider for support. He ran a hand through his damp, tousled hair.

The mother cow began lapping the calf, cleaning off the traces of embryonic sac and fluid. The calf responded with eager little bounces of its head. Maude squeezed Ryan's arm affectionately. "We'll make a farmer of you yet, Sweetie!" she proclaimed. Crisis averted, Maude had reassumed her good-natured, grandmotherly persona.

"You were amazing, Ryan!" Rebecca gushed. The calf bleated, and struggled to rise up. "Oh, my goodness – it's just about the cutest thing going!"

Ryan felt the full emotional weight of his effort. He examined the cow and calf with an expression of proud parental fondness. "It is extremely cute," he agreed. He wiped his sweaty forehead with a clean piece of shirt sleeve.

The high-powered attorney had settled lawsuits worth millions of dollars, but he had never experienced anything close to the elation he now felt. He became vaguely conscious of the fact that the only thing that would make this accomplishment more meaningful would be assisting at the birth of his own child!

Strange emotions roiled his heart, almost too indescribable for words. Ryan MacDonald, an only child, an orphan, the sole remaining offshoot of his family tree, would have been hard pressed at that moment to put his feelings down on paper. But I think we can safely say that a new root was firmly established in the deep, fertile soil of Scotch Broom Acres.

When Trudy arrived home from work about an hour later, she encountered Ryan's black sedan parked in the yard. Her father was nowhere in sight, but Trudy hadn't expected to see him, knowing as she did that Leland had planned to spend the afternoon yarding out wood with Cain and Abel. She exited her four-wheel-drive, and warily stepped into the barn, harboring a suspicion that Amber had plotted another romantic set-up with Ryan MacDonald.

When Trudy spotted the little group loitering outside Rosebud's stall – from which favorite heifer she was eagerly awaiting a first calf – she abandoned her hesitation. She tossed her purse onto a hay bale, and dashed forward. "What happened?" she cried, anxiously examining her beloved bovine. The calf was now up on its legs, sucking loudly at its mother's teat. Trudy accosted Maude, whose Sunday dress was certainly ruined. "Oh, my God! Was there a problem?!"

Maude patted the younger woman's arm. "Now, now, Sweetie, there's no need to worry. It was a breech birth, but thanks to Ryan, everyone is safe and sound!"

Trudy turned to Ryan, and for the first time she noticed his dirty hands, unkempt black hair and soiled clothes. "*You* did this?!"

He nodded, suddenly tongue-tied.

A grateful cry escaped her parted lips. Trudy threw herself into his arms, taking him by surprise and almost knocking him over. He stumbled backward, grasping the edge of the stall to steady them both. Once re-balanced, his arm dropped to the curve of her neat waist, and he instinctively drew her closer. Because of her height, he discovered that Trudy's head fitted perfectly into the crook of his shoulder!

"Oh, thank you, Ryan! Thank you!" she sobbed, clinging to his neck. He felt her warm tears bathing his sweaty skin and his heart filliped. His groin tightened, and he clasped her possessively.

Perhaps it is hardly necessary to add that, in that moment, two strong roots from their lonely hearts intertwined, and thus, despite Trudy's vow to the contrary, there would likely be an "old MacDonald" on her farm!

Chapter 25
. . . .
Duty Calls

"Ex-wife," Bruce corrected, hastily. "Sheila is my ex-wife." He stood self-consciously behind the paper-strewn desk in his office, facing the woman who had once been his wife and the woman who he hoped to make his future wife. And he didn't know what to say to either of them!

"Pooh," Sheila sniffed. "Picky, picky." She shifted the baby from her shoulder to her ample hip.

Amber stared at Sheila, a befuddled expression upon her youthful face. The situation had taken her so much by surprise that she also didn't know what to say. She'd already introduced herself, and there certainly seemed to be nothing in common between herself and this other woman except—Bruce Gilpin!

Fortunately for them all, the baby started blubbering, providing a mutual focal point.

"Does it need changing?" Bruce asked.

"Her name is Olivia," Sheila replied, tartly. "She's not an 'it'."

He ran his hand through his short hair. "Sorry, right. Does … Olivia … need her diaper changed?"

"I just changed her an hour ago!" Sheila joggled the infant, and the sobs condensed to heavy wet sighs.

"Maybe she's hungry?"

The brief disruption gave Amber a chance to regain her composure and reconnoiter the situation. She didn't know why Bruce's ex-wife had reappeared on the scene after all these years, although she thought it was most likely something to do with Gray. She'd obviously interrupted an uncomfortable situation, however, and realized that her presence was only compounding Bruce's distress. "I'll just wait upstairs," she said. "Don't mind me." She made a move toward the new stairwell that had been added to the front office.

"Wait," Bruce interjected. He hesitated, a thousand thoughts running through his mind. They all boiled down mostly to one looming issue: What was he going to do with Sheila?!

Amber looked over at him, expectantly. Her eyes filled with reassuring love. "Mmm?"

"I might be a while, Amber," he continued, lamely. "Why don't you go home, and I'll stop over to your place tonight. Seven o'clock OK?"

For the first time, Amber felt icy fingers of fear touching her heart. She was too secure of his love to suspect a threat to their relationship. The difficulty must be something else – most likely the blonde-haired, blue-eyed elephant in the room! She didn't know why Sheila was in Sovereign, but she hoped for his sake that his ex-wife's visit was of a short duration.

"Sure," she said, forcing a smile. "No problem." She retraced her steps to the door, bobbing her neat dark head at the other woman. "Nice to meet you," she added.

"Yeah, right," replied Sheila.

Amber exited, closing the office door behind her. Head down, she crunched across the packed snow toward her mother's car. She'd parked fifty feet away from the building, thoughtfully leaving plenty of space for potential customers to park. As she walked, a dozen or more concerns popped into her mind, all clamoring for attention at once.

He hadn't called her Amber in months! Not in months! She was his "Sweets!" And why was he asking if seven o'clock was OK? Since she'd known Bruce Gilpin, he'd come and gone at all hours at the old Russell homestead almost as though he owned the place! She recollected how he had let himself into the hen pen the morning of the church breakfast – how he'd moved confidently toward her through the coop, brown eyes twinkling, looking so handsome in his Maine Army Guard sweatshirt! And yet now he was asking permission to come over at 7 p.m., just as though he was an acquaintance from the city?! Something was wrong; something was definitely wrong. Her step quickened.

"Too cute," Sheila said, watching Amber's progress through the office window. "She won't last," the ex-wife prophesied.

"The pot shouldn't call the kettle black," Bruce retorted, immediately regretting his words. Sheila always brought out the worst in him!

"And doesn't she just know she's cute, too! With that cute little hat and cute little walk!"

"Look, Sheila …" he broke off. What was he going to do with her? Should he allow her to stay? Or should he just give her more money so that she could take Olivia to a motel? Weren't there social programs to help women in situations like hers? Suddenly, the thought of his ex-wife – whom he had once vowed to cherish and protect – being destitute and homeless, almost made him sick to his stomach.

Sheila picked up on his hesitation, and recollected her position. She allowed the alligator tears to reform in her eyes. "I just need someplace to crash, 'til I get my act together," she continued, whining. "Won't take me long, I promise!"

The baby sneezed again. Bruce felt his heart softening, not toward her, but toward Olivia. His mind flew back to his recent time in Afghanistan. One of the things he had missed most during his tenure in the war zone was the sight and sound of children: children playing, children laughing, even children crying. His heart was suddenly touched by the fate of this innocent and now homeless child. "OK, OK, you can stay. Take Olivia upstairs," he said. "It's too cold for a baby down here. Do you have stuff in the car? Do you even have a car?"

"Yeah, Taylor gave me the old Subaru the last time he threw me out. But really, honey, I need to get some smokes, first. Can you just watch Olivia for a minute while I run over to the store?"

The sound of her old nickname for him – "honey" – made his skin crawl. He almost regretted his offer. "Can't you go without a cigarette for a few hours? It's not good for Olivia, you know."

"Do you want me to start climbing the walls? I promise I won't smoke inside. It'll only take a sec!"

Bruce sighed, and reached across the desk for the child. She passed the infant into his outstretched hands and stepped toward the door. She stopped, right hand fondling the two folded $50 bills in her pocket. "Need anything at the store?"

"Milk, I guess. I wasn't expecting visitors." He placed the baby on his shoulder and instinctively began patting her back. Olivia's stomach gurgled. "Dad probably won't be thrilled to see you," he warned.

"Pooh. Who cares! I'm not afraid of Ralph."

She disappeared out of his office with a gay wave, leaving him holding the chubby, watery-eyed child. He sighed. "Now what?" he asked himself aloud.

He strode over to the chair, and, keeping his hand carefully behind the infant's head, returned Olivia to the child carrier. He pulled the blanket up over her fat pink legs. "Don't go anywhere," he directed the infant.

He fished his phone out of his pocket, and sent a quick text message to his son, informing him that Sheila was in town. He didn't know whether or not Gray was working at the general store tonight, but he thought it was better for the boy to have a heads-up about his mother's return. He also asked Gray to bring his sleeping bag and camp out with them overnight. That would get him through the first twelve or fourteen hours with Sheila. But what was he going to do with her after that?

Olivia began whimpering, reclaiming his attention. He replaced his phone, and scooched down next to the baby's face, leaning against the arm of the chair. "Hey, Sunshine," he cooed. "What's a pretty girl like you doing in a place like this?" He wriggled his fingers above her head. She reached for his hand, momentarily distracted.

Bruce was no stranger to babies, although it had been quite a few years since he'd cared for an infant. He was the one who had risen in the middle of the night to feed his own infant son, certainly not Sheila. When their baby had wailed hungrily, Sheila only lamented that she'd ever had a child in the first place, then put a pillow over her head and rolled over. Everything came back to him now: the jet lag feeling from lack of sleep that first year; the endless diaper changings; Gray splashing and giggling during his nightly baths with the yellow rubber ducky; the preciousness of Gray's first steps; the frustration of potty training; that scared, empty feeling the day he'd put his son on the bus for his first day of school! As he hovered over Olivia, the early years of Gray's childhood flooded back in a flash. The baby reminded him so much of Gray, yet there was no father in this child's life to pick up Sheila's slack as a parent. Poor Olivia ... Olivia? He didn't even know the baby's last name! But it certainly wasn't Gilpin!

Instinctively, he checked the child's diaper. Just as he'd suspected, the disposable diaper was just like early-set cement. He searched the plastic carrier, and found a spare. He liberated a towel and wet wipes from the bathroom, cleared his desk, and in less than two minutes, the baby was clean and dry.

He wasn't done, yet, however. While changing the baby's diaper, Bruce had noted a sore-looking red slash next to Olivia's right ear. He grasped one of her fat wrists and inspected her fingernails. Sure enough, they were at that deadly stage. Sheila never noticed things like that, or, if she did, she never did anything about it. He fished through the top drawer of his desk and located his Swiss Army knife, which had a midget scissors attachment. He tried to trim the infant's teensy-weensy nails with the gadget, but soon gave up and carefully bit the nails off one by one, a trick an old maid aunt had taught him when Gray was a baby.

Olivia was cute and completely lovable, as all babies are. But she wasn't his child! Bruce, sensing his vulnerability, tried to caution himself against becoming attached to her. He needed to harden his heart, which he realized was overly susceptible thanks to his time in Iraq and Afghanistan. He closed his eyes, and prayed silently that he and Amber would have plenty of pointy-eared babies with dirty diapers to change and fingernails to trim!

His eyes flew open. Amber!

He groaned. What must she think of him, after seeing Sheila? Only a saint would have failed to compare herself to his ex-wife! Amber must be wondering what kind of sorry young man he must have been to have first married – and then been divorced by – such a sad example of womanhood!

One single mistake in his youth had brought him to this moment, he realized. If he had only restrained his physical lust with Sheila – as he had later taught himself to do – he wouldn't be faced with this dilemma. But then, he wouldn't have Gray, either.

While thinking once again of his son, he realized with a sudden start, that – although Olivia was nothing to him – she was in point of fact—his son's half-sister! *Jesus!*

Things were getting more and more complicated!

Bruce leaned an elbow against the arm of the chair, and covered his eyes in despair. What was he going to do?

While raising Gray, he had tried to teach the boy the Golden Rule – do unto others as you would have them do unto you – hoping that Gray would one day become a caring, compassionate man. And so far, with the help of his parents, he had succeeded. So how could he now tell his son that in a few days he was going to throw his mother and his half-sister out into the cold?!

The one mistake of his youth was like a debt that had never been fully paid, despite multiple attempts to discharge it over the years. The interest on that debt had kept compounding and compounding, until now the balance was astronomical. Would he ever be free and clear of Sheila? Wouldn't she always be, to some degree, his responsibility?

The more he pondered his dilemma, the more Bruce felt stuck in a terrible morass, a black, sucking quagmire. And the more he flailed around searching for quick relief, the faster he sank.

How could he ensure Sheila's safety and security, and remain true to his love for Amber? How could he help this poor unwanted child? He couldn't have two women and two families in his life, vying for his attention! And he certainly couldn't afford to keep Sheila and Olivia on the side, and yet give Amber everything that she deserved as his wife!

Amber Johnson had been the one bright shining star in his life. She had provided him renewed hope, joy and happiness. Over the past few months – almost since the moment they had met – he had pictured the happy life they might share together. He was planning to propose to her on Valentine's Day, and even carried the ring in his pocket, a purplish-blue Maine tourmaline that matched her pretty eyes.

He had grown up in a household filled with love, kindness and joy. Even today, his parents' marriage was the epitome of a happy marriage. Of course there had been difficulties over the years, but he had witnessed his parents face those difficulties together, and had seen their love become stronger, deeper as a result. Bruce had never had this kind of relationship with Sheila. But after she divorced him, he had begun to hope for such a union, two hearts sharing common goals, filled with mutual love, admiration and respect. He had never found anyone with whom he thought he could share this perfect love, until he had met Amber on the bus ride from Boston.

But where could Sheila take herself off to now? What could she do to support herself and Olivia? She had never learned a trade nor had she even finished high school. She had dropped out the summer between her junior and senior years, when Gray was born. In the fourteen years since she'd left his care and protection, Sheila had simply been passed around from one man to the next, almost without volition on her part. The pattern was always the same. She'd find a man; they'd cohabitate until he tired of her; he'd throw her out; she'd move on to the next. Now, he realized, Sheila was probably too old and too unattractive to secure a man, especially with a new baby in tow. Nor would he want her to continue that way of life.

Bruce idly toyed with the infant's fat hand. The poor thing didn't stand a chance, having Sheila as a mother! Perhaps he could persuade Sheila to put the baby up for adoption? That would help lighten her load.

He shook himself. He realized his thoughts were all over the map. On top of that, he was already trying to take command of the situation, as though Sheila and Olivia were indeed his responsibility. He felt the chains of duty coiling around his ankle.

To whom did he owe the highest and first duty? His son? His ex-wife? Amber? (It never occurred to Bruce to put himself on the list.)

That evening, as promised, he put in his appearance at the old Russell homestead. He looked tired and haggard. Amber was shocked when she saw him. He looked as though he had aged fifteen years in three hours!

Still wearing his winter jacket, he dropped down into his usual chair and tossed his baseball cap carelessly onto the kitchen table. Amber pressed eager warm kisses upon his face. He smiled wanly, accepting her caresses. But he didn't return them.

"Want some tea?" she inquired, anxiously. Tea was the most common remedy in the Russell household, generally heavily-laced with some of Wendell's sweet honey. "I think there's a piece of blueberry pie left, too?"

"Nothing, thanks," he replied. He picked up a pen that Wendell had left on the table, and absently began drumming it against the wood. His mind had already reverted back to the dilemma at hand, and he frowned without knowing it.

Amber noted the complete change to his demeanor. The bounce was altogether gone from his step, and the loving twinkle had disappeared from his brown eyes. His face was set and stern. She felt an icy hand squeezing her heart. She had seen that look before – on the bus ride from Boston! She recalled how, upon first learning who she was, Bruce had metamorphosed from a good-humored, pleasant companion into a distant, hard-hearted soldier. Now, it was happening again!

But why was it happening? And what could she do about it?!

She knelt next to his chair, forcing him to look at her. "Tell me what's wrong, Love?" she pleaded. She leaned familiarly across his knees. "Has something bad happened to Sheila? Is that why she's here?"

He nodded, glumly. "She got kicked out again. Her latest boyfriend told her to take Olivia and go. She's got no family, no money. They're gonna stay with me for a while, I guess." He avoided her eyes.

"With you?!" She would have given anything to retract her words, hearing in them the mix of disdain and accusation that they carried.

"She's the mother of my son," he reminded her. "And Olivia is Gray's half-sister."

"I hadn't thought of that," Amber admitted, honestly. His words shed fresh light onto the dilemma he was facing. She had never fully considered the ramifications of what it meant to share a child with another person. Now, she realized that the lives of Sheila, Bruce, Gray – and even Olivia! – were all intertwined, despite what the divorce papers might say to the contrary. The father was necessarily still connected to the mother and her new offspring through their shared son.

"Gray's gonna stay with us, too," he continued. "For a while, anyway."

"Oh, that's great! He'll get to spend some quality time with them!"

But he didn't seem to share her enthusiasm. Instead, he took her by the hand and maneuvered her up into the chair next to him. He laid her arm on the table, and pulled away from her. "Amber, I don't know how long Sheila and Olivia are gonna be with me," he said. "I don't think, well, I think maybe we shouldn't see each other for a while."

She heard a buzzing in her ears, a loud chattering and clamoring of noises confusing her senses. OMG, Wendell had that TV blaring so loud she could hardly hear herself think!

Surely, he didn't say what she thought she'd just heard? That they shouldn't see each other for a while?! She felt sick with fear.

"At least, until I get this thing with Sheila and Olivia figured out, anyway." He reached out, and squeezed her hand, which had suddenly gone limp. "OK?"

Her heart shrieked: *No, no! It's NOT OK!*

Heroically, she bit back her words, actually biting her lip with her sharp teeth to keep herself from crying out. She must think of him, first! Not of herself!

She nodded, eyes filling with tears.

Awful as it was, she did understand. He needed some time to figure out the right thing to do. Unfortunately, there was only one person who could figure out the answer to that and – alas, alas! – that one person wasn't her!

"I knew you'd understand!" he said, gratefully. He rose, kissed her awkwardly on the cheek, and fumbled for his baseball cap.

It wasn't until after he'd closed the shed door behind him that Amber noticed the warm taste of blood on her lip. Instinctively, she licked her lip. Then she put her head onto the table and burst into tears.

Chapter 26
. . . .
The Old Wooden Cradle

The arrival of two additional souls into a town of 1,048 often has the power to tip the emotional scales one way or another, affecting the community's sensibility. With the return of Bruce Gilpin's ex-wife and her child, a pall had been cast over the sleepy little farming hamlet of Sovereign.

No one could say that Sheila didn't have a perfect right to be there. She was the mother of Bruce's son, after all. In addition, the town was proud of its open door policy – locks and bolts were foreign objects – and no one was ever turned away in Sovereign, Maine. But there were many who, in the sanctuary of their kitchens or the sanctity of their bedrooms, wished that Sheila had never returned. Among them were necessarily those most closely concerned: Rebecca Russell and Maude Gilpin.

"What are we going to do?" Rebecca lamented to Wendell, from the security of their marital bed. She spoke in a low voice, not wanting Amber to overhear. Sounds did sometimes carry through the cavernous old post-and-beam at night. Usually, however, what was heard was the soughing of the wind in the eaves or the nibbling of the mice in the horsehair plaster. "We can't let it go on like this! She spends all her time with her eReader and the chickens. She's hasn't even left the house!"

"Wal, you know, 'tain't much we kin do," Wendell replied, laconically. He tucked his arm around his wife, attempting to provide some physical comfort since he knew that his words would probably fail to provide emotional comfort. "'Tain't any of it up t'us."

"How could Bruce be so foolish?!"

He squeezed her reassuringly. "Now, now. Sheila's only been heah a few days."

"Six days! That's almost a week!"

"Wal, she won't be heah long; jest long 'nuff to git what she come for."

Rebecca sat up, actually sat up in bed. She confronted her husband. "What does she want? Why doesn't he just give it to her!"

"Don't git yerself all worked up, Mrs. Russell," Wendell chided her. He maneuvered his pretty young wife back down next to him in the comfy feather bed. "Course, she's only come back for his money."

"Oh! Does Bruce have money?!" Rebecca wondered, eyes widening.

"He will, when them fancy papers gits auctioned off."

"The Emily Dickinson letters?"

Wendell grinned and nodded, his gold tooth catching the winter moonlight. "Thet's likely what she come back for. I predict she'll be gone, soon 'nuff."

Rebecca made a sound of protest. "No! Bruce is planning to use that money to renovate the old canning factory!"

"Don't bet on thet," he advised.

Across town, a similar conversation was occurring.

"Why doesn't she just go away?!" Maude exclaimed, settling herself back onto her flocculent pillows for a heart-to-heart with her *caro sposo*. "Surely there must be one of those other men that will take her back!"

Knowing what was coming, Ralph groaned inwardly. He reached for his reading light and gave the switch a meaningful snap. The bedroom was thrown into a state of half-darkness, as though one of the room's eyes had been closed.

But his wife failed to get the message, and she soldiered on. "I can't believe what all this must be doing to poor Amber! Rebecca says she hasn't left the house all week. She's such a pretty little thing, too!" Her hands absently fingered the embroidered hem of the sheet. "And Gray is so fond of her!"

Ralph saw the hook and worm dangling in front of his eyes, but like the curious trout he couldn't resist. "I thought ya didn't want them two gettin' together?" he parried.

"Sometimes I think you don't hear a word I say!"

"'Tain't likely!" he opined. He sat up. To an outsider's eyes, the bedroom scene resembled something from *'Twas the Night Before Christmas*. With the moon on the new-fallen snow outside, and Ralph and Maude inside in their matching blue striped pajamas, the addition of bed caps would certainly have suggested Santa's imminent arrival, despite the January calendar. "'Twarn't more 'n three months ago ya was belly-achin' 'bout them two, right here in this very bed!"

Peas, Beans & Corn

Maude brushed aside her husband's dart. "Oh, that? That was ages ago! Why, even you can see how happy Bruce and Amber are together! I think she'd make him a wonderful wife. You want a granddaughter, don't you?"

This was another fat worm she jiggled in front of his face. Ralph was partial to his grandson, Gray, and fond of Penney's two boys; however, he did think maybe he'd like a pretty little granddaughter to spoil. "Don't go countin' ya chickens afore they're hatched," he warned, fluffing his pillow and settling himself back down into their Queen-sized bed. "Not unless ya want to count thet baby Sheila brung back as one of ya chicks!"

"Heaven forbid!"

Ralph chuckled, picturing Sheila's roly-poly baby. He'd taken his wife's bait, he might as well enjoy the worm. "Thet Olivia – she's awful cunnin'," he continued. "She'll make more hay with Bruce's heart 'n Sheila evah could! If ya ain't careful, yer brother'll be draggin' thet old Hodges cradle ovah from Winslow fer Olivia," he predicted.

Maude let out a little shriek. "How can you even think such a thing!" She daubed the side of her eyes with the hem of the bed sheet. "That would be awful!" A plaintive sob escaped her. *"Awful!"*

He scooted his skimpy frame over next to her in bed, which act of comfort was in fact his enjoyment of the worm. He threw a skinny arm across her ample breasts. "Now, now, Maude," he said. "'Tain't like the world's comin' to an end!" He pressed a dry kiss against her plump warm cheeks.

She batted him away half-seriously, half-playfully. "Oh, go along with you, Ralph Gilpin!" she declared. "You know that lovey-dovey stuff doesn't work with me!"

"I guess maybe it has, leastwise once or twice," he corrected her. He bussed her again, this time full on her ruby lips.

"He, he, he!" she giggled. She snuggled closer, perhaps enjoying a little of the fat worm herself.

The next day dawned sunny, temperate and bright, signaling the opening strains of the annual January thaw. That afternoon, Wendell's honeybees would be flying, exiting their hives for the first time in weeks in order to take their cleansing flights. Hibernating Maine black bears would begin birthing their cubs, despite their slumbers. The sugar maples would unfurl their aching bones and reach for the sky, considering whether or not the time had come to let down the sap.

Encouraged by the fine day, Amber, after completing her morning chores and consuming her breakfast, strapped on her snowshoes and tramped off across the snow-covered fields. A fresh southerly breeze teased the tip of her nose, and rustled the tops of the pine trees. She caught a tantalizing whiff of spring, as though the earth, like the birthing black bears, had shifted in her winter sleep allowing for the change of air. Amber began to feel new hope swelling like the buds on the hardwoods, radiating thrillingly out from the center of her core.

She would not give him up! She would wait, patiently, faithfully. He loved her! She knew this with perfect confidence. He would find a way to do the right thing for Sheila and the baby, and then, once that mission was accomplished, he would come back to her. They would pick up where they had left off, and their relationship would be replete with deeper understanding, stronger love, and firmer commitment.

She almost wept with relief. She stomped along across the crusty snow — *crunch, crunch, crunch* -- repeating to herself the mantra: *He loves me! He loves me! He loves me!* The blue sky above seemed to approve of this conclusion, as did the chickadees, which in their fanciful flights mirrored her exultation. She inhaled deeply of the hint of spring that was in the air, and cried out: "I know you're in there!" speaking not only to spring, but also to the joy that was bubbling up within her soul.

When she returned to the old Russell homestead, the feisty red squirrel greeted her at the Staircase Tree. He immediately began his usual scold.

"Ha, don't even try it!" she cautioned him, exuberantly. She caught up a handful of snow in her mittens, fashioned it into a ball and playfully lobbed a warning shot into the tree. "There's more where that came from, if you keep it up!"

The red squirrel put its rust-colored tail between its legs, and darted into the security of its hidey hole, which was a good-sized cavity in the crotch of the tree. Amber laughed, leaning an arm against the tree to catch her breath. She instantly recollected the October afternoon that Bruce had rested back against the Staircase Tree, arms folded across his chest, bragging: *I know who carved the steps in the Staircase Tree!*

She smiled lovingly at the memory. He had been just about to kiss her, when the red squirrel had interrupted them!

She returned to the house, heart happy and spirits high. She changed out of her work clothes and dressed for town. At two o'clock, she had an appointment in Waterville with the owner of a natural foods store, who wanted to purchase organic eggs wholesale from *The Egg Ladies*. Unfamiliar with the city of Waterville, Amber left home at eleven o'clock, unsure not only how long the trip would take her but also where the store was located. When she reached the junction of Route 139 and the Sebasticook Bridge Road in Winslow, she knew she was going to be too early. Instead of turning right and proceeding to town, Amber decided to explore some of the unfamiliar countryside. She drove straight across the intersection into the quaint town of Benton Falls.

She pressed on through the village, past the little white church and the matching Meeting House. The woods converged, and she followed the road down a long sloping hill, until the blacktop stretched out next to the Sebasticook River with nothing but guardrails between her and the snow-covered river. The road dipped at an old WPA concrete bridge, and Amber slowed her pace to cross the narrow bridge. She could hear the gurgling of a stream as it flowed beneath the bridge, joining the half-frozen river. She paused to ponder the pretty scenic view upstream. When she gently accelerated forward she spotted a prominent sign swinging from an old pine tree to her left, proclaiming: *Oaknole Farm, Registered Jerseys*.

Amber slowed the car again. Oaknole!

Immediately Miss Hastings' words came to mind. *If he gets you over to Oaknole, you'll never want to leave—the two of you will spend the rest of your days clishmaclavering among the cows!*

Since that afternoon with the retired music teacher, Amber had heard much more about Oaknole Farm from Bruce, who had regaled her with stories about the place he'd spent his summers as a boy, and where he'd learned from his grandfather his love of mechanics and mechanical conundrums. Bruce had spoken so often of his uncle Peter that sometimes Amber felt as though she knew the older man. Unable to restrain her curiosity, Amber pointed the car up the well-plowed gravel lane. She wouldn't stop; she would just get a quick glimpse of the place, and turn around. What harm could there be?

She motored carefully down the tree-lined lane, impressed by the height and breadth of the stolid old oak trees, the tips of their branches nearly touching across the twenty foot divide. Her car window was partially rolled down, and she soon caught the pleasing odor of the barnyard. When she arrived at the turn-around, she spotted the cows mingling at the western end of the elongated red barn. She stopped to watch the pretty fawn-colored Jerseys chewing their cuds and enjoying the afternoon sunlight. There was no one around, and she thought perhaps she would just sit a minute, basking in the pleasant sunlight herself.

However, Bonnie the border collie, who had been resting peacefully in the barn, keeping an eye on the latest batch of barn kittens in lieu of any other chores, had heard the tires on the gravel almost as soon as Amber turned onto Oaknole Lane. The alert border collie had slipped out through the open door on the south side of the barn, and now trotted forward to greet the visitor, offering up several sharp yelps. Amber rolled her window down the rest of the way and spoke a few encouraging words to the small black and white dog. Her voice only served to whet the animal's hopes, and Bonnie yipped even louder. In a moment, Amber noticed a man exiting the statuesque, two-story white homestead. Her heart nearly failed her. She'd been discovered! How embarrassing!

"She won't hurt you!" he called, shrugging into his winter coat and striding down the long farmer's porch. Amber popped open her car door, and leaned over to pat the sleek animal. The dog immediately began sniffing her. "Her name's Bonnie," he continued, advancing down the four front steps. "The worse she'll do is try to lick you to death."

Amber shyly stepped forward to introduce herself. As they drew closer, her breath caught in her throat—he was the spitting image of Bruce, only twenty years older!

"You're Uncle Peter!" she proclaimed. Reassured by the familiar countenance, she held out her hand.

"And you must be Amber," he replied. He took her warm hand and held it between his calloused paws for several moments. His brown eyes twinkled. "What a nice surprise!"

"How did you … ?"

"I recognized your mother's car," he admitted, grinning. Bonnie was now jealously vying for his attention, and he bent down momentarily to fondle the dog's head. He straightened back up. "I'm like Bruce—I never forget a vehicle!"

Amber laughed. "You are so like him!"

"People used to say that he was like me. Now, it's the other way round!"

She giggled. It felt perfectly natural being with him.

He indicated the house behind them with a bob of his head. "Got time for a cup of tea with a lonely old bachelor?"

Intrigued, Amber nodded. Her heartbeat quickened, and with heightened interest, she followed Bruce's uncle into the house.

I fear that my old friend Peter Hodges had more than tea in mind when he solicited Amber's company. Information flows freely in both directions from Sovereign to Winslow, and Peter had learned of Sheila's recent return to Sovereign. Lately, he had been worried not only about the disposition of Oaknole Farm, but also about the disposition of his nephew's heart. He knew how much Bruce loved Amber, and I'm almost ashamed to admit that Peter had decided he couldn't pass up such an excellent opportunity to secure two fish with one worm.

Inside the front hall, they hung up their coats and then he led her past the gleaming oak staircase into the cozy country kitchen. Peter poked the fire and tossed two sticks of maple into the wood cookstove. He set the tea kettle on top. "Would you like to see the rest of the house?" he suggested. "It'll take a while for the kettle to boil, I'm afraid. The fire was almost out."

Amber nodded eagerly.

Peter led Amber though the gracious old farmhouse, revealing to his guest in minute detail the glories of the two-hundred-year-old homestead. Since his mother's death, there had been no mistress at Oaknole Farm, and the place had been left almost exactly as it had been on the day she died. Over the past forty years, Peter and his now-deceased father had led bachelor lives, with only Mrs. Smiley, the housekeeper, providing them a smidgen of feminine companionship and comfort. Mrs. Smiley still came in daily to fix the meals and straighten up a bit. Before Amber had even set her booted foot inside the front hall, Peter had already determined that it was time to retire the seventy-year-old housekeeper and turn over the keys to this pretty young woman!

As Peter and Amber passed from one stately and yet comfortable room to the next, he pointed out this and that beloved attribute. He showed her the matching daguerreotypes of the ancestors on the white painted mantelpiece, the 19th century Maine pastoral oil paintings, the lovely hand-embroidered linens, the colorful Depression glass, the polished silverware with the letter "H" in beautiful scrollwork on the handle, the wrought-iron hardware, the bundling beds, the sweeping views of the Sebasticook River from the house's windows, the mysterious stuff squirrelled away in the old attic, the winding back stairwell that led down to the office, and much, much more. Amber was completely enthralled, and perhaps we can understand why the tea kettle had been steaming merrily away in the kitchen for nearly twenty minutes before she even noticed that five minutes had passed!

But my old friend had saved his *coup de foudre* for last. He now led Amber into the south-facing nursery, which room he knew at that time of day would be awash in the bright mid-winter sunlight. The glorious light haloed a hand-carved wooden cradle the size of a bassinette resting on a braided rug in the center of the small room. A black state of Maine rocker sat expectantly next to the cradle, as though a new-born baby was imminent.

"It's beautiful!" Amber gushed, moving quickly forward to examine the cradle and accoutrements. The baby's bed was made up with precious little linen sheets and topped with a soft, hand-knitted yellow blanket threaded with yellow ribbons. She touched the blanket carefully, enjoying the feel of the silken ribbon beneath her fingertips. She ran her hand lightly across the bow of the cradle. She turned to her companion, whom she'd momentarily forgotten. "How old is it?"

He regarded the cradle tenderly. "We're not sure. Family tradition says nine generations have used the old wooden cradle. I'm afraid Bruce was the last, though."

Amber felt a quickening in her ovaries. Her midsection radiated with strange and wonderful yearnings. "How sad that it's been empty for so long!"

Peter stepped on the treadle with his foot, and the cradle began rocking, rocking, rocking. Mesmerized, Amber watched the cradle swinging back and forth, back and forth. Suddenly, she experienced a confusing spatial sensation, as though time had warped, allowing her a glimpse of the future. She saw herself in her white nightdress, perched on the edge of the chair, rocking the cradle.

"I'm afraid this old cradle won't ever rock another baby," Peter allowed in a sad voice. "It's a shame, really. When I die, the old thing will probably go to the auction block."

Amber awoke with a little cry. "Oh, no! Why?!"

"Aw, there's nobody to take over this place. I was hoping when Bruce came home from Afghanistan he'd come back here to Oaknole." He sighed deeply. "But that doesn't look like it's gonna happen, and there's nobody else to take over the farm." He appeared to recollect himself. "Listen to me, carrying on like an old maid! You don't want to hear about my troubles … let's go have that cup of tea!" He moved to go.

"Oh, but I do want to hear them!" she assured him, catching his strong arm. "I do!"

He smiled, gratified. Peter Hodges knew how to bait a fishhook almost as well as his sister Maude!

Chapter 27
. . . .
The Sleighing Rally

Revitalized with new hope and, thanks to Peter, an interesting new vision to ponder, Amber returned to her old life calmly and confidently. She even went about town just as she used to before Sheila's arrival, as though there were no burden weighing upon her heart. She didn't visit Bruce at his garage, of course, or even call or text him; however, she spoke about him to others in a tone of voice that was very matter-of-fact. Most of the townspeople took their cues from her, and thus life in Sovereign almost settled back to normal.

Out of sheer boredom, Sheila had taken to hanging out at Ma Jean's Restaurant. Bruce didn't have a TV set, nor would he install one on her behalf. Maude had given her some ladies magazines to consume, but these she had found slow to digest, so she sought out more immediate comfort food. Around ten o'clock every day, Sheila settled herself and Olivia into the restaurant's corner booth, and there they remained for the next four hours until Ma Jean's closed.

One would expect, given Rebecca and Maude's animosity toward the interloper, that Sheila would have received a cold shoulder at the restaurant. But this wouldn't have been in keeping with the older women's true motherly natures, and I might as well admit that both had become fond of the baby. Who can resist a roly-poly infant? Even Ralph had fallen victim to her drooling baby charms! But the two women could not resist talking about Sheila.

"Why doesn't she get a job?" Rebecca whispered to Maude, from behind the server's window. "I know I'd be bored out of my mind just sitting there all day!"

"She's never worked," Maude replied. "I don't think she knows how."

"Maybe somebody should teach her?" Rebecca suggested. "After all, there's nothing more satisfying than a job well done!"

"Maybe somebody *should* teach her," Maude agreed.

And the two put their heads together and came up with a plan. The next afternoon, Rebecca invited the young blonde woman to follow her back into the kitchen, where Maude introduced her to the stainless steel sink filled with soapy water and dishes. Both women took turns holding forth on the joys of independence, and Maude flat out named a very fair wage at which they would remunerate her for her services in the sink.

Not surprisingly, Sheila balked at the first fence. "You want me to wash those old pots and pans! No f***ing way!"

"Oh, dear!" said Rebecca.

Sheila speedily made her exit, only pausing long enough to pick up Olivia. As soon as the door was closed behind them, Maude and Rebecca held another parley in the kitchen.

"Perhaps we've made a mistake," Maude admitted.

"That certainly didn't go very well!" Rebecca agreed. She squirted some additional dish soap into the hot water, and proceeded to tackle the dirty dishes herself. "Maybe she'd rather wait tables?"

Maude handed her partner a soiled pot. "What?! And let her scowls chase away all our customers! I'm sorry, dear. I'd like to help her, but I don't think we should stoop to that!"

So the two older ladies gave up attempting to inculcate the younger woman with the joys of personal responsibility. Instead, they provided Sheila with endless cups of coffee and pieces of Maude's lemon meringue pie, all of which naturally went on Bruce's tab.

On Wednesday morning, Amber arrived at the restaurant with the bi-weekly egg delivery. She and Maude had worked out a mutually agreeable price for the eggs. She spotted Sheila in the corner booth, and offered up a friendly smile. "Hi there," she said, carefully maneuvering around the corner of the bar, into the kitchen, carrying a raft of corrugated egg flats.

"Hey," Sheila replied, glancing up, curiously. She soon returned to flipping the pages of her magazine.

When Amber was done unloading the eggs, she approached the corner booth. "How's Olivia?" she inquired of the other woman. "I noticed she was sneezing a lot the other day. I hope she didn't come down with a cold?" She smiled and cooed at the chubby infant in the baby carrier.

"She's fine," Sheila replied, warily. She was unsure whether or not there was some intended sarcasm in Amber's remark. She examined Amber's face. Finding no hidden scorn, Sheila warmed to the conversation. At least Amber was somebody to talk to! "She's fine – except that everybody around here spoils her."

"Oh, babies are meant to be spoiled!" Amber said, waxing enthusiastic. After her recent experience with the old wooden cradle at Oaknole, she considered herself an expert on all things baby.

"Yeah? Well, I don't think it's such a hot idea. And Bruce is the worst offender!"

Sheila's rejoinder grated disagreeably upon Amber's ears. In addition, her stomach roiled slightly at the thought of her beloved becoming attached to this fat little baby. What if Bruce decided he didn't want any more roly-poly babies of his own? What if Olivia and Gray were enough for him? What would she do, then!

She felt the heat of blood rising in her face. "You've got a good point. There's a fine line between caring and spoiling."

"Yeah," Sheila replied. "Like I said."

Amber suddenly realized that her hands were clenched and that she was inwardly wishing Sheila would take Olivia and depart Sovereign for good! Feeling guilty, she herself turned to leave. "See you later," she added.

"Sure," Sheila replied. "Why not?"

Saturday was the day of Sovereign's annual sleighing rally, sponsored by the Ladies Auxiliary. The rally was held in the large field located across from Gilpin's General Store, and was scheduled to begin at ten o'clock. Firewood for a bonfire had been hauled into the field in advance, as well as other necessities such as portable toilets, and about a dozen bleacher seats from the high school. Snowmobile trails had been groomed for use by four-legged creatures, and owners of modern sleds all agreed to park their motorized toys for the day. Sleigh rides were made available to everyone (for a small donation to the Auxiliary, of course), and the Ladies also sold hot chocolate, tea, coffee and donuts. The event, which had been held annually for more than twenty-five years, was widely anticipated and drew attenders from as far away as Kittery.

The state of Maine was still in the middle of her January thaw, and the morning dawned beautiful and bright. Eighteen teams of horses from Sovereign and the surrounding towns converged on the field, their sleigh bells jingling and the polished brass and nickel of the leather harnesses flashing in the sunlight. The horses pranced through the knee-deep snow, ferrying cheerful cargos around the field, their heavy hooves showering snow upon many an unwary bystander.

Sleighs of every type were represented at the rally, from the two-seated bob-runner to the romantic-looking Canadian-Russian sleigh made famous by the movie *Dr. Zhavigo*. Several one-horse Portland cutters were present, including the old Gorse sled, which light-weight, one-seater Cain zipped easily across the field, while Abel stood patiently at the ready as back-up. Leland's pretty antique sled had received a fresh coat of black paint for the rally, and was trimmed with plush maroon velvet upholstery. Trudy had thoughtfully added an old fur robe to the sleigh, in case the light south breeze took a northerly turn.

Trudy and Ryan had been selected to act as ambassadors of the event, answering questions, directing customers to the food, and ensuring innocent bystanders stay out from under the horses' hooves. Bruce and Amber had originally been conscripted for this important post, but the selection had necessarily changed after their break-up. Even Miss Hastings put in an appearance, her arrival at the cash box cheering the Ladies no end, knowing as they did that with the retired music teacher in the driver's seat (rather than Shirley Palmer) the donations would increase by 100%. "I'm so happy to see you, dahrrrling!" Miss Hastings purred to seven-year-old Jemma Peabody, Betty Peabody's granddaughter. "So good you brought your parents with you, too, Jemma, you dahrrrling!"

The sleighing rally was an event to which Amber had long looked forward. A sleigh ride had been on her "Bucket List" for many years, and Bruce had promised her that she would be able to cross this item off at the annual sleighing rally. But Amber had determined in advance that nothing on earth could make her get into a sleigh, no matter how romantic-looking the sled was, unless, unless—Bruce Gilpin was already in it! She wasn't going to go for her first sleigh ride without him! She would wait for next year's rally, if that's what it took.

Therefore, Amber was glad when her mother asked for her help at the restaurant, giving her a bona fide excuse to avoid most of the event. Ma Jean always chalked up one of her best days of the year during the sleighing rally, and Maude had suggested that Amber help her mother wait tables. Maude wasn't worried that Amber would chase customers away. Instead, she possibly calculated that Amber's pretty face and trim figure might lure diners into that second piece of pie.

The restaurant closed at 2 p.m. per usual, and Rebecca immediately urged her daughter to attend the rally. "We'll clean up here," she said. "When I'm done, I'll come right up and join you."

Unable to think of a good excuse – and curious to see the lovely antique sleighs – Amber obediently hiked the short distance up the Bangor Road to the rally. She smelled the wood smoke from the bonfire and heard the sounds of laughter and sleigh bells as she drew near. She arrived on the snowplowed part of the field to discover hundreds of attenders still milling about, laughing, chattering and enjoying the old-fashioned winter event.

Trudy spotted Amber in the crowd and quickly made her way to the younger woman's side. "I'm so glad you finally got here! I was worried they were going to keep you enslaved at the restaurant all day!" Trudy had become exuberant of spirit lately, these her halcyon days of the romance with Ryan.

"They let me out for good behavior," Amber replied, smiling. She surveyed the crowd. "Looks like you've had a good turnout?"

"Yes, but now if I can just make sure nobody gets trampled, I'll be a happy woman!"

But Amber realized that her friend was already happy. In fact, she was radiant! And no wonder! In a moment, they were joined by an equally ebullient Ryan. The couple exchanged meaningful smiles, and surreptitiously began holding hands.

Amber felt a pang of latent disappointment. Oh, how she had looked forward to this day! How she had longed to take a romantic sleigh ride through the woods with Bruce! She didn't begrudge Trudy and Ryan their happiness, however.

Ryan gallantly offered Amber his free arm. "Would you care to come for a sleigh ride with us? I've got one standing at the ready!"

Amber managed a weak smile, attempting – unsuccessfully – to hide her pain from her friends. "No thanks," she said. "Maybe … maybe another time." She watched Ryan lead Trudy happily toward a beautiful *Dr. Zhavigo* sleigh, her heart almost sick with desire for the sight of Bruce's face and the sound of his voice. His hands! How she loved his capable hands!

But there were forces at work in Sovereign, of which she was unaware, ready to confer upon Amber her heart's desire. I'm sorry to say that the Old Farts – normally so indolent and dilatory – had taken an informal straw poll and had decided to intervene in the sadly truncated love affair. Sheila's baby was cute and all, but Bruce deserved to be happy. The Old Farts, in their infinite wisdom, knew that Sheila couldn't and wouldn't make him happy. After all, he'd been down that route once before, and how'd that work out for him?! The Old Farts also knew that Bruce was head over heels in love with Amber Johnson, who perhaps had not left many of their own susceptible hearts untouched.

Wendell ambled over to where Amber was sadly staring off into space. He hitched up his jeans. "Kin you come ovah heah a minute?" he said. "Miss Hastings don't feel so good."

Amber became instantly concerned. "Is she sick again?"

"Wal, you know, 'tain't nuthin' to worry 'bout."

"Where is she?!"

Wendell nodded in the general direction of the smoldering bonfire, and Amber anxiously followed along behind as he wound his way back through the crowd. Head down, she didn't notice until the last moment that he'd led her to where Leland and Abel were awaiting them in the Portland cutter. Wendell paused at the side of the black sleigh, and indicated that she should climb up into the seat next to Trudy's father.

Amber stopped short. "Where's Miss Hastings?" she asked, glancing around dubiously. She recollected her promise that nothing could make her get into a sleigh without Bruce today.

Wendell hesitated. His was a lead role in the Old Fart's Plan, but he wasn't a very good liar. "Wal, you know ..." he broke off.

"She's up ahead," assured Leland, whose conscience was perhaps not as finely tuned as that of his brethren to the difference between a fib and a bold-faced lie. He patted the plush seat beside him. "Come 'long, now, I'll take ya."

Unable to think of any suitable way to escape, Amber allowed Wendell to help her up into the sleigh. She settled herself into the padded velvet seat next to Leland, and he poked the fur robe around her hips. He clucked to his patient steed, and gave a little shake to the reins. "Let's go, Abel. Git 'long now, hoss!"

Abel's ears perked up, and the horse proceeded to break into a slow trot. Leland clucked again, and they were soon speeding quickly across the slippery snow.

Despite her reservations, Amber found she enjoyed the feel of the fresh breeze in her face and the unusual vantage point offered up by the one-horse open sleigh. "I didn't realize we'd be so high up!" she exclaimed. Abel took a sharp turn onto a snowmobile trail and the sleigh listed slightly. Amber grasped the side of the wooden sled for support.

"We ain't hard up," Leland corrected, pretending to mishear her remark. The necessity for further conversation thus neatly avoided, they glided on through the Sovereign woods, the sleigh's runners *swishing* over the well-packed snow.

They soon approached the intersection of two snowmobile trails. Without warning Leland pulled back on the reins, bringing the horse and sleigh to a halt. Amber glanced around. Nothing and no one was in sight! "Where's Miss Hastings?" she inquired of her charioteer, beginning to suspect a plot.

Leland shrugged. He handed her the reins. "Hold 'im a moment, will ya? I got to take a …" he broke off, realizing at the last moment the sex of the person to whom he was speaking.

"But, I don't know how to drive a horse!" she protested.

"You don't gotta drive Abel – jest hold 'im still!" Leland hopped down, and disappeared into the thick greenery of the balsam fir branches, leaving Amber completely alone!

"I will not panic," she said aloud, reconnoitering her situation. At the sound of her voice, Abel perked up his ears. "Nice horse," she said, clutching the reins. "Please don't go anywhere!"

On the other snowmobile trail, unbeknownst to her, another sleigh was fast approaching. The luring of Bruce from his garage had presented more of a challenge to the Old Farts – he being savvy of their characters – but Maynard Nutter had succeeded in convincing Bruce that Leland's harness had broken beyond repair, leaving a Portland couple stranded. The "beyond repair" part had piqued our hero's interest, and Maynard and his team soon pulled up just short of the intersection, where Leland's sleigh could be glimpsed through the trees.

"Hop out here; 'twill be easier for me to turn the team 'round without yer weight," Maynard suggested.

Bruce obligingly leaped out onto the snow-covered trail. He stepped back, allowing for Maynard and the horses to proceed. He followed along in the sleigh's wake, startled to see that, instead of turning or stopping at the intersection, the selectman whizzed straight on through!

"Hey!" he called, running after the sleigh. "Maynard!" But the old man kept going, with nary a backward glance. At that point, Bruce did suspect a plot, but it was too late. He turned, and caught sight of his sweetheart, all alone in Leland's Portland cutter, a look of astonishment upon her pretty face.

Jesus!

It had been an agonizing two weeks since he had seen her, although her eyes had been in his mind every moment of the day. He had day-dreamed of her while stoically turning wrenches in his garage, and her face flashed upon his closed eyelids at night as soon as his head hit the pillow. "Sweets!" he cried, involuntarily.

A sob of joy escaped her. She rose to her feet, stretching her hands out to him. Abel, hearing her voice and sensing the release of pressure on the reins, started forward. The sleigh lurched, and Amber tumbled backward into the seat. In a moment, he was in the sled with her, wrap-ping his arms protectively around her. He hugged her to his chest. "My love! My Sweets!" He couldn't resist pressing kisses upon her face and eyelids, satisfying the intense cravings of his heart.

She laughed and wept, overwhelmed with love and relief. She was safe in his arms again! The euphoric sensation was almost more than she could bear. She tilted her head, eagerly offering up her lips. But when the expected kiss did not come, she opened her eyes in bewilderment. He groaned, and relaxed his grip.

Oh, God! Was she losing him again?!

"What have I done?!" he lamented loudly. He smashed his right hand against the side of the sleigh.

He had the ring in his pocket! Her ring! He still carried the ring ev-erywhere with him – he even slept with it at night. He could pull it out now, now! And take her by the hand and demand that she become his wife!

He could do it! He should do it! He loved her now and forever. He would always love her!

He could do it—except on that very morning he had finally decided to offer Sheila and Olivia a permanent home!

Sheila had been sitting on the couch, flipping through the pages of her magazine, while he was once again changing the baby. The mental and emotional quandary had become too much for him, and he tenta-tively broached the topic of making their non-sexual cohabitation legal. He even suggested that he would like to adopt Olivia, to whom he was in fact becoming deeply attached. But all the time he was talking he was hoping and praying to himself that Sheila wouldn't take him up on his offer. Instead, she shrugged at his words. "Sure," she replied. "Why not?"

Why not?!

Jesus! What had he done?!

In abject misery, he apprised Amber of his awful decision. And then he had the further agony of witnessing her pain, watching as the joy drained from her face and eyes. What must she think of him?! How she would hate him!

She stared at him dumbly at first, almost unable to believe her ears. How she got herself out of the sleigh, she wasn't sure. But she knew she heard his voice crying out for her to stop, as she blindly pushed ahead through the dense green undergrowth, trying to follow the scent of wood smoke back to the others.

It was over. Over! Now there was no hope—no hope for them at all!

Chapter 28
·······
Peas, Beans and Corn

As I've said, news travels fast in Sovereign, and the news that Bruce had decided to recommit himself to his ex-wife was all over town by eventide the next day. I heard the news from Maynard Nutter, who came to my home on the Cross Road to seek me out. Although Maynard and I had been friends for fourteen years, this was the first time he'd crossed my threshold, deeming it unseemly to visit a single woman alone in her home. These were extenuating circumstances, however, and he shucked off his wool hunting jacket and foisted the plaid coat onto the back of my kitchen chair. He took the proffered seat and faced me across the table.

"'Tain't right," Maynard allowed, his blue-veined hands trembling with emotion. "He's in love with t'other gal!"

"That's a fact," I agreed.

"'Cain't you do somethin', Maggie?" he pleaded, twisting his wool cap round and round. A gentleman of the old school, Maynard was one of the few men in Maine who removed his hat in the presence of a lady.

"What do you want me to do, Maynard? I'm a minister, not a magician!"

He stared glumly at me, his romantic bachelor heart bleeding all over the place. In a quavering voice, he proceeded to tell me about his lifelong love of Mabel Jean, and the letters that had been penned shortly before her death. I listened to his lamentations for nearly half an hour. "Life's too short for them kids to muck it up!" he concluded.

There's nothing that torments us older folks so much as witnessing younger people make the same stupid mistakes we did, knowing all the while that the kids will reject our well-meaning advice, just like we did at their age! Ah, well. Youth is wasted on the young, and wisdom is wasted on the old.

"I'll do what I can," I assured Maynard.

Maynard collected his coat and departed, possibly as gratified to have shared his own personal story as he was to plead for intercession on behalf of Bruce and Amber.

But what was I to do? What could I do?!

I tossed another stick of rock maple into my wood-burning cookstove, and sank back into the rocker to think. The comfy rocker was situated next to the hot stove, and faced the window overlooking the road. It was a pleasant seat, and I often sat and rocked, watching the cars pass by, as I pondered the fate of my flock.

As the minister of the local church, every soul in Sovereign is my responsibility, whether the owner of that soul attends church or not. Some might ask: Who died and left you in charge? And in reply I can only point to the sky or tap my heart. If you don't know the answer to that question, I can't explain it to you.

Part of what motivates me is my belief in the goodness of God, of course. I believe that God loves us, and truly wants each and every one of us to be happy, not just the pretty ones, or the rich ones, or the healthy ones – *every one* of us. Also, I do feel I'm called to share with my flock this Word and its consort Comfort. But a lot of my motivation comes from just plain fear, fear that when I get to Heaven God's gonna call me on the carpet and grill me, asking me stuff like why I didn't do everything in my power to keep Bruce Gilpin from making such a stupid mistake!

In Bruce's case, the task of intervention wouldn't be easy. I could already see that he was avoiding me. Maynard had told me that he had asked Shirley Palmer to perform the marriage ceremony. Shirley was a Notary Public, and notaries can marry people in the state of Maine. But the very fact that my young friend had selected Shirley to do the deed after he and I had shared so much in his youth only suggested to me the depths of his despair. Bruce knew he was making a terrible mistake, but he was so pig-headed he didn't want anyone – like me – to try and talk him out of it.

There's a strain of stubbornness in the Gilpin clan, of which I was only too well aware. Ralph and I had had our tug o' wars over the years, and frankly both of us had ended up on our tushes in the dirt. While Bruce had inherited the good looks and physique of the Hodges men, he had inherited some of his father's contumacy.

I plotted my strategy, picked my time carefully, and drove over to his garage. Bruce was inside the shop working on a vehicle, but a little bell rang when I opened the door to alert him of a customer. The doorknob was new, and had one of those push button locks. I glanced up at the heavens and depressed the lock. I didn't want us to be disturbed.

The door to the shop from the office was open, and I passed through. A rusty red truck was on the lift closest to the door, with Bruce's head under it. "Anybody home?" I said, loudly.

His handsome head quickly appeared, and his arms followed. "Maggie!" he exclaimed. He pulled a rag out of his back pocket, and wiped his hands. "I didn't hear the bell. Having car trouble?"

He knew why I was there – and I knew that he knew why I was there. Normally, I would have called him on it. Today, however, I let it go. "Where's Sheila?" I asked, ignoring his question. Of course he knew that I wasn't having car trouble.

"At the restaurant. She spends most of her time there. She and Olivia."

"You're getting very fond of Olivia, aren't you?"

He bristled. "So what if I am? She doesn't have anybody else to look out for her and she's just a baby!"

"She's not your baby," I reminded him.

Angrily, he retreated to the workbench, and tossed the dirty rag on top. He leaned back against the wooden bench and folded his arms across his chest. "I know why you're here, Maggie, and it won't work," he declared. His brown eyes flashed defensively.

"Now, now, Bruce, don't get your back up."

"Just say what you have to say, and I'll listen. Then you can go away!"

I advanced a few steps, oblivious of where I was walking.

"Watch the air hose," he said. He pointed to the long black hose near my foot. He ran his fingers through his hair, and I could see that he was almost at the breaking point. There was a smudge of grease on his cheek, which if Amber had been present would have been lovingly wiped away.

The smudge reminded me how human Bruce was, and made me more determined than ever to help save him from a life of misery. Sometimes the best way to help someone is to make him or her feel sorry for you. I'd planned in advance to use this approach to get around Bruce's stubbornness so that I might touch his heart. "Your uncle came to see me a couple of months ago," I began.

"Peter?"

I nodded. "The day you first went to look at the old corn shop. I hadn't seen him in a long time, not since your grandfather's funeral, I guess." I paused.

Bruce wasn't sure where the conversation was going, so he remained stubbornly silent.

"I made a mistake with Peter that I've regretted all my life," I continued, earnestly. "He asked me to marry him when we were both young – young and foolish. I was so stupid I didn't know my own heart, although I was pretty sure about his. My grandmother told me to take him; she told me not only that Peter was a good man but also that he was the love of my life and I'd regret it forever if I turned him down. But I didn't listen. I was proud and stubborn and stupid. I thought I knew what was best for me, but I didn't. And so I ruined two lives, not just my own, but your uncle's also."

Bruce's arms had unfurled as I shared my story. He absently picked up a wrench from his workbench and began turning it in his hands. "I figured it must be something like that, why Peter never married." He tossed the wrench back on the bench. It *clinked* against another iron tool. "Yikes! You could have been my aunt!"

"Exactly!" That wasn't my point, but I'd take it. His pronouncement seemed to give me some familial authority, as well as spiritual authority. "I don't want to see you make the same mistake, Bruce."

"Who says it's a mistake?!"

"You do. Your own heart tells you it's a mistake! You love another woman, and she loves you. Don't just think of Sheila and the baby, think of …"

"Olivia," he interrupted. "Her name's Olivia."

"Don't just think of Sheila and Olivia, think of Amber! You have a responsibility to Amber that is greater than the responsibility I know you feel to those two lost souls. Don't tell me you didn't think of marrying Amber before Sheila turned up, because I won't believe it!"

He put his hand into his right pants pocket. "I did," he admitted. "I did think of marrying Amber. I even bought the ring." He pulled out a green velvet ring case, and held it out to me.

I was so surprised I almost lost my focus. Instinctively, I reached for the velvet case and flipped it open. A beautiful purplish-blue tourmaline in a simple gold setting sparkled under the fluorescent lights. "Oh, my! It's beautiful!" I proclaimed. I shut the case, and handed it back to him.

He returned the ring to his pocket. "I was gonna propose to Amber on Valentine's Day, but then Sheila came back to town, with Olivia."

"Why did you wait?!" I cried. "Why didn't you go to Amber the first moment your heart told you that she was the one!"

He smiled. "That would have been when I sat down next to her on the bus from Boston."

I started to speak, but he held up his hand. "Listen, Maggie, I've thought this thing through until I can't think anymore. I have a duty to Sheila, and even to that innocent baby. I can't have my ex-wife wandering the streets taking up with any man she can find, just because she needs a roof over her head!"

"We can help her!" I protested. "All of us in Sovereign will help her! And there are social programs to help Sheila and the ba--, Olivia!"

"It's not just that. There's a season for everything and everything has its season."

"Oh, God! Please don't quote Ecclesiastes to me! I hate that quote. People only use it when there's something they want to justify or there's something they aren't happy about, like death."

He shrugged. "There's a Natural Order of Things, then," he continued, resorting to the lecture his mother had given him when he'd first returned home. "You don't plant the corn before you plant the peas, 'cause it won't grow. You plant stuff in the natural order: peas, beans and corn. I'm in the season of peas, and Amber is in the season of corn."

"That's bull crap," I said.

He winced.

"Pure malarkey! You know in your heart that there's no difference between the two of you. You're simply two people who've fallen in love."

"But I'm nearly fourteen years older than Amber!"

"What?! Do you think that Love is so weak it's bound by time! That Love could ever be confined or constricted or tugged or twisted by any human hand! No! Love is Lord of All, my young friend, and you can no more escape Love's fate than you can escape Death. But Love is more powerful than Death, because Love lasts well beyond the grave. You might go to your grave without Amber by your side, but you'll have her heart with you every step of the way and into the hereafter! And you know it, too!"

He was weakening. I could see him turning my words over in his head. I could almost hear the throbbing of his heart, beating with the desire to throw off the chains of duty and rush over to the old Russell homestead and throw himself at Amber's feet.

The bell on the office door *jingled*, startling both of us. In a moment, Sheila appeared, carrying Olivia in the baby carrier. "Hey, the door was locked," she apprised him. "Good thing you gave me a key the other day. I thought you said you never locked the door?"

The spell was broken. Bruce recollected himself, and straightened up to his full six-foot-one. His eyes hooded over. I could see that he had retreated back into his solider self.

"Sorry about that."

Sheila shifted the baby carrier. "No problem."

I nodded at Sheila, hoping that she would realize we were busy and go away.

"Hey," she said, instead. "Aren't you the minister? I remember you."

"Maggie Walker," I replied. "Bruce and I were just having a little private conversation here."

But Bruce had taken the opportunity to retreat to the workbench. He retrieved a wrench, and flipped it in his hand. "Thanks for stopping by, Maggie. I'll think about what you said."

But I wasn't done yet. He couldn't get rid of me that easily. I thought of Amber, and I thought of that old wooden cradle in the nursery at Oaknole. Possibly there was some additional impetus on my part when I considered that I myself might have provided an infant for that cradle, had it not been for my own stubbornness. Fortunately, patience is the flip side of stubbornness, and I patiently waited for Sheila to leave.

When she had taken the baby upstairs, I changed my tack, lowering my flag. "Look, I'm sorry if I'm butting in where I'm not wanted, Bruce," I apologized, meekly. "I just can't help myself! Ask Peter, he'll tell you."

"Aw, I know you mean well," he admitted. "But there's only one person who can make this decision, Maggie, and you're not it."

"OK, but if you do decide to go through with this thing with Sheila, at least let me be the one to perform the wedding service," I pleaded.

Bruce was clearly taken aback. "You'd do that?"

"Of course! Just because I don't agree with you, doesn't mean I care for you any less, or that I don't want to be part of your lives!"

He pondered my words for a moment. "OK, how about Saturday? That'll give me time enough to get the marriage license."

My heart nearly stopped. Was he serious? Or was he testing me? "This Saturday?"

"Do you have a problem with that?"

I turned things over in my mind, and concluded that Bruce was testing me. When push came to shove, he wouldn't go through with this faux marriage. He couldn't possibly have made his final decision that quickly. "Saturday's fine," I said, warily.

"Great. It's a date, then. I'll call you later about the time."

Frustrated, I threw up my hands. Clearly, it was time to move on to Plan B!

Chapter 29
·······
Plan B

Things were certainly not cheerful at the Gilpin households – either of them – leading up to the wedding on Saturday. For starters, when Gray came home from school the day of my conversation with his father, Bruce asked his son, now sixteen, to act as his best man. Gray adamantly refused.

"I think what you're doing is wrong," the boy said, stubbornly. Alas! The Gilpin contumacy had carried on to the next generation, proving once again that what goes around comes around. "I love Mom and everything," he continued. "But you don't. You love Amber. I think you ought to marry her!"

Gray then packed up his belongings and his sleeping bag, and moved back over to his grandparent's house. This act of desertion probably hurt Bruce as much as the boy's refusal to participate in the wedding, for it left Bruce alone in the evenings with Sheila. His free time had been gloomy enough before without Amber, but without Gray to enliven his daily life he was almost beside himself with despair.

"Hey," Sheila said to him the night that Gray left. "What should I wear?"

Bruce, still sore from his son's defection, answered her angrily. "I don't care what you wear!"

Sheila looked hurt. "You don't have to yell at me. It was just a stupid question."

Bruce immediately felt ashamed of himself. "Don't you have a dress or anything?"

She shrugged. "Maybe. But I don't think it'll fit."

Bruce recollected all those pieces of pie on the tab that his mother had presented him recently and he began to have a glimmer of understanding. He opened his wallet and drew out some money. "Here, go buy yourself a dress. Nothing fancy, though." He had wanted to add, "And nothing white!" But he didn't because he felt sorry for her.

He realized that it wasn't entirely Sheila's fault she was in the situation she was in, nor was it his fault. He knew on some level that society was to blame, for perpetuating a pattern among families of poor, uneducated women where they ended up having babies with different men simply as a means to provide themselves with a roof over their heads. He was unable to hold society accountable, however, and so he was doing what he believed to be the honorable thing by taking responsibility for Sheila and Olivia himself.

"Is that enough money?" he worried. "I don't have any idea how much a dress costs these days."

Sheila accepted the cash. "Sure. Thanks."

Bruce, still scrambling for a best man, considered asking some of his buddies from the Guard to stand up with him, many of whom were now back in the area thanks to the accelerated draw-down in Afghanistan. But he was too embarrassed by what he was doing to explain to any of them that his marriage wasn't a love match but an act of charity. He finally decided to ask Peter, although he knew his uncle wouldn't approve of his remarriage to Sheila.

Fortunately, I'd already contacted my old friend to apprise him of the situation and alert him to the particulars of Plan B. Therefore, Peter was ready when the phone call came.

After explaining the situation as best he could – and this was difficult for Bruce to explain over the phone, but certainly much easier than in person – he asked for his uncle's support. "Can you do it, Peter?"

"No problem," Peter replied. "I'd be honored." That was probably laying it on too thick.

"Really?" Bruce asked, somewhat suspiciously.

Peter caught himself. "Son, I might not agree with you, but I'll always support you. That's what family's for."

The time of the wedding was initially problematic, since Maude and Peter had conflicting schedules. The restaurant didn't close until 2 p.m. and yet Peter needed to be back at Oaknole by 3 p.m. for afternoon milking. In the end, Peter asked a former dairy farmer friend to cover for him, and the 3 p.m. time was selected for the wedding.

There was still some Gilpin contumacy to be dispatched on the North Troy Road, however. Before I was able to enlighten Maude about Plan B, she and Gray both threatened to boycott the wedding. Ralph, normally the most stubborn member of the family, suddenly found himself pressing the other two to do that which he himself didn't really want to do!

"He's ya own flesh 'n blood, Maude," Ralph reminded his wife, perhaps unnecessarily, since she was the one who'd given birth to Bruce. "Ya gotta stand by him!"

Maude sniveled. "He's making a terrible mistake!" She began to weep.

He pressed his skinny arms around his wife. "Now, now, 'tain't the end of the world!"

"Waaa!"

Ralph finally prevailed, and Maude agreed to put in an appearance at the wedding. His grandson, however, was dug in like a tick. "Ya don't gotta say nuthin' or do nuthin'," Ralph pleaded, looking up at Gray. The boy had grown four inches in the last six months, and was now taller than his grandfather. "Ya jest gotta be there. Even Peter's gonna come!"

"I don't think what Dad's doing is right," Gray declared, folding his arms across his thin chest. He had never resembled his father, but at that moment Ralph thought he looked exactly like Bruce!

"Course 'taint right!" Ralph agreed, reassuringly. "But there's lots thet ain't right in this world, 'n the sooner ya git used to thet fact the bettah off yer gonna be!"

Eventually, Gray capitulated, but only grudgingly.

Amber's life was now one long nightmare of despair, sadness and longing. She would force herself to rise in the morning, stoically performing her chores. But then her feelings would become too much for her and she would hasten back to bed for a few hours, eager to curl up with her eReader and Emily Dickinson. Since Bruce had informed her of her fate, she had taken to lounging in bed or moping about the house despondently in her pajamas. At best, she would wander aimlessly through the woods on her snowshoes. Rebecca wisely left her daughter alone, recognizing the symptoms of the grieving process. But Wendell's soft heart had got the better of him, and once or twice he'd tried to tempt Amber back to the pursuit of happiness and joy.

On the day of Bruce and Sheila's wedding, Wendell valiantly attempted to entice Amber away from Sovereign, even suggesting a trip to the Fairfield Antiques Mall, where free hot coffee and donuts were on display as well as thousands of antiques. But Amber stubbornly decided to stay at home alone, hoping against hope that Bruce would come to his senses and seek her out.

She was in the middle of drowning her sorrows with chocolates and Emily Dickinson, when she heard a car honking its horn annoyingly in the driveway. Determined not to stir from her repining – even though it might cost her an egg customer – she ignored the noise for several minutes. But when the honking persisted she resignedly slipped into her jeans and a shirt, and headed to the shed. She threw open the door, astonished to see Maude Gilpin puffing up the steps!

"Good heavens, Amber!" Maude uttered, stopping to catch her breath. "Hurry up! We haven't got much time left! Why didn't you come right away when I blew the horn?"

Fearful that something awful had happened to Bruce, Amber clutched at the shed door for support. "Mrs. Gilpin! What's wrong!"

"Everything's wrong! I can't find that letter and I've looked everywhere! Maggie thought you might be able to help me. We need to hurry, though, the wedding starts in less than an hour!"

Amber felt a thrill of hope. "What letter?"

"Bruce's letter, the one he wrote to himself years ago! Maggie said that when Sheila left him, he wrote a letter to himself – sort of a warning – in case he ever thought about getting married again. I tore his old bedroom apart, but I couldn't find it! Maggie thought you might know something about it?"

Amber's heightened senses were slightly titillated. "You went through Bruce's things?"

"My dear, when you have children, you'll understand all about it! Do you love him or not?"

"I love him with all my heart!" Amber vowed. She reached for her coat, which was hanging just behind her on a peg. "Tell me what to do!"

"Find the letter! Do you have any idea where Bruce might have put it?" Maude inquired, anxiously. "I've looked in all his secret hiding places – all the ones I know about, that is – and I didn't find a thing!"

An image flashed into Amber's mind of Bruce leaning up against the Staircase Tree. She recalled his words: *Hey, have you ever climbed up to the top? … All my hopes and dreams are in this tree.*

All my hopes and dreams are in this tree!

"I know exactly where it is! Follow me!"

She shrugged into her coat and raced to the Staircase Tree, Maude hustling down the driveway behind her as fast as her fat legs would carry her. The *papier-mâché* chickens had been put away for the winter, and the pegs had been removed from the steps. Amber carefully balanced herself on the bottom step, and began climbing agilely, hanging onto the sides of the downed tree limb for support as she moved upward.

"Be careful, dear!" Maude called, shielding her eyes from the afternoon sun so that she could better follow Amber's progress.

Amber reached the top step, and hoisted herself across the rough bark into the crotch of the old tree. She slid her legs around into a comfortable position, and began fishing through the good-sized cavity in the tree that had served as the red squirrel's hidey hole. Fortunately, the red sentinel had temporarily abandoned his post, and Amber made good headway emptying out his hole. She pulled out dank decaying leaves, broken pieces of nuts, crumbling bark and other cold, damp trash. Suddenly, her hand struck something large and hard – a tin box! She finagled her hands underneath the box, and liberated it from its hiding place. She brushed the black dirt off the top.

"I have something!" she called down to Maude. "Looks like an old tackle box!"

"Open it up, quick! Good Lord! It's almost three o'clock!"

With shaking hands, Amber flipped up the latch and opened the rusty lid. Inside she found a treasure trove of boyhood memorabilia: a scuffed baseball with missing threads, two quill-sized feathers, an old wooden nickel, a tarnished brass key, several square-shaped buttons, a scouting patch, and much more. Tucked beneath the souvenirs was a sealed white envelope. Amber slowly pulled the envelope free, and turned it over in her hands. She recognized Bruce's careless scribble: *To Be Opened by Myself in the Event I Ever Think About Getting Married Again.*

"Oh, my God, I found it!" she cried, hugging the letter to her chest. She closed and latched the tackle box, and scooted quickly down the tree to show Bruce's mother the prize.

Maude took one look at the letter, and clasped Amber to her ample breasts. "My dear, I know you're going to make him a wonderful wife!"

Time was of the essence however, and Maude quickly released her hoped-for daughter-in-law. In less than a minute, she shared with Amber the rest of Plan B.

Meanwhile, back at the little white church, the wedding party and a few guests had already assembled. Bruce hadn't sent out any kind of announcement nor had he invited anyone to attend the wedding other than his immediate family. So he was surprised to see that a smattering of townspeople had preceded him and Sheila to the church, including Maynard Nutter, Leland and Trudy Gorse, Ryan MacDonald, Clyde Crosby and the Palmers.

Bruce was dressed in the black suit he'd purchased for his grandfather's funeral, unable to bring himself to wear his military dress uniform. He'd imagined too many times himself in his dress blues standing at the altar with Amber to wear that! Sheila had on her new dress, a new pair of shoes, and had even taken extra effort with her hair. My old friend Peter looked as cute as he did when he stepped onto the bus in Winslow more than fifty years ago, and I discovered that he did indeed have hair left on the top of his pointy-eared head.

Olivia was happily tucked away in a new baby carrier, and Bruce carefully set the seat into one of the front pews. Shirley Palmer had agreed to stand up with Sheila, and I collected the little wedding party into the chancel, that area behind the white railing which supposedly separates the holy from the profane. Bruce had asked me to perform a simple service, and had not wanted a rehearsal. I steadied everyone into their appropriate spots, and glanced at my watch. I had stalled as long as I could, and it was already after 3 p.m. I offered a little silent prayer, and began reading the wedding service.

I had selected a service of marriage from one of my particularly medieval clergy guides, and more than a few eyes glazed over as I droned on. I paused for effect every now and then, but mostly to kill time. Finally, I reached that all-important part. "If any man can show just cause why these two may not lawfully be joined together, let him now speak, or else hereafter forever hold his peace," I proclaimed solemnly. I stopped reading, and peered expectantly at those gathered in the white pews.

Nobody said anything for a moment. The church was so quiet you could hear the chalice's flame flicker.

Sheila spoke first. "Who put that in there? Do you have to say that?"

Leland obligingly hollered a reply from the back pew. "Doncha know, them's regular words in a weddin' ceremony!"

Sheila glared at the old farmer. "Pooh!"

Trudy, who was sitting up front with Ryan, turned around and reprimanded Leland. "Hush, Father!"

I flipped the clergy guide book around so that Sheila could read the words for herself. She shrugged. "Whatever," she conceded. She resumed her position, clutching the small bouquet Bruce had bought her.

I could see the wheels turning in Bruce's head, but he said nothing. He stared grimly down at the red carpet.

Sheila's interruption had given us more time, and also enabled me to repeat that dastardly charge, which I've certainly never used in any other wedding ceremony! "Is there any reason why these two should not be joined together?" I paraphrased, loudly. The entire church held its breath.

Clyde Crosby shifted uncomfortably in his hard seat. His conscience finally forced him to speak up. "I guess probbly!" he bellowed out.

Maynard Nutter vehemently nodded his agreement. "'Tain't right," he cried, from the second pew. "'Tain't right at-tall!"

A general commotion broke out and the noise was further increased when Amber flung open the front door and burst into the church. "I have it!" she cried, waving the letter in her hand. She flew up the center aisle, her beautiful hair streaming behind her. "Is it too late! Oh, God, please don't tell me I'm too late!"

"Holy God Almighty, you're just in time!" I replied, in great relief.

"Amber!" Bruce exclaimed. "What are you doing here?!"

She stopped at the white railing, and regarded him lovingly. "I'm here to stop you from making the biggest mistake of your life Bruce Gilpin!"

"But Sweets, you told me yourself, there's only one person in the world who can make this decision, and …"

"And you're it!" she declared. Triumphantly, she handed him his own letter.

I knew what was in the letter, of course, because I'd encouraged my young friend to write it nearly fourteen years ago. In it, Bruce had vowed to himself that he would never marry again—except for love. Sometimes it's good to write important stuff like that down, just in case the world is too much for us and we forget our own vows.

Bruce re-read the letter with shaking hands. Seeing his own words on the white paper had a powerful effect on him, and his heart was turned immediately in the right direction, the direction that he'd wanted to take all along. His stubborn pride and his overly developed sense of duty were no match for the rush of love that overwhelmed him. He uttered a little cry, and dropped the letter to the floor. "Amber!"

After handing Bruce the letter, Amber had rushed back down the aisle, embarrassed to discover so many pairs of eyes upon her. He vaulted over the railing and dashed after her, catching up with his beloved on the front steps.

He swept her up to his breast, sobbing with pent-up emotion. "Can you ever forgive me, Sweets?! What a fool! What a stupid fool!"

Needless to say, she offered him a non-verbal reply, and he greedily kissed her lips, her face, her throat and her hands. He wrapped her hair around his wrist, proclaiming: "I'll never let you go again! Never! I swear it!"

Back inside the church, havoc had broken loose. The baby had begun to cry, and Leland was shouting in an attempt to explain to Clyde exactly what had just occurred. Maude, who had followed Amber into the church, immediately took charge of the chaos. "Here, Shirley, give that baby to me! Peter – don't just stand there, help Sheila into her coat! Leland, hush! I think Clyde's got it figured out by now!"

And that's how we successfully implemented Plan B.

Chapter 30
. . . .
The Auction

Needless to say, the Maine tourmaline ring that Bruce carried with him in his pocket and with which he slept at night wasn't long in finding its rightful owner, a pretty young woman with eyes the color of late-season asters. While Maude was marshaling order inside the church, Bruce knelt on the steps, took Amber's hand, and formally proposed. I wasn't surprised when I discovered later that he'd had the ring in his pocket the whole time he was standing at the altar with Sheila. And I certainly wasn't surprised that Amber accepted his proposal!

There were other tasks to dispatch before everyone involved could become quite comfortable again, however, especially our hero. Bruce still had the problem of what to do with Sheila and Olivia. He couldn't throw his ex-wife and the child of whom he'd become increasingly fond out onto the street, and yet they couldn't continue to live with him, either. He, his new fiancée and his parents discussed the situation in a huddle that evening. Unable to find immediate resolution, the dialogue continued over the course of the next few days. All sorts of solutions were proposed for Sheila, while she herself sat quietly at home in the apartment over the garage, apparently content to flip through the pages of her magazines.

In the end, the solution came from an unexpected quarter. Maynard Nutter had spoken a few words to Sheila at the church during the wedding-that-wasn't, and had taken pity on her. His soft bachelor's heart was touched by her plight, and one night while the Gilpin clan was holding a powwow on the North Troy Road, Maynard stopped by the garage and offered Sheila and Olivia a home with him.

"I been rattlin' 'round thet old place by myself for fourteen years, since Mother died," Maynard explained beforehand to his colleague John Woods. He hadn't quite made up his mind whether or not such an addition to his household would be a good idea. "I ain't got no family and I'm downright tired o' being alone."

"Course you got plenty of room," replied the laconic Woods. He leaned back in his desk chair at the Town Office, and shifted his lanky legs.

This was an argument that hadn't occurred to Maynard, and he immediately cobbled onto it. "Seems sinful to waste all thet space, don't it?"

"Sure do."

Much to Bruce's surprise, Sheila took Maynard up on his offer. "You don't want me," she pointed out. "And he does. Besides, he's got a TV."

And so Sheila, Olivia and their few belongings moved into the old farmhouse on the Bangor Road with Maynard Nutter. Although Bruce was grateful to Maynard for providing a home to his ex-wife, he felt to some degree that he was shirking his duty to Sheila. He and Amber privately considered the situation, and together they decided to give Bruce's share of the proceeds from the sale of the Emily Dickinson items to Sheila and her daughter.

Although Bruce was the one who proposed the gift, he was understandably dejected by their decision, since it meant that the money wouldn't be available to fund his dream of saving the old corn shop. "What'll we do now?" he asked his bride-to-be. The couple was enjoying a rare moment of privacy at his apartment over the garage.

"We'll find other ways to fund the museum project," Amber assured him. "It might take us a little longer to get everything the way we'd like, Love, but we'll make it work!"

He dropped a kiss on the tip of her nose. "That's why I love you, Sweets! No matter what happens, you're always so positive!"

She smiled, inwardly grateful that he hadn't seen her moping about the old Russell homestead over the past few weeks! "I'm certainly positive I've made the right decision to spend the rest of my life with you, Bruce Gilpin!" she'd replied, as a balm to her conscience.

The next day Bruce consulted Ryan MacDonald about the matter, and the lawyer advised him to set up a trust for Olivia, funding the trust with the proceeds from the auction. Ryan offered to prepare the legal paperwork, and also act as trustee. While the trust would be for the maintenance of Olivia, Sheila would necessarily be provided for as well. In addition, Ryan took upon himself the exploration of state and federal social welfare programs, to see what might be available to help Sheila and the baby.

"You don't need to carry this burden by yourself," the attorney said, putting a reassuring hand to his friend's shoulder. "There are plenty of others who want to help Sheila."

Bruce, overwhelmed by gratitude, marveled at his feelings of affection for the other man. "And to think I was jealous of you once, MacDonald!"

"I'm a happy man now, Gilpin – thanks to you!" Inspired by Bruce, Ryan had proposed to Trudy on that very afternoon, and the couple was already planning a spring wedding.

"I think Amber had more to do with getting you and Trudy together than me. I'm just glad everything worked out for you two!"

"Well, I think honesty demands that we also give some credit to the cow," Ryan conceded. "I suppose I'll be delivering all the calves at Scotch Brook Acres now." He sighed heavily, in mock despair.

Still even greater things were in store for our friends. At the next meeting of the Sovereign Canning Factory Museum Board of Directors, which was the final meeting before the auction of the Emily Dickinson letters, Ryan surprised them (all but Trudy) with an altogether different offer.

"The Ladies Auxiliary has asked me to formally offer to take over the museum project," he announced. This time the little group was meeting at Miss Hastings' house, the retired music teacher having mostly recovered from her illness.

"I don't get it," said Bruce, puzzled.

"We decided everything at our last meeting, Bruce!" Trudy interjected, unusually animated. "When the Auxiliary heard that you were going to give your share of the Emily Dickinson money to Sheila and Olivia, we knew we needed to do something. The Ladies Auxiliary has more than $350,000 saved up in our principal account, which is separate from our endowment account. So we voted to change our policy, and spend the money in our principal account – that is, *if* you'll let us take over the museum project. The vote was unanimous!"

"Yikes!" Bruce exclaimed. "$350,000! You ladies have been busy!"

"That's wonderful, darhhhlings!" cried Miss Hastings.

"Wow! I had no idea the Auxiliary had so much money!" Amber declared. "Mom never said a word!"

Trudy nodded, her hazel eyes gleaming. "Auxiliary policy from the very beginning, in 1851, was always to save half the money the group raised and donate the other half," she explained. "Our cookbooks and bake sales might not bring in much at the time, but after one hundred and sixty-three years, the money adds up!"

"Behold! The amazing power of compounding!" Ryan added. "Benjamin Franklin knew all about it. What do you say, Gilpin? Want to turn everything over to the Ladies?"

Bruce, still confounded by the amount of money the Auxiliary had managed to save, almost didn't know what to say. He nodded, bemused. "I think it's an offer we can't refuse!"

The much-heralded auction of the Emily Dickinson items was slated for the end of February, and, when the day finally arrived, it seemed as though half the town of Sovereign turned out at the James Julia auction house in Fairfield to witness the event. The auction was scheduled to begin at 10 a.m., and the pleasingly rustic room in which the event was held was filled to its capacity, with auction workers busy squeezing in more folding chairs. In addition, a bank of twenty phone lines had been established to handle all the remote bids that were expected to come in on the Dickinson letters. Two employees were designated to handle the live online bidding.

Bruce surveyed the crowd with amazement. He and Amber had appropriated seats with Gray and his parents, in and amongst a smattering of friends from the little community. When he spotted Sheila with Olivia in her baby carrier sitting next to Maynard Nutter on the opposite side of the room, he excused himself and approached his ex-wife. She was wearing another new dress – one that his money hadn't purchased – and her hair had been recently cut and styled. Most surprising to him, however, was the fact that Sheila was smiling – actually smiling! For a moment, Bruce glimpsed the pretty blonde-haired, blue-eyed teenager he'd first met seventeen years ago.

"You look very nice," he complimented Sheila, after his initial greeting to both her and Maynard.

"I bought myself a new dress," she replied, proudly. "Ryan got me hooked up with some program for single mothers. It's not welfare money, either; I'm gonna pay 'em back."

"Good for you!"

"And I'm taking classes at KVCC. I'm gonna be a radiographer," she further informed him.

"A radio what?"

"A radiographer – we help radiologists take X-rays." Sheila hesitated. She had never yet thanked her ex-husband for his gift, nor had she even acknowledged it. "Thanks," she said, now. "For helping me 'n Olivia."

Embarrassed, Bruce accepted her thanks with a nod. He didn't know what to say, so he fondled the baby's head, and turned away before anyone could see the tears in his eyes.

This exchange should serve as a reminder to us that we shouldn't give up on a horse just because it has balked at the first fence. Sheila didn't want to wash dishes at Ma Jean's Restaurant; however, she didn't want to spend the rest of her life flipping magazine pages or waiting on men, either. With the support of Ryan and Maynard, she'd revisited the interesting idea about a woman's independence that Rebecca and Maude had put into her head at the restaurant, and she decided to go back to school to get a career. Sheila liked the idea of not having to beg a man for money, and was already dreaming about the nice things she would buy for both herself and Olivia when she was able to pay her own way in life.

I also must take the opportunity to point out that Wendell had misjudged his horse. Sheila had not returned to Sovereign because she had set her sights on Bruce's share of the proceeds from the sale of the Emily Dickinson letters. In fact, she'd known nothing about the discovery. She'd returned simply because she'd run out of places to lay her head. She knew that if anyone would take her back with a child in tow, Bruce Gilpin would open his doors to her.

Later, Bruce caught up with Maynard Nutter alone at the food table, where hot coffee and fresh pastries from Hillman's Bakery in Fairfield had been provided for the sustenance of those who attended the auction. "How's it going with you, Maynard?" he asked the older man. "I can see for myself that Sheila is doing great!"

"You know, it's kinda good to have someone besides me 'n Toffee 'round the old place," Maynard answered. Toffee was Maynard's yellow lab. "I didn't realize how lonely I was. Sheila's a good girl, too. She jest needs someone to take a real interest in her, is all."

"Olivia doesn't disturb you too much?" Bruce worried.

"Oh, thet baby ain't no trouble at-all! Sheila's only takin' classes three days a week – she ain't gone long, neither. 'Tain't no problem to watch out for Olivia while she's gone."

"You're babysitting Olivia?!"

Maynard chuckled. "Don't look so shocked, son. You ain't the only man in Sovereign who kin change a di-a-per!"

While Bruce was gone, Amber found herself eavesdropping on Shirley Palmer, who was sitting directly behind her. The former Sovereign

Post Mistress was regaling a Connecticut couple with stories about the town's old canning factory. The couple had heard that part of the money from the sale of the Dickinson discovery was to fund a restoration of the corn shop, and they were curious about the factory's history.

"I remember one summer Father worked at the canning factory alongside German POWs," Shirley shared with the middle-aged couple. "'Twarn't 'nuff men in town, you know; they was all off fightin' the Germans!"

Both husband and wife appeared startled by this information. "There were German POWs in Maine? On American soil?" the husband inquired, punctiliously.

"Oh, yes – lots of 'em! 'Twarn't nuthin' to be scairt of! They was regular folks, jest like you 'n me. When I was 'bout ten, Father worked husking alongside this one big handsome fellar—did I have a crush on him! After school, I used to sit on the grass nearby 'n watch him work. One day I got up my nerve 'n I asked him if he was married. He could speak a little English, you know. He winked at me. 'My wife is married, but I'm not!' he said. Did I blush up something fierce! Oh, how Father laughed!"

Just before the auction began, Bruce reclaimed his seat. He squeezed Amber's hand affectionately. "Here we go, Sweets!"

When an image of the first Emily Dickinson letter to be auctioned off flashed onto the projection screen, the excitement in the audience was palpable. Jim Julia, the auctioneer and co-owner of the auction house, proceeded to hold forth on the particulars of the discovery in the old carriage shed. Although Julia knew that most of the bidding would be done by those not present, he took the trouble to explain to the audience something of Emily Dickinson's singular history and her importance to the field of American arts and letters. He then lifted the gavel, slammed it against the wooden podium, and opened the auction.

When the bidding on the first letter commenced, all twenty phone lines were active with bids coming in from around the world. It seemed as though every Emily Dickinson fan alive – whether an individual or bidders representing a museum or university – was hoping to acquire something penned by the iconoclastic 19th century poet from Amherst, Massachusetts!

"And I have one thousand, now two, now three – is that all you're willing to pay for this FABULOUS piece of literature?!" Jim Julia pleaded, affronted. "And now I have five thousand, and six, and seven ...

and ten thousand dollars! TEN THOUSAND DOLLARS! Ladies and gentlemen, remember, once these letters are sold – they're GONE! And so is your chance to own a piece of Emily Dickinson!"

Amber trembled with excitement. Ten thousand dollars! She herself had held that very letter in her hands! She almost wished that she had money enough to bid. But then she stole a fond look at Bruce's handsome face and decided that fate had rewarded her more than enough!

When the first of the letters sold for $15,500, Bruce was convinced of two things. First, he knew that he'd never have to worry about Sheila and Olivia again. And second, he knew that his dream of rescuing the old corn shop was going to become a reality!

And he was right. Twelve of the letters, which were more or less alike in nature, averaged $15,000 each. One Emily Dickinson epistle that contained the germ of an early poem sold for $45,000. The bidding on the rare copy of *Forest Leaves* was even more intense, and the winning bid came from an undisclosed phone bidder, who offered nearly $150,000 for the old Amherst Academy publication. When all was said and done, the Emily Dickinson ephemera that Bruce and Amber had discovered stashed away in a trunk in Ma Jean's carriage shed netted an astonishing $376,500!

"But wait … where's the fourteenth letter?!" Amber puzzled, when the auctioneer's gavel had fallen for the last time. "He only auctioned thirteen!" She reexamined her catalog. Something didn't add up!

Bruce liberated a yellowed envelope from his shirt pocket and held it up for her perusal. "It's a little early, but here's my wedding gift to you!"

Amber's breath caught in her throat. She looked at the fragile, faded envelope with a mixture of awe and confusion. She hardly dared to move, lest she awaken from a beautiful dream.

He indicated the auction hall with a little movement of his hand. "This is all because of you, Sweets," he said. "You took the trouble to go through those old papers, and you recognized their value. It's only right that you have your own personal piece of Emily Dickinson." He leaned over and kissed his addled bride-to-be. "Besides, I never forgot what she wrote about the fields being quiet when the dew falls, and all that meckling stuff!" he added with a grin.

Amber laughed, and wiped away a few tears of joy. "*Mechlin,*" she corrected, gaily. "Oh, Love! You shouldn't have!" Nevertheless, she eagerly accepted the letter.

He shook his head. "No, I should have. And I did."

Chapter 31

. . . .

Conclusion

It now only remains for me to wrap up the few loose ends of our story, and then say "goodbye" to all of you, who have so kindly spent some time with us in our little town of Sovereign, Maine.

The Ladies Auxiliary, utilizing their new-found wealth from the auction proceeds, in addition to their hard-earned savings, did indeed take over Bruce Gilpin's dream to restore the Westcott Canning Factory. Ryan MacDonald, who shortly became licensed to practice law in the state of Maine, coordinated all the paperwork, and the Ladies thus became his first paying client. The Ladies also soon elected to formally change their name to the Ladies Corn Shop Museum Auxiliary. Since they had been forced to become simply the Ladies Auxiliary – instead of the Ladies Fire Auxiliary – the spirited group of service workers had been searching for a new identity. This new identity they now found in preserving the town's old canning factory, which place had touched so many of their lives and the lives of their ancestors over the past one hundred and forty years. The Ladies hired a full-time museum director, and several part-time workers to clean, paint and restore the building and machinery.

"We've got the money; we might as well do it up right!" Maude announced at the decisive meeting of the Ladies Auxiliary.

Not to be outdone, the Sovereign Historical Society took over Ma Jean's lovely brick Federal-style house on the Bangor Road, and is in the process of a major fundraising effort, to which the Ladies have contributed a sizeable amount. The two groups are coordinating their efforts, and the Grand Opening of both the Sovereign Historical Society and the Sovereign Corn Shop Museum is slated for August of 2014. Mark your calendars – August is a lovely time to visit Maine! In addition, you'll have the opportunity to view a letter penned by the youthful Emily Dickinson, as Amber has permanently loaned her epistle to the corn shop museum.

Not all in Sovereign is good news, however. Miss Hastings' pet chicken Matilda died unexpectedly in April, and Miss Hastings herself took another turn for the worse. "No more, dahrrrling!" she declared, when Amber attempted to give her a replacement chicken. "There are only so many 'goodbyes' left in this old bird!" It seemed to all her friends as though the spunky and beloved Miss Hastings had become frail and elderly overnight. We suspected then that she had performed her last musical parade at the Sovereign Elementary School. Doctor Bart was sent for, of course, and although he pronounced her heart was still strong, he noted that her spirit was weak.

"She's losing her desire to live," Metcalf confided to me, after his examination of the retired music teacher. He had stopped by my house on the Cross Road on the way back to his office in Unity to alert me that my recent mammogram had picked up a lump on my breast. "It's probably nothing to be alarmed about, Aunt Maggie. But let's schedule a lumpectomy soon, OK?"

Needless to say, I didn't mention the lump to my daughter Nellie. I knew that she was swamped with papers and finals at Columbia, and I didn't want her to worry unnecessarily. I did feel a bit glum about the news, and to brighten my own spirits I spent the afternoon with the Old Farts down at Gilpin's General Store.

"Whatcha preachin' on this week, Maggie?" Leland bellowed affectionately at me as I entered, as though there was actually a remote possibility he might attend church.

"Jonah and the whale," I replied. "That is, unless you've got a better idea, Leland?"

The others hooted and hollered, and Clyde guffawed. "I guess probbly he don't!"

Ryan and Trudy were married in April at the Sovereign Union Church, with yours truly officiating. After a brief honeymoon, the couple returned to Scotch Brook Acres, where Ryan hung out a shingle at the end of the Gorse driveway. He appropriated the rarely-used front parlor for his law office, and, shortly after he settled in, a steady stream of clients came and went via the even rarer-used front door. Like me, most folks in Sovereign had put off attending to their important legal affairs, not wanting to motor out of town to seek legal advice.

I sought Ryan out not long after he hung out his shingle, having become keenly aware of my mortality thanks to the impending lumpectomy.

I arrived at the farm one afternoon to talk with him about my will, and discovered a paper sign posted to the front door: *Honk if you need me, I'm in the barn.* I peeked into the barn and spotted Ryan leaning up against the wooden stall, enthralled by his new wife, who was singing a beautiful love ballad as she milked her cows. I turned around and drove back home. The will could wait; love could not.

Ryan MacDonald, the big city attorney and forlorn orphan who had first arrived in our town last year seeking love and a place to put down roots, had finally found a home at last! And we are blessed to have him.

At the end of April, my old friend Peter Hodges suffered a terrible accident on the farm, breaking his arm and his leg and crushing several ribs when his bulldozer flipped over on him. He was lucky to escape alive! I never knew how much I loved Peter until I got the call that sent me terrified to his hospital bedside in Waterville.

"That's what I get for being careless, Maggie," he said. Peter attempted a weak smile, but he altogether failed to convince me that his injuries were anything to laugh about.

I took his good hand lovingly. If Peter had had the strength to ask me to marry him at that moment, I would finally have said, "Yes!"

After the accident, Bruce immediately assumed the milking and other farm chores at Oaknole. Since it was obvious that Peter was going to be laid up for a while, Bruce moved to the farm, subletting his garage to George Palmer, Asa's grandson. The man who had built the little apartment over the garage, shortly moved into it!

Bruce and Amber had been planning a big summer wedding in Sovereign; however, that plan was now off the table. They were understandably unhappy being apart, and Amber also hated the thought of Bruce and Peter being without feminine companionship at Oaknole. Therefore, she suggested immediate nuptials. The license was procured, and, in early May, when the blue squills and yellow daffodils were in full bloom, I performed the wedding service for Bruce and Amber on the farmer's porch at the old homestead in Winslow. Needless to say, the bride was wearing white, and the bridegroom was wearing his dress blues! Gray served as Best Man, and most of the couple's friends attended, including several of Bruce's buddies from the Maine Army Guard. The guests watched the service from comfortable chairs on the lush green lawn, with Bonnie happily making new friends. It was a beautiful day; one that many of us will never forget. My old friend was wheeled out onto the porch for the service, and I could see by the tears in Peter's eyes that he was praying that the old wooden cradle wouldn't be empty much longer!

Amber's move to Winslow necessitated the dissolution of *The Egg Ladies*. The organic egg business had been losing money, and so with a saddened heart Amber sold off most of the chickens. Some went to Scotch Brook Acres, where Trudy now offers her customers organic eggs as well as butter and yogurt. And some of the hens Amber brought with her to Oaknole. But, by and large, most of the chickens were sold to a middle-aged woman from Brooks, who had recently moved to Maine to escape the rat race of big city life and corporate America.

Rebecca, who had moved to Maine for much the same reason, was sad to see the chickens go. "It's an idea whose time has come," she said to Wendell, from the comfort of their marital bed. There was no need for whispering now that Amber was gone. She snuggled against her husband. "It's time that people returned to a simpler way of life. Think how much happier everyone would be! The chickens brought us together – maybe they can do the same for Susan!" Susan Wachtel was the single woman who'd purchased *The Egg Ladies'* hens.

"Wal, you know, 'tain't many more like me 'round heah!" Wendell replied, flashing his gold-toothed grin.

"Then I'm glad I got one of the last ones!"

Gray Gilpin decided to stay on with his grandparents, who were gratified by the boy's decision to live with them. But Maude felt somewhat dejected, thinking that Bruce and Amber were living so far away.

"'Tain't very far off," Ralph pointed out to his bride of nearly fifty-four years. "Ain't much more 'n twenty-two miles ovah to the farm!"

Maude heaved a heavy sigh. "I suppose Rebecca and I could visit them after we close the restaurant? We wouldn't be able to make it back by five o'clock, though."

Too late, Ralph realized his mistake. He eyed her suspiciously. "Who's gonna cook my suppah?"

"Maybe it's time you learned to cook yourself, Ralph Gilpin!"

To no one's surprise, Bruce and Amber settled comfortably into their married life at Oaknole, so comfortably in fact that the couple elected to make the place their permanent home. Thus the prayer of my old friend's heart – one of them at least – was finally satisfied. Bruce would take over the farm from Peter, and the couple would care for him in his declining years, which were still a good ways off. Bruce's mechanical services soon became common knowledge in the community, and he shortly became the go-to person for every broken truck or tractor or piece of farm equipment within a twenty mile radius.

By June, Peter was up and about, and feeling well enough to assist in the milking and some of the lighter daily chores. He urged Bruce to take Amber on their honeymoon trip to Niagara Falls, which honeymoon they'd delayed until Peter had fully recovered. Bruce agreed, and late one morning in mid-June Charlemagne was finally packed for that cross-country adventure. But just as the couple was about to depart, Bruce received a call on his cell. A local farmer's baling machine had broken down mid-field, and rain was imminent. Unless Bruce could help the farmer get his baler going, his friend was going to lose the entire crop of hay!

"It'll only take me an hour, Sweets," Bruce promised, taking the opportunity to kiss his pretty young wife. "Two hours, tops!"

Amber sat down on the front porch steps of Oaknole, and regarded him lovingly. "Oh, go ahead," she said. "You know you want to! Charlemagne and I will be right here when you get back."

She was waiting for him on the porch when he returned eight hours later, watching the fireflies sparkle in the warm evening air. And that's where they've been ever since, at Oaknole Farm, clishmaclavering among the cows.

The End

Author's Note: *clishmaclaver* is a Scotch word made famous by the 18th century Scottish poet Robert Burns, known as the Ploughman Poet, who captured the common dialect in his poetry. The word has various definitions including "idle talk" or "idle conversation," often of a loud nature. In the 19th century, Sophia Peabody (before marrying Nathaniel Hawthorne), sought a cure for her migraine headaches in the countryside of Dedham, Massachusetts; however, not long after her arrival she wrote home to her family that she was bothered by the "clishmaclavering among the cows." Miss Hastings has given the term a playful twist in *Peas, Beans & Corn* meaning as she does that Amber and Bruce will be "frolicking among the cows."

THE SOVEREIGN SERIES

TRADE MARK

I went to Heaven—'Twas a small Town—Emily Dickinson

The Sovereign Series is a four-volume work of fiction by Maine farmer and itinerant Quaker minister Jennifer Wixson. The books are set in the mythical town of Sovereign, Maine (pop. 1,048), a rural farming community where "the killing frost comes just in time to quench all budding attempts at small-mindedness and mean-spiritedness." Good-hearted and lovable characters, such as the old chicken farmer Wendell Russell and the town's retired music teacher Miss Hastings, weave in and out of the four novels like beloved friends dropping in for a cup of tea.

Visitors to Sovereign partake in the felicity that abounds in the picturesque hamlet of rolling pastures and woodlots, whether while sharing a picnic with our little group of friends at the Millett Rock or wandering with a lover beside Black Brook. Readers, like the residents of Sovereign, become imbued with a sensation much like that described by Ralph Waldo Emerson, "a certain cordial exhilaration … the effect of the indulgence of this human affection."

Book 1, *Hens & Chickens* (White Wave, August 2012) – Two women downsized by corporate America (Lila Woodsum, 27, and Rebecca Johnson, 48) move to Maine to raise chickens and sell organic eggs—and discover more than they bargained for, including love! *Hens & Chickens* opens the book on Sovereign and introduces us to the local characters, including Wendell Russell, Miss Hastings, the handsome carpenter Mike Hobart, and the Gilpin family. A little tale of hens and chickens, pips and peeper, love and friendship, *Hens & Chickens* lays the foundation for the next three titles in the series.

Book 2, *Peas, Beans & Corn* (White Wave, June 2013) – The romance of a bygone era infuses Book 2 in *The Sovereign Series*, when Maine Army Guardsman Bruce Gilpin, 35, returns to Sovereign with the secret dream of restarting the town's old sweet corn canning factory. He's encouraged in his mission by the passionate young organic foodie Amber Johnson, 21, who reawakens his youthful heart. The course of their true love becomes muddied by their well-meaning mothers, however, and by the arrival of Bruce's ex-wife Sheila and the handsome corporate attorney Ryan MacDonald, who hits town to rusticate. History pervades this little tale of hummingbird moths and morning mists, horse-drawn sleighs and corn desilkers, and the words of the poet Emily Dickinson, who could have been describing Sovereign when she once wrote: "I went to Heaven – 'Twas a small Town."

Book 3, *The Songbird of Sovereign* (White Wave, 2014) – In Book 3 of *The Sovereign Series*, Miss Hastings reveals the secret of her youthful heart, a tragic lost love that has lasted a lifetime. While gracing the stages of New York as a teenage musical prodigy, Jan Hastings' career is cut short by consumption (tuberculosis), the wasting disease. Panicked, her parents seek a cure for their daughter at a sanatorium in central Maine, where she meets and falls in love with fellow TB sufferer Henry Graham, 27. His gentle goodness transforms the young Miss Hastings, and his love reaches beyond the grave to positively touch the lives of hundreds of Sovereign schoolchildren over the course of the next seven decades.

Book 4, *The Minister's Daughter* (White Wave, 2015) – Although she is tall, blonde and lovely, Nellie Walker, 22, the daughter of Maggie Walker, minister of the Sovereign Union Church, is also selfish, supercilious and vain. When an unforeseen event leaves Nellie alone in the world, she returns to Sovereign and initiates a desperate search for the father whose identity her mother has never revealed. Helping Nellie through this dark time is the compassionate country doctor, Metcalf Bartholomew Lawson, 31, known locally as "Doctor Bart." Doctor Bart's love for Nellie has long been suspected (and encouraged) by her mother, although to date Nellie has exhibited little use for her pedantic suitor, a man more at home among herbs and rose bushes than cityscapes and boardwalks. Maggie's childhood friend Peter Hodges also provides Nellie with much needed comfort and support, when Nellie is forced to face – and overcome – some long-held prejudices. As we say "goodbye" to our old friends from Sovereign in this fourth and last book of *The Sovereign Series*, we are again reminded of the importance of unconditional love, "the fountain of youth upon which our ageing and aged selves will return to drink again and again." And while we sit with Nellie Walker watching the Sovereign sun set for the last time, we know that the sun is rising elsewhere with new hope.

All Things Old and Antique

A Maine native, Jennifer Wixson, author of *The Sovereign Series*, fell in love with history as a child growing up on the old family farm in Winslow. That love for the past stayed with her throughout her early adult years, and some of the happiest days of her youth were spent attending local auctions with her family. Today, she still enjoys a good auction or a browse through an antique mall. Here are some of Jennifer's favorites:

James D. Julia, Inc. – One of America's top ten auctioneers located in Fairfield, Maine. This world renowned firm makes an appearance in *Peas, Beans & Corn*, when it auctions off (fictitious) letters penned by the iconoclastic poet Emily Dickinson. Jennifer regularly attends both the winter and the summer fine art and antiques auctions. *www.jamesdjulia.com*

Houston Brooks Auctioneers – Known locally as the "Burnham Auction" due to its location on the Horseback Road in Burnham. The Burnham Auction holds an auction every Sunday (except for a few weeks in the winter) where the contents of old Maine households and other interesting items, including books, art, dishes, furniture, dolls and toys are put up for sale. *www.houstonbrooks.com*

Poulin Auction Company – Another fine auctioneer and antique dealer located in Fairfield, Maine, next door to James D. Julia, Inc. Known for their firearm and estate auctions. *www.poulinantiques.com*

The Fairfield Antiques Mall – It's worth a visit to central Maine to see the thousands of items on display in Maine's largest antiques mall. In addition, the free coffee and donuts attract lots of locals, including Wendell Russell, who tries to tempt Amber away from grieving her lost love in *Peas, Beans & Corn*. *www.fairfieldantiquesmall.com*

The Roller Rink Antique Mall – formerly a skating rink, this new shop is located in Detroit (Maine) and features sixty dealers, offering a wide variety of antiques and collectibles from all over the world. Furniture, dishes, jewelry, small collectibles, tools and more fill every nook and cranny of this large building. *www.rollerrinkantiques.com*

Maine Corn Shop History

For readers looking for more information on Maine's historical sweet corn canning industry, the following short list is a good place to start:

Canning Gold *Northern New England's Sweet Corn Industry: A Historical Geography*, by Paul B. Frederic. For more information on this fascinating and informative book or to purchase a copy, please contact Professor Frederic at *frederic@myfairpoint.net*.

The Maine State Museum, 230 State St., Augusta, Maine. Wonderful revolving exhibits relating to Maine history on display in three floors. (207) 287-2301 *www.mainestatemuseum.org*

The Brooks Historical Society, proud proprietors of the historic Pilley House, which was donated to the Society by radio personality Bob Elliott. Some of the stories in *Peas, Beans & Corn* come from former workers at the now defunct Brooks canning factory. For more information please contact Betty Littlefield, President. (207) 722-3633.

Minot Maine Historical Society – Located at 329 Woodman Hill Road, Minot, Maine 04258 This little Maine town was home to multiple corn shops, including Corn Shop #5, at which the cover insert and back shadow photographs were taken. For more information please contact Lucille Hodsdon at *lhodsdon1@roadrunner.com*.

Stepping Back into the Past in Minot, Maine

The following photographs are from the Don Mills Collection, Poland, Maine, courtesy of the Minot Maine Historical Society. All the pictures were taken at the Burnham & Morrill Co. Corn Shop #5, which was located at Minot Corner between the Methodist Church and the Little Androscoggin River. Our thanks to Lucille Hodsdon of Norway and to the Minot Historical Society for giving readers an opportunity to step back into this fascinating piece of Maine's past.

Husking corn.

Baskets and baskets of sweet corn!

Is romance in the air?

Corn shop workers of yesteryear.

A social affair.

B&M Corn Shop #5

Jennifer Wixson

M aine farmer, author and itinerant Quaker minister, Jennifer Wixson writes from her home in Troy, where she and her husband raise Scottish Highland cattle. A Maine native, Jennifer was educated at the School of Hard Knocks, and also admits to a Master's degree in Divinity from Bangor Theological Seminary.

You can follow Jennifer's adventures on Twitter @ChickenJen and visit her Facebook author's page: *www.facebook.com/Jennifer.Wixson.author* for the latest on her writing.

For more information on *The Sovereign Series* visit: *www.theSovereignSeries.com*

Praise for Peas, Beans & Corn

"*Peas, Beans & Corn* is a delightful, folksy story that could be almost any small town in Maine. Jennifer Wixson blends the descriptions of the people and the area together so well that one can picture the Men's Club, the Ladies Auxiliary and the old canning factory. I liked the references to the German POWs. They were here in Houlton, and I remember POWs picking potatoes for my Dad during the war…Once I started reading this book, I did not want to put it down. Now, I'm waiting for the next one!"
– *Dorothy Fitzpatrick, Houlton, Maine*

"Reading *Peas, Beans & Corn* is like 'coming home to a place I've never been before.' The second installment of Jennifer Wixson's *Sovereign Series* brings back characters that are familiar and comfortable. Her blend of history and romance creates an inviting story that makes you want to pull up a chair and listen awhile. Devoid of today's artificial drama and narcissism, *The Sovereign Series* is a glimpse of old-fashioned graciousness, morality and charm."
– *Tami Erwin, Salem, Nebraska*

"Life in Sovereign, Maine isn't idyllic or perfect—it's real. The characters are warm and friendly, the Old Farts are genuine, and the food isn't just good, it's organic and delicious! Once again, Jennifer Wixson brings central Maine to life with friends you'll grow to know and care about in *Peas, Beans & Corn!*"
– *Robin Follette, Talmadge, Maine*

Praise for Peas, Beans & Corn

"This book is a wonderful glimpse into the lives of caring, loving, and sometimes eccentric folk in small town Maine! I liked the multi-generational aspect of the characters and the very descriptive language. If you're looking for a story that will take you away from the hustle and bustle of your busy life, curl up with *Peas, Beans & Corn* and catch up on the heartwarming happenings in Sovereign, Maine!"
– *Viletta Knight, Fairbanks, Alaska*

"*Peas, Beans & Corn* is a superb novel, reminiscent of such classics as *Come Spring* by Ben Ames Williams and *As the Earth Turns* by Gladys Hasty Carroll. So many diverse and interesting facts are woven seamlessly into the plot, including the operation of an antique canning shop, the breech birth of a calf, and the writings of Emily Dickinson. The story has just the right amount of romance, too! ... I'm anxiously awaiting the third book in *The Sovereign Series*."
– *Wini Mott, Paris, Maine*

"Jennifer Wixson has a gift of bridging the gap between young and old, the present and the past... She paints a lovely picture of rural Maine and sprinkles it with heart-warming stories of everyday folk who come together in good times and in bad to provide each other love, friendship and support. *Peas, Beans & Corn* shows just how nice the world would be if the world were only like Sovereign, Maine!"
– *Sally Beaty, Springfield, Ohio*